**Praise for the novels of *New York Times*
and *USA TODAY* bestselling author
DIANA PALMER**

"Fans of stark outer space military science fiction
will appreciate this sobering at-war thriller."
—*The Best Reviews* on *The Morcai Battalion*

"A high-octane and gritty space adventure."
—*RT Book Reviews* on *The Morcai Battalion*

"Palmer…is the queen of desperado quests
for justice and true love."
—*Publishers Weekly* on *Dangerous*

Brought to you for the first time in paperback…

New York Times bestselling author Diana Palmer presents readers
with her Harlequin HQN series, The Morcai Battalion. A thrilling,
romantic space opera and adventure, The Morcai Battalion features
passionate romance and intense action as unforgettable warriors
fight for peace in the galaxy.

Also available from Diana Palmer

Other books in the Morcai Battalion series
The Morcai Battalion

And coming soon
The Morcai Battalion: Invictus

THE MORCAI BATTALION: THE RECRUIT

DIANA PALMER

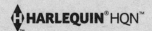

Recycling programs
for this product may
not exist in your area.

ISBN-13: 978-0-373-77923-9

The Morcai Battalion: The Recruit

Copyright © 2009 by Susan S. Kyle

Revised text copyright © 2014 by Susan S. Kyle

Printed in U.S.A.

www.Harlequin.com

Dear Reader,

It is my great pleasure to have this novel, the second in my Morcai Battalion series, in mass market paperback. It was released previously, in 2009, under the Harlequin LUNA imprint, only as an ebook, so I am very grateful to have it in print. I have also added new content to this edition of the novel, as I did to the rerelease of the original *The Morcai Battalion* in June 2013.

It is fun to create a science fiction series, especially around characters with whom you have lived for over forty years. This is the second book of several in my Morcai Battalion series. It follows the adventures of Dr. (and Lieutenant Commander) Madeline Ruszel, the only female ever to serve as a member of the Cehn-Tahr/Human commando unit known as the Holconcom. She is a combat vet, and her alien C.O. doesn't think women belong in combat. Watch for sparks to keep flying. Also watch for the next sequel, which continues Ruszel's stormy relationship with her commander, in *Invictus* in 2015.

A lot of people helped give me ideas for this book. I am grateful to James Daniel Clayton, to whom it is dedicated. He served on a number of U.S. Navy nuclear submarines, and he was kind enough to let me pick his brain about the routine on a vehicle submerged for long periods of time away from port (sort of like being in space, you can't just walk out of a nuclear sub and take a stroll when you feel like it). He is also Donovan and Selena Marie Kyle's other grandfather, and part of a very nice family, which includes his wife, Jane; his son, Daniel; and his daughter, Christina (Blayne's wife and Selena and Donovan's mama!).

I owe Dr. Rob Wainberg, who is a biology professor at Piedmont College in Demorest, Georgia, a debt, too, because I forced him to revisit both graduate school and his days as a researcher to help me flesh out the Cehn-Tahr. He will find a surprise when he reads the book. Thanks, Rob! (And thanks to Dr. Carlos Camp, who was so understanding when his name was misspelled in the dedication to the first book in 2007!)

I hasten to add that any mistakes in this novel are strictly mine. As I age, the little gray cells become more rigid and less efficient with information. I do write primarily to entertain, not to educate. But I do spend a great deal of time reading studies in theoretical physics and hanging out on medical and science and NASA websites. Hope you like the book.

Visit me at www.themorcaibattalion.com and www.dianapalmer.com.

Susan Kyle

Habersham County, Georgia

2013

To James Daniel "Danny" Clayton, submariner
and retired veteran of the United States Navy, with many thanks

CHAPTER ONE

BATTERED AND SORE, Dr. Madeline Ruszel stood at attention in front of the Holconcom commander, Dtimun. The tall alien perched on the edge of his liquiform desk with his arms crossed, glaring at her. His cat-eyes, which changed color to mirror his mood, were the dark brown of anger.

She knew she looked unpresentable. Her red Holconcom uniform was stained with synthale and her own blood. She was disheveled and bruised. Her long, wavy reddish-gold hair was in a tangle all the way to her waist, and also sweaty from her recent activities in the base officers' lounge. Contacted by the base military police unit, after her apprehension, Dtimun had ordered Ruszel brought to the *Morcai*, the flagship of the integrated Cehn-Tahr and human commando unit known as the Holconcom.

He hadn't said a word since she arrived, with bruises just coming out on the soft skin of her face, around one of her green eyes. She'd been standing at attention for several minutes, waiting for the explosion. Holconcom were forbidden to engage in brawls. That included not only the Cehn-Tahr complement, but the humans as well. The elite and feared military unit had, unknown to the human commanders of the Tri-Galaxy Fleet, genetically engineered superior strength, plus microcyborg enhancers that made brawling extremely dangerous. Besides that, Madeline was a combat surgeon. By constitutional galactic law, medical personnel were denied that sort of recreation.

Of course, they were also denied the use of sidearms. Madeline tried to conceal the one she was carrying tucked in her waistband, under her tunic, from the alien's penetrating gaze.

Finally, he spoke. "You are out of uniform, madam," he growled, indicating her uniform, unbuttoned at the throat.

She raised one hand and quickly fastened the button.

"And you are carrying a firearm," he continued. "Firearms are forbidden to medical personnel. You are a doctor."

Technically, she wasn't only a doctor of medicine, but an internist in Cularian medicine, an anthropological group which included the Cehn-Tahr—or Centaurians, as they were incorrectly known by humans—and their worst enemies, Rojoks. In her past, Madeline had captained an Amazon commando squad and had routinely carried a service weapon. But she wasn't going to push her luck by reminding him of that fact, given the state of his temper. His expression might be benign, but his elongated slit-pupiled cat-eyes were still brown. Grimacing, she tugged the Jebob disruptor from her belt, stepped forward and laid it gently on the desk beside him. She returned to attention.

"Would you care to explain the purple discoloration around your left eye?" he added.

"It's called a black eye," she informed him merrily. "That would be from Flannegan's fist. Sir."

He made a rough sound deep in his throat and folded his arms across his broad chest. "I assume that you do have some justification for throwing Flannegan through the expensive antique glass patio doors at the officers' club?"

She brightened, although she still hadn't quite met his eyes. "Yes, sir!"

"Which is...?" he prompted.

"Flannegan called you a cat-eyed benny-whammer. Sir," she added formally.

He just stared at her, as if he had doubts about her sanity.

"How can I justify the dignity of your position aboard the *Morcai*," he began solemnly, "as the only female, human or otherwise, ever to serve aboard her, when you spend hours in various bars across the base embarrassing both the Holconcom and me?"

She shook her head. "Sir, the honor of the unit was at stake," she said earnestly. "You must see that we..." She cleared her throat. "I mean, *I*, had to defend your honor."

"We." His eyes grew darker.

"Me. I. Myself." She gathered speed.

"And Stern," he guessed, "and Hahnson and Komak." The other two human officers, Captain Holt Stern and Dr. Strick Hahnson, were Madeline's longtime comrades. Komak, a Cehn-Tahr, was Dtimun's second in command.

She met his eyes, aghast. "Sir, I never said that...!"

He drew in a breath. "It is useless to try to deceive me."

She straightened even more. "I'm really very sorry, sir," she said. "I waded in to punish Flannegan, and his buddies in the First Fleet attacked me. I was out-numbered, so the others intervened to save me from them."

"A pity," he muttered darkly, "that they are not here to save you from me."

"I was about to say that myself, sir," she returned brightly. Her green eyes were twinkling, despite all her efforts to appear sincere.

The humor was contagious, apparently, because his cat-eyes flared into a green smile, if only briefly, before the angry brown returned.

"Brawling," he scoffed. "Not only does it reflect poorly on your profession, but you have no business displaying a firearm to the entire base."

"I had to relieve Flannegan of the firearm, sir— he'd taken it from a Jebob officer and he was using the grip to batter my head."

His eyes narrowed. "I will remind you once more that medical personnel are not allowed sidearms. Lawson insists on it, and so do I."

Her green eyes glittered at him defiantly. "With all due respect, sir, I'm not going into a combat situation unarmed, whether or not Admiral Lawson likes it."

Dtimun stood up, shaking his head. "Your pre-vious combat history as a captain with the Amazon Division is at war with your professional credentials as a healer. It will lead to grief."

"I always hide the firearm, sir," she assured him.

He turned, scowling, and gave her a long look that took in the nice fit of her red Holconcom uniform. There were no pockets. Neither was there room for a weapon. "Should I ask where you hide the firearm?" he questioned unexpectedly.

She gave him a horrified look. "Sir!" she exclaimed with mock embarrassment.

"At least reassure me that all of your Cehn-Tahr crewmates removed their microcyborgs before you engaged in this senseless slaughter," he replied, trying to salvage something from the encounter. This was a deliberate deception, also. The microcyborgs were strength-enhancers, used by the Cehn-Tahr clones of the Holconcom. But their contribution to Dtimun and Komak's physical superiority was minute. Dtimun and Komak were not clones. The humans had no idea of the real nature of the Cehn-Tahr.

"Komak collected them the minute Flannegan called you a cat-eyed...called you a name," she amended quickly, "and I threw a bar stool at him," she assured him with a muffled grin.

He let out a long sigh and waved a hand at her. "Get out of my office," he muttered. "And stay out of the base officers' club until I give you official permission to return there."

"Yes, sir!"

"And, you are grounded until further notice."

"Yes, sir!"

He glared at her as she started to leave. "Take that weapon and give it back to Flannegan. And if I catch you carrying a firearm into combat," he began with the threat in his tone and his posture, "I will stand you up in the brig and let Komak use you as a practice target for his novapen. Am I understood?"

"Oh, yes, sir, you are," she assured him, grabbing the weapon off his desk.

"Ruszel," he called as the door powered apart at her movement.

Her hair flew around her face as she turned back to him, her eyes questioning.

"Does Flannegan have a similar souvenir of the encounter?" he asked unexpectedly.

She grinned. "Indeed he does, sir. Two of them!"

Once again, there was the faintest flash of green in his elongated eyes. "Carry on."

"Yes, sir!"

She was chuckling as she went out of the room and down the deck toward her medical quarters.

DTIMUN WATCHED HER go with mixed emotions. She was so unlike women of his species, who were not allowed in the military, much less in combat. It had been a point of contention between himself and Ruszel since she and her Terravegan Strategic Space Command comrades, Captain Holt Stern and Dr. Strick Hahnson, had become part of the legendary Cehn-Tahr Holconcom unit now known as the Morcai Battalion. The humans frequently tested his patience to the limit. But they were fierce fighters, loyal and honorable, and they complemented the Cehn-Tahr soldiers in ways he hadn't imagined.

In the almost three years since the Holconcom had escaped from the Rojok death camp, Ahkmau, the war between the Rojok dynasty and the Tri-Galaxy Fleet had intensified. The Cehn-Tahr of the Holconcom, except for Dtimun himself and Komak, were all clones. So were Captain Holt Stern and Dr. Strick Hahnson—through no fault of their own, since their originals had been killed by the Rojoks. Dtimun had carefully concealed this knowledge about Stern and Hahnson from the brass of the Tri-Fleet military, due to the inexplicable human contempt for clones.

His men and the humans, formerly of Stern's ship, the SSC ship *Bellatrix*, had been a volatile mix in the first days of the unit. Holconcom were not used to touch without combat, and the Terravegan humans were a physical race. Therefore, brawling had been strictly forbidden for fear that a massacre might ensue, and not only because of the secret tech used by the Cehn-Tahr members of the Holconcom to boost their already formidable strength.

Not that it did any good to forbid brawling. Komak, Dtimun's executive officer, had gotten around the no-brawling rule by having the clones remove their microcyborgs, the tiny, highly classified strength modifiers that all members of the Holconcom had embedded in their scalps. His comrades enjoyed the physical sparring with other races. Now the humans aboard the *Morcai* and their Cehn-Tahr comrades frequently trashed bars; but usually not on Trimerius, the headquarters planet of the Tri-Galaxy Fleet. Admiral Jeffrye Lawson was not going to take Ruszel's participation in the sport lightly. He felt that a Terravegan lieutenant commander, as Madeline was ranked aboard the *Morcai*, should not brawl. Of course, he also felt that doctors should not help to create patients. But he had a soft spot for Ruszel, which was why she got away with so many infractions of regulations.

Besides Ruszel's brawling, Dtimun had two more equally disturbing problems. The first had to do with the living machines aboard his ship, the *Morcai*. There were four *kelekoms* aboard the *Morcai*. The living, sentient machines bonded with their operators and were capable of incredible intelligence-gathering abilities. On Ahkmau, the ship had lost one of its operators and the unit had gone into hibernation after its companion had died.

None of the *kelekoms* had ever lost a companion since Dtimun's accession to head of the Holconcom. Because the joining was so intimate a relationship, it was also emotional. The unit had gone into advanced hibernation mode. Two attempts had been made, over the past two years, to find it a new companion. The first had seemed encouraging. The *kelekom* had made an effort to give the Cehn-Tahr officer time to become familiar with it. It had forced itself to go on missions with him, had functioned almost normally during the weeks that followed. The officer was delighted to be part of the elite unit. The *kelekom* accepted him in the months that followed and allowed him to join with it. Mission after mission had followed. And just when Dtimun was sure the match would be permanent, the young Cehn-Tahr officer had walked into an ambush and died instantly.

The *kelekom*, now robbed of two linkeds Cehn-Tahr companions by death, had gone into depression and had finally shut down all over again. Months had passed with no interest from it as Dtimun presented it with new candidates, none of whom seemed to be acceptable. Now, it seemed possible that it would die. That, Dtimun could not allow to happen. He had to find a replacement operator, but none of his men aboard ship had inspired any interest in the declining bionic machine. So the ship had had to operate with only three units. He thought that perhaps

Lawson might have a human computer technician to spare, one whose very strangeness might appeal to the depressed living machine. It was a long shot, but it might work.

His second problem had to do with a complement of ambassadors who were holding an emergency meeting on Ondar, a neutral planet in the nearby Cerelles system. They were discussing the unexpected death of Rojok tyrant Mangus Lo while he was in Tri-Galaxy Fleet custody, pending a retrial in his conviction on war crime charges, and the latest incursion by his nephew and successor, Chan Ho, who had seized another star system in the New Territory with the help of Chacon, his respected field marshal.

Apparently, Chacon had managed to explain his part in Mangus Lo's arrest on Ahkmau. He had permitted the Morcai Battalion to escape from the horrors of Ahkmau, but no one outside the unit had been privy to that knowledge. Presumably, even if the explanation was sketchy, the Rojoks' new emperor was afraid to test his own power as commander-in-chief by attempting to try the people's favorite soldier, Chacon. There was interspace chatter, however, that Chan Ho favored his late uncle's terror policies and had gone head-to-head with Chacon about their renewal. It was worrying.

The Tri-Galaxy Council was working on a diplomatic solution to the Rojoks' latest appropriation in the New Territory, claimed by member planets of the Tri-Galaxy Council. The Rojoks had already seized Terramer and its system, now they were spreading out to another nearby system, which contained abundant natural resources. The ambassadors were on Ondar to vote on sanctions against the so-called neutral member-worlds of the Rojok dynasty, as well as a modified budget to fund the war against the Rojoks. It was a controversial meeting. The Rojoks might attempt a kidnapping.

Dtimun had word from a spy in his circle of acquaintances who said that a contingent of Rojoks was planning to establish a covert base within skimmer distance of the council chambers. He'd taken that information to Lawson, who advised patience. Dtimun had none. Despite the Holconcom's alliance with the Tri-Fleet, it was autonomous. Dtimun could ignore Lawson's dictates and do what he pleased.

Since the chambers were on neutral ground, in a neutral system, the Tri-Galaxy Fleet had been ordered to stand down while the diplomats debated.

Just to annoy Dtimun, the Cehn-Tahr emperor, old Tnurat Alamantimichar, had sided with Lawson on the issue and insisted that the Holconcom stay away from Ondar. He interfered frequently. It was ongoing payback for his Holconcom commander's deliberate provocation of his chauvinistic policies by allowing a female—and a human female at that!—in the Holconcom. The old emperor had been outraged at the news. He and the Imperial Dectat had tried to have Ruszel arrested and executed. Dtimun and Lawson had spiked his guns with the Tri-Galaxy Council. Over the years the emperor had been making the *Morcai's* commando raids more difficult. His word carried weight with the Council. Most of the member worlds were terrified of him. Dtimun was not. Nor was the old emperor going to keep him planetside if he had intel that the delegates on Ondar were in immediate danger. But for the time being, Dtimun sought more confirmed intel.

Meanwhile, he'd grounded Ruszel, forbidding her to leave her medical unit planetside as well as her office on his flagship until further notice. He would have put her in the brig, but grounding her, along with the threat of the brig, might be enough to keep her in line. For the time being, at least.

Privately, he admired her fighting spirit and valued her in combat situations. Even though she frequently pushed his temper past the breaking point, she pulled her weight aboard ship, and she was popular with the whole crew, including the Cehn-Tahr element. She was capable, intelligent and afraid of nothing. She was also beautiful. He found himself watching her and had to work at controlling his impulses. It was fortunate, he considered, that she had no emotional attachment to him. There were dread secrets in the past of his people, scientific experiments, genetic tampering, which had resulted in terrifying behaviors beyond their control. The Cehn-Tahr were so ashamed of them that they never permitted any knowledge of their social patterns or mating rituals to be known by outworlders. Had Ruszel displayed any physical interest in him, the results might be lethal. It was a good thing, he decided, that the human military mentally neutered its crewmen and officers for duty.

He was more wary than most of his race about interspecies relationships. In his youth, his defiance of the rules had ended tragically. It must not happen again. However, he had to admit that Ruszel was the most interesting, and desirable, female he had ever known. If regulations forbidding it had not carried the death penalty in both their societies, and the difference in their species not so great, his reaction to her might have been very different.

As it was, he put her out of his thoughts and went back to work.

MADELINE RUSZEL WAS animated as she explained her confrontation with Dtimun to Holt Stern and Dr. Strick Hahnson in her office at the base medical center.

"He was furious!" she chuckled, her green eyes gleaming. "But he let me off with a lecture. I didn't even draw brig time for the gun. Of course, it was Flannegan's gun," she added.

"Not really." Dr. Strick Hahnson grinned. "Flannegan knocked out a Jebob tech and stole it from him to bash you in the head."

"You're going to get yourself in serious trouble one of these days, Ladybones," Stern said somberly. "The old man won't overlook these infractions forever."

"He's been overlooking them for almost three years," she reminded him.

"Yes, but the casualty lists are growing longer, and he's more somber than I've ever known him," Hahnson put in. He sighed. "He's worried."

"Aren't we all?" Stern agreed. "I thought capturing Mangus Lo would end the Rojok threat. Was that naive, or what?"

Madeline could have answered that he was naive, in a sense. His entire life span amounted to only a little under three years. Like Hahnson beside him, he was a clone. The Rojoks had killed their originals; Stern on Terramer during the rescue of the colonists, and Hahnson on Ahkmau in a bout of torture that still could make Madeline sick to her stomach. Stern had fought off his conditioning and helped save his comrades. Hahnson had been cloned and returned to them by Dtimun as compensation, as he put it, for pulling them out of the Terravegan military and into the Holconcom. The human clones of her friends still had most of the memories of their originals. So the bond between the three officers was as strong as it had ever been.

That was nonregulation, of course. All members of the Terravegan military were mentally neutered before they ever put on a uniform if they were slated for space duty. The authorities had decided that most conflicts were based on sexual or violent emotional issues. They simply used chemical means to remove the ability to bond from members of the military. But once in a while, a candidate fell through the cracks. Madeline was one. So was her father, Clinton Ruszel, a colonel in the SSC Paraguard Wing. Although she'd been reared in a government nursery, Madeline was one of the few children who actually knew one of her birth parents. Her father had contacted her when she was very small. In fact, he and Dtimun had saved her from terrorists in the Great Galaxy War. Dtimun didn't look it, but he was eighty-nine human years of age. He could have passed for a human in his thirties. He was only in the middle years of his life, at that. He could look forward to another eighty-nine years or more before he died.

"You drifted off again," Hahnson mused, tapping her on the hand.

"Oh! Sorry." She smiled self-consciously. "I was

thinking about…" She started to say Ahkmau, but that would have brought back really awful memories for all three of them. "I was thinking about how I ended up being the first woman on a Holconcom ship."

Stern whistled through his teeth. "Now, there's a story of legend."

"You aren't kidding," Hahnson laughed. "Old Tnurat Alamantimichar, the Cehn-Tahr emperor, had a screaming fit about that."

She grinned. "We heard that he sent the officer who reported my assignment to the brig for a standard month."

"Well, the C.O. does do everything he can think of to tick off the emperor," Hahnson commented. "They've had an ongoing feud for decades. Nobody knows what started it, but it's heated up in the past few years. Your assignment to the Holconcom tied the old emperor up in knots. He can order people killed on Memcache, the home planet of the Cehn-Tahr," he added, giving the true name of the race that humans in first contact had mistakenly called Centaurians, thinking they came from the star-system nearest old Earth.

"He's an emperor," Madeline pointed out. "Couldn't he just order the C.O. to give me back to Lawson?"

"That's a whole other story," Hahnson mused. "You see, old Tnurat was the first commander of the Holconcom. He gave it, and its commander, absolutely autonomy during the Great Galaxy War and thereafter. He can't command it. Neither can the Cehn-Tahr Dectat, their parliament. Dtimun has absolute authority."

"I begin to see the light," Madeline said, grinning. "Poor old emperor."

"He is, sort of," Hahnson said thoughtfully. "He only has one child left, a daughter, the princess we rescued from Ahkmau. All his sons are dead, including the one you tried to treat on Terramer, the day we met the Holconcom for the first time."

"I'd forgotten that his son died that day. Does he have a wife?" She frowned. "Do Cehn-Tahr have wives, or do they have harems?" she continued absently.

"You're our resident Cularian medicine specialist," Stern pointed out. "Shouldn't you know the answer to that?"

She gave him a droll look. "Cehn-Tahr social behaviors, and mating rituals, are forbidden knowledge. We aren't even allowed to research them." She had an angelic expression on her face.

Hahnson raised a blond eyebrow. "There are black-market vids that purport to explain them."

She shifted some virtual paperwork. "I've heard about those."

"Have you also heard that they're filmed in a studio in Benaski Port by people who've never even seen a Cehn-Tahr?" Hahnson persisted.

She gasped. "They're what? Those pirates!" she raged. "I paid two hundred mems for...for..." She broke off. They were giving her odd looks. She cleared her throat and lowered her voice. "I mean, why would someone pay so much money for misinformation?" she corrected innocently.

Her comrades laughed.

"There's a much easier way. Ask the C.O.," Stern suggested.

Madeline actually flushed. "Are you nuts? They'd space him for even listening to such a question. They'd space me for asking it."

"I was assigned to medical duty with the Cehn-Tahr during the Great Galaxy War," Hahnson recalled. His eyes lowered. "There are things humans are never allowed to learn about them."

Madeline was openly curious. "Such as?"

He looked up and smiled sadly. "Just things."

"Didn't you learn something you could tell me?" she persisted.

He hesitated, as if weighing his answer. "Well, Cehn-Tahr mark their mates in some ancient rite of passage."

Madeline was taking notes. "Mark them. How?"

Hahnson shook his head. "Don't know. But it does leave a scar." He lifted his eyebrows again. "Does that help?"

"Not a lot," she sighed. She leaned her chin on her elbow. "Rojoks are a lot more forthcoming. But their customs aren't the same as Cehn-Tahr. I mean, what if I ever have to treat a social disease or give counseling to a Cehn-Tahr woman? I'd be useless."

"They don't have social diseases," Hahnson said. "Because they don't frequent brothels. They're amazingly pristine in their intimate habits. They also don't mate outside their own species, ever. It's a capital crime."

"I know," Madeline said quietly. Her companions tried not to notice the hollow tone of her voice. Her covert glances at the Holconcom C.O. hadn't gone unnoticed by her longtime friends.

"Dr. Ruszel?" A small, pretty blonde woman in a green SSC Terravegan medical uniform popped her head in the door. Bright blue eyes glanced from one officer to the other. They lingered on Holt Stern just a few seconds too long for polite interest. "We've got an Altairian diplomat with a nasty cellulitis. Do you want to treat it, or shall I?"

Madeline smiled. Lieutenant (J.G.) Edris Mallory was a sweet woman. She'd actually started out in Cularian medicine on a military scholarship. But just after graduation from medical school, she'd wanted to become a breeder. In fact, she'd come back to the medical unit from a breeder colony after tests had found her ineligible as a host parent. Any slight defect in genetics could disqualify a candidate and Mallory had recessive genes whose inheritable traits—light eyes and hair—were out of fashion the year she applied. She'd been devastated by the rejection. She'd gone back to the military and been assigned to combat training. She'd even agreed to the mental neutering, dangerous in a woman of twenty. But she flunked out of combat school with the lowest score in academy history. After that, she landed in the SSC medical corps. Madeline liked her. She was a hard worker and she never shirked a task, even the unpleasant ones. She was only twenty-two. Ruszel, approaching thirty, found her shy presence comforting, in some odd way. She and Hahnson had conspired to protect Mallory from a Three Strikes provision, a covert and shaming law that could land an offender in stasis, to be used for medical experimentation. Mallory had two

strikes already, and they kept a secret that could make
it three. She was a sweet, kind woman.

"Go ahead, Edris," she said. "I'll be around if you
need me."

She grinned. "Thanks, Dr. Ruszel," she said.
"Hello, Doctor," she greeted Hahnson warmly. She
flushed a little as she glanced at Stern and then
quickly away. "Captain." She darted back through
the door.

"She knows I'm a clone, doesn't she?" Stern asked
a little irritably. She'd barely looked at him.

"Oh, it's not that." She leaned toward him. "She's
shy. But she thinks you're hot."

He frowned. "It's cool in here."

"She thinks you're desirable," she corrected.

He flushed. "That's not allowed."

"She wanted to be a breeder," she reminded him
with a wicked grin. "But her genetics disqualified her
to produce a child for the state, so when they expelled
her from there, she decided to try combat medicine.
She already had her degree in Cularian medicine."

Stern glared. "How nice for her."

Madeline shook her head. She knew it was the
memory of Mary, his only love, that prompted that
response. The original Stern, too, had come out of the
neutering basically unaffected. He'd loved a woman
named Mary who sacrificed her own life to save the
lives of children. He carried a piece of blue velvet
ribbon that had been attached to the posthumous
medal they'd given her. He and Hahnson and Madeline passed it around between them as an accolade
for heroic deeds. It was one of their best-kept secrets.

Hahnson's wrist unit alarmed at the same time

Madeline's did. They looked at each other and grimaced.

"New medical transports are coming in from the
occupied territories," Madeline explained to Stern. "I
guess we've got work again, Dr. Hahnson."

"I guess we have, Dr. Ruszel," he agreed. "Good
thing we're in port for a few days. Medical is over-
whelmed already."

"Mallory, casualties coming in!" Madeline called
to Edris. "Call in all off-duty personnel, if you
please."

"Right away, Dr. Ruszel," she replied.

"She and I are the only two Cularian specialists
on the base until the graduates from the Tri-Fleet
Medical Academy arrive," Madeline commented. "I
suppose we'll do double duty again. Not that we get
many wounded Rojok prisoners to treat."

Stern was somber. "Good thing. Three cadets who
were in the last firefight tried to break into sick bay
and hang a wounded Rojok when the last medical
transports came in."

"Sadly for them, the commander was here reading me the riot act for another bar brawl when it happened," Madeline recalled with a faint chuckle. "You
never saw cadets run so fast. Pity they bothered. He
had all three of them before they made the front door.
They were so shaken up that the military police didn't
even have to cuff them." She shivered with mock fear.
"The C.O.'s pretty scary when he loses his temper."

"To everybody else except you," Hahnson mused,
tongue-in-cheek. "He could space you if he wanted
to. But all he ever does is ground you."

She leaned forward. "He's not sure that I didn't

sew up a boot or a glass of synthale inside him when I operated on him at Ahkmau," she said with malicious humor. "He wouldn't dare space me until he's positive that I didn't."

"He keeps you for a pet," Hahnson said with a chuckle.

"Eat worms, Hahnson." Madeline made a face at him before she followed Mallory into sick bay.

CHAPTER TWO

SICK BAY WAS FULL. Not only were there combat casualties brought in from all parts of the battlefront, but a new type of influenza was making itself felt among members of the Tri-Galaxy Fleet. There was no vaccination so far, and hardly any treatment that worked.

"I remember Dr. Wainberg, head of the Exobiology Department at the Tri-Fleet Military Academy, lecturing us on viruses," Madeline said as she and Edris Mallory worked side by side on combat wounds encountered by two Dacerian scouts who'd been ambushed near Terramer.

Edris laughed. "So do I. He and our human anatomy chief, Dr. Camp, gave lab exams that were, to say the least, challenging."

Madeline grinned. "Challenging to cadets who thought they could pass those courses by dissecting holospecimens instead of the real thing. The medical sector didn't tolerate slackers. They meant us to be taught proper surgical techniques, and we were." She frowned. "You know, it's still fascinating to me that viruses aren't actually alive. They're like a construct, an artificial construct."

"Who knows," Mallory agreed, "maybe they were originally part of some long forgotten engineered bioweapons tech."

"Viruses are already dead, Mallory," Madeline repeated.

Mallory frowned. "But, ma'am, how can they be dead if they were never alive?"

Madeline rolled her eyes. "That controversy still rages. They are alive in one sense, not in another. And I'm not joining that debate," she added on a laugh. She finished a restructuring job and motioned for one of the medtechs to take the unconscious patient in his ambutube out to the floor. She stripped off her glove films and smiled at the younger woman. "We can debate that over a nice cup of java after lunch."

The younger woman hesitated. Her blue eyes grew large. "Java? You don't mean, real coffee?"

Madeline leaned closer. "I have it shipped in illegally from the Altairian colony on Harcourt's Planet," she confided. "Then I grind the beans and brew it in my office."

"Coffee." Mallory's mouth was watering. "I dream about it. What passes for coffee in the mess hall is an insult to a delicate palate."

"I agree."

She pursed her lips. "Ma'am, are you going to tell me something I won't want to hear? Is that why I'm being treated to such a luxury?"

"You have a suspicious mind," her colleague replied. "Hurry up. We don't have a lot of time. There's a medical transport coming in from Terramer in about a standard hour and we may have more work."

"Yes, ma'am."

"I have to go over to Tri-Fleet HQ and report to the commander about this latest batch of casualties.

You can flash me if there's anything urgent before I get back."

"Yes, ma'am."

MADELINE LOCATED DTIMUN in his temporary office at Tri-Fleet HQ. It was smaller and more cramped than the one he maintained aboard the *Morcai*, but closer to fleet operations.

He frowned when she was admitted. "You have never reported to me directly on battle casualties. Is there a reason for this deviation from protocol?"

"Yes, sir," she said, standing at parade rest. "It's about Mallory."

His eyebrows lifted.

"Lieutenant J.G. Edris Mallory?" she prompted. "My assistant?"

"Yes. What about her?"

"Sir, she needs to be familiarized with the routine aboard ship, in case I ever have to bring her with me on a mission."

He stood up, cold and unapproachable. "I will not authorize the presence of a second human female aboard my flagship," he said flatly.

"Only to observe," she persisted. She let out an exasperated sigh. "What if I were captured by Rojoks on the battlefield?"

"I would send them my condolences," he returned.

She glared at him. "You'd have nobody aboard who could save you from a health crisis," she tossed back.

"It amazes me that you have never questioned the reason I carry no complement of Cehn-Tahr medics aboard the *Morcai*."

She blinked. "They said you had a fine contempt

for medics of your own species. I assumed that was the explanation."

His eyes narrowed and became a steady, searching blue as they explored her face. "You know nothing about us except what we permit you to know."

"You can pin a rose on that," she returned bluntly. "I've had to resort to black market vids to find out anything at all about Cehn-Tahr society."

His eyes flashed green with humor. "Those vids are made at Benaski Port…"

"…by pirates who never saw a live Cehn-Tahr, yes, I know. Hahnson informed me after it was too late to demand my money back!" she muttered.

The green grew broader in his eyes. He cocked his head. "It did not occur to you to ask me?"

She cleared her throat. "I wouldn't dare!"

"I have found very little that you would not dare, Ruszel," he retorted.

She shifted restlessly and averted her eyes. It would be embarrassing, even for a physician, to put any of her burning questions to him.

"I realize that," he said softly.

She grimaced. "I wish you wouldn't walk in and out of my mind, sir. It's very disconcerting."

"You are far too easy to read," he pointed out. "Telepaths learn to block unwanted intrusions at a very early age."

She lifted her eyes to his, searching them quietly. "You healed the little Altairian child with nothing more than your mind," she recalled. "I've never spoken of it, but I think your mental abilities are greater than you allow us to see."

"Much greater," he said in her mind.

"You keep secrets very well, as a species," she pointed out.

"Some are best kept," he returned silently. "If your species knew the true nature of mine, few humans would feel secure enough to serve with us."

That was a revelation. It disturbed her at some deep level. "We've seen you fight," she said, assuming that was what he referred to.

His eyes became solemn. "You have seen a greatly restrained version of our fighting style," he said surprisingly. "We modified it for the benefit of our human crewmen." He looked at her closely. "Why do you think our emperor was able to conquer over one hundred and fifty worlds with little more than the Holconcom?"

That was a question she'd never asked. "I never thought about it, sir."

"Some races who were victims of his first conquests still remember the Holconcom attacks. The fear alone kept them in line. It does, even today." His face grew hard. "We are an aggressive, violent species. Mercy is unknown to us."

"My little Altairian patient might disagree with you," she said, smiling in memory.

"The child was not my enemy," he pointed out.

She studied his hard face in silence. "Why don't you want other races to know anything about your society?"

"It would serve no useful purpose," he said curtly. "We never mate outside our own species."

She felt cold inside. She wasn't quick enough to divert her mind. He saw the sadness, and understood it all too well.

His eyes narrowed. "You are a fragile race," he said.

She stared at him, uncomprehending. "I could remind you that I took down several Rojok soldiers when we were in Ahkmau."

"I could remind you that only Chacon's intervention saved your life during the escape."

"Rub it in," she muttered, flushing. "I was intent on saving a patient. I didn't see the Rojoks rushing me."

"Your impulsive nature could lead you to tragedy," he said. "You must exhibit more control of yourself."

"I do try, sir. But human nature is what it is. We can't change what we are."

He grew contemplative. "No," he said, an odd bitterness in his tone. "We cannot."

"About Mallory, sir..."

"You can use the comps to give her a virtual tour of the ship," he said firmly. "I do not need any more distractions aboard. You and your temper provide quite enough already."

"My temper?" she exclaimed. "Look who's talking!"

"Remember to whom you are speaking!" he shot back.

"I didn't break a Gresham in half with my bare hands when I lost my patience...!"

"Dismissed!"

She almost bit her tongue off keeping the reply back that she wanted to make. She saluted sharply, turned and marched out of the office. Behind her, she heard muffled curses in Cehn-Tahr, and marched faster.

LIEUTENANT (J.G.) EDRIS MALLORY'S expression was one of pure joy as she sipped the illegal caffeine in Madeline's office. The use of stimulants, even natural ones, was prohibited by Tri-Fleet regulations. Not that anyone enforced the law, especially since Admiral Lawson himself sneaked in java from the Altairian colonies. Of course, he was an admiral and could get away with it. Madeline might not fare as well.

Edris closed her eyes and savored the taste and scent as she lifted her head. "Oh, bliss," she sighed.

Madeline laughed. "It is pretty special, out here in the big black, isn't it? We're so far away from anything that can't be grown in solution." She sipped her own coffee. "I have to talk to you about something."

Edris grimaced. "I've screwed up again, haven't I?" she asked. "I'm just not suited to life in our present age, you know. I washed out of combat school with a memorable low grade, after I couldn't get accredited as a breeder. Now here I am doing combat medicine, and I fumble more than I fix…"

"You're doing well," Madeline interrupted. "All you lack is confidence in your own abilities. Well, that," she added hesitantly, "and the ability to talk back to people. To the Cehn-Tahr specifically."

The slender young blonde moved restlessly in her chair. "They're very intimidating, especially the Holconcom commander," she replied. "He glares."

"You have to learn to glare back," Madeline told her. "They're a misogynist culture. Their own women are denied access to the military, much less combat. The Cehn-Tahr think our military is mad to permit women to serve in it, mentally neutered or not."

Edris finished the last precious drop of her coffee. "I'm just glad it's you and not me serving aboard the *Morcai*."

"That's what I want to talk to you about," Madeline told her. "Since Holmes and Watts shipped out, you and I are the only experienced Cularian specialists on base right now. There are twenty in graduate school, four of whom are due to be assigned to Trimerius when they graduate. But if something happens to me, you're the only backup around."

"Nothing will happen to you, ma'am," Edris assured her with a smile. "You're one of the bravest people I know."

Madeline hesitated. "Anyone can die. The Holconcom can't function without a medic who can operate on Cehn-Tahr soldiers in an emergency. The commander hates medics as a rule, and he won't permit the Dectat to assign physicians to him. He's reluctant to have me aboard, but Ahkmau convinced him that it was lunacy not to carry a Cularian specialist into battle."

"He scares me to death," Edris commented, wrapping her arms around her slender figure. "I don't know what I'd do, if I ever had to substitute for you in the Holconcom."

"That's just the point. The commander agrees with me, that we need to start letting you come with us on certain missions aboard the *Morcai* so that you can get used to the routine aboard ship." She deliberately didn't meet Mallory's eyes as she lied to her. It was in a good cause.

Edris lost two shades of color. "No," she said at once. "Oh, no, I can't do that. I can barely manage

here, when you're away with the unit. I could never...
I mean, I can't..."

"You can," Madeline said, and in a tone that didn't
brook argument. "You got through medical school.
You'll adapt to the *Morcai*."

Edris bit her lower lip. She looked hunted.

"They're just men," she said, exasperated. "Alien
men, but males are pretty much the same anywhere."

"Not the Cehn-Tahr," Edris argued. "I've heard
stories."

Madeline raised both eyebrows.

Edris hesitated, but the gossip was too juicy not to
share. "They say," she said in a conspiratorial tone,
"that a Cehn-Tahr soldier ate a young Jebob recruit
during the Great Galaxy War...ma'am?"

Madeline was doubled over, laughing. That story
had gone through the ranks over the years like a fever.
Some people did actually believe it.

"Well, they said," Edris said defensively.

"Edris," Madeline replied, wiping away tears of
near hysteria, "I can give you proof that no Cehn-Tahr
has ever eaten another soldier."

"You can?"

"The C.O. has never eaten me," she reminded her
colleague. "And nobody over the years has given him
more cause."

"You do wear on his nerves, I hear."

Madeline laughed. "His nerves, his temper, his patience. He's dressed me down, grounded me, brigged
me on occasion," she recalled. "But he's never taken
a bite out of me."

That was true. The battles between the commander
of the Holconcom and his chief medic had assumed

the mantle of legend. Once, Madeline had followed Dtimun off the ship raging about his refusal to let her suture a bone-deep wound in his leg. He trailed blood out the airlock and just kept walking, even when she threw a cyberclamp after him in impotent rage.

"Isn't it amazing that he never busted you in rank?" Edris mused.

"He did try," Madeline assured her. "But my father is a colonel in the Paraguard Wing and best friends with Admiral Lawson. They ganged up on the commander and refused to let the demotion go through." She grinned. "The C.O. was livid! And did he get even! He requisitioned my billet for storage and I had to sleep in the cargo hold for a solid week. He only relented when I borrowed a player from Hahnson and flooded the hold with ancient human drum and bagpipe music."

"I heard about that," Edris chuckled. "Didn't he break a Gresham in half…?"

"With his bare hands, and lucky for him that the power pack was drained." Madeline nodded enthusiastically. She pondered that. "You know, they really are incredibly powerful."

Edris toyed with her java cup. "Do I have to go?"

Madeline nodded.

Edris sighed. "Okay, then."

Madeline smiled. "Good girl," she said affectionately, as she would have to a younger sister; if she had one. The government restricted information about the parents of children raised in government nurseries. It was one of many laws that she simply accepted, because she was educated to accept it, without question. But after serving with the Holconcom, her attitudes about her government were undergoing some serious alterations. Not that she could speak of them to Edris. Not now, anyway. She went back to work.

EDRIS MALLORY HAD never been aboard a Cehn-Tahr ship before. Everything about it fascinated her, from the way personnel ran to and from positions down the wide corridors to the temperature, which was several degrees cooler than SSC ships.

"Their core body temperature is three degrees higher than our own," Madeline reminded her as they jogged toward the Cularian medical sector. "They cool the ship to make them more comfortable."

Edris was looking at the alien script on the compartment hatches as they passed them. She shook her head. "I don't know how anybody ever reads that."

"It's not so hard," came the amused reply. "It's a lot like old Asian languages on Terravega, mostly symbols. Pronouncing it, though, that's hard."

"They pronounce names differently according to kinship and relationship status, too, don't they?"

"Yes."

Edris frowned. "Why are they so secretive? I mean, we know a lot about their physical makeup, but nothing about their culture or even their behavioral patterns."

"They don't volunteer information," Madeline said, still smarting about her black market vids that had been a scam. "I've spent years trying to dig it out of Komak. He won't tell me anything."

"You could ask the C.O.," Edris suggested.

"Only with a good head start," Madeline assured her. "You just don't bring up those topics with him."

"I suppose not. I wonder if..."

"Who authorized you to bring Mallory aboard?" came a terse, angry deep voice from behind them.

Madeline stopped with easy grace and turned. Edris was frozen in place, her blue eyes like saucers as she stared uneasily at Dtimun.

"If I go down sick, you have to have a Cularian specialist aboard," she said simply.

"You are never unwell," Dtimun pointed out.

"I could catch that Altairian flu and be laid low for a week," she replied. "We have to have backup, and there isn't anyone else."

"Holmes," he began.

"Holmes shipped out to the Algomerian sector last week," Madeline told him. "Besides, he wasn't comfortable aboard the *Morcai*." She said it with a hint of reproach.

Dtimun's eyes narrowed and his jaw firmed. "I have competent physicals on my own planet, given by my own physician," he replied. "I do not require the services of a Terravegan Cularian specialist!"

Madeline pursed her lips and smiled. "Ever?"

He glared at her while Edris tried to melt into the deck.

"If I hadn't been at Ahkmau," she began, "you'd be dead now. Sir."

"Will there ever be an end to the constant revisiting of that medical procedure?" he wondered.

"Well, not as long as I'm alive, sir," she said with twinkling green eyes. "You are, after all, my greatest medical accomplishment."

He didn't speak. He was still glaring.

"Some surgeons couldn't have managed what I did

under laboratory conditions," she continued, warming to her subject. "I did it with a couple of purloined tools and almost no pure water, with Rojok patrols right outside the prison cell."

His lips were now making a thin line.

"You know, I don't recall that you ever even thanked me for it," she continued.

He bit off some comments in his own language.

"Sir!" she exclaimed.

He made a rough noise in his throat and turned his attention to Mallory. "Make sure that Ruszel acquaints you with shipboard protocol. No wandering is allowed, especially in the *kelekom* sector."

Mallory saluted, rigid as a board. "Sir, I never wander. I've never seen a *kelekom*. I mean, I don't want to see one. I mean, not that they aren't interesting, I'm sure…!"

Dtimun turned back to Madeline, exasperated. "There is no one else?"

She glared at him. "Edris is perfectly competent."

"To do what?" he demanded.

Edris made a hunted sound. She looked as if she wanted to hide under something.

"Sir, don't you have some pressing military function to perform that requires your attention elsewhere?" Madeline asked pleasantly. "Lives must be at stake somewhere."

"One day, warwoman," he bit off.

She raised both eyebrows. "One day, what, sir?" she asked innocently.

He darted a killing glance at Mallory, another at Madeline and turned on his heel, muttering in his own tongue as he stalked off.

"Can you translate that?" Edris asked timidly.

"Oh, you don't want me to do that," Madeline assured her. "Let's get you settled. It's going to be a long few days."

ON THAT SCORE, she was absolutely right. There was an emergency on one of the Coromat system planets near Terramer which required the skills of a Cularian medical specialist. Madeline elected to take Edris along, to let her get the feel of an away mission.

Sadly, no one had thought to tell the new recruit that the commander did high grav landings. He put down at six megs and Mallory threw up all over the deck. Dtimun was eloquent.

When he left the scout ship, Hahnson and Stern and Komak roared with laughter.

"Sorry," Hahnson told Edris, "we aren't laughing at you. It's just that the C.O. does line himself up for these mishaps. I mean, who puts down at six megs?"

Stern raised his hand.

"Not in a Cehn-Tahr scout, you never did," Madeline pointed out.

"I'm just so sorry," Edris moaned, pressing a medicated wipe to her face. "I'm so embarrassed! I've never done anything like that." She dotted an enzyme eraser onto the mess she'd made on the deck, cleaning it efficiently.

"I threw up the first time I did a high grav landing," Madeline assured her.

"Not on Dtimun's ship, you didn't," Hahnson reminded her.

"Oh, like you know," Madeline muttered.

"Actually, I threw up, too, the first time I had to fly

with Dtimun," Hahnson confessed. "He's just short of suicidal when he's piloting a small ship. But that high grav landing really weirds out enemy combatants. They never expect it."

"I suppose it would give us an edge in battle," Edris commented weakly.

"I don't suppose you'd know why the C.O. looks as if he's been chewing on the hull plates?" Stern asked Madeline.

She gave him an angelic smile. "I'm certain it doesn't have anything to do with me," she assured him.

"What did you say to him?" Stern persisted.

"I only mentioned how lucky he was that I was with him at Ahkmau when he needed emergency surgery," she replied. "And there was the matter of bringing Edris aboard."

"But you said the commander wanted me to learn the routine aboard the *Morcai*," Edris burst out.

"He did say that. Sort of," Madeline hedged.

"What exactly did he say?" Hahnson piped in.

Madeline shrugged. "That I could give her a virtual tour of the premises." She blinked. "Virtual, real, I mean, with the vid systems we have today, really, is there a difference?"

Edris put her face in her hands. "He'll kill me."

"Yes, but he can't eat you," Madeline assured her. "And we've already had that discussion. That Jebob soldier they said the Cehn-Tahr ate during the Great Galaxy War—he was actually eaten by a Rojok, wasn't he?" she asked the men.

Edris covered her mouth with her hand and went pale.

"Rojoks don't eat Jebob nationals," Stern scoffed. "They're far too stringy." He yawned. "It was an old Altairian, and they'd just run out of rations...Mallory? You okay?" He winced. "Damn, and you just cleaned the deck already!"

Madeline hit him. He just laughed.

"I AM CERTAIN that I don't want to serve aboard this vessel," Mallory said when they'd treated the diplomatic patient and were safely back aboard the *Morcai*, heading back to Trimerius.

"You just had a bad introduction to Holconcom routines," Madeline said soothingly. "First times are always difficult."

"This first time will give me nightmares every night from now on," Edris assured her. "How could you bring me aboard without telling the C.O.?" she moaned.

"Well, if I'd actually told him, he wouldn't have let you come," Madeline said reasonably, "and you have to learn someday."

Komak came up beside them, running backward to keep pace. He was grinning. "Have you shown Lieutenant Mallory the *kelekoms*?" he asked.

"No, sir, and she's not going to," Edris interrupted firmly before Madeline could get her mouth open. "I've done enough damage for one mission. With my luck, I'd sneeze on one and give it some fatal disease."

"They are quite used to humans now," Komak chuckled. "It has been a long time since one of them was ill."

"Has the C.O. had any luck finding a new partner for the inactive *kelekom*?" Madeline asked.

Komak shook his head. "Lawson will not provide him with any candidates."

"Brave Lawson, to refuse the commander," Edris murmured.

"He intimidates her," Madeline explained to Komak.

"Who, Lawson?" he asked.

"No. The commander."

"Oh." Komak grinned. "He does not intimidate you, Madelineruszel," he said.

"I've had all my shots."

Komak frowned. "Excuse me?"

She chuckled. "Private joke."

The intership speakers blared with Dtimun's deep voice speaking in Cehn-Tahr.

Komak grimaced. "I am told to mind my own duties and refrain from delaying other crew members from attending to their own."

"How did he know?" Edris asked, looking around warily.

"AVBDs," Madeline said, bending the truth. She knew that Dtimun was a telepath, but she'd never told anyone. "They're everywhere, except in the C.O.'s own office. You won't see them," she added. "They blend. See you, Komak."

He smiled, turned and put on a burst of speed, leaving them behind.

"THAT OFFICER, KOMAK," Edris commented as they jogged down the corridor of the *Morcai* on their way to the airlock, "he doesn't seem a lot like the rest of the Cehn-Tahr."

"I know. He's spent so much time around humans

that he's taken on human characteristics," Madeline laughed. "Odd, though, when we were in the death camp on Enmehkmehk's moon, I was using Komak for blood transfusion for the C.O. When I synched and synthed compatibility factors, his blood seemed to have human elements." She sighed. "And that's impossible. We know the Cehn-Tahr never mate outside their own species."

"Why?" Edris wondered.

Madeline blinked. "I suppose it's their racial laws. It carries the death penalty."

"Just like our military punishes any sexual fraternization with death," Edris replied. "Isn't it odd that both societies are so xenophobic?" she asked. "I've heard it said that all Terravegans were originally tea-colored with dark hair."

"I've heard that, too," Madeline said. "But I think you and I are proof that it's just an old legend," she added, smiling. "Your coloring and mine put paid to that theory."

Edris fingered her blond hair and eyed Madeline's reddish-gold hair and nodded. "Will the C.O. get over it? That I threw up all over the scout, I mean?"

Madeline stopped and looked at the other woman. "He's amazingly tolerant sometimes," she said. "He does have a temper, and he can be irritating and stubborn. But he's the best commanding officer in the fleet. All of us would follow him out the airlock if he asked us to. Of course, he does have this deplorable, primitive attitude about medics being unarmed, and I do have to sneak weapons off the ship in my equipment bag…"

Edris's eyes had widened and she was staring apprehensively over Madeline's shoulder.

Madeline's teeth clenched. "And he's standing right behind me, isn't he?"

Edris only nodded.

Madeline turned with a sigh. Dtimun was glaring down at her with both hands locked behind his back, looking stern and unapproachable.

"Shall we lengthen the period of your confinement to the base by two standard weeks?" he asked.

"Now, sir, why would we want to do that?" Madeline asked innocently.

He pursed his lips. "From now on, I intend to have your equipment bag searched every time we leave the ship."

She groaned.

He nodded curtly, turned and jogged off down the corridor.

Edris, wisely, didn't say a word. Dr. Ruszel's face was almost as red as her hair with bad temper.

CHAPTER THREE

MADELINE WAS CATCHING up on reports on her virtual desk when a flash came in from Admiral Lawson.

She answered it at once. "Yes, sir?" she said respectfully.

He grimaced. "I hate to have to ask you to do this, Ruszel," he replied, "but everybody else cut me off the minute I mentioned a personal dispatch I needed to send to Dtimun…" He waited. She didn't protest. He grinned. "I knew you had the guts to do it."

She sighed. "Everybody else is afraid of him, especially lately," she confided. "He's been in a sour mood. Not my fault," she added at once. "I haven't done a thing to upset him."

Lawson reserved judgment on that, but he didn't say so. "I'm flashing the dispatch to you. Top secret. Eyes only. I can't trust anyone else to transport it."

She blinked when it appeared, in solid form, in her cyberreconstitutor "in" tray. "Sir, you couldn't flash it to the C.O.?"

He shrugged. "I could, if he'd answer his unit. He won't." His face tautened. "He won't like the dispatch, but I have to give it to him. You'll find him at the Cehn-Tahr embassy, by the way, getting ready for some big reception at the Altair center. He's not happy that he has to go and represent his government. Their own ambassador refused to go and was recalled."

She pursed her lips. "My, my, imagine that. It must be something big."

"Something. Get going. He'll be leaving shortly. If you have to chase him down to the Altair embassy, the Altairians will never let you through the door in uniform."

"They'd have to," she commented, "because I'm not changing my uniform for skirts even for diplomacy's sake."

He chuckled. "I don't blame you. Not a lot of human females in the Holconcom," he added with a grin. Her place as the only female in that crack unit made him proud.

"Yes, sir," she agreed, smiling back.

He cut the connection. She looked at her screen with dismay. There were eight reports left to do. It was going to be a long night, she thought as she disabled the unit. But, hopefully, this wouldn't take long.

SHE HAD TO GET a military skimmer to the embassy. The building was, like most things Cehn-Tahr, smooth and rounded and elegant, a fantasy of blue and gold lights, the colors of the Cehn-Tahr Imperial Royal Clan. She dismissed the robot transport and walked up the steps, declining the vator tube. She wondered how much trouble she was going to have getting inside the embassy. Humans weren't exactly welcome here, even if a whole detachment of them served with the Holconcom.

A uniformed sentry waited at the door. With a hopeful smile, she started to present her arm, with its ID chip, but he saluted her at once and activated his comm unit.

"Dr. Madeline Ruszel of the Holconcom to see the commander," he spoke into it.

Her surprise was visible. She hadn't realized that she was known here. There was a long pause.

"Send her," came the terse reply.

Madeline grimaced. "Oh, boy," she said to herself. "He's not in the mood for company."

"It is the Altairian reception," the sentry confided. "None of us like the Altair delegation..."

A rush of angry Cehn-Tahr poured forth from the comm unit.

"Yes, sir!" the sentry said into his unit, motioning Madeline through the door with a clenching of teeth and a look of apology.

Poor guy, she thought.

"You are not required to pass time with my subordinates," came an angry, deep voice into her mind. "Why are you here?"

"You won't like it," she thought back.

"Lawson and his dispatch," he muttered, adding a few choice words in his own tongue.

"Sir!" she protested, because she recognized some of them.

He stepped into the hallway. She almost didn't recognize him. It wasn't just the absence of facial hair that made him look different—he hadn't regrown the beard and mustache he'd sported when the complement of the Morcai ended up in Ahkmau and Madeline had shaved him to disguise his face. It was his clothing that was different. He was wearing robes of blue and gold, the imperial colors, in some fabric as sleek as silk. The robes clung to the muscular lines of his body and draped over one shoulder to touch the floor at the tip of his highly polished black boots. He looked...different. Elegant. Regal. It was the first time she'd ever seen him out of a Holconcom uniform in the nearly three years she'd been part of the Morcai's crew.

"HE SENT YOU," Dtimun said with faint hauteur. "Why?"

"Because everybody else hid under a desk," she muttered. She held out the dispatch.

A flash of green amusement touched his eyes. "You were afraid of me, too, at first."

"That was years ago, sir," she reminded him. Her own eyes twinkled. "As soon as I realized that the Cehn-Tahr didn't eat humans, I stopped worrying."

He chuckled. He read the dispatch. His lips made a thin line. "More predations on our forward supply transports. I cannot turn the Morcai into an escort ship. Lawson will have to find another way."

"That was the job the Altairians were doing," she reminded him. "Then the Terravegan ambassador, Aubrey Taylor, ticked them off and they withdrew their support vessels."

"Taylor is what you humans call a bigot," he replied.

"I could think of a few better names," she murmured. Taylor had been vicious in his verbal attacks on the Cehn-Tahr, and the Amazon Division as well. He thought women in combat were a disgrace. She pursed her lips as she looked up at Dtimun. "You and Taylor should get along. He doesn't think women have any place in combat, either. I hear he's going to the

Altairian reception, too—probably to tick off even more of their military. Pity you can't think of some way to irritate him even more than you did when you withdrew his transport privileges on Cehn-Tahr vessels. Sir."

He gave her an odd, intense scrutiny. "Sadly for you, I can think of a better way. You will accompany me to the reception." He clapped his hands. Two younger men in uniform ran up and saluted. "Take Ruszel to the weavemaster and have him weave her robes to wear to the Altair reception. Tell him he has ten standard minutes."

"Robes? Reception? I will not…!" she burst out.

"Does Lawson know that you brew contraband coffee in your med lab?" he interrupted smugly.

Her mouth stayed open. She closed it. "Admiral Lawson does it, too," she began.

"He is an admiral." He looked at his immaculate fingernails. "I understand the penalty is revocation of all base privileges for a period of four standard months." He eyed her with evident amusement.

She glared at him. But she saluted, turned and followed the younger soldiers upstairs. She really hoped he was reading her mind on the way.

EXACTLY FIFTEEN STANDARD minutes later, she made her way down the winding staircase. Dtimun was looking at messages on his small virtual unit. He heard her steps—amazing, since the whole embassy was carpeted—and turned. His expression was too complex to classify, like the warping colors in his eyes.

She was enveloped in silken blue robes with gold trim. The robes covered her discreetly from her neck to her toes. The neck of the robes was draped in back just to the beginning of the creamy skin over her shoulder blades, displaying her nape. Her long reddish-gold hair had been pulled up and pinned in draping curls from a position high on her head by the weavemaster's assistant, who had also applied the lightest touch of makeup. She looked elegant. Regal. Beautiful.

She felt awkward. She moved the rest of the way down the steps, watching carefully so that she didn't trip over the unfamiliar skirts. "Next time could you just shoot me in the foot when you want to punish me, sir?" she asked.

He lifted an eyebrow. "You would grace a palace, madam," he said quietly. He drew in a long sigh. "It is a great pity that there are so many differences between our species."

She frowned. "Not that many," she protested.

He laughed bitterly. "You have no idea. Come. We cannot be late."

He moved in front of her and then stood aside at the door to let her exit first. There was a long, elegant diplomatic skimmer at the top of the steps, floating in midair, waiting for them. They entered quickly, standing by the rail, as the doors closed and the flyer zipped to the next row of buildings where the Altair embassy was located.

"I know where we could start a brawl," she murmured to herself, provoking him.

His eyes cut around to meet hers. "I know where we could find a brig."

She made a face. "I hate parties."

"No more than I do, I assure you," he returned stiffly.

They arrived at the Altair embassy and he stood aside to let her precede him. At the door, two blue-skinned officers were waiting to validate invitations.

"See, they have two guards at their doors. You only have one," she said under her breath.

"One Cehn-Tahr suffices to keep out any number of intruders," he replied. "Be quiet."

"Yes, sir."

He extended his invitation, indicated Madeline and was admitted to the flashy, neon-accented ballroom of the Altair embassy by vator tube.

"Fancy," she mused, looking around.

"I have seen ragged carnivals with better taste."

Her eyebrows arched. "You have?" she asked with pure mischief.

He glared at her.

"Commander Dtimun," the Altairian ambassador said as he joined them. He was smiling, but cool. "I did not expect so high ranking an official at my poor reception."

"Our ambassador was called away unexpectedly," Dtimun said formally.

"And your companion…human? How…unorthodox. But she is lovely," he added, giving Madeline a long look.

Madeline thought of planting her fist right in his teeth.

"Madam!" Dtimun said aloud.

She cleared her throat, flushed and smiled at the Altairian. "How kind of you to say so, sir," she said.

He nodded and returned the smile.

"You do not recognize Dr. Ruszel?" Dtimun commented.

The ambassador did a comical double take. "Dr. Ruszel?" He peered closer and caught his breath. "No, I did not recognize you, Doctor. Forgive me."

"I am out of uniform," she sympathized with a cold glance at her commander.

"We are honored to have the Holconcom's medical chief of staff among us," he replied. "Please, enjoy our hospitality."

"Thank you."

Dtimun jerked his eyes toward the buffet table, a blatant hint that she was to leave him alone with the ambassador. She excused herself and set out to sample what she could stomach of the buffet. She sighed sadly when she realized that most of the dishes were what humans would describe as sushi. Not that she didn't like it, when they docked at oceanic continents. But the Altairian idea of sushi came from sea lizards of a particularly poisonous species. She helped herself to a glass of synthale and nibbled on a dish of what she hoped was ground nuts.

The commander rejoined her shortly, clearly pleased.

"I'm glad you're happy, sir," she said. "I'm hoping to get drunk enough not to mind the taste of the canapés…"

"Do not dare embarrass me here," he bit off.

She gave him a wry look. "Would I do that, sir?"

He lifted an eyebrow.

"Hey, look at the sweet little lady," came a heavily accented, drunken voice from beside her. A fat little Terravegan in an expensive suit sidled up to her. "Aren't you pretty?"

The voice belonged to the Terravegan ambassador, Aubrey Taylor. Highly positioned politicians weren't bound by the neutering policy of the military. They could, and did, amuse themselves with women of all species. They, of all Terravegans, even chose where they wanted to marry.

Madeline gave him a cold look. Taylor glanced at the Cehn-Tahr beside her. "Some weird, unlawful combination, aren't you?" he asked with disgust. "Does she know that trying to mate with you would kill her?" He sidled closer and put an arm around her. "But you'd do just fine with me...!"

She jerked back from him just as Dtimun made an odd rumbling noise, in the back of his throat. Madeline didn't understand what it was, but she risked his temper by kicking him, covertly, in the leg. He made another sound, dismayed and angry. Madeline turned quickly and pretended to stumble. Her foot shot out efficiently, just covertly enough to trip the ambassador and knock him flat on his rear.

"Oh, my goodness, Ambassador Taylor, I'm so sorry!" she exclaimed loudly, and rushed to his side as he sat up on the floor, cursing. "Sir, I'm very sorry!" she exclaimed. "I turned too fast and tripped over my big feet! I'm not used to skirts."

"You clumsy cow!" Taylor raged. "I ought to...!"

"You don't recognize me, do you, sir?" she asked Taylor quickly as the commander stepped forward angrily and heads turned toward them at the ambassador's loud exclamation. "I'm Dr. Madeline Ruszel, medical chief of staff of the Holconcom. The commander is my C.O." She indicated Dtimun, who was glaring at the ambassador with eyes a color she couldn't quite classify. His posture was oddly threatening.

"Commander?" Taylor blinked. He looked from one face to another and registered his surprise. He struggled to his feet. "What are the two of you doing here, dressed like that?" he demanded.

"Covert ops, sir," she whispered to Taylor.

He swayed a little, then blinked. "Covert...? Oh. Oh!" He put his finger to his lips. "Shhhh."

"That's right, sir," she agreed, forcing a smile. "Shhhh."

He blinked. He was clearly over his limit. "I get it. Well, carry on, carry on!"

"Yes, sir."

"I'm all right. Just tripped!" Taylor told his colleagues as he turned away from Madeline and stumbled toward the buffet table. "Will somebody get some more ice? These drinks are hot! Have to drink, this food is inedible!"

Muffled conversation began again. The Altair ambassador was even bluer with anger. Dtimun took the opportunity to leave the room, followed closely by Madeline.

They were outside, heading for the skimmer, when a curt laugh escaped him. "I should have you courtmartialed," he muttered. "The problem is deciding which charge to press—striking a superior officer or assaulting a diplomat."

She grinned. "The diplomat deserved far more than that, sir," she commented. "Sorry I kicked you, but I was afraid you meant to add to the ambassador's condition."

He didn't answer her. He couldn't admit that his temper had almost slipped its bonds when the drunk human had dared to put his hands on Ruszel. It was a behavior that was of some concern to him. It had not happened before with Ruszel. He was uncertain why it was happening now.

The skimmer lifted and moved off toward the Cehn-Tahr embassy.

Madeline was looking at him oddly. She was recalling what Taylor had said; that shocking comment that made no sense.

Dtimun read it in her thoughts, but he said nothing. The ambassador was quite correct. If he attempted to mate with Ruszel, with his genetically enhanced strength, he would kill her instantly. But he couldn't speak of that to her. It was forbidden. Intimate contact was, of course, impossible. He looked down at her, at her radiant beauty, and had to force his eyes away. She was unlike females of any race he had ever encountered. He found her intriguing. But that still did not explain his violent reaction when Taylor touched her. It was disturbing. It was not a military response. It was a very personal one.

"Anyway, the sushi was nice," she remarked, for something to say.

He pursed his lips. "Yes. We prefer our meat and fish raw as well." He wasn't adding that they could eat them whole, as any feline predator could.

She paused and looked up at him with open curiosity.

"Stop there," he said in her mind. "Some questions are taboo, even among Clan. We are forbidden to speak of cultural habits to any outworlder. Even a Holconcom physician," he added with a smile in his tone.

"We do know some things about your species," she ventured.

"From your black market videos?" he asked with amused green eyes.

She gasped. "Sir!" she protested, flushing. "It has to be a breach of some sort of ethics for you to walk in and out of my mind!"

He chuckled. "Of course it is. But, then, madam, I have a reputation for bending the law."

She had to admit that. It had saved their lives in many desperate situations, too.

"As for probing your mind, that is not intentional. I read only what lies on the surface."

She gave him a demure look. "Good thing. I don't fancy a court martial if you dig too deep," she said with a gamine grin.

He repressed a laugh and changed the subject. "Ambassador Taylor's behavior should be reported," he said instead.

"Oh, please, sir, be my guest," she invited. "If I report him, I'll be mopping bathrooms, excuse me, heads, out on the Rim in the farthest outpost he can find for the rest of my military career."

He laughed. "Surely not."

"Afraid so. He, like all the politicians, has immense power in our society. It's something we have to live with, in the military."

"I might drop a word in Lawson's ear," Dtimun pondered. "He, too, has connections in high places."

"That wouldn't be a bad idea, sir." She laughed. "But it is rather amazing, how much he seems to know about your race," she commented.

He didn't answer. It was just as well that it didn't occur to her to wonder why Taylor had such intimate knowledge of a race he purported to hate, which was the Cehn-Tahr. Although it was the Rojok dynasty into which Taylor had been initiated, for some years now. Rojoks, both allies and enemies to the Cehn-Tahr in times past, knew a great deal about their culture, and would share that knowledge with even a human who was working for them. Madeline didn't know, and he couldn't tell her. He didn't want to admit how correct Taylor's remarks had been.

He was brooding. She could sense it; and not about the ambassador's behavior. He wasn't heading toward the skimmer. He seemed to have forgotten it was waiting for them.

"Sir, there's something more," she began hesitantly, wary of his hot temper. "It wasn't just having to sub for your ambassador at the Altairian embassy."

He turned and glared at her.

"Oh, right, it's okay for you to wear ruts in my mind, but I can't discuss what's going through yours. Sir," she added. She cocked her head and looked up at him quietly. "Something is really disturbing you. I'm not prying. But if there was any way I could help, I would," she added very gently.

He hesitated. For once, his expression was almost vulnerable. His eyes narrowed, deep blue with solemn thought. "You are remarkably perceptive, Ruszel." He drew in a long breath and when he spoke, it was only in her mind.

"We have, in my culture, a day of remembrance when we honor the dead. It takes place in the Hall of Memories on Memcache. But if we are too far away, we observe the ceremonies here, on Trimerius." His tone in her mind was somber. "I place a glow stone, a virtual collection of music, verses, poetry, for each of my two brothers."

"I'm very sorry for your loss, sir."

"This happens in war. The youngest was close to me. It is…difficult." He straightened. "I would be glad of the company."

Her eyebrows arched. "You mean, I could go with you?" He nodded. "But, sir, isn't it against the law?"

He smiled. "Yes."

She caught his mood and smiled back.

"Come." He led the way to the skimmer. A few minutes later, they landed at the Cehn-Tahr embassy. He led her down a long hall. All along the way, Cehn-Tahr soldiers bowed respectfully and saluted.

He glanced at her confusion. "They bow to me," he said. "However—" and he sounded amused, in her mind "—they salute you."

"Me?" she faltered.

"The Holconcom's human warwoman," he explained. "They find you fascinating. In fact, a group of our elite troops on Memcache refer to you almost in reverent tones. Considering their prejudice against humans, the behavior is remarkable."

She was left speechless. He noticed that, and smiled.

But when the guards opened the door into a huge indoor conservatory, with trees and plants which were, presumably, native to Memcache, she found her voice. "It's incredible," she whispered as the doors closed behind them. The species of plants and trees were unfamiliar, but gloriously beautiful.

"A taste of home," he remarked.

They approached a huge statue of a galot. This one was jet black with glowing green eyes. "Magnificent," she thought, fascinated.

"Cashto, from whom we obtained some of our genetic material many ages ago." He looked down at her. "You will not speak of this."

"No, sir," she promised. Later, she would recall these confidences with curiosity. He had said it was taboo to speak of culture with outworlders.

He turned back to the statue. He pulled three softly glowing pastel stones from a platform on one side of the statue, placed them on the other side and spoke words of remembrance in the Holy Tongue, which was spoken only by Cehn-Tahr elite—and which Ruszel would not understand. If he had been alone, he would have pulled up the images of his brothers. But that would be unwise. Ruszel had an excellent memory. He stepped back from the altar and stood quietly for several minutes. Ruszel, beside him, didn't make a sound. While she'd lost comrades—in fact, her whole Amazon unit from the *Bellatrix* during the Rojok attack three years earlier—she'd never lost a family member. Well, except for Hahnson, on Ahkmau. She had his clone now, and he had Hahnson's memories. It was infinitely sad to remember the original Hahnson's death. She could only imagine how hard it was for the commander, to lose two brothers. The pain must be terrible.

"Quite," he remarked. He was staring at Cashto's

statue, which towered over both of them under a spread of leafy trees. "Are you religious, Ruszel?"

She smiled faintly. "Well, I am, although not in any conventional sense," she replied. "I've seen enough unexplained recoveries in my career not to discount miracles. There has to be something far more powerful than we are. Even science has its limits."

He only nodded, as if her answer satisfied the question.

He led the way back out, lost in his own memories, his own pain. He had placed a stone as well for a woman he lost on Dacerius, decades ago. That was a memory he would not share with his companion.

She noticed that he placed three glowing stones at the altar, but she put the thought away. It wasn't her business. However, she was very curious about the purpose of Dtimun's visit to the embassy, when he hated Altairians.

He glanced down at her. "You wonder why we went to the reception."

She nodded.

"The Altairians have a treaty with the Nagaashe, a race who live on a world near our borders. They have great stores of Helium 3, which we employ in reactors to provide heat and cooling for our cities. Our resources of this element are diminishing, but the Nagaashe will not trade with us. After many decades of diplomatic persistence, the Altair ambassador has agreed to present our case to the Nagaashe," he added. "But considering the usual speed of their negotiations, I fear the treaty will not be created in my lifetime."

"Who are the Nagaashe?" she wondered.

He smiled. "So many questions whirling in your mind, Ruszel. But answers must wait. Thank you for accompanying me."

"It wasn't as if I had a real choice, sir," she pointed out, and he chuckled. She made a face. "And their idea of synthale is an abomination."

"They do not consume alcoholic beverages in their culture," he reminded her.

"No wonder!"

He laughed. He motioned for one of the young officers. "Show Dr. Ruszel to the room where she left her uniform, and then accompany her back to the medical center."

"Sir," she protested. "I can hardly be in danger during that short hop…"

He held up a hand. "I do not trust Taylor," he said flatly. "You are one of my officers. I will not have you troubled by drunk politicians, regardless of their so-called power. Do as I say."

She sighed, but she saluted. "Yes, sir."

He nodded. His eyes roamed over her one last time, openly appreciative of her delicate beauty and the excellent fit of the robes she was wearing. But all at once, his expression became distant. He walked away without looking back.

MADELINE WONDERED FOR days about Taylor's odd remark, that Dtimun would kill her if he tried to mate with her. She couldn't find any reference to Cehn-Tahr customs or culture in any of her resources. In desperation, she key holed Hahnson, who knew more than anyone in her acquaintance about the aliens.

She told him what Taylor had said in his drunken state. "What did it mean?" she asked.

Hahnson only smiled blandly. "How would I know?"

She glowered at him. "You know a lot. You knew that Cehn-Tahr mark their mates."

"A bit of gossip I picked up," he said evasively. He lifted an eyebrow. "If I were you, I'd leave the subject strictly alone."

She shrugged. "I guess I'll have to. But it's intriguing. We know so little about their culture, their behavioral traits. We know a lot about Rojoks, but they have reptilian DNA. Cehn-Tahr are supposed to be descended from felines." She gave him a wry look. "I'm no geneticist but I'm not stupid, either. They have eyes that change color...nobody else in the galaxies does. And they may have feline traits, but the only way you get galot DNA is to be injected with it."

He put a finger to his lips. "Don't even joke about that."

"Strick, we've been friends for a long time," she persisted. "Can't you tell me anything?"

He averted his face. "Some mysteries are best left unsolved," he said flatly. "Now how about giving me your opinion on this new treatment for Altairian flu?"

Diverted, she turned to the virtual display. Since there was no way to satisfy her curiosity, she let the subject drop. For the time being. Privately, she wondered about the window her commanding officer had given her into his culture, something he'd never discussed with her in almost three years. It had been intriguing, and flattering, that he shared the remembrance ceremony with her. She really wondered why, when it was such a breach of custom. As she'd promised, however, she hadn't said a word to Hahnson about that, even if she had picked his mind on Cehn-Tahr mating habits.

CHAPTER FOUR

THE WAR, LIKE all wars, had periods of monotony and boredom. It also had sudden spurts of urgency. This was one. The Rojoks had landed an advance force on a planet in the Dibella system and were preparing a staging area for a far larger command. Lagana was the largest continent on the planet; a rich source of clean water and foodstuffs, of which the Rojok supply lines were desperately in need.

Dtimun called in all off-duty personnel and set a course for the planet. The Dibella system was a link in a chain leading to the home planets of the Tri-Galaxy Council members. The advance, which was small at the moment, had to be stopped and the staging area destroyed. Lawson, for once, didn't oppose the commando mission. Madeline had wanted to take Edris Mallory along on the mission, even if she'd had to conceal her on board. But once the *Morcai* put down on Lagana, the Dibella system's fourth planet, she was glad she hadn't. It was no milk run. There was a considerable Rojok presence in a staging area near one of the continent's major cities—although on this jungle world, that meant a population of less than two hundred souls. The Rojoks obviously planned a takeover here, and had just landed troops with that intention, in two makeshift camps. The resources of the planet were extensive.

Dtimun called a briefing before the Holconcom left the ship. He pulled up a virtual map in the center of the room and indicated the Rojok staging area.

"We must destroy their communications equipment first. Jennings."

"Yes, sir!" the human comm chief said, saluting.

"This will be your job. Coordinate with Komak's forward unit."

"Yes, sir!" Jennings grinned. On a human ship, he'd never have been allowed in combat. Communications personnel of Jennings' command rank were not allowed on away missions in the Terravegan military. But here, duty descriptions were different. He loved these assaults; odd for a communications guy, Madeline thought amusedly.

Dtimun glanced at her and his eyes flashed green as he read the thoughts in her mind.

"You must take your bodyguard with you," Komak told the C.O. abruptly.

Dtimun gave him an odd look.

Komak didn't back down. "You must."

Dtimun sighed. "Very well." He indicated the four Holconcom who performed that function. "You will come down with me."

The ranking officer in the small unit saluted.

Madeline found it unusual that Dtimun agreed to Komak's suggestion. Often, the younger Cehn-Tahr had premonitions about difficult missions. Apparently, he had one about this one. Strange, because it was such a small Rojok command. But, Madeline thought, might as well err on the side of caution. She

studied Dtimun covertly as he outlined the order of
battle. She recalled him in sweeping robes at the Altair embassy. He had looked…very nice.

His eyes shot around and pinned her.

"Sorry, sir," she thought at once, and forced her
mind back to military thoughts. These irrational
flashes were starting to get the better of her.

THEY HAD HOPED to land undetected, but the Rojoks
had new state-of-the-art sensors and they worked.
The minute the scout ships touched down, the Rojoks were waiting for them.

The onslaught was fierce. Two Rojok squads
armed with *kremoks*, the new rapid-firing plasma
rifles that fried internal organs, tore through the
human infantry like fire through forests. Madeline
saw two soldiers she'd served with since basic training go down, dead before they hit the ground. She
checked them, anyway, but it was far too late for any
medical technique to bring them back other than as
clones, a living death in Terravegan society. She rose
and moved quickly to the sound of plasma fire, forcing herself to be professional, not to let her emotions
get the better of her. She had to tend to the living.

The medical research facility on Camcara was developing a counterweapon, a chemical screen that
would be woven into the newest uniforms issued to
the SSC. Madeline had adapted the technology for
the Holconcom and Dtimun had authorized the addition and made it standard issue. But the uniforms
were still in quality control tests.

Some of the commando squads were still using the
older *chasats*, and one of those units had wedged it-

self between Dtimun and his bodyguard in the thick, muggy green jungle of vines and plants that covered this continent. Madeline cursed as she tried to move past a tangle that resembled a spiderweb. Then she remembered the illegal Gresham she'd tucked in the small away kit over one shoulder. She pulled it out and activated the power pack. With that, she cut through the vegetation in no time. She pressed ahead. The urgency grew as she heard the thum-thum sound of *chasat* fire close by.

"Ruszel!" She heard the ranking member of Dtimun's four-man bodyguard unit in the tissue-thin monitor pasted just behind her ear.

"Yes!" she spoke into the matching monitor that rested like part of the skin at her lips.

"The commander has been hit!"

For an instant, the world went black. She was very still. "Critically?"

"Unknown. We saw him go down. Afterward, he did not move. We cannot get to him from our position. He has not answered our comms."

"Where is he?" she asked tautly.

He gave coordinates. She didn't speak to her comrades, who were mopping up the Rojok attack force. She motioned her medics toward three wounded Cehn-Tahr and then, with her heart racing at her throat, she sprinted toward the position where the commander was located. She didn't dare think about his injury. With his greatly modified strength, if he was unconscious…!

Terror welled up in her. She didn't see where she was going, she only ran, seeing the coordinates in the ether display that popped up from its concealment at the corner of each eye, produced by a film of circuitry which she wore over her corneas. She followed the blip, her illegal Gresham ready to fire. She wasn't going to be captured. The C.O.'s life might depend on her, if he was still alive.

If he was still alive. She felt the words, like knives. He couldn't be dead. He couldn't be! She realized suddenly that if he died, the light would go out of the world. There was nothing that would make up for his loss.

Forbidden thoughts, she told herself, and she must clamp down on them at once. She was a doctor, and a patient was waiting. That was what she needed to be thinking about.

She rushed through a cover of native vegetation and saw the commander flat on his back with two Rojok soldiers standing over him, *chasats* drawn.

She yelled, commanding their attention before they could fire. As they turned, surprised, she took them down in a heartbeat with two quick blasts and never even paused to check, to make sure they were no longer a threat. She was a dead shot, especially under combat conditions, having been battle-tested as a child.

"Sir!" She slid onto her knees at his side, her wrist scanner already busy, searching out clues to his condition. "Sir?"

The members of his bodyguard suddenly came running from the direction of the worst fighting. Their uniforms were torn and one had a bloody arm.

"Why did you leave him?" she raged at them from a face as red as her hair. "Your job is to protect the commander, not to act as regular combat troops!"

In her mind a familiar, furious voice made itself heard. "Remember who you are, madam!" it demanded.

Her eyes turned to his. They were open, brown with pain and anger, but open and alive. She was shaking. She hadn't even realized it.

"Remember who you are," the angry voice sounded again in her mind. "Pull yourself together! You disgrace the uniform with this display of hysterics."

She forced her mind to work, her body to relax. Her face reverted to its usual serene expression. "I beg your pardon," she told his bodyguard in her usual, measured tones. "I spoke out of turn. We lost some of the Terravegans in the first wave, two of whom I had served with for years. It…affected me."

"No apology is necessary, Ruszel," the ranking bodyguard officer spoke for all of them. "We were pinned down in a gulley and could not get to the commander in time. Had you not been armed, the Rojoks would have killed him."

"What…Rojoks?" Dtimun gritted as she opened his tunic and revealed a penetrating chest wound. "And what do you mean, had Ruszel not been armed?" he demanded, his angry voice gaining strength.

Madeline, busily working on his wound, tried to look invisible.

"Two Rojoks were in the act of killing you when Ruszel fired on them," the officer said respectfully.

"You were armed?" he demanded of her.

She ground her teeth together as she pulled out another tool and began to repair the cellular damage. "So court-martial me."

"I intend to!" he shot back. "How many times

must I tell you that medics are not permitted weapons in combat? It draws fire from the enemy directly to you!"

"She saved your life, sir," the eldest of his bodyguard interjected solemnly.

"Yes. And that's twice…" Madeline began with defiant humor.

"Silence!" he growled. He tried to sit up while she was still working on him.

She pushed him back down. "Stay there!" she grumbled. "I can't mend tissue on a moving target!"

The bodyguard stood rigidly, waiting for the explosion. To their amazement, the commander only made a sound in his throat and lay back down in the grass while Ruszel's deft hands reduced the wound.

"After all the time and effort I put into saving your life at Ahkmau, I'm not letting some stray Rojoks take you out," she muttered as she worked.

"We have already agreed that you most likely repaired me in such fashion that I will never function properly again," he reminded her.

She made a face. "You could look for years in the Tri-Fleet and not find another Cularian medicine specialist who could operate on you under combat conditions."

He didn't answer. The rigid lines of his face began to relax. Madeline realized belatedly that he had been concealing the extent of the pain. It must have been horrific, she reasoned, considering the extent of the damage.

She finished the sutures and applied a sterile bandage. "You're lucky that the Rojok hit your lung and not your heart," she said absently.

"Your misfortune," he replied, touching the invisible bandage with the tips of his fingers. "You have been warned repeatedly about flouting the regulations forbidding weapons to medics. This time you will pay the price."

She got to her feet, trying not to notice the broad, muscular chest with its thick wedge of black hair confronting her as he followed suit.

"You'll file charges," she said nonchalantly, "the board will ask for my side of the story, I'll call your bodyguard as witnesses and everybody will note that you would be dead if I hadn't disobeyed orders. You'll lose your case, I'll get a commendation, and the Tri-Fleet will foot the bill for all the legal wrangling." She gave him a smug look from twinkling green eyes.

"We would be required to tell the truth under oath," the chief of Dtimun's personal bodyguard interjected. "Sorry, sir."

Dtimun closed his uniform shirt. "Get back down there and check the Rojok camp for intel," he growled at the officer.

The other Cehn-Tahr saluted, grinned at Madeline and led his unit back to the dwindling sounds of combat from above.

Madeline knew she was in trouble. She didn't even have to note the color of his eyes. It was bad enough that she'd carried a Gresham. It was worse that she'd forgotten herself so completely that she'd shown her fear for the danger he was in. She toyed with complex mathematical computations, hoping they might prevent him from seeing too much.

He didn't say anything at first. He checked his virtual combat array to see how the mopping-up was proceeding, and he noted the position and strength of the remaining Rojok troops.

"Well, I couldn't let them kill you," she said defensively when he finally glared down at her. "I'm a doctor. I took an oath to save lives."

His eyes narrowed. He seemed deep in thought. Something dark and painful made shadows under his eyelids.

Suddenly, she saw shapes. Humans. No, Cehn-Tahr. And Dacerians. Rojoks, too. There was sand; a village in the deep desert of Dacerius. There was a beautiful woman with jet-black hair that fell to her hips, and eyes like almonds. She wore the thinnest of black lace veils over her nose and mouth. She was smiling. Then she was yelling, held firmly by Cehn-Tahr soldiers in royal blue uniforms. A shadowy figure was raging at a younger version of Dtimun as he held the female by the arm. She whirled, moved toward him aggressively. The shadowy figure raised his hand and grabbed something from a nearby wall. A razor-sharp golden sword sliced downward. There was an anguished shout, a short scream, blood...!

She had to sit down. The images were horrifying, even to a physician who'd worked under combat conditions.

Dtimun was scowling. "Impossible," he said harshly, visibly shocked. "You have no *psi* abilities. I checked your medical records!"

She was still trying to catch her breath. That beautiful, helpless woman. The barbarians! She shivered.

"Only six other minds in the three galaxies have ever penetrated mine, and they were of my own Clan!" he bit off.

The telling reference went right over her head.

"She was so beautiful," she murmured, feeling sick.

He turned away from her. "We must go."

She knew she should never have spoken aloud. Now she was going to catch hell for that, too. She got back to her feet, shaky and unsettled. She checked the medical banks in her wrist scanner for something to do.

"You will never repeat what you have seen," he said, but his lips didn't move.

She heard him in her mind. "Of course I won't," she replied, and her lips didn't move, either. "I never repeat anything you tell me in confidence."

They stared at each other for one long moment while the realization penetrated. Now it worked both ways. He was reading her mind; but she could read his as well. She wondered how Cehn-Tahr learned how to block probing minds. Before she could ask the question, even silently, the bodyguard came down the hill with a hostage.

Madeline left the commander with his bodyguard and rushed back to the rest of the command, to see what she could do for the wounded. Hahnson was directing his own medics among the humans of the unit. Madeline motioned to her medtechs and started toward another small section of the jungle battlefield. The sound of weapons firing seemed unusually loud.

Her contretemps with the commander had unsettled her, or she might have noticed the ambush. She'd gone ahead to search for more casualties when she heard the snap of a fallen limb just behind her. As she turned to see who was following her, there was a sharp pain in her head and then, darkness.

"WHERE IS RUSZEL?" Dtimun asked Hahnson as he and his bodyguard joined the rest of the unit.

"Maddie?" Hahnson looked dazed. "Sir, I haven't seen her."

"She came this way. She must be here."

Hahnson called one of his assistants over. "Have you seen Dr. Ruszel?" he asked.

"Yes, sir," the younger man acknowledged. "She went ahead to look for any casualties we might have missed. She's only been gone for a few minutes…"

Dtimun was a blur of red, moving so fast that his own bodyguard was hard-pressed to close the distance between them. He looked for her in his mind. But he couldn't find her. The lack of communication was…disturbing. His red-haired medic tended to overshoot her mandate in battle, often rushing into trouble. He recalled Chacon's timely interference at Ahkmau during the escape of the Morcai Battalion from imprisonment, when Madeline had been treating a wounded comrade and didn't see Rojoks creeping up on her with deadly intent. Her courage was legendary. But she sometimes had poor impulse control. He didn't like this. It was very unusual that he couldn't touch her mind when he liked. He did it more often than he cared to admit lately, and often without her knowledge.

He tossed a curt order to his men, insisting when they were reluctant to leave him. He had no basis for his concern, but he felt somewhere inside him that Ruszel was in trouble. She got on his nerves, she irritated him, she frequently made him furious. But if he lost her…

He put on another burst of speed as he looked for any sign of her. He found her boot prints in the soft dirt. They were joined by two larger pair. Rojoks! Her footprints vanished and those of one of the Rojoks deepened. She'd been carried out of here. But to where? If he couldn't access her mind, he couldn't find her!

He closed his eyes and searched for her thoughts. "Ruszel," he called silently. "Ruszel, answer me. Where are you?"

There was a hesitation that he actually felt. "Sir?" Her thoughts were disoriented and layered in intense pain. But she was alive! He hated the intensity of relief that he felt. His overreaction to her danger was disturbing.

"Where are you?" he persisted.

Madeline's head was splitting. She sat up and caught her breath. She was in a Rojok camp atop a mesa, overlooking the battlefield. The ranking officer of the Rojok squad was staring down at her with an expression that made her want to kick him.

"So you wake," he said. "You are Ruszel," he added surprisingly. "We have heard of you. The Holconcom has caused the deaths of many of our comrades. How fitting that we should now cause yours." He gave an order. Two of his men jerked Madeline to her feet, worsening the headache.

The Rojok gave her a scrutiny that, if she had been herself, would have propelled her fist into his thinlipped, slit-eyed face.

"You are comely, for a human female," the Rojok

purred. He reached out a six-fingered hand and ripped her tunic open. "Such white skin," he laughed, gripping her soft flesh in his fingers.

She kicked him as hard as she could and was trying to land another blow when the Rojok's hand connected with her cheek. She took the blow without flinching and used a Rojok word she'd heard from Komak. It made the officer furious.

"Here," the small, muscular Rojok called to them as he poised on the edge of the cliff. "Bring her! We will show this bad-tempered, worthless female how we reward bad behavior among our own people!"

The taller aliens half dragged her to the precipice. Below, she could see the red uniforms of her colleagues. Her eyes weren't focusing. She could barely think for the pain.

"Where are you?" Dtimun demanded again.

She blinked. "I'm on the edge of a cliff," she thought to him. "Above one of our units. My head is killing me. These two-legged lizards must have hit me on the head. Which is nothing to what this little tyrant just tried to do…" She pictured it in her mind.

"Holconcom!" the small Rojok officer interrupted her, calling down to her comrades. "Can you hear me?"

Dtimun looked up. There was Ruszel, in the grasp of two tall Rojoks. A smaller one was posed there, his hands on his hips.

"We have your warwoman!" the Rojok officer yelled down. "Retreat, or we will throw her down to you!"

Dtimun felt the others group around him. Hahnson

moved to his side. The husky blond medic was tense, still. His concern was almost physical.

"The Holconcom do not bargain. Return our crewman, or face the consequences," Dtimun called back, in a tone like steel hitting rock.

The small Rojok only laughed. "I did not think you would bargain. But this one is much known among soldiers. Even our commander in chief has respect for her," he spat. "She is nothing special. Just a female." He caught Madeline's arm and dragged her closer to the edge of the cliff. "But you will not replace her easily, Commander of the Cehn-Tahr," he added. He laughed again. "What a shame, to kill her! You should obey me, and quickly, if you wish her to live. Which would break first when she landed, I wonder—her back or her skull? Perhaps we should remove her brain before we toss her down to you!"

"Dear God," Hahnson whispered, his voice barely audible as he saw the certainty of what was going to happen next. "He's crazy."

Dtimun tensed. "Be still," he shot at his comrade. He closed his eyes. "Madeline," he called silently, using her name almost unconsciously. "Do you trust me?"

"With my life, sir," came the quiet reply.

"You must close your eyes, hold your breath and throw yourself over the cliff."

She didn't question him, or argue. She knew it would be a leap to her death. No being in the galaxies could possibly save her without a force net, and she knew that her unit carried none of those. He wasn't going to let the Rojoks have the satisfaction of causing her death. He expected her to die like a soldier, and bring honor to her command. And she would. Lack of courage had never been one of her faults.

"Now?" she asked.

"Yes."

She didn't even hesitate. "*Malenchar*!" she yelled, giving the battle cry of the Holconcom. At the same moment, throbbing head and all, she jerked out of the shocked Rojok's grasp, took a breath and dived head-first over the edge of the cliff. She closed her eyes. Free fall was exciting. Of course, there would be a sudden stop, she thought with gallows humor. Hopefully, she wouldn't feel it.

About halfway down, she felt something warm and solid wrap itself around her. She opened her eyes, startled, and found the commander enveloping her. He made leaps against the face of the cliff that her mind told her were impossible. She'd seen great cats bound from high place to higher place, liquid with grace and strength, but she'd never seen a Cehn-Tahr do it.

With grace and elegance, holding her easily against him, he flew like the wind, finding a foothold, using it to leap to another foothold. Claws extended on one hand, and he used them to help keep his balance as he jumped. He made his way down the cliff in a matter of seconds, his strength unbelievable. Belatedly, Madeline wrapped her arms around his neck and held on for dear life. She was dead of course, but her mind had somehow lapsed into dreams before she hit bottom. None of this was real. No species in the universe could do what her mind told her that Dtimun was doing.

With a soft thud, he hit the ground at the bottom of the cliff, still holding Madeline close in his arms. The momentum cost him his footing. He rolled with her, protecting her with his body, so that the hard ground didn't bruise her too badly. His grip was painful, like steel, and the genetically engineered claws that his hands produced in combat had come out involuntarily with the stress of the rescue. She flinched as they bit into her back like knives.

He felt the pain in her and forced his claws to retract. But there was a more intense reaction, which he could not control, prompted by her nearness and the flood of pheromones suddenly exuding from her soft body at the almost intimate contact.

As they rolled to a stop, he lifted enough to see her face. He looked down into her wide, shocked eyes and fought to catch his breath and control his hunger. A low, dangerous growl echoed deeply from his throat, involuntarily, as he stared at her without blinking.

Madeline was shell-shocked. She was still alive; the pain told her that. Her head hurt. There were deep punctures where his hands had gripped her, in her lungs, making breathing painful. She felt the sudden tension in his body and was amazed not only at its strength, but at the weight of it above her. The Cehn-Tahr were feline in origin, or so the legends went, but cats were lightweights. The commander was as solid as a wall, and he was heavy. She stared into his eyes with mingled fascination and scientific curiosity. The growl was puzzling. She'd only ever heard it in combat. No, that wasn't true. She'd heard it at the Altair embassy, when Ambassador Taylor had touched her...

"You...caught me," she stammered. "But that's impossible! I fell from over a hundred feet!"

"One hundred and fifty," he corrected, slowly calming. He scowled. "Your body is cool."

"No, sir," she said unsteadily. "Your normal body heat is three degrees higher than that of humans. I only feel cool to you." She swallowed. His nearness was producing some odd sensations. "You must weigh three times as much as you appear to weigh…"

"Genetic engineering," he replied tersely, something else he was forbidden to tell outworlders, that he'd already shared with her at his embassy. He was disturbed by her, and not thinking logically. "Density and mass, a result of enhanced tensile strength in the muscle tissue and bone."

She was only barely aware of the words. He smelled of spices. He was very warm. She felt safe in the shelter of his strength. But the sensations were frightening to a woman who'd never felt them.

He searched her eyes quietly. "I damaged you in the process of saving your life," he said curtly.

"Hahnson can heal the wounds," she said simply, fighting to breathe. Claws had punctured her lung in one of the lower lobes. Still…"I would have been dead, had you not intervened. Thank you."

He hadn't blinked. "You obeyed me without question. Yet you thought I was commanding you to leap to your death."

"Of course," she said, puzzled. "I've never refused a command from you, sir. Well, not unless it involved carrying a firearm," she added facetiously.

That was true. It touched him, at some deep level, that blind trust.

His eyes had darkened again and narrowed. His

lean hands, propped beside her ears, tensed. The low growl came again.

"Sir?" she whispered, uneasy.

"We are predators," he said in a rough tone. "There is a saying among us, that nothing in the known galaxies is as dangerous as a Cehn-Tahr male who is hunting."

She wondered what that had to do with their present situation and what he meant by "hunting." Did he mean the combat with the Rojoks? She started to ask. But even as she nursed the thought, the sound of footsteps, running, broke the tense silence.

Dtimun got to his feet in a quick, graceful motion and drew Madeline up with him, steadying her when she stumbled.

Hahnson came into view, huffing a little from the exertion. "We saw her fall!" he exclaimed. "Is she all right?"

Several human crewmen, and Dtimun's Cehn-Tahr bodyguard, fetched up beside them. The humans were astonished.

"A tree broke my fall," she lied with a laugh. She couldn't admit that Dtimun had touched her. If anyone repeated the story, he could be spaced for breaking such a basic law among his own people as contact with a human female, even in the act of saving her life. "Well, several trees broke my fall," she amended. "I'm fine, except for a hell of a backache," she told Hahnson with a wan smile. She winced as she moved. The punctures were deep. "I got hit on the head, too. I need some patching up."

Hahnson glanced at Dtimun, who was looking

more dangerous by the second. "I can do that. We need to get you back aboard the scout ship."

"That can wait," she returned. "There's a battle to win."

"Indeed," Dtimun said coldly. He whirled, shooting orders in his own language at his bodyguard. "The rest of you, wait here. And you will say nothing of what you see to anyone outside this unit. Is that clear?"

There was a chorus of affirmatives. Even as they died on the air, Dtimun and the four members of his bodyguard vanished like red smoke. The Terravegans had seen their C.O. move fast before, but never like this; not in almost three years.

Hahnson ran his wrist unit over Madeline while the other crewmen spread out, looking for survivors of the battle, along with a handful of medics.

Hahnson gritted his teeth. "These wounds are bad. One of them would have been fatal if I hadn't been close by," he added as he mended bone and muscle.

"He didn't mean...to do it," she panted, wincing as the pain bit into her. She'd hidden it from Dtimun, but she didn't have to hide it from Strick. It hurt to breathe. "He saved me, Strick," she said in a low tone. "He came up the cliff and caught me in midair, leaped from rock to rock to get me safely to the ground. I wouldn't have believed it if I hadn't seen it with my own eyes."

"They have incredible strength and flexibility," he said as he worked.

"You won't mention this?" she worried and relaxed when he shook his head. "I wouldn't want to land him in trouble with his own people. I'm not sure it's safe to tell our own crewmates that he carried me down."

"They wouldn't tell."

"They wouldn't mean to tell," she corrected. The pain eased as he mended the punctures. "The Cehn-Tahr keep so many secrets."

"More than I can ever tell you," he returned solemnly.

She studied him curiously. "He said an odd thing."

"What?"

"That there was nothing in the galaxies more dangerous than a Cehn-Tahr male who was hunting."

He let out a breath. His eyes met hers and concern was in them. "Oh, dear."

"What do you mean, oh…?"

Suddenly, in the distance there were horrible screams. They were coming from the top of the mesa. Everyone looked up.

Bodies erupted from the bare rock and, falling heavily from the mesa, came to rest in the forest, breaking tree limbs as they careened down toward the canyon floor. Seconds later, Dtimun appeared with the small Rojok officer who'd taunted him with Madeline. The humans gathered close, fascinated. They'd never seen such speed.

Dtimun had the alien by the collar of his uniform. He shook him and threw him at Madeline's feet while the nearby humans gathered closer.

"I…apologize," the Rojok said in a thready voice.

"Again!" Dtimun prompted.

"I…am…sorry," came the obliging reply.

The little alien had rips all over his uniform, and lacerations on every visible inch of skin. It occurred to Madeline that he was much like a mouse that had been caught by a cat.

"An appropriate analogy," Dtimun thought to her.

She looked at him with surprise. "You were playing with him," she thought back, shocked.

He cocked an eyebrow. He still spoke only in her mind. "It is not a game. He would have allowed us to watch him cut you to ribbons before he killed you. He is a sadist who enjoys torturing his victims. He has killed females who did not please him."

She blinked. "There are still laws. Even a prisoner is entitled to trial…"

He closed his eyes. The Rojok arched. There was a loud, violent snap. He lay still. Dtimun's eyes opened, stormy and cold, and looked, defiantly, right into Madeline's.

No one spoke. Their commanding officer had killed an enemy combatant with the power of his mind alone. For the first time, Madeline realized what he could have done at Ahkmau if the *dylete* hadn't caught him unaware. Perhaps it was also why Mangus Lo had been so desperate to capture him. Had the Rojok tyrant known the power of Dtimun's mind?

"That is not a question I will permit you to ask," came the terse reply, but only in her mind.

The humans had unconsciously moved closer together in the wake of their commander's violent response to the Rojok. He glanced at them, slowly calming.

"There are things Holconcom never share with outworlders," he told them quietly. "We have genetic enhancements which give us great advantage in combat, far beyond our natural strength. In addition to the enhancements, I can kill with my mind. Of this, you will never speak." He had broken another taboo. But, then, they were his people, these humans. He was protective of them.

Higgins, the engineer, moved forward. He was pale, but not intimidated. "Sir, we are Holconcom, too," he said with dignity. "It would never occur to any of us to betray any confidence you share with us."

"Exactly," Lieutenant Jennings, the communications officer, agreed somberly.

A chorus of affirmatives ran through the small unit.

"We'd follow you right into hell, sir," Stern agreed, his dark eyes steady on the alien's.

"Without hesitation," Higgins said.

"Absolutely without hesitation," Jennings seconded.

Dtimun managed a faint smile. "I chose well, when I requested your transfers. Search the casualties for any hidden tech or communicators. We must lift before their reinforcements arrive."

Stern grinned. "Yes, sir!"

He and the others moved off.

Madeline, meanwhile, bent over the dead Rojok officer. She was still trying to reconcile what she knew of the commander with what she'd just learned about him. It was a fascinating lesson, to a Cularian specialist who'd been taught that the Cehn-Tahr had nothing more formidable than superior strength produced by microcyborgs.

Dtimun joined her. His eyes, as he studied the Rojok, were merciless.

Madeline got to her feet. The alien's neck and back

were broken. The violence of the attack had stunned her. She lifted her eyes to Dtimun's. It wasn't like him to single out a combatant for attack.

His eyes narrowed on her. He stepped closer, so that she had to look up to see his face. She felt the heat of his body with fascination. He made a faint sound, deep in his throat, the same sound she recalled from the embassy reception when Taylor had tried to humiliate her, the sound she remembered after her tumble down the cliff when they were lying on the ground. It sounded for all the world like a low growl.

"So many secrets," she said hesitantly.

"More than you can ever know," he replied, and his tone was bitter. His eyes moved over her lovely face with a delicate touch. He was experiencing sensations that he thought never to know again in his long life. His concern for her, his fear for her, had manifested in violent action. He had gone through the Rojoks like a firestorm as he searched for the officer who had toyed with Madeline's life. When he found him, there had been no thought of capture or mercy. There was only revenge.

Madeline frowned as she read the violent emotion in him. "Your species is so mysterious," she said absently. "We study you, we fight alongside you in battle, but we know almost nothing about your social structure, your behavioral patterns. We know only the physiology, and not a great deal of that. We know far more about Rojoks."

"Be thankful," he said, his voice harsh. "What you learned would give you nightmares."

She cocked her head and her eyes softened. "Are you certain?"

He didn't reply at once. His chest rose and fell a little heavily. "Almost three years as a Holconcom," he said softly, "and it has not yet occurred to you how dangerous we truly are. Other races have sampled our combat skills and retain the memory as a nightmare terror which they have no wish to revisit. Old Tnurat conquered a hundred and fifty worlds with only that memory."

She was looking at him with odd intensity, trying not to allow the emotion in her to dominate. She was a scientist. It was curiosity, she told herself. That was why she wanted to know more about him. "We've seen you fight."

"And I have told you once before, you have not seen us fight as we can fight," he replied solemnly. "The concept of mercy is unknown to us. We are a violent, aggressive species."

He was saying something, but she didn't understand.

"You have injuries which I inflicted involuntarily, in the act of saving you," he continued. "One was potentially fatal."

"You're very strong."

"Even without the addition of microcyborgs, I have greater strength than a human male," he said bluntly. "Komak has taught our own soldiers to reduce their physical strength in brawls with yours by removing their microcyborgs. He employs some sort of tech that he will not share to control his own. But like Komak, I am not a clone, and my strength does not come from any artificial means. In some circumstances, it is not possible to exert control."

"You mean that if you didn't pull your punches, you could kill without meaning to," she translated.

"It is not possible to 'pull punches.' Not for me." His eyes narrowed. "Your human body is far more fragile than I realized," he said quietly. "I damaged you badly, and I was not angry."

She smiled. "You have been. I tested your temper a lot when I first joined the unit."

He let out a sharp breath. "You are not hearing me, madam."

The smile became quizzical. "I don't understand."

"Obviously." He turned away. "We must lift. Regroup your medical teams."

He was gone before she could wonder exactly what he'd been trying to tell her. Strick had been hinting at something more, too. She tried to get a minute to pump him for information, but he became suddenly elusive. When they reached Trimerius, he was still dodging her. Ambassador Taylor's intriguing remark haunted her, and now there were other bits of information adding to it. She was determined to solve the mystery, whatever it took.

CHAPTER FIVE

THE MEDICAL STATION on Trimerius was overrun with battle casualties, and Edris Mallory was heading up a trauma team when Madeline walked in.

She looked up and visibly relaxed when she saw her superior officer. "Oh, thank goodness," she said fervently. "There wasn't enough of me to go around!"

Madeline only smiled. She activated her surgical field and went to work.

"CAN YOU TELL ME what happened?" Edris asked hours later when they were washing up after the last surgery.

"What do you mean?" Madeline asked.

"While I was on break, I overheard Dr. Hahnson talking to someone about injuries you sustained when the Rojoks threw you over a cliff," she said in a hushed, incredulous tone. "I didn't believe it!"

"It's true," she replied. "I had a close call. Luckily, there were plenty of trees to break my fall," she added without meeting the other woman's eyes.

Edris stopped washing her hands in the chemical field and just stared at her.

"Trees," Madeline repeated. "Big, soft trees."

Edris was still staring.

"Be a nice colleague and believe my lies."

Edris just shook her head. "I feel like a mush-room."

"What a coincidence," Madeline exclaimed, "because that's exactly how I feel most of the time!"

"You aren't going to tell me, are you?"

Madeline just grinned.

"I do work with you."

"So does Stern, but I'm not telling him, either," came the droll reply.

"Well, at least that makes me feel a little better," the younger woman sighed. "It's something damaging to someone else, I gather?"

Madeline's eyebrows arched. "Now you're a telepath?"

Edris gave her a hunted look. "Trees won't break a fall of over a hundred feet without breaking you in the process."

The older woman averted her eyes.

"The commander caught you, didn't he?" Edris asked in a hushed tone. "And you can't admit it without getting him in trouble."

Madeline's eyes mirrored her shock.

"I'm not totally hopeless," she said firmly. "And I do understand things, even if I seem slow and fumbly from time to time. I won't tell a soul. I'm just glad you got to come home."

Madeline was touched. "Thanks, Mallory."

Edris's blue eyes twinkled. "Too much work here for one Cularian specialist," she teased.

Madeline threw a sponge at her. She ducked, laughing.

THE CONFLICT WITH the Rojoks was heating up. So was Madeline's private life. The unexpected contact with Dtimun on the last mission had shaken her. She'd never had close physical contact with another being. Well, she had hugged Stern and Hahnson from time to time in a comradely way. But this was different. There was no one she could discuss it with. Not that there was anything to discuss. There was no possibility of anything outside a military formality with the mysterious commander of the Holconcom.

From birth her path through life had been chosen for her. She'd been part of the military since she was a child. Emotion was not part of her makeup. She'd been taught that fraternization was a deadly taboo. She was mentally neutered. Or...was she?

Now, the memory of that contact wouldn't go away. Worse, there was a sudden distance between herself and her commanding officer. He went out of his way to avoid her company. She didn't understand why, but she thought it might have something to do with their last mission.

The situation on Ondar was heating up, too. The ambassadors had finally agreed on sanctions, just about the same time that contact with them had been lost.

Dtimun went to Lawson and insisted on a rescue mission. Lawson stonewalled and refused to let him go.

Dtimun simply shrugged, gave him a green-eyed laugh and walked out the door.

"I'll have you shot down if you lift!" Lawson yelled after him as he walked away. "I swear I will!"

Dtimun didn't even answer him.

"LET'S GO!" MADELINE called to Edris. "We've got a mission!"

"But, ma'am, you don't need me, and there's a backlog of patients…!" Edris tried to protest.

"We've got two new residents and three new interns working the unit, starting today," Madeline muttered, grabbing the other woman's arm. "I'm not going on a rescue mission to a diplomatic conference alone, not with the ratio of Cularian species represented and their importance to the Tri-Fleet," she returned. "You're coming with me."

"But the commander said…!" Edris protested.

"Flame the commander," Madeline retorted curtly. "I need backup and you're coming with us."

"He'll eat me!" Edris wailed.

"He'll have to kill and dress you first, and he won't have time," Madeline returned, still pulling. "Now, let's go!"

THE VATOR TUBE operator was motioning frantically as they approached the ship.

"He won't lift before we're in the vator tube, will he?" Edris worried as they sprinted toward the big copper-hued saucer ship.

"No, but he will lift while we're still *in* the tube, so let's hurry!"

Edris was panting as they dived headfirst into the tube with the operator and rolled. Sure enough, the ship was already lifting when the tube surged up through the opening.

"Oh, no!" Edris wailed, pointing toward a wing of interceptors heading right toward them. "Surely they aren't going to shoot at…aaaahhh!"

The scream came as tracers winged their way at the vator tube. It retracted into the *Morcai* just in time to keep the two women, and the amused Cehn-Tahr vator tube operator, from being vaporized.

"Those were our ships! They were shooting at us!" Edris shouted. "Why were they shooting at us?"

"Well, I'm just guessing, but I imagine Lawson told the commander to stand down, and he refused," Madeline chuckled as they ran toward the medical unit, flanked by the vator operator who was also rushing to his post. "It isn't the first time he's tried to enforce an order with attack ships."

"It will do no good, save to give their gunners some target practice," the vator operator laughed.

The ship weaved, almost throwing the women to the deck, even in the high grav interior.

"What if they hit us?" Edris queried, holding on to the vator operator for support as the ship reeled again.

"Hit the *Morcai*?" He chuckled in a very human fashion. "The commander pilots us now," came the amused reply. "No gunner alive can hit us at such times."

"He's right," Madeline assured her. "The C.O. has tech in this ship that even Lawson doesn't know about. We're almost invincible. Besides that—" she traded a grin with the vator operator "—the C.O. is the best pilot in the fleet."

"Indeed he is," the alien agreed. He put on a burst of speed and vanished down the corridor.

"I expect he's laughing while he dodges the emerillium bursts, too," Madeline laughed. "He does love a good fight."

"I think I'm going to be sick," Edris moaned as the ship lurched, and then lurched again.

"You'll get used to it. Honest. You got used to six meg landings," she added.

"I did not! I just stopped throwing up during them!"

Madeline looked at one of the vid screens in the corridor. The Tri-Fleet interceptors were flying toward them one minute. The next, the *Morcai* was cutting through open, empty space with only a tiny shudder to indicate the increased acceleration, thanks to the *Morcai*'s delicate pressurization systems.

"Oh, that's impossible," Edris told her, stunned. "No ship can move that fast!"

"The *Morcai* can," Madeline said with pride. "Come on, Edris, just a few more feet to sick bay, and I'll give you something for that nausea."

"I'm never going to make a spacer."

"Yes, you are. Like everything else, it's only a matter of practice."

Edris didn't reply. But her eyes did, and they said she didn't believe it one bit.

THEY PUT DOWN on Ondar, just outside the main city but short of the spaceport. Dtimun dictated the formation of the shore party. Madeline had wanted to send Edris, but Dtimun insisted that Madeline go with Holt Stern to check out the council quarters and see if there were casualties. The bulk of the Holconcom was headed to the spaceport, where a Rojok battle cruiser had been detected.

"But I don't need to go searching for phantom casualties," Madeline protested. "The *kelekoms* didn't pick up a single sign of a Rojok in the council chambers. Sir, Edris is more than capable...!"

He held up a hand, silencing her instantly. "These are diplomats," he reminded her. "They will expect my most experienced medical officer."

She glared at him. "Can I at least carry a sidearm? If there is a Rojok ship at the spaceport, no doubt they'll be looking for ways to get to the diplomats before we can."

"We will not revisit that argument now."

She sighed. "Very well, sir."

"Why do you not wish to go?" he asked abruptly. "You usually pester me to include you on away missions."

"This isn't an away mission, it's a milk run," she said curtly. Her eyes were accusing on his face. "The Holconcom is going after Rojoks. You're sidelining me from the action."

He looked away. "You are a healer, not a soldier," he said shortly.

"I am a soldier," she pointed out. "I can fight."

He looked uncomfortable. His chin lifted. "Your assignment on the *Morcai* is to treat the wounded, not wade into battle alongside the Holconcom."

"It would be, if you'd let me," she muttered.

He lifted an eyebrow. "Madam, your inclination toward physical violence is at variance with your chosen profession."

She blinked. "Could you occasionally speak in Standard, sir, so that I don't need a translator hub?"

He glowered at her. "You will search for injured diplomats and, if you find any, you will treat them."

"Yes, sir," she said heavily. "Well, maybe a stray

Rojok will jump into my path on the way to the council chambers."

His eyes narrowed on her face. "If that happens, Stern will be with you." An odd look crossed his face as he said it, almost as if he found the thought distasteful.

"Of course," she replied, and averted her eyes. She was getting fanciful.

"You have served with Stern for many years," he said abruptly. "Have you never felt anything other than comradeship for him?"

Both her eyebrows tried to meet her hairline. "Sir, my ability to feel physical attraction for any other soldier has been neutered. It's regulation for all soldiers in our military."

"Which is no answer at all," he replied curtly. Except that his lips didn't move. He knew that sometimes the neutering drugs failed. In her case, and Stern's and Hahnson's especially. He was wondering at his own behavior. It was disturbing that he had such thoughts about her. He'd shared a very private memorial service with her, taboo to outworlders. He'd been ready to kill the human ambassador for touching her. This behavior was dangerous to her. It should not even be happening.

"Stern was my commanding officer once, and he's still my friend," she thought back to him. "Only ever that. Sir." The way he was looking at her made her feel odd. Was it possessiveness? She dismissed that at once. He was her commanding officer. It was concern for any breach of regulations, that was all it meant.

He stared down at her with conflicting emotions.

He had to get this under control. He straightened. "Carry on, Ruszel."

"Yes, sir."

She didn't understand why he asked that question about Stern. Things hadn't been the same between them since the last away mission. Life was becoming complicated.

"IF THE OLD man's punishing you by making you look for lacerated diplomats, why do I have to be punished with you?" Stern groaned.

She glared at him. "Because I'm not allowed a gun. I guess the C.O. is afraid I might accidentally get my hands on a Rojok when he wasn't looking." She shrugged. "I can't even hide a sidearm from him anymore. He overheard me telling Mallory that I tucked one into my kit, and now he has it searched every time I leave the ship!"

"Shouldn't have said that in front of him," he chuckled.

"Tell me about it." She looked around. The planet was mostly deserted. There was a scattering of buildings, here in what passed for the town square. But there were no signs, in Standard or any other tongue, and no virtual map hubs.

"Now where do we go?" Madeline asked irritably.

"Let's split up and see if we can find someone to ask. If I haven't flashed you in five minutes, meet me back here." He indicated a tall light under which they were standing.

"Fair enough. You don't have a spare Gresham…?"

"If I did," he mused, smiling, "I'd be nuts to give it to you. The old man would have my head on a stick."

"Oh, thanks so much," she muttered.

"You're welcome." He bowed.

She tossed him a sarcastic look and walked off in the other direction.

On the way, grumbling about being put out of the action, she made a wrong turn and got separated from her former captain. Worse, she stepped on an accelerator pad that she didn't see…

CHAPTER SIX

MADELINE CURSED WITH every step she took down a red valley that looked as if it had once been a river. This continent was largely desert, and there were *chova* mounds everywhere. The giant ants had a potent venom, a neurotoxin that killed quickly. She kept to the sheer wall at one side of the valley, avoiding the mounds.

She hadn't noticed a *caspidas* ramp—a linear accelerator used for long jump rapid transit—until she'd stepped on it just after she and Stern separated. The next thing she knew, she was miles from the city, on a rough path that led to some sort of power substation. The accelerator devices weren't commonly used in this part of the galaxy, but she assumed that this one was for the convenience of utility workers repairing power grids, to allow them to avoid the dangerous *chova* mounds where colonies of the deadly giant antlike creatures lived. She could have kicked herself for the mistake; especially when she noticed that the engine in the device was smoking. She wouldn't be able to use it on the return trip, not unless she could repair it, which was an impossibility. In a less dangerous situation, it would have been a joke. But she wasn't laughing now.

She heard the rapid fire of Rojok *chasats* as she

moved between two large boulders that flanked a rough path up into the hills. She didn't even have a weapon, thanks to the commander's improved vigilance. Well, she mused, it was obvious that the Rojoks were armed. They probably had more weapons than they needed anyway, so she'd just have to appropriate some of their firepower.

Stealthily, she worked her way halfway around the next boulder and froze. There was a mean-looking young Rojok facing an elderly wounded Cehn-Tahr, who was prone on the grainy desert path. The old fellow, a tall, husky alien with a leonine head full of thick white hair, was gripping his leg, which was bloody. He glared defiance at the Rojok, despite his injury.

"Beg for your life, Cehn-Tahr," the Rojok taunted. "I might spare you."

"I will never beg," the old alien said in a deep, gravelly voice. He raised his pugnacious chin. "Kill me."

"That will be a pleasure," the dusky-skinned alien said with a twist of his thin lips as he aimed the *chasat*.

But before he could fire, Madeline yelled and made a flying leap at him, hitting the surprised alien in the stomach with both feet. Paralyzed momentarily by the unexpected loud yell, he was unprepared for the body blow. He went into the ground on his side, with his head inches from the old Cehn-Tahr's leg.

The Cehn-Tahr kicked out with a booted foot, dislodging the *chasat* at the same time that he rendered his enemy unconscious.

Madeline got to her feet and rushed in. She threw

the Rojok on his back, activated the drug bank in her wrist scanner and laserdotted a large dose of narcotic into the main artery at the Rojok's throat.

"So much for you," she muttered.

She turned to the elderly Cehn-Tahr. He was a big fellow, with thick snow-white hair and the same elongated cat-eyes that she'd become so familiar with after serving with the Holconcom. His uniform was royal blue with gold trim—the colors of the Alaman-timichar empire. He had a chest full of medals as well. He must be a Cehn-Tahr regular, she thought. A high-ranking officer.

She saluted him. He glared at her, openly hostile, and didn't return it. His distaste was evident in every hard line of his face.

She dropped the salute, feeling foolish. Her green eyes went to his bloody leg. Obviously, she thought, not the one he'd kicked the Rojok with. "Do you have other injuries, besides this one, sir?" she asked him formally.

He was watching her warily. "No," he said, after a minute. He noticed that she wore the red uniform of the Holconcom. His scowl grew blacker.

She saw that, but she pretended innocence of his dislike. She picked up the Rojok's fallen *chasat* and stuck it in the mission belt of her uniform, looking around to make sure there weren't other Rojoks in the vicinity.

"We have to hurry," she said, kneeling beside him. He jerked away from her.

Her face softened. "Look, I know this is against protocol," she said quietly, "that your culture forbids the intercession of alien medics and that your law

forbids me even to touch you." She aimed her wrist
scanner at his bloody leg for a diagnosis. It, thank
goodness, was still functional because of its superior shielding. "But you're in rather a tricky situation.
Your leg is broken," she added, meeting his eyes. "It's
a compound fracture. I don't have the equipment to
do a restructure job here. I can make a temporary fu-
sion of the bones, but you won't be able to walk far
on the leg, even if I can find you some sort of stick
for support."

Having given her medical opinion of his case, she
remained silent beside him, resting on one knee, waiting for a reply.

He was suspicious of her. He seemed to find her
very presence offensive. Well, she reasoned, he was
elderly and humans were held in contempt by his
race. He might refuse her help, despite the desperate situation he was in. But she didn't dare treat him
without permission. Not unless she wanted Dtimun
to court-martial her. She had no doubt that the C.O.
would enjoy that, given her mutinous record.

The old fellow was in obvious pain. He tried to
hide it, but he grimaced involuntarily when he tried
to move. He muttered something under his breath in
his native tongue that was unprintable. Komak had
taught her those words in Cehn-Tahr for a joke, and
roared with laughter when she started to show off her
new linguistic skills for the commander. The explosion that resulted had been quite colorful. The commander had been even more eloquent than usual. She
cocked her head and waited, saying nothing.

"Very well," the old Cehn-Tahr said finally, biting
off the words. "Mend it. But be quick."

"Yes, sir."

She slid back the panel in her wrist, which contained her medicomp and tools, and pulled out a tiny tool that mended bone through fabric and flesh. It was one of the newer instruments developed by Tri-Fleet Medical Command, a welcome addition to her other tools. She noticed then that she'd left her ring communicator on the ship. The flux in the accelerator had fried her compass. Fortunately her wrist scanner and the mender, new tech, had better shielding.

"You weren't out here alone?" she asked as she focused on her work.

"No," he confirmed. His anger-dark eyes narrowed, watching the skillful movements of her hands. "A Rojok fighter disabled our scout ship, stranding us here. In the firefight that ensued, I was separated from my squad. The Rojok you knocked down hit me with a *chasat* blast before I could defend myself." He watched the instrument in her slender hands. "Old age is dangerous."

She smiled. "You aren't old, sir," she replied. "You're aging like a nice synth brandy."

He made a rough sound in his throat, which passed for laughter in a Cehn-Tahr, and then cleared his throat, as if to disguise it. "You wear a Holconcom uniform," he said after a minute.

"Yes. I'm Cularian specialist and medical chief of staff aboard the Holconcom ship *Morcai*."

There was a pause. "You are Ruszel."

She glanced up, her green eyes wide and surprised. "Yes."

"We know of you," he replied. "Although until

today, I thought what we heard of you must be exaggeration."

She laughed, finishing the last suture. "That's what my C.O. says," she told him, "every time he has to chew me out for brawling. He has no respect for people who defend the honor of the *Morcai*, or himself." She put the tool away. "The First Fleet guys called him a cat-eyed benny-whammer. I ask you, how could we sit back and take that sort of insult about our commanding officer? Of course we had to mop the floor with them!"

His eyes flashed green, so quickly that she wondered if she'd imagined it. He didn't seem to be a man with a sense of humor.

"As I mentioned, this is just a stopgap measure," she said, indicating his leg. "I carry minimal supplies in combat—only what fits in my wrist scanner. You'll need to have your own medics check it before you start kicking people again," she added with a wicked little smile. He'd made short work of the Rojok with his good leg.

He eased up, using a boulder for a prop, and stood. He seemed surprised. "There is no pain."

"The instrument produces a painkiller matched to the DNA of the patient," she explained. "It's a revolutionary invention. In the old days, mending one of the long bones of the body would have required a cyberscalpel and sterilization modules. The instrument I just used is cutting-edge tech, a mender that works through fabric as well as flesh."

"Amazing," he mused. He glanced at her. "Are you here alone?"

She grimaced. "I was with our astrogator, Holt

Stern. He was my captain when I served aboard the SSC starship *Bellatrix*. We were dropped on the other side of the spaceport and I was ordered to look for casualties among an ambassadorial party holding hearings on the planet while the Holconcom targeted a Rojok ship at the spaceport. Stern and I separated to get directions to the council chambers, and I accidentally stepped on an accelerator ramp that I didn't see. I ended up here. It fried my compass. My medicomp is about the only thing I have that's still functional."

He only nodded, giving away nothing. "For a physician, you have something of a flair for combat."

"Oh, that." She took her wrist scanner offline and pulled down her sleeve. "I commanded an Amazon attack squad for many years before I studied medicine." She grinned, and her green eyes twinkled. "In other words, I learned to create patients before I was taught how to repair them."

This time he did laugh. "You are not what I expected when they spoke of the human female aboard the Holconcom flagship."

Her eyes twinkled. "I get that a lot." She looked around, listening. "Do you have any idea how many Rojoks we're going to have to disassemble before we can get to a ship? It's a long walk back to the city." It wasn't, for her. Several miles was nothing for a soldier in good condition. But she was thinking of her companion, who would never manage the hike.

His eyes, inexplicably, flashed green as she processed the thought. "We will have to commandeer a vessel, and I think it will require the disassembly of many Rojoks to accomplish this," he replied. He straightened. He was very tall, and there was a parade of medals on the royal blue tunic of his uniform. He had to be regular Cehn-Tahr military, she concluded, but despite his lack of rank insignia, she imagined he was an officer.

"I accidentally left my ring communicator in my quarters aboard the *Morcai*, and my compass is dead," she added. There must have been some leakage of electromagnetic flux in the accelerator unit she'd stepped on before it malfunctioned. The units had sustained similar damage once before due to radical electromagnetic fields. "Can you determine the direction of the spaceport from here?"

He closed his eyes for an instant and then opened them. They were an opaque blue; the same shade, in fact, that the Holconcom commander's turned when he was reading minds. "The spaceport is just east of the direction my squad took, looking for a secret Rojok base here. That way. North." He pointed. "A long walk," he added, but without complaining.

She looked worried. "Yes. And that suturing won't hold if you trek so far."

"In that case," he replied, staring toward a formation of rocks some distance away, "we must require my troops to come to us. We must call them." He grimaced as he checked his comm unit. "I fell on it when the Rojok shot me. It is useless."

She held her hand out, palm up. "If you can call soldiers without a communicator, be my guest. I only know how to call Meg-Ravens."

He seemed interested. "Truly? How did you learn such a skill?"

"One of my patients was a Jebob ornithologist," she said with a smile. "I always take advantage of free knowledge. You never know when it may come in handy."

"I can also call Meg-Ravens, and communicate with them in their own language," he said surprisingly. "I frequently seek the nests of Meg-Ravens, to track changes in their young," he said. "It is a… hobby…of mine."

"You're only the second person I've ever become acquainted with who studied them. It's a hobby of mine as well. I wish there were time for you to teach me how to talk to them," she added whimsically. "It's a skill I covet." She stared out over the desert. "How can we attract your troops without giving away our position to the Rojoks?"

There was something oddly familiar about the twinkle in his eyes, suddenly green. "Observe."

He cupped his hands over his mouth and made a sound like a galot. It was such a good facsimile that Madeline shivered. The great cats of the Eridanus sector were fierce and aggressive. Few who came across them in the wild ever lived to tell the tale. They moved like blurs and devoured their prey. Even their matings, from what little information Madeline had ever gleaned, from a single survivor of such an assault, a researcher, were so brutal that the females occasionally died of injuries incurred in them.

Almost instantly, there was a reply. Blurs in royal blue uniforms raced toward the old man and the female officer, so quickly that they were standing beside her before they came into focus. Despite having been in the field with the Holconcom, Madeline was impressed by the speed of these aliens. She'd only ever seen her commanding officer that fast rarely, most recently just after he'd spared her a killing fall on their last mission.

One of the younger Cehn-Tahr scowled at Madeline and the *chasat* in her belt and produced a weapon, as if he thought she'd wounded the old fellow.

The old Cehn-Tahr held up his hand. "This is Ruszel," he told them.

The weapon was lowered. The men stared at her as if they'd never seen a female before.

"*The* Ruszel?" the tallest and most authoritative of the newcomers asked the old one, surprised. He was wearing a line of medals, almost as many as the older alien. Of the unit, only he wore a helmet.

He nodded. "She saved me from the Rojok, there." He indicated the fallen enemy.

"I helped," she corrected with a smile. "I only knocked him down. You immobilized him so that I could hit him with a tranquillizer."

His eyebrows arched, as if he was surprised by her modesty.

"Ruszel, this is the *kehmatemer*, a bodyguard unit of the Dectat. Captain Rhemun leads them," he added, indicating the soldier in the helmet. Madeline saluted them respectfully, curious that she'd never heard of them in her years with the Holconcom. But, then, the C.O. had little contact with the Dectat. His feud with the emperor was legend.

The old fellow turned to his men and spoke to them in rapid-fire Cehn-Tahr. They replied with the same rapidity. She could only make out a word here and there. It seemed to be an ancient dialect, not the modern Cehn-Tahr language that Tri-Fleet personnel learned.

The old one turned to Madeline. "There is a squad of Rojok scouts between us and an outstation which may contain a transport vehicle. We shall not be able to avoid them. They have biosensors capable of detecting even phantom movement. No doubt they are already aware of our presence here."

She pulled the *chasat* from her belt. "If we can't avoid them, then we can neutralize them," she said calmly. "Then we can appropriate a ship to get us back to our lines."

"I will certainly require one." The old Cehn-Tahr moved a little awkwardly.

"You must make slow movements, even when you turn, sir," she cautioned quietly. "The bone is only partially mended. If you break the suture, a blood clot could end your life."

His eyes softened as he looked at her, measuring her easy courage and her beauty. Even with her long, red-gold hair damp with sweat and her uniform stained, she was attractive. Dtimun's efforts to merge the two races were laudable, but the humans still had little knowledge of what the Cehn-Tahr were really like behind their mask of civilization. Nor did Ruszel know how hopeless were her carefully hidden feelings for Dtimun, which he saw quite clearly in her mind. What a shame. She would be a fit mate even for a Cehn-Tahr, if only their species were compatible; which they were not.

"In that case, you must command the unit," he told her bluntly.

She gaped at him. "Sir, I'm certain that these soldiers are of higher rank than I am," she protested. "They won't follow me."

"Ruszel, you are Holconcom," he said simply. "Holconcom always leads in battle."

She looked at the stern alien faces with a little trepidation. These were seasoned veterans. At least two of them, including Rhemun, were wearing campaign ribbons and battle stars that denoted superior command rank. Surely, with their prejudices they would never allow a human female to command them!

To her surprise, the men straightened into formal fist to heart salutes.

"You lead. We will follow," the tallest of the Cehn-Tahr squad said respectfully.

"Very well." She pushed up her sleeve and brought out a small Milish Cone. It was an emergency water synthesizer, taking oxygen and hydrogen out of the atmosphere to produce water. She handed it to the elderly soldier.

"It isn't much, sir, but it will keep you alive in this heat until we make a path to the spaceport."

He took it, his eyes warm as they met hers. "You must not let yourself be killed," he told her. "Your commander would have my stripes for it."

"I don't think he would miss the aggravation, sir," she said with a grin. "He once offered to trade me for a Yomuth in the Dacerian colonies."

"I am certain the Yomuth could not treat broken bones," he replied, tongue in cheek. "Be wary, warwoman," he cautioned as he found a bit of shade to sit in. He glared at his men and shot something at them in commanding tones.

"The threat is not necessary, sir," the ranking officer replied in the same language with a flash of green eyes. "It will be a story to tell around campfires."

"Captain Rhemun will translate for you," the old fellow told her. "Some of the younger members of our squad do not speak English."

Madeline nodded. "Very good, sir. *Comcamrion*," she added in passable Cehn-Tahr as she faced Rhemun and the others. "*Ca Makesh*!"

The command to form the unit and move out, in Cehn-Tahr, seemed to surprise all the aliens, including the old fellow, but the unit snapped to attention, and became solemn as she took the lead. The old Cehn-Tahr watched her with quiet admiration. Whatever he had expected when he first learned of Dtimun's effrontery—the installation of a human female aboard the *Morcai*—his attitude had undergone a rapid revision since their meeting. There was more to this human than he had anticipated. Much more. He was curious to know if the Holconcom commander had feelings for his human medic. But, then, it was impossible to read Dtimun's mind. He had often tried, and failed.

Madeline led off at a rapid trot, her movements almost as graceful as theirs. She knew she couldn't match their speed, but she was a combat veteran. She knew how to lead.

The captain didn't speak as they neared the camp and became stealthy. He gestured, using sign language that only Holconcom or Cehn-Tahr troops would understand. He hesitated, not certain she would understand. But she smiled and replied in the same way, directing a two-pronged assault on the Rojok camp, which was enjoying a brief meal under the blistering sun. Unlike the Cehn-Tahr, and humans, Rojoks had minute traces of vestigial reptilian DNA, proof of genetic tampering. Nothing pleased them more than hot sun and desert.

She looked toward Rhemun and nodded, once.

The *decaliphe*, the famous death cry of the Cehn-Tahr warrior, echoed through the rocks around the Rojok camp, softly at first, and then building and building like the scream of a hundred cats. Even Madeline, accustomed as she was to the sound, shivered at the menace of it. The Rojoks, surprised, took precious seconds to react. By the time they did, it was too late.

"*Malenchar*!" she yelled, and rushed forward.

She jump-kicked the first Rojok in her path, knocking him down and using a nerve-pinching blow to temporarily paralyze him. Another came at her, firing his *chasat*. She walked right into the fire, a trick she'd learned from her C.O. It shocked the Rojok. He missed her at point-blank range. She backhanded him against a boulder, brought her leg up and snapped a kick into his solar plexus—which was, in Cularian species, just below his navel rather than above it. He gasped and fell. "That will teach you to mess with a specialist in Cularian medicine," she told the sidelined alien.

Her senses, honed to incredible sensitivity by serving in the Holconcom, alerted her to a rear attack. She whirled as the Rojok started to fire, knocking the *chasat* out of his hand, following with a second kick that was even faster, rendering him unconscious even before he hit the ground. Not for the first time, she was grateful for Dtimun's insistence on frequent combat practice.

Around her, the Cehn-Tahr were making quick work of the Rojok patrol. Genetically modified, their lean hands produced steel-hard claws in battle, a function of nanotechnology that was beyond anything the Tri-Fleet had invented so far. Of course, the Holconcom had cutting-edge technology, which was never shared, or discussed, with outworlders. Even Lawson, head of the Tri-Fleet, was not privy to such information.

She looked around her, smiling. The Cehn-Tahr were victorious.

"Ruszel, we have won," Captain Rhemun told her with a green smile in his elongated eyes.

She beamed with pride. "Was there ever any doubt?" she asked, chuckling. "We'd better disarm them." She got another *chasat* and, more valuable, a sensor sweeper.

She spun it around, watching for any sign of approaching patrols. She stopped dead when she read a high concentration of Rojoks to the north, in the path of the retreat to the spaceport; but these were behind a barrier of some sort. There was also a force net that would alert them to the presence of anything approaching. She grimaced.

"There's a fortress," she said as she joined the alien Cehn-Tahr. They were so tall that even with her moderate height, she felt small among them. They all had the height of the commander, and Komak. They must be crack troops, too, even if they weren't Holconcom. They fought like tigers.

"A fortress?" the ranking officer Cehn-Tahr asked, his eyes revealing a blue curiosity.

She nodded, frowning. "It's at least twenty feet tall. North of here. About a fourth of a *klek*. And it's broadcasting sensor waves."

They looked at each other. "We can scale the wall without difficulty," the officer told her. "But they will be waiting for that."

She pursed her lips. Her eyes twinkled. "I think I have a solution. Do any of you have a sensor web screen?"

The youngest of them came forward and saluted. "Yes, Ruszel," he agreed. He pulled out a small packet and handed it to her.

She grinned. "I can't keep up with you scaling a wall," she said without envy, "but I can create a diversion to help you get over it past the sentries without detection."

"How?" Captain Rhemun asked.

"You'll see. Just keep a close watch."

She tossed the lightweight net over her head. It would blind sensors and even sight to her approach, as it scattered light in all directions. It was like being invisible.

She ran to the wall, which was a true fortress, complete with guard stations at each corner and a huge, immovable metal gate. The guards were thick on the front wall.

She tossed a tiny disc flash grenade at the gate. While it erupted, blinding those around it, she lay down on the desert floor about twenty yards from the gate. She spread-eagled her body and stripped off the web.

When the flash died away, she was visible to the guards on the wall.

She heard them talking to each other, questioning each other about the female who lay unconscious just outside the gate.

"She wears the red uniform of the Cehn-Tahr Holconcom!" one called to his officer.

"No woman serves in that unit!" another scoffed.

"But, yes!" came the reply. "They have a warwoman. A human!"

More talk, but excited now. Capturing a member of the Holconcom would make them heroes. They fought over who would go out and fetch her back.

In the end, most of the soldiers on the front wall came through the heavy gate as it was opened.

"She might be dead," one said.

"It might be a trap," another muttered, looking around.

The officer glared at him. "A trap, when she is the only living thing on the continent besides us?" he exclaimed. "And what do you expect to find…the entire Holconcom lying in wait for us?"

Madeline slitted one eye. Behind the arguing Rojoks, blue blurs went noiselessly up the walls and over into the fortress.

"Is she alive?" one Rojok asked as he approached her.

"Shoot her," another suggested, "and see if she moves."

Uh-oh, she thought uneasily. That was a suggestion she hadn't anticipated. But maybe they'd just wound her and she could repair herself…

The *decaliphe* sounded just as the thinnest Rojok was aiming a *chasat* at her stomach.

The Rojoks whirled at the terrorizing sound and broke into a run, back toward their fortress. Except for the one with the *chasat*. "So it was a trap, warwoman," he spat. "You will not live to see it sprung!"

"The web, Ruszel, throw the web over you!" The voice, unrecognizable, echoed in her mind, but she heard it as if it were shouted at her.

Her hand slid under it and flicked it between her and the Rojok, and she rolled away just as he fired.

The Rojok suddenly stiffened. The weapon fell from his hand as he clutched his throat and began to choke. He fell to his knees, turning even redder than his race usually was. His eyes fixed and he fell forward, dead.

Madeline stood up, stripping off the sensor web, staring at the Rojok with wide, shocked eyes. There was no one in sight. Who had saved her? And, how?

"Run!"

She heard the voice again even as she heard the skimmer screaming through the sky, heading toward her. She threw the sensor web back over herself and zigzagged to the gate. She ran through it and side-stepped, just in time to miss the strafing run. Even as the skimmer shot up over the wall, there was a flash of light, followed by a loud report, and the skimmer exploded, cartwheeling all the way to the ground.

Her heart was beating double-time. She didn't understand what had happened. She should be dead.

The Cehn-Tahr had made short work of the Rojoks on the walls. She got a glimpse of bodies thrown in a pile. None were moving and there was more blood than she'd ever seen in an attack. She averted her eyes. Even the Holconcom was not so savage in their assaults.

Captain Rhemun looked at her with an odd expression, as if he read those impressions in her mind.

But he averted his attention to a hangar and she dismissed the thought.

There was a small troop transport inside, and they piled into it without hesitation. There was enough room for the squad, with a little to spare. Captain Rhemun took the controls and gunned the small craft into the sky. As it soared away down the canyon, Madeline went down on one knee to examine a wound on the youngest of the Cenh-Tahr.

"You have a compromised blood vessel," she told him. "May I mend it?"

He looked toward his commanding officer, who nodded. "Yes," he replied.

She pulled out her tool and sutured the cells together. He watched her with a rapt expression that she didn't see. It only took a few seconds, and he was as good as new.

"Thank you," he said formally.

"My pleasure," she replied, smiling.

Before she could remind them about the elderly Cehn-Tahr waiting nearby, Rhemun had turned the craft and was easing it down onto the desert soil. Two younger officers jumped out, ran to the old Cehn-Tahr who was sitting on a large boulder, bowed, and lifted him, one on either side. He clung to their broad shoulders as they ran him, in a blur of motion, to the ship.

"Welcome aboard, sir," Madeline told him with a grin as they eased him gently into a seat across from Madeline.

He gave her an odd look. "I thought I knew enough about human females from ancient texts we have archived in our libraries, collected from multisystem wave scanners. We have ancient vids that show human females in immodest clothing being attacked by various space creatures," he told her. "They run and scream."

"Oh, yes, the ancient entertainment films made on old Earth centuries ago. Neat propaganda for the primitive epoch, wasn't it?" she asked, putting up her mending tool. "Not very convincing now, however."

"Not to anyone who saw you fight today, Ruszel," Captain Rhemun said solemnly, his solemn blue eyes meeting hers. "It was an honor to serve with you."

She was touched, and a little surprised. She'd heard from many sources that Cehn-Tahr males were deeply prejudiced about women in combat, not to mention humans of any sort. "Thank you," she said quietly. "I can say the same."

The old Cehn-Tahr, the commander of the unit, was watching her with open curiosity. "I am...surprised," he said, choosing the word carefully, "that your commanding officer had no objection to your presence aboard his vessel."

She looked innocent. "He had no choice, sir."

"How do you calculate that?"

"I saved his life when we were held captive in Ahkmau," she said simply. "Since only I know exactly what I did to his insides, while I was saving him, he needs to have me aboard in case he needs emergency surgery again."

There were curious looks all around her.

"What did you do?" the old alien persisted.

"He went into the *dylete* while we were imprisoned," she said, her voice very quiet. "I had to perform open-heart surgery with jury-rigged equipment, under battlefield conditions. The soldiers in our human crew, and his Cehn-Tahr one, bought the time with their lives. The Rojoks cut up my colleague, Dr. Strick Hahnson, like a wild animal to try to make us give up the commander. We refused." The memory was still painful. "The Rojok field marshal, Chacon, arrived in time to stop the torture, but it was too late for Strick. The commander cloned him for Stern and me." She smiled. "It was a bittersweet reunion after we escaped."

The old man was listening with rapt attention. "The Rojok field marshal himself stopped the torture?" he asked.

She nodded. "Chacon and his men put the jailers in their own ovens, and gave the prisoners food and fresh water and medical care. We called the *Freespirit* to get the survivors out. Then we blew up the camp."

The silence grew poignant. These aliens all knew the commander, she was certain.

"I understand how you must feel, to know that," she said softly. "No Holconcom commander has ever been captured in battle. But they had no chance to hurt our C.O. We made sure of it. He got us out. He saved us."

The oldest of the aliens leaned back against the bulkhead. His heavily lined face seemed even older. "We had heard about the escape, but not the particulars." He looked at her evenly. "Now I understand how you came to be aboard his vessel, warwoman. He values you."

She managed a smile. "He won't when he hears how I've fouled up this mission," she said with a grimace. "He ordered Stern and me on a very simple assignment to the diplomatic mission. He didn't say to get separated, lost in the desert and involved in a small war." She looked around at her comrades. "You'll all come and visit me in the brig, I hope? I expect to be there for some time," she added with resignation.

There were amused sounds from the others.

"If he puts you in the brig, Ruszel," Captain Rhemun assured her, "we will come and break you out."

"Would you, really?" she asked, beaming. "How kind!"

There was a sudden shock that threw them against the bulkheads.

"The Rojoks want to play some more," she guessed, certain that a skimmer was following them, and shooting.

"Then let us raise the stakes," the eldest Cehn-Tahr said, with amused green eyes. He got up, limped to the command console and sat down in the copilot's seat. His hands flew on the buttons, making quick work of the weapon controls.

He shot a command at Captain Rhemun.

"Hold on to something," he warned the others.

The small ship stopped abruptly, reversed and moved backward at blinding speed. The Rojok ship shot past it. Seconds later, a spray of emerillium beams hit the Rojok ship and knocked it out of the sky like a swatter.

"Wow!" Madeline exclaimed, laughing. The old one was as good a pilot as her commanding officer, who was in a class of his own.

The old alien glanced at her, his own eyes laughing as well. "Their pilots have no imagination. It will lead to their ruin."

"Let us hope so," she agreed.

She wanted to mention the voice that had saved her life, but she was uncertain of the wisdom of it. The old one might think she was crazy. So, instead, she asked him how to communicate with Meg-Ravens, and he taught her a few very basic phrases. She had just time to memorize them before they came within sight of the spaceport.

THE SMALL SHIP put down at the spaceport. Dtimun was standing with Stern and several ambassadors, scowling. He advanced at the sight of the Rojok scout ship. A crewman, a weapons specialist, shouldered a nanomissile and prepared to fire. Dtimun knocked the barrel into the air.

"Would a Rojok ship land here among enemies with no show of force?" he shot at the young man. "Put yourself on report, Jones."

The young crewman grimaced. "Yes, sir. Sorry, sir."

The panel on the Rojok skimmer slid open and Madeline Ruszel jumped out. Behind her was a contingent of Cehn-Tahr, but Dtimun didn't recognize their unit in the brief glimpse he got of them. Madeline didn't give him a chance to. She waved to her companions and started toward Dtimun at a dead run. The ship's doors closed and it lifted immediately.

"Where have you been?" Dtimun demanded. "We sent out search parties!"

"Got lost," she confided. "Sorry, sir."

"Who was in that Rojok ship?" he persisted.

"Some Cehn-Tahr regulars who got caught in a cross fire," she said. "They gave me a lift." She recited mathematical formulae in her head to deter any probing.

He glared at her. "What Cehn-Tahr regulars? I had no intel about that."

"What about the diplomats?" she asked to divert him.

"Safely aboard ship. We had to fend off a double Rojok attack, from the spaceport as well as from a hidden base nearby," he replied. "We must send a team back in to deal with the Rojoks at the base, but not until we get the diplomats to safely."

The Rojoks at the hidden base were no longer a threat, but she didn't dare say so. She rushed into the ship, still solving math problems until she was safely back in her own sector.

CHAPTER SEVEN

DTIMUN GAVE HER a silent glare when she came aboard the *Morcai* behind him. But if she thought she'd have time to explain her absence further, she was wrong. He motioned her to her own department and jogged toward the bridge access ladder.

She glared after him, almost colliding with Komak as he ran to his post.

He flashed green eyes at her. "You are late, Madelineruszel."

"I am, but I have an excuse. Not that the old man's going to give me the opportunity to tell it to him," she fumed. She stopped and frowned thoughtfully. "Komak, you always run my names together. But the guys back on the planet didn't."

"Guys?" he asked curiously.

She hesitated. Perhaps she wasn't to mention the group to anyone else. Dtimun had seen the Cehn-Tahr planetside, but nobody else had.

Komak made an odd sound and looked shocked.

"What's the matter with you?"

He started to speak and grimaced. "I am not permitted to say. I must run!"

He took off before she could question his strange behavior. His eyes had been blue—that same odd blue that the commander's turned when he was probing her mind. Ridiculous, she thought as she ran toward her department. Komak certainly could not read minds!

They'd been back on Trimerius for two hours before Dtimun called Madeline into his office aboard the ship.

She stood at parade rest in front of his desk and stared at the wall. He seemed busy with a compudisc. He didn't speak for a full minute.

"Komak had something disturbing to say about your absence on the planet."

She wouldn't meet his eyes. "With all due respect, sir, Komak doesn't know what happened. I haven't told him."

He got to his feet, moved to the front of the liquiform desk and perched on the edge of it, facing her. He was so tall that even in the half-sitting position, he was still taller than she was. His elongated eyes narrowed, so that their color was difficult to classify.

"What contingent were you with, when you became separated from us?" he asked.

"A group of Cehn-Tahr regular military," she replied. "They were cut off from their main assault force and their leader was wounded. He had a compound fracture."

He scowled. "Their leader?"

"Yes. An elderly Cehn-Tahr, very tall, with white hair. He was sitting on the ground and a Rojok officer was about to *chasat* him when I intervened."

"Translation?"

She shrugged. "I attacked the Rojok, the old Cehn-Tahr officer kicked the *chasat* away and I knocked the Rojok out with an injection."

"And?"

"I fixed the break in his leg."

He started to speak, his eyes a stormy-brown.

She held up a hand. "I asked permission first. He gave it. But he was still unable to walk properly because I had only minimal supplies with me."

"Komak said you went into battle with the group."

"Sir," she told him, "I didn't tell Komak…"

"What group was it?"

She bit back a sharp reply. But she hadn't been ordered not to mention the encounter. "I've never heard the word before, and I can't translate it. But he said they were a squad of *kehmatemer.*"

He got to his feet and moved to the door in a blur of motion. He locked it, activated a mute screen from a console on his desk and then stalked back to Madeline.

His hands shot out, cupping her face. While she was getting over the shock of his touch, he added, "Show me."

It was no use pretending she didn't understand what he wanted. She replayed the episode in her mind, trying not to notice how warm his hands were, that there was an odd, spicy, clean scent to his skin that made her giddy. She wasn't supposed to be able to notice these things, much less feel them.

After a minute, he lifted his head. But he didn't release her. "You led them into battle," he said slowly.

She nodded. "Their leader said that Holconcom always command, regardless of the rank of other officers. I led them into battle. Then I created a diversion so that they could scale the walls of the fortress and clear it out."

He let go of her and moved away. His breathing

was slow and labored. He searched her eyes quietly. "You must never speak of this to anyone else."

"I won't," she assured him. She studied him, trying to understand the implications of what he was saying. "Who was he, sir?" she asked. "He was wearing more medals than Lawson."

"He is a career soldier of some considerable power on Memcache," he said after a minute. He seemed troubled.

"Memcache. The home planet of the Cehn-Tahr."

He nodded.

"He knew of me," she said, meaning it as a question.

"That is not surprising. He was the most vocal of my critics when I announced your appointment to the Holconcom."

"Really? Perhaps he's changed his mind."

"Perhaps." He didn't elaborate on just how vocal the old one had been.

He was watching her, very closely. "You did not carry a weapon with you?"

She glared at him. "You'd have seen it when I left the ship, sir. As it was, I had to attack an armed Rojok barehanded…!"

"Barehanded?" he exclaimed.

She grimaced at his expression. "Sir, he would have killed the old fellow if I hadn't intervened. I had no weapon and no choice."

He was scowling, as if the possible consequences of her actions were playing out in his mind. He looked troubled.

"I came to medicine as a combat veteran," she reminded him. "I know how to disarm people."

His eyes narrowed. "You are no longer a young cadet."

Her high cheekbones flushed. Her eyes blazed. "Are you insinuating that I am too old for combat?"

His eyebrows arched. "Madam, in any other branch of the military, you would be sitting at a desk."

Her fists clenched at her sides as she reacted to the insult. "Why don't you ask the *kehmatemer* how I diverted a Rojok squad and facilitated their entry into the enemy camp?" she asked hotly.

He stared at her with that pale blue inquisitive stare that touched her mind. His face hardened. "You take chances," he said curtly. "Far too many."

"I belong to the Holconcom," she began.

"You are a physician," he shot back, interrupting her. "You have no business in combat!"

She glared at him. "I was an Amazon captain, sir," she reminded him in an icy tone.

He cocked an eyebrow and his eyes flashed green for just an instant.

"I amuse you?" she demanded.

"At times, yes."

"You sound very superior, sir."

He locked his hands behind him. "You know nothing about us," he said quietly.

"I'm a specialist in Cularian medicine…"

"Which gives you knowledge of blood and bone and cell structure. Nothing more." His eyes darkened. "We reveal nothing of ourselves to outworlders, and little even to you humans who serve with us in the Holconcom."

She didn't want to react to that. She'd heard stories,

of course. All the services had their gossip about the fearsome Cehn-Tahr. But she'd seen them fight.

"You have seen us fight," he agreed out loud. "But in controlled situations." His eyes took on that odd color that gleamed from them in the dark. "You are children, playing at war," he said in a soft, dangerous tone.

"If you have such contempt for us, why ally yourselves with us in the first place?" she asked.

"The Rojoks would have decimated your numbers, after which they would have taken over whole star systems in the New Territory," he said simply. "We have a long history with them, both as allies and as enemies. Your people and, consequently, the allied worlds, stood to lose precious worlds of resources. We had to intervene."

She was too wary of more detention time to say anything aloud.

He saw that. Her spirit amused, and touched him. She was so beautiful. So brave. So foolhardy. She acted without thought. Her actions had saved the old fellow on Ondar, certainly, but could so easily have ended her life. It...disturbed him, to think of seeing her dead. Not for decades had he permitted himself to feel such things. Nor could he afford to, now. She was not for him. The differences were far too dangerous to her. But, still...

His chin lifted as he studied her with something like arrogance. "You must learn to control your impulses," he said flatly. "It would give me no pleasure to have you urned for burial."

Her eyebrows arched. "Are you certain, sir? Because you've threatened to make soup out of Komak, and I know I irritate you more than he does."

A short laugh escaped his throat, and she flashed a grin at him.

"Only marginally," he confessed.

She frowned. "Why does Komak run my names together, when none of the other Cehn-Tahr did?"

"The coupling of names among us indicates affection," he told her gently. "Komak is fond of you."

She smiled. "I'm fond of him, too." She laughed. "He seems so...well, so human, sometimes."

He frowned, as if the thought hadn't occurred to him before.

"He isn't, of course," she added, but her mind went back to the sensor readings at Ahkmau, when she'd fought to save the commander's life; the ones that found human elements in Komak's blood. They must have been glitches, she told herself.

Dtimun's eyes narrowed. "Of course," he said aloud.

She grimaced. "Sir, it's not ethical for you to read my mind," she protested, as she had once before.

"By all means, let us speak of ethics. You brought Mallory aboard my ship after I ordered you not to."

She shifted restlessly. "We have to have backup," she said. "What if the Rojok had been quicker on Ondar?" she asked. "You'd have been without any Cularian specialist aboard."

The thought was like a knife in him. He turned away abruptly, all amusement gone.

He removed the sound locks, and turned back toward her. "The next time I give you an order, I will expect it to be obeyed. Especially concerning side-arms."

She saluted him.

He glowered at her.

"I'll try to improve, sir," she said formally.

He didn't reply.

She paused in the open door. "The Altairian Space Service requires their medics to be armed," she began stubbornly.

He closed the door in her face.

She threw up her hands and jogged back down the hall. "You bend over backward to help people and they serve you up fried every time," she muttered to herself.

"What is fried?" Komak asked, jogging up beside her.

She glared at him. "You sold me out, you traitor," she accused. "And just how did you know what happened on Ondar? I didn't tell you."

He thought for a moment and then grinned. "I have listening devices."

"You do? But I didn't say anything out loud!"

He only laughed. He ran off before she could continue.

She wandered back into the Cularian medical sector, where a flustered Edris Mallory was trying to contend with a wounded Cehn-Tahr who was attempting to leave the unit untreated.

"Get back in there," Madeline told him firmly, "or I'll flash the C.O. and tell him you filched the last of the *entots* fruit out of the galley on a midnight raid," she added smugly, as he flushed. "The C.O. is partial to *entots* fruit and was very unhappy that they went missing, I hear."

The officer frowned. "You would not do that, Ruszel?"

"Let Edris heal that wound and I'll reconsider."

He sighed. "Very well," he said, and went back to the treatment cubicle.

Edris gaped at Madeline. "How did you know that?"

"I have spies," she whispered with a grin. She whistled. "Boy, did you miss an engagement," she added as they moved into the space set aside for their medics. "I almost got fried by a Rojok."

"What happened?" Edris asked.

"Tell her, and you can explain the coffee to Admiral Lawson," Dtimun said in her mind.

"Damn!" she thought furiously. The voice went away. Flushed, she glanced at Edris, who was all eyes. "It's classified," she gritted. "Sorry, Edris."

"No problem, ma'am," the other woman said with a smile. She sobered. "But it seems that it was a good thing the C.O. sent you to the council chambers instead of me."

Madeline considered that for a long time afterward. Yes, it was a good thing. She'd had an experience that she would have been loath to miss. It had improved relations between her and at least a few of the Cehn-Tahr, and she'd saved a life. In her place, Edris might have folded at the most crucial moment, due to her lack of combat experience. But the voice in her head that had warned her about the Rojok attack, and the mysterious destruction of the ship that was strafing her—that was a puzzle she wondered if she'd ever solve. She'd have liked to. It had saved her life.

CHAPTER EIGHT

THE STAFF MEETING had none of its usual passion. Probably, Madeline thought, because they were just past the difficult mission of rescuing the diplomats from Ondar and with no new objective in sight for the time being. Lawson was massing for a new offensive, and he never advanced without proper supply and communications lines. It would probably be weeks before the *Morcai* saw action again.

"We are within easy reach of Dacerius," Komak spoke up. "Would shore leave not be a fitting reward for our latest ordeal of combat?"

"Hear, hear!" Madeline seconded.

Everyone else agreed, all at the same time. Hopeful looks claimed the faces that turned toward Dtimun.

He sighed, sitting on the edge of his liquiform desk, his arms folded across his broad chest. "Dacerius is far too dangerous a destination for shore leave," he told Komak. "Rojok forward patrols have recently erected bases in the desert regions."

"There's always Benaski Port," Stern suggested.

Dtimun glowered at him. "The most notorious port of call in the galaxy and, as you know, off-limits to Tri-Fleet personnel because of the war. I would turn my back for five standard minutes, and Komak would have sold Ruszel into slavery."

"I would never...!" Komak exclaimed.

"In a heartbeat," Madeline interrupted, glowering at him.

"If I did, I would ask a very high price for you," Komak assured her merrily.

"I thought we might visit Memcache," Dtimun said quietly.

There were looks of utter delight among the Cehn-Tahr. It was their home planet. Even Hahnson and Stern looked interested. Madeline was, too, but she tried not to show her enthusiasm.

Dtimun glanced at her. "One of the religious in the Mahkmannah compound has expressed a wish to meet Ruszel," he said. "They are a private sect who live far away from cities and civilization."

Madeline's eyebrows arched. "But how would they know about me, sir?"

"A question which had also occurred to me," he replied. "I have no answer." He straightened. "A female of our species has the gift of prophecy. She is elderly and important. She wishes to speak with you. The request was passed to me by a high government official and condoned by the Dectat itself."

"I would very much like to go," Madeline told him.

"The rest of us could proceed to Kolmahnkash," Komak suggested. "It is a beautiful city. It has the most fascinating exhibitions of cyberart..."

Hahnson and Stern raised their hands. "We love art," they said almost in unison. "We'd love to see the cyberart exhibitions!"

Dtimun glared at them, and at Komak. "Gaming domes do not deal in cyberart," he returned. "Kolmahnkash is notorious for them." He stared pointedly at Stern. "As you well know."

Stern grinned sheepishly. "Sir, we haven't had liberty for months."

"Hint, hint," Hahnson added.

"My whole department is depressed," Lieutenant Higgins interrupted. "I know a little gaming would improve their efficiency."

"My whole department is more depressed than his whole department," Lieutenant Jennings added.

Dtimun held up a hand. "Very well but Stern will be held responsible for any problems that occur," he added, looking at the grinning human.

"We won't have a single problem. I swear it on the lives of my children," Stern said.

"You don't have any children," Hahnson reminded him.

Stern put his finger to his lips, frowned and said, "Shhhhhh!"

Even Dtimun laughed. "All right. You can rotate departments for R&R and use the scouts for transport. Ruszel and I will take the skimmer to Mahkmannah."

Madeline hardly heard the rest of the briefing. It had always amused her that the somber Cehn-Tahr could conceive of and build a virtual reality complex as intricate and exciting as Kolmahnkash. The complex boasted hundreds of virtual gaming sites with tech so cutting-edge that the scenarios were virtually undetectable from reality. Engineers used them to configure fantastic designs, soldiers to test weapon concepts. No one knew what the Cehn-Tahr themselves used the tech for. Perhaps they were, like most of the soldiers, secret gamers who coveted the latest innovations in gaming.

She wondered how many of her crewmates would tag along with Dtimun and herself. She was curious about the request and the elderly woman who had made it. She must be a person of some authority if her request was approved by the Cehn-Tahr Dectat itself. She still wondered how the woman knew about her.

SHE JOGGED DOWN to the flight deck when she was called, a few hours later. She was excited about her first visit to the Cehn-Tahr home world. She'd seen vids of it, but they were never much like the real thing.

When she arrived, it was to find Dtimun waiting beside a small scout ship, the series that Cehn-Tahr referred to as "skimmers." They were all-terrain vehicles as well as spaceworthy transport. Only one of them was assigned to each ship, and only the commanding officer was allowed its use.

He motioned her inside. She buckled up in her seat, surprised that it appeared to be only the two of them making the trip.

"It's curious, isn't it," she asked on the way down, "that a stranger would know about me?"

He glanced at her with dancing green eyes. "Caneese is a seer," he replied, his hands flashing over the controls. "One of the few we recognize as infallible."

She bit her lip. "Has she seen something terrible in my future, I wonder?"

He didn't look at her. "A question I have been asking myself."

He turned the skimmer in the general direction of the capital.

Madeline glanced at him. "Sir, isn't this the way to the city?" she asked, having studied maps of the planetary capital.

"Yes. I have been asked to meet with an official at the offices of the Imperial Dectat. It will only mean a slight delay," he added.

"Of course." One could hardly refuse such an order, she thought. She remembered that the *keh-matemer* were headquartered here and wondered idly if she might get a glimpse of the old soldier she'd met and ask about his injuries.

MADELINE HAD NEVER set foot on Memcache. The Cehn-Tahr capital was like a softened contour of Ter-ravegan architecture. The buildings here were so far conformed into the ecology that they seemed to be a part of it. There were no skimmers allowed in capi-tal airspace. The avenues were wide and paved with natural stone, the sidewalks grassed and groomed. Pedestrians and motorists traveled in one- and two-person conveyances, which caused no pollution as they moved around the city.

The headquarters of the Cehn-Tahr military was taller than the buildings around it, glowing in muted blue and gold imperial colors. The transports inside moved freely, arching up to the second floor when they felt added weight. They reminded Madeline somewhat of the old moving sidewalks of ancient Earth that she'd seen in vids.

As she and Dtimun entered, he excused himself and went to announce them to the guard in his small post. Madeline turned and was suddenly enveloped in a blue wall of *kehmatemer*, with the old fellow himself in their midst.

"Ruszel!" he exclaimed, smiling as he went to take both her hands in his, an alarming and flattering greeting since Cehn-Tahr were forbidden to touch outworlders. Presumably the old fellow was of such high rank that he didn't have to worry about the consequences. "It is good to see you again."

"And you, sir," she said at once, returning the gentle pressure of his hands and smiling. She glanced around her. "Good to see you guys, too," she added.

Their leader, Captain Rhemun, wearing his helmet even inside the building, chuckled. "Have you come to give up the Holconcom and join us, Ruszel?" he asked with green eyes.

"Now, just a minute," she began with a laugh.

Dtimun came toward them, noting the camaradcrie of Madeline and the *kehmatemer,* who were notorious for their hostility to any alien race. The old fellow turned, releasing Madeline's hands. His demeanor changed at once. He became cold and threatening.

"Commander Dtimun," he said curtly.

Behind him and Madeline, the *kehmatemer* started to bow. The old fellow, unseen, waved his hand behind his back and forced them back erect.

Dtimun stopped in place. He did not salute, or smile. "Sir," he said.

The old fellow followed suit. "I will see you in my office," he said. He glanced at Madeline, and his expression softened. "I will see you again before you leave, warwoman," he said with something akin to affection.

"Yes, sir," she replied, smiling. But she saluted, too. The salute was returned.

"May we remain?" the leader of the *kehmatemer* asked hesitantly. "We wish to ask Ruszel about her command combat experiences."

The old fellow smiled, amused. "Very well."

They gathered around Madeline again.

The old fellow led the way up the arching staircase and then into his office. He waved his hand over the controls, shutting the office in a stealth mode that denied access, either physically or electronically.

He sat down behind his desk.

"You sent for me?" Dtimun asked stiffly, and he remained standing in front of the freeform liquiform desk at which the elder Cehn-Tahr sat.

"I did," he replied tersely. "I am aware that Caneese has asked to see Ruszel. She senses a new danger, one which may place the warwoman at risk of death."

"Do not ask me to believe that the death of a human female would affect you," the younger Cehn-Tahr said.

"Ruszel's would," the old man replied quietly. "She is unique. I have not met her like in my lifetime, save once."

Dtimun's eyes narrowed. They were cold. Ice-blue. "May I ask how you came to know her at all?" he asked.

The old fellow cocked his head. "Some years ago, your tone of voice alone would have gained you living space in the brig," he said softly. "I am still your superior." The very softness of the old one's voice carried the threat.

Dtimun stood more respectfully, but did not speak. His eyes still rebelled.

There was a soft sigh from across the desk. "I led the *kehmatemer* to Ondar. I had heard that there would be an attempt on Chacon, the Rojok field marshal. He was rumored to have been in the party that kidnapped the ambassadors," he said surprisingly. "Also, Princess Lyceria had heard of this and we could not locate her. It was feared that she was en route to Ondar to warn the Rojok. We know that she still has contact with him, despite the war. I took a great chance leading the *kehmatemer* into hostile territory myself, but I thought it necessary, under the circumstances."

Dtimun frowned. "We had no inkling of this."

"We informed no one. Nor was our information accurate," the old one replied. "As it turned out, the intel was faulty. Chacon was not on Ondar; neither was the princess Lyceria. Like a rank private, I allowed myself to become separated from my unit. A Rojok spotted me, *chasated* me and would have killed me. Ruszel attacked him physically, brought him within reach of my boot and, when he was down, she tranquillized him." He laughed. "She is a warrior of some skill."

Dtimun nodded. "I am aware of her combat abilities."

"My leg was broken, the bone shattered. She mended me—not, I add, without some show of anger and resentment on my part. I had never been in the company of a female human, and I had reason to dislike Ruszel before I met her," he added pointedly. "You added her to the Holconcom, I expect, to cause such resentment in the Dectat, as well as the *keh-matemer*."

"I did," Dtimun had to acknowledge.

"Despite my bad temper, the fire-haired medic restored me at least to a less painful state, but she had not the tools to repair the damage. I could not walk, and our transport had been destroyed by the Rojoks."

Dtimun seemed to be less rigid. "Her wrist scanner is an emergency store only."

"So I realized. But we had to appropriate transport and I could not lead my men. Since Ruszel was the only serving Holconcom among us, she had to lead the *kehmatemer* into battle."

Dtimun scowled. "Until a few minutes ago, when I saw their reaction to her, I would not have believed that possible. They are notorious for their hatred of aliens, especially your captain Rhemun, and they have never seen a female in combat. I would not expect them to willingly follow a female of any species, but especially a human."

"Nor would I, so I ordered them to." He chuckled, a very human sound. "It was unnecessary. They were eager for the experience. They said it would be a tale to be told around campfires." He leaned forward. "As it has been. Ruszel has already become legend among them."

Dtimun's face softened. "She is…a surprising sort of human."

"Surprising indeed. She not only led my men into battle, but she did it by subterfuge and stealth worthy of even you. She made it possible for the *keh-matemer* to wipe out a Rojok outpost and steal one of their transports. They came back for me. The rest you know."

Dtimun was quiet for a minute.

"I am surprised," the old one commented, "that you did not see this in her mind when she returned to you on Ondar."

Dtimun's lips made a thin line. "I saw a great deal of it, but not all. She recites multiplication tables."

The old one's white thick eyebrows arched. "Excuse me?"

"When she wishes me not to read her thoughts, she recites mathematical formulae or tables. It is remarkably effective, especially when we are in dangerous straits and I have no time to penetrate the barriers."

The old one chuckled again. "Will you take her to the fortress, when you visit Caneese?"

Dtimun was hesitant. "I have not set foot there in many years."

"It is time you did." The old one stood up. "Introduce her to Rognan, too. I told her many things about Meg-Ravens. He will teach her more."

"Rognan is still there?" he asked.

The old one nodded. "More abrasive than ever… it comes of having no mate, I think, an estate with which I can sympathize." He studied the taller Cehn-Tahr closely. "Komak has told me many things that he dare not speak of to you." His eyes narrowed. "You have some idea of who he is."

Dtimun nodded curtly. "There is no such Clan as Maltiche."

"Yet it is your second given name," came the reply. "Yes. He has knowledge of things that have not yet occurred, like Caneese. But he is no seer. He knows the pattern of events, but not the details."

"You think he comes back from another period of time."

"Yes," the old one replied. "He is careful not to say too much."

"But he betrays himself in many ways," Dtimun agreed. His eyes narrowed. "He insisted that I take my bodyguard with me to Lagana, in the Dibella system, where we decimated a Rojok outpost. I would have died, had I not followed his advice. He knew that I would be wounded. My bodyguard found Ruszel and sent her to me."

The old one grimaced. "I regret that I opposed her assignment to you. Much time has passed. My ambition destroyed my family," he said, shocking his companion. "I have many regrets and no way to mend the wounds I have perpetrated. Ruszel has caused me to do much soul-searching, as the humans call it." He met the other Cehn-Tahr's eyes. "I cannot change the past. But I am hopeful of securing a better future for my family, starting with the interspecies edicts."

Dtimun's eyes reflected his inner turmoil. "I would be interested in knowing how you propose such a change in policy to be accomplished."

"With much gnashing of teeth and dissent," he announced with a sigh. He glanced at Dtimun. "You are surely aware of Lyceria's...affection...for the Rojok field marshal?"

Dtimun moved restively. "It is unfortunate."

"Caneese does not think so."

Dtimun scowled. "And you?"

The old one actually grinned. He moved around

his desk and clapped Dtimun on the back. "Go and see Caneese with the warwoman. It will be a happy reunion for her. Tell her...tell her that I begin to see from her point of view, many years too late. She will understand."

He led the way out the door and back down the staircase, which moved them eloquently to the first floor without seeming to move at all.

The *kehmatemer* were on the floor, kneeling, around Madeline, who was sitting, bent over, her face animated as she explained a stealth tactic she had used with her unit to attack a much superior force during her time as an Amazon captain.

Dtimun watched her with an expression to which he was oblivious. His companion noted it with amusement and approval.

"She has them hypnotized," Dtimun murmured.

"They have never seen a woman in combat." He made a face. "Now I am being asked to consider the organization of a female military component."

Dtimun stared at him, surprised.

The old one lifted a shoulder. "I would have fought them even two standard months ago. Now, however..." He smiled with pure affection at the human female in the distance. "It is a great pity that she is not Cehn-Tahr," he said softly. "A great pity."

Dtimun refused to rise to the bait, even if he was thinking the same thing.

The old one saw it in his mind, a rarity. His eyes narrowed. "They have no idea how different our species really are, have they?" he wondered.

Dtimun sighed. "I considered it wiser to reveal as little as possible to the humans."

"Yes." He glanced at the younger alien. "But I wonder how much difference it would make now? The humans revere you, I am told."

"That is an exaggeration."

The old one just smiled. "Perhaps our friend Komak knows of a way in the future to permit us to bond with humans," he murmured dryly.

Dtimun glared at him. "Ruszel is a member of my crew. Nothing more."

The old one's eyes changed into an opaque, searching blue.

"Stop that," Dtimun muttered, resorting to Madeline's use of mathematical tables to keep the old one out of his mind.

He only laughed. "*Kehmatemer*!" he called.

They jumped to their feet and rushed, like blue blurs, into formation immediately. Madeline followed suit, snapping to attention.

The old fellow, delighted, returned the salute. "You must come back another time, Ruszel," he told her. "I would hear some of these stories with my own ears."

She grinned. "Anytime, sir. It would be my pleasure to hear some of your stories, as well."

The old fellow looked at Dtimun. "She knows how to smooth egos," he said in the Holy Tongue, a rare dialect used only by the *kehmatemer* and a select few Cehn-Tahr officials. "Look to your own."

Dtimun gave him a glare.

"Caneese will be waiting," the old fellow added in Standard.

"Yes. We should go." He motioned to Madeline, who moved toward the door.

Dtimun stopped as they reached it. He straightened, as if deep in thought. Then, slowly, he turned. He stood at attention, and gave the old fellow a terse salute. He did not wait for it to be returned.

As he went out the door, he missed the sudden wetness in an old pair of eyes. In sixty-five human years, it was the first time he'd saluted the old man.

IN MINUTES THEY were off again, this time to the rural province where the secr Caneese lived with a group of religious Cehn-Tahr. Below, the terrain was hilly and green and beautiful. Madeline, who had lived for many years on the artificial military colony on Trimerius, hadn't seen a blade of real grass or a mountain in her adult life.

Dtimun reversed the engine and set the ship down with his usual astounding speed, landing it like a feather on the air.

They stepped out onto a lush green plain with scant trees on the horizon and jagged, purple mountains in the distance. Closer, there was a small group of gray stone buildings with ancient carved runes, linked by towering stone walls that seemed endless. The air was crisp and fresh-smelling. Underneath was a faint musk scent, like the exotic perfumes one found on Dacerius. Overhead, there were two suns, a yellow one and a smaller blue one. The sky was an odd shade of blue, and there were puffy white clouds like the ones on Terravega itself. She recalled from her reading that Memcache also had two moons, the largest of which, reasonably close to the planet in its orbit, was colonized and contained a mining sector. She'd love to have seen them at night. Two moons in a night sky would have been beautiful. Trimerius had not a single one.

She drew in a full breath, her eyes closed to savor the scents of exotic flowers that bloomed abundantly nearby. Among those scents was that of canolithe, which she knew only from textdiscs. The rare flowers were indigenous only to Memcache and were known for some legendary, and probably fictitious, abilities.

The forest of trees, which resembled the bamboo forests she'd seen ancient depictions of from old Earth, were green from trunk to feathery leaves, and stretched off toward the mountainous horizon. Somewhere, there were faint violinlike tones. Wind chimes, she wondered, or insects?

"Wind chimes," Dtimun answered absently, watching as a metal gate slowly opened and a woman in blue silks moved toward them with such grace that Madeline couldn't keep her eyes off the sight.

"It's so beautiful here," she said slowly.

"I have always thought so," he replied. "My own lands are here in this valley. My family inhabits another, larger, property across the mountain range."

It was the first time he'd spoken to her of his private life. She was flattered and even more curious, but she didn't reply to the statement. "Is this the seer?" she asked instead as the elderly woman approached.

He nodded, his hands linked behind his back as he walked toward the old woman.

He made a slight bow and kept his eyes lowered as the woman approached him. She was Cehn-Tahr, Madeline noticed, but her hair was silver and fell to her waist in back, over the simple, long robes she wore. She smiled at Dtimun and reached up to touch his jet-black hair.

"*Mecaache*," she said softly as she smoothed his hair. "It has been far too long!"

He smiled back, and touched her hair in a similar manner. They touched foreheads briefly. Ritual behavior, Madeline was certain, but she had scant knowledge of Cehn-Tahr behavior among their own people.

The elderly woman spoke to him in their native tongue. He replied the same way.

They both turned toward Madeline. She wished she knew more Cehn-Tahr. Sadly, except for basic military commands, what she'd picked up from Komak turned out to be the most awful swear words. Komak had encouraged her to exhibit her Cehn-Tahr linguistic skills for the commander. It had been a memorable occasion that she often wished she could forget. Dtimun had called her—and subsequently Komak—on the carpet for it.

The woman, tall and elegant, stopped in front of Madeline and studied her curiously. "So you are Ruszel," the woman said in her soft, quiet voice, and in perfect standard English. "Welcome."

Madeline smiled, surprised. "Thank you."

The woman nodded, returning the smile. She was taller than Madeline by a head, and her elongated eyes were a soft brownish color that the Morcai's medical chief of staff had never noticed in other Cehn-Tahr eyes.

"You are wondering how I know about you," the old woman said gently, and smiled at Madeline's reaction. "I have the gift of prophecy. I am the only one in my Clan to have received such a gift."

Madeline studied her curiously. "Should I ask you about my future?" she wondered aloud.

The elderly woman laughed softly. "How interesting that you should connect it with me."

Madeline's cheeks flushed and she smiled self-consciously. "Forgive me for making assumptions."

"Unnecessary," the other woman replied. "You are intelligent and you have great courage." She laughed when Madeline flushed even more. "Now you begin to wonder if I have been speaking with persons who know you. I must confess that I have. Not him," she added when Madeline shot a suspicious glance at her companion.

Dtimun chuckled softly. "You have spies everywhere," he commented.

"I do," the woman replied without conceit. "And I use them." She turned back to Madeline, and this time she didn't smile. Her eyes took on an odd, watery shade of blue that was reminiscent of Dtimun's eyes when he was looking into her mind. The elderly woman closed her eyes and made an odd humming sound.

Madeline, confused and fascinated, stood quietly, her eyes involuntarily darting to the tall alien at her side. Dtimun met her searching glance and his eyes narrowed faintly. A shock of pleasure rippled through her body as they looked at each other.

"Yes." The elderly woman was staring at Madeline, who hadn't realized her own preoccupation with Dtimun.

Madeline struggled to regain her composure.

The old woman only smiled; a human trait that Madeline had often noticed in Komak. "I have been given a prophecy," Caneese began softly. "It concerns a human female."

Madeline's eyebrows arched.

"Yes," the woman replied, "a curious element, is it not? Especially considering that our culture has denied humans entrance here since the Cehn-Tahr race settled on Memcache. I saw the prophecy as a child, but I had put it aside. Then I heard of you. The prophecy is that in a time of great turbulence a human female will bring peace to a kingdom torn by tragedy." She closed her eyes. "There will be signs when she comes among us…giant serpents which she will befriend…a great war with a former ally, days of torture ended by an unexpected alliance." Her eyes opened. "There is also a description of the human female. She will be a healer, and veteran warriors will follow her into battle."

Madeline was trying to wrap her mind around all this. The part about warriors following the healer into battle was disturbing, and she thought of the *kehm-atemer*. But, she'd said nothing about it to Caneese. The older woman knew anyway—her expression betrayed the knowledge. How?

She smiled at Madeline. "You are the only female ever to serve with the Holconcom in its history," she continued. "I have heard stories of your courage under fire. It was you who saved the Holconcom commander here from death during the dylete."

"Well, I did do that," the medic agreed slowly. She glanced up at Dtimun. "Not that he ever takes that into consideration when I defend his honor…"

"His honor?" The seer seemed puzzled.

Dtimun glowered at Madeline. "She wrecks bars."

"It was only one bar, and the First Fleet is responsible," Madeline defended herself. "I would never have attacked them if they hadn't referred to you as a, and I quote, cat-eyed benny-whammer! Sir."

The old one laughed out loud. "Our emperor has steadfastly refused to allow our females to serve in the military," she mused. "But I think he is weakening on this point. Your exploits have even reached his ears."

Madeline bit her lower lip. "Oh, dear."

The seer held up an elegant, graceful hand. "Not in a bad way," she corrected instantly. "I am told that his…" She frowned. "I have not the words in Standard to explain his personal guards." She looked to Dtimun for help.

"According to Stern," Dtimun said, glancing at Madeline, "emperors on your ancient homeworld, Earth, were protected by a personal bodyguard of great capability. They were called the Praetorian Guard."

"Yes," the seer agreed. "That would be a proper description. The emperor's Praetorians speak of Ruszel in whispers. They have great respect for her."

Madeline was confused, because she'd never been around the emperor of the Cehn-Tahr, or his soldiers; only the *kehmatemer*, which were dispatched by the Dectat.

The old seer chuckled at her confusion. "Yes, the *kehmatemer* also know of you, do they not?" she queried the younger woman, and now Madeline knew that she, too, could read minds. "Nevertheless…"

A horrible high-pitched scream interrupted the seer. Madeline turned along with her companions to see a small white cobra-looking animal shooting across the green valley. Right behind it was a galot, one of the legendary big cats, native to Eridanus, that roamed the Cehn-Tahr homeworld. Cehn-Tahr were rumored to trace their beginnings to Cashto, an ancient cat-human mutation, although Madeline found that hard to believe. However, galots were endangered, and on the protected list.

Which meant that Madeline couldn't shoot it, even if she'd been able to sneak her Gresham off the ship past the commander. But there was another way to rescue the small, screaming hot lunch that even now, for some inexplicable reason, streaked toward Madeline for protection. There were Meg-Ravens on Memcache. And Madeline knew how to call them. They were natural enemies of the galot

Without mentioning what she planned to do, she cupped her hands, inserted the tip of one finger into her mouth and made the call of a Meg-Raven.

The seer watched, astonished, as did Dtimun, when a small flock of the huge, elegant black birds suddenly appeared and swooped down on the racing galot. In seconds, the huge cat was stopping, turning away from the little serpent. One of the Meg-Ravens flew toward Madeline and circled, making its merry cry.

Madeline, laughing, cupped her hands and made a second call, one of only a handful in the avian language that she'd painstakingly learned on her own after being tutored by the mysterious old Cehn-Tahr when the ambassadors had been rescued by the Holconcom on Ondar. The Meg-Raven dipped its wing and then rejoined its friends as they circled and dived at the retreating big cat.

Beside her, the little white serpent panted. Madeline bent and cupped her hands in front of it. She'd played with the friendly little white serpents on Dacerius and at Benaski Port, where they were sold as exotic pets on the black market. She was fond of them, and had almost bought one. They were as endangered as the galot, and they weren't predators. They had intelligence and they liked humans.

The serpent crawled right into Madeline's hands. She lifted it, to look into its pretty blue eyes. It swayed back and forth, purring, and then rubbed against Madeline's cheek.

"Ruszel!" Dtimun called urgently. "Put it down!"

She was about to ask why when she felt a soft stirring of wind on either side of her. Before she could turn her head, two giant white serpents with blue eyes were suddenly flanking her. They were both hissing. Partially coiled, they were still taller than Madeline. Her body froze in position while her heart raced madly. They were terrifying, even to a human who'd been around serpents, as Madeline had. She'd never seen snakes of such size and strength. One bite and she would be dead.

She started to put the little serpent down, very slowly, but it refused to go. It leaped onto her shoulder and rubbed against her hair, still purring.

"Sir?" she groaned to Dtimun, certain that she was about to die.

CHAPTER NINE

DTIMUN STARTED TOWARD Madeline at once. Both adult serpents moved in front of her and spread their hoods. Amazed, as he read their thoughts, he stopped in his tracks.

The serpents moved gracefully to face Ruszel. For a few seconds, while the baby serpent rubbed her cheek and purred, she waited for death.

And then, without warning, the two adult serpents moved on either side of her, swayed and purred, and rubbed their heads against hers. The two Cehn-Tahr stood spellbound a few feet away.

The little serpent jumped from Madeline's shoulder to the hood of the larger of the two big serpents. All three looked at Madeline and suddenly vanished.

Madeline let out the breath she'd been holding and gaped. "What the…?"

"And she will befriend the serpents," the seer quoted, breathlessly.

Dtimun was in front of her, his elongated eyes dark blue with lingering faint traces of the concern he'd felt. Involuntarily, his hand touched her long hair.

Fearful for him, because this was a taboo that could have him spaced by his own people, she stepped quickly back, her expression betraying her fear.

"*Camaashe*," he said softly.

She'd heard the word before. He used it with humans when fear overcame them. It was comforting, even without a translation. She began to relax.

"Your concern is not necessary here," he said, but his lips did not move. "No regulations bind me on my own land."

She felt her heart skip at the way he was looking at her. The feelings that kindled were new and frightening.

"Your...land?" she faltered.

"Indeed," the seer agreed, joining them. "Your commander allows us possession of the retreat here, on his estate." She indicated the stone buildings. "This is an ancient temple. It has been here since far before written history documented it."

"It's very beautiful," Madeline replied, still fighting to regain her composure.

"You can call Meg-Ravens," Dtimun murmured, fascinated. "How did you learn this rare skill?"

Madeline smiled. "An acquaintance of mine studies them as a hobby. He taught me."

There were raised eyebrows from the Cehn-Tahr, followed by amusement that seemed out of proportion to the discussion.

"Effective for rescuing serpents," Dtimun replied, tongue-in-cheek. "The Nagaashe."

Her heart skipped. "Those...were Nagaashe?" Now their visit to the Altair embassy made sense. "How did they vanish like that?"

"They jump through time," he told her. "They have a planet, not too many parsecs from Memcache, but we have no diplomatic embassy with them, despite our endless efforts at detente. That was the purpose of our visit to the Altair embassy. The Nagaashe have resources that we need. There is a very small colony of them on Dacerius, in the mountain country, evolved to a diminished size. There are only a male and a female here. This pair has occupied a catacomb on my land as long as the estates have existed. We protect them. Their child, however, was unknown to us. I shall have to find a way to protect them from the galot." He didn't add that he knew the galot in question, who was going to get a stern lecture for frightening the Nagaashe child.

"They were going to attack me," she began.

"Only in the act of protecting their child," the seer told her kindly. "They rarely produce more than one offspring during their lifetimes. It is why they near extinction. The child grows at a very slow pace, during which it is vulnerable. Poachers have decimated their numbers on Eridanus Three, where they, like the giant feline galot, originated. Their fangs are said to have healing properties. They were once killed by the thousands for that reason. Even now, you may find such fangs in clandestine shops."

"What a pity, to kill something so intelligent for such a reason," Madeline said.

"Yes," Dtimun replied. He cocked his head. "How is that you have no fear of serpents? Most of your colleagues would have reached for a weapon."

She flushed a little when she remembered that she'd had that in mind herself at first.

Dtimun only smiled. "It was a natural reaction," he told her.

The seer's eyes became narrowed. "He does not allow you a weapon in combat?" she exclaimed.

Dtimun glowered at her. "Medics may not carry weapons. It is a universal regulation."

"Which she disobeys," Caneese said, amused.

Madeline chuckled.

"You have not answered the question," he persisted.

"Oh, about the snakes?" She smiled. "My father kept serpents, years ago. I visited him at his station. He had three or four species of snakes in his quarters, which resulted in charges more than once. He always managed to talk himself out of them. His snakes were very poisonous. He taught me how to handle them. Of course, none of them were intelligent, like these white serpents. How did they vanish?" she asked again.

"They are multidimensional," he said simply.

She blinked. "Multiwhat?"

"Dimensional." He frowned. "You must have heard of the string and membrane theories. Did you not have theoretical physics as part of your medical training?"

"Of course. We're required to study all fields of science, not just medicine, so that our education prepares us for any military space assignment. But the super-string and membrane theories are hundreds of years old and, at the moment, out of vogue with our physicists."

"We consider it quite logical, that we exist in multiple dimensions that reflect different choices we make in this life. The serpents can travel between the dimensions, an ability our scientists have labored to assimilate. Sadly, it seems linked to an extrasensory organ that cannot be replicated."

"Just as well," Madeline said. "I don't want to run

into another version of myself, or multiple versions of myself. I have enough trouble managing the one."

Dtimun said nothing, but his eyes were unusually thoughtful.

The seer moved forward. "Come," she said, taking Madeline's arm with her soft hand. "Let us sip tea and discuss the many anomalies of theoretical physics and quantum mechanics and their application to exobiology."

Madeline was fascinated by the woman. She knew Cehn-Tahr were intelligent, but this surpassed her expectations. She was happy here, with her companions. She wondered what other surprises were in store for her. But she didn't ask. Some things, she reasoned, were dangerous to know.

CANEESE ASKED QUESTIONS delicately, without overt curiosity. She was graceful and intelligent. Madeline liked her very much.

When Caneese looked toward the commander and nodded, he rose and left them, walking out into the courtyard.

Caneese became serious. "You have an…attachment to the Holconcom commander," she said, holding up her hand when Madeline involuntarily tried to protest. "It is dangerous. Far more dangerous than you realize."

"I don't understand," Madeline replied uneasily.

The older woman let out a long sigh, and her eyes were sad. "We are not permitted to discuss certain aspects of our culture with outworlders. I deeply regret this, because the lack of knowledge could cause your death. I must speak in abstracts, but you must try to hear what I cannot say." Her eyes became a somber blue. "We are not what we seem. You think of us as humanoid because we appear so. But there are differences which are not apparent..."

" My feelings were mentally neutered," Madeline began gently. "I can't feel..."

"You must never attempt to lie to me," the older woman said gently. "It is useless." She softened the words with a smile. She put her hand over Madeline's on the table between them. "Your 'feelings' may trigger a behavior in your commander which is not subject to his control. Regardless of your inclination, you must never permit him to have physical contact with you...what is it?"

The younger woman's breath caught. She was remembering what had happened when the Rojok tried to throw her over a cliff and Dtimun, against all odds, had saved her.

Caneese was uneasy. "Then it is too late."

"Excuse me?"

Caneese chewed her lower lip, an oddly human action. "Listen to me. You must take care not to be completely alone with him, away from other humans or Cehn-Tahr, and you must never let a male touch you in his presence. Do you understand?"

"No," Madeline stammered, and was recalling Dtimun's odd behavior even at the embassy, when he growled at Taylor. That was long before he touched her in the act of saving her on Lagana.

Caneese frowned worriedly. "It began without touching?" she said, astonished. "I do not understand, either. The prophecy is quite specific, but there is no way known to science that it could be realized," she said, almost to herself. "And there is another matter. A far more deadly one. A traumatic time approaches for you."

Madeline wondered what she meant.

Caneese's eyes became dark blue and intense. "A change is coming, Madeline," she said. "A great change, a very dangerous change, for you."

"Can you tell me what sort of change?" she asked. "A promotion?"

The older woman's eyes became sad. "Is this life that you have so rewarding that you can conceive of nothing better?"

Madeline frowned. "My career has always been my life," she faltered. "Our society is very strict. We are chosen for the work we do. It is not possible to refuse."

"If you could refuse?"

Madeline was confused. She bit her lower lip. Involuntarily, her mind went back to the commander and she felt a jolt of emotion.

The older woman sat straighter. "I see."

Madeline met the other woman's eyes evenly. "You won't tell anyone that the commander touched me?" she worried. "They would kill him…"

Caneese caught her breath at the wave of emotion emanating from the fragile creature before her. "Of course not," she said gently. "Never!"

She let out a sigh of relief. "I would have died. He told me to throw myself over the cliff and I did. I thought he meant to spare the unit's pride, to deny the Rojok the power to harm me. He caught me." Her voice betrayed her wonder. "It was…unbelievable."

Caneese looked unsettled. "He told you to throw

yourself over a cliff and you obeyed him without protest?" she asked, aghast.

"Of course," Madeline said simply.

The older woman saw it in her mind, saw everything. She looked down at her own hands. "I had forgotten," she said in a wistful tone, "how very powerful such emotions are."

"Oh, the commander doesn't feel anything like that," Madeline assured her, flushing. "I'm just one of his people. One of his crew. He's possessive. Of all of us," she added quickly.

Caneese suddenly looked her age. "It is tragic," she said in a whisper. "More tragic than I realized."

"I don't understand."

She looked up at Madeline with troubled blue eyes. "You will be forced to make a decision you do not wish to make," she said heavily. "A sacrifice. I see death." She grimaced. "I brought you here to warn you, to counsel you. But I can see little of the danger. Only that it involves a hidden agenda." Her eyes closed. "I had no idea."

"Excuse me?"

Caneese drew in a long breath. "The prophecy is true. I am certain of it. But I cannot see how to resolve what I know with the reality of the present." She searched Madeline's confused eyes. "You are so fragile a species."

Madeline laughed. "Armed with Greshams, we're not all that fragile."

Caneese wasn't thinking of conflicts. But this was not the time to instill even more fear. She forced a smile. "There will be a way. There must be. I cannot see it, but I know the prophecy is not a false one."

"The prophecy...is there more to it than you told me?" Madeline asked.

The alien woman looked troubled. "Yes. You must not ask," she added very softly. "I have already said too much. You must keep as much distance from your commander as possible, once you leave Memcache. At least," she amended, frowning, "until I can do some covert research on the problem."

"Research." Madeline nodded, but she looked totally stunned.

The old woman smiled at her. "We will find a way. We must." She smiled. "Now, sip your tea and tell me what you think of Memcache."

DTIMUN RETURNED MINUTES later. When the tea was finished and the commander stood, Madeline followed suit. "Thank you," she told the other woman. "I really enjoyed meeting you."

"I have also enjoyed it," Caneese said softly. "We will meet again. Soon." She paused at the door. "Madeline, if you would not mind waiting for your commander outside in the compound, there is something I must say to him. Something private."

"Of course," she said at once, returning the smile. "I'll be outside, sir."

He nodded.

She walked out the door and closed it gently behind her.

Inside the room, Caneese was more solemn than Dtimun had ever seen her.

"The prophecy cannot concern her," he said curtly. "You and I both know that what you envision is impossible."

"Yes, but my visions never lie," she replied. "You know that."

His face hardened. "What you envision would kill her. That is certain. I rescued her from a fall of almost one hundred and fifty terrestrial feet. In the process, as careful as I was, I punctured her lungs. The wounds would have been fatal, had Hahnson not been handy with his medical kit."

She searched his eyes with concern. "You have touched her."

His face closed up. "It was unavoidable. I could not let her die."

"Of course not. But it began long before that, did it not?" she questioned very softly. "I saw in her mind that you reacted violently when a human ambassador touched her, at the Altair reception."

He averted his eyes. That was true.

She probed gently and then frowned. "The gown. You gave her a gown to wear to the Altair embassy."

He scowled. "Yes, but she returned it when we arrived back at our embassy...."

She held up a hand. "It was a gift. You gave it, she accepted it."

He groaned. In his culture, the giving and receipt of a gift was a prelude to courtship. He hadn't considered the gown in that light. "It was a mistake," he added quietly. But his mind went back to the image of Madeline wearing the gown, her beauty that had stunned him.

Caneese saw that. She smiled indulgently. "Yes. She is quite beautiful. But as fragile as canolithe," she added gently. "It is now only a question of time. You know that."

"I will manage it," he said flatly. "I must find a way to distance myself from her."

"You do not wish to," she perceived gently.

His eyes were bitter. "Where hope does not exist, practicality must."

"If the prophecy is true, and I think this likely, then a solution must exist which we have not found."

"If there was one, it would have been discovered in four hundred years," he said curtly.

"You are forgetting Komak," she said, peering into his mind. "Ruszel's 'old fellow' thinks he comes from the future. If that is so, then he may hold the key to the solution."

He had forgotten the conversation. His heart lifted, but quickly fell. "Who knows how far in the future that solution might be?" he said flatly. "Humans do not share our life span. In fact, they have no idea what it really is."

Her old face quieted as she acknowledged the truth of his comment. "Yes. I know. I am sorry."

"So am I," he said stiffly.

"But I will not relinquish hope. In the meantime," she added firmly, "you must distance yourself from her, for your own good as well as hers. At least for a time, distance may spare her." She touched his face with a lean, soft hand. "Having said that, I thank you for bringing her to me. She is not what I expected. She is far more."

"So her 'old fellow' said, in the capital city," he replied, with a smile in his eyes. "She captivated him as well."

She eyed him warily. "Is he...as uncompromising

as ever?" she asked, averting her gaze as her hand fell back to her side.

"He is not," he said. "In fact," he added quietly, "he has already begun to change. Ruszel has changed him."

She exchanged a long glance with him. "She is the catalyst," she said. She nodded. "That, too, is the prophecy. I know it."

"Perhaps it is only a partial prophecy," he said heavily.

She shook her head emphatically. "No. She carries the future inside her."

He started to speak.

"Something will happen," she said. "Something that will provide a solution."

He only sighed. "I long ago lost hope."

She smiled. "So did I. But now, I think, we may find it again. Go to her. But be cautious," she added worriedly. "You know what could happen. You must take precautions."

"Yes. They will not be pleasant ones," he added quietly.

She didn't add to his worry by telling him what she'd said to Madeline. She concealed it behind barriers in her mind. The human was going to be in great danger in the very near future, and not just from Dtimun. There was a tragedy in the making. She only hoped the outcome would be something short of death. Perhaps the details would come clear in time to warn Ruszel.

As MADELINE REACHED the outer gate of the compound, the sky suddenly opened up and it began to rain on the green fields.

She had been in swampy places during her military career, but too occupied to enjoy weather. Most of her work was in pressure domes with controlled climates. But this incredible green forest with its wind chimes and flowers and real grass fascinated her. Astonished, because she had rarely felt natural rain in her adult life—having been raised in a military compound on the ecologically modified Trimerius—she was spellbound at the soft, silky feel of it on her upturned face. She laughed with pure delight and whirled around and around in its misty embrace, her eyes uplifted and closed as she savored the unexpected gift of nature.

Dtimun had said his goodbyes to Caneese and was out looking for Madeline when he spotted her, dancing in the rain. He stopped and stood very still, his eyes soft and embracing, and shocked, as he watched. The female physician did engage in brawls from time to time, but he'd never known her to act with such uninhibited pleasure. She was more beautiful at that moment than he'd ever seen her. He felt a jolt of pleasure far too intense for the reality of the situation, and forcibly clamped down on it.

"Ruszel," he called shortly. "We must go."

She stopped dancing and turned, her eyes quiet and curious. He sounded as if she'd offended him. She flushed self-consciously as he turned and led the way through a part of the compound toward the parked skimmer.

Women in flowing garments and men in robes glanced toward the visitors, all smiling. Madeline felt odd. There was something familiar about this place, but she was certain she'd never seen it before.

Dtimun opened the doors of the skimmer and seconds later, they shot up to treetop level. But instead of heading back to the spaceport, he sped across a small group of mountains to a deep valley. They flew over a silvery waterfall, and a field of deep blue flowers. In the distance was a compound that reminded Madeline of archived vids of castles on ancient Earth. It was a huge square constructed of oversized dressed gray stones, and in its center was a castle with square towers. There were skimmers in a large isolated area, and flowers and shrubs and trees covered every available free space. The grass, if it was grass, was neatly trimmed. A stone pond of mammoth proportions stood to one side of the main entrance.

He put the skimmer down at the front entrance and cut the engine. A man in long white robes came out of the castle, bowed to Dtimun and smiled at Madeline.

Dtimun spoke to him in warm tones. He bowed and went to move the skimmer into the parking lot.

"It looks like a fortress," Madeline said, awed by the size and strength of the stone blocks.

"It is," he replied, leading the way inside. "In ancient times, it was a refuge for the colonists who claimed this planet. More recently, a warrior of some notoriety settled here with his family."

"I'll bet he never lost a battle," she mused, looking around curiously.

"He lost one, at least," he said enigmatically.

A tall, silver-haired woman came forward, her deep blue robes trailing gracefully behind her. She greeted Dtimun with a smile and a bow, her elongated eyes going curiously to Madeline.

He said something to her in his own language. She nodded, smiled again and withdrew.

Madeline was fascinated by the statues and paintings and wall hangings and carpets. She'd never seen anything like them. Her attention was drawn to a huge image of a hunting galot over the great stone fireplace in the hall. There were different colors and patterns in the coats of the great cats. This one was jet-black with emerald eyes and fierce white fangs.

"The galot is threatened, even here, where it is protected," he said quietly. "That one—" he indicated the painting "—spends time here, occasionally, on my estates."

"Sir, that looks like the one who ran from the Meg-Ravens," she remarked slowly.

He only chuckled.

"They're beautiful creatures. And lethal to visitors on Eridanus Three," she commented.

"Yes. They have a deep-seated fear of Meg-Ravens," he added in a faintly humorous tone.

She glanced up at him and grimaced. "I couldn't let the galot kill the little serpent," she defended herself. "They're so gentle…"

"Having now faced adults of the Nagaashe, you might reconsider your opinion," he chuckled. "However, you seem to have made friends of two alien species today, the Nagaashe as well as the Meg-Ravens."

She grinned. "Meg-Ravens are fascinating."

His eyebrows arched. "Have you ever seen one face-to-face?"

"Not really. Only from a distance."

He led the way into a spacious room with a giant perch overlooking a force-field endowed patio. There, on the perch, was a black Meg-Raven, pecking its way through a fruit of some sort. It lifted its noble head to look curiously at Madeline.

"Oh!" she exclaimed softly. "It's beautiful!"

"He," Dtimun corrected. "His name is Rognan."

"Rognan." She stared at the bird, fascinated. It was huge. If it had been on the floor, it would have come up to her shoulders. It had bright, intelligent yellow eyes and a threatening large beak. Its plumage was blue-black, like the commander's hair. It had claws the size of Madeline's fingers. One of its legs was bent and twisted, as if from a very old injury.

Dtimun saw her looking at the leg. "He was injured many years ago, saving the life of a Cehn-Tahr military leader," he told her, "and no female of his species would mate with him. He was brought here, where he would be safe, and given refuge. Were he returned to his flock, they would either drive him out or kill him. It is the way of things in nature," he added quietly, when she looked stricken.

The Meg-Raven cocked its blue-black head and stared at her with its large, bright yellow eyes. It made a soft, purring sound, adding a few clicks.

She laughed delightedly. Her face grew radiant. The alien beside her couldn't drag his eyes away from her beauty.

"Can you communicate with him in his own tongue?" Dtimun asked.

"I'm not sure, but I'd love to try."

He motioned her ahead of him.

She realized that the bird was much larger at close quarters. It stood on a perch, but not in a cage, and the patio was open to the sky. She studied it, spellbound.

It seemed equally fascinated with her. It made a soft purring sound again, with a series of clicks while its eyes fastened on hers.

She imitated the purring and added a series of clicks of her own, hoping she hadn't forgotten what the elderly Cehn-Tahr had taught her.

The bird nodded its head and danced on its perch. She laughed again.

"What did you ask him?" Dtimun wondered.

"If he liked music," she replied. She smiled sheepishly. "I only know three or four phrases. There wasn't much time when I was being tutored in their language."

"We call him Rognan. In his own tongue, I am told, that means Brave One. He came here when I was a child and became my companion." Dtimun went closer to him and touched the noble head. The Meg-Raven made a purring sound. "My mother could never tolerate him. They were enemies." He withdrew his hand and seemed to withdraw from the world around him as well. "It was a long time ago."

Madeline pretended not to notice his preoccupation. She smiled at the Meg-Raven. "Rognan," she said softly. "What a very handsome bird."

He purred at her. "Ruszel…pretty." She laughed. Her mind went back to the interlude on Ondar when the old fellow had taught her some of the Meg-Raven dialect. She recalled suddenly what Caneese had said about her future, and about the danger the commander might pose to her.

It was a mistake to think of that, and she knew it at once. Dtimun scowled suddenly. His eyes went the odd blue shade that denoted a link between her mind and his. Suddenly, he drew in his breath.

She gnawed her lower lip. "Is something wrong, sir?"

He was still staring at her. His eyes were a color now that she couldn't classify. "What, exactly, did Caneese say to you?" he asked.

Now she was in for it, she told herself worriedly. Caneese hadn't said that the information was classified, but it certainly should be. She started reciting multiplication tables in her mind to cloud it. Maybe, she thought, it would be enough to keep him out...

CHAPTER TEN

INEVITABLY, HER QUICK mind rebelled against the boring and endless task of adding infinite numbers toward the absolute value of pi, and the instant she lowered her mental guard, Dtimun was right there in her mind.

"Sir, you mustn't," she protested urgently.

He hesitated. But then she felt his mind withdraw. He turned away from her, toward a second huge open fireplace that dominated the room. In it was a holographic fire, complete with popping and crackling sounds and real heat. Above it was a painting. It depicted a fierce battle during the Great Galaxy War. A tall Cehn-Tahr was leading a charge on foot, holding a huge, glowing energy sword in the air over his head. His features were generic, although he seemed to be bristling with authority even in the static setting.

She glanced at her commander and knew that he'd never brought another person here, not even one of his own species. It was an honor. She stared at him with mingled emotions. Strongest of all was curiosity.

"Do you have family, sir?" she asked respectfully, and then flushed, aware that she was breaking conventions by asking him what was a very personal question. "Sorry," she added formally. "That was presumptuous of me. I had no right…"

He turned, studied her for a moment and then smiled. "We will agree," he said, "that anything we say here will never be repeated. I have your word?"

"Yes, sir," she said at once.

He drew in a long breath. "Many years ago," Dtimun said quietly, "a family occupied this compound. My parents, my two brothers and my sister. Tragedies combined to separate us forever."

She felt her heart skip a beat. She knew that he shared his private life with no other being. Clan was everything in his culture, yet he advertised no Clan allegiances, wore no familial colors. He was very alone.

"Are they still alive?" she asked hesitantly, reluctant to pry into something so private.

"Some of them," he said nebulously.

"Are your families like those of ancient humans?" she probed. Her knowledge of Cehn-Tahr customs was sketchy at best. "I mean, do several generations live under one roof, and do you marry and remain bonded for life? Or does the government dictate professions and reserve breeding for a single class of citizens?"

He turned slowly. His eyes searched hers. "You have no real concept of freedom, have you?" he said abruptly. "In a truly free society, the decision to mate or have offspring, to belong to a profession, is a matter of choice. Not even the emperor himself may dictate those choices here, save for the species intermixing, which is forbidden by constitutional law."

She frowned. "Well, we aren't allowed a choice, of course. But we do have efficient committees that make the decisions in our society…"

"You live in a cold, totalitarian state," he interrupted. "You have only the illusion of freedom. No honorable culture would mentally neuter its military."

"Emotional ties disrupt function and duty," she said defensively, quoting her service manual.

"Propaganda, engineered to maintain the status quo. Even your violent ancestors lived more sensibly than humans enslaved by the military and denied offspring."

She stiffened. "Yes, well at least we have voluntary breeders to produce our children. We don't have to participate in violent, barbaric rites to create them!" She flushed when she realized what she'd said. That comment would have seen her court-martialed if any other military personnel had overheard it.

But he didn't seem to be offended. If anything, her retort seemed to amuse him. "You have been attempting to research our mating rituals, I gather."

Her cheeks were fire-red by now. "It was part of my graduate work," she lied.

"It was not," he shot back. "We do not speak of our intimate customs, and nothing has been written about them which is sanctioned by our government. Whatever you learned, it was only an approximation of the truth."

"Yes, well, I bought these black market vids that turned out to be bogus. But I do hear gossip in the course of my professional duties. A lot of races contend that Cehn-Tahr have barbaric mating rituals. It isn't just speculation by exobiology professors in our own military academy," she said defensively.

He cocked his head and studied her with open curiosity. His eyes narrowed as they searched hers.

"Perhaps the rituals might seem barbaric, to an out-worlder," he said finally. He moved toward her.

Instinctively, she moved back a step, still standing at parade rest.

He smiled at the telltale movement. "Yes. Like us, you are unused to a close approach without combat."

She drew in a breath. "Yes, sir." It was a lie. It was his nearness that made her nervous.

"A Cehn-Tahr warrior marks his woman during their first mating. His teeth inflict a wound, there." He indicated a spot just below her collarbone without actually touching her. "It leaves a faint scar that is worn proudly by the female. It denotes the ceremonial tie of bonding, much as other races exchange rings or bracelets. The female marks the male in the same fashion." He pursed his lips and his eyes went green. "I understand that in some of the Rigellian colonies, a male is required to exchange nose hair with his intended. Hardly emotionally stimulating, one would think."

She laughed in spite of herself. "Hardly." She was remembering what Hahnson had told her about the mark. This was fascinating. She couldn't contain her curiosity. "Do your people mate for life?"

"Yes," he replied quietly. "The object of bonding is always children, and for that reason alone, we sanction relationships which offer stability."

Her heart jumped. "But what if one of the couple is infertile…?"

"Our religious people have retreats, like the one here," he explained. "There is a certain prejudice toward members of our society who are unable to breed.

They usually volunteer for deep space patrols or enter a religious order."

"But there are surgical means…" she began.

He shook his head. "Our culture will tolerate no artificial means of either conception or prevention of pregnancy. This is what you might call hardwired behavior, like the scar of mating, and other—unsavory—aspects of our culture that we have tried in vain to modify. It was not possible."

It was taboo for him to say such things to her, or for her to listen to them. But she was fascinated. She was learning things that she would never know in the ordinary course of her profession.

"The mating…they say the process is violent." She hated her own stammering query. She was a seasoned warrior, and a good doctor. But she had no knowledge of men or intimacy.

He couldn't afford to explain it to her. The conversation was disturbing enough already. His fingers moved to her long, soft red-gold hair and tested its silky softness. "Passion is always violent," he replied very quietly.

She was aware of so many things at once; of the cool, clean scent of his body, of its strength, of its warmth so near her own. She felt uncomfortable, yet she also felt safe, as if nothing could harm her when he was near. She wanted to touch him. She wanted him to touch her. Forbidden thoughts. Dangerous thoughts.

He let go of her hair, but his eyes still held hers. "Your curiosity will be your undoing one day," he said enigmatically, his voice unusually harsh. "Our species are far more different than you realize."

He turned away from her to the fireplace. As he paused in front of it, he reached up, covertly, and turned the animated images of a woman so that they faced the wall.

"It still amazes me," he murmured absently.

"What does, sir?" she asked.

He chuckled. "The sight of the *kehmatemer* gathered around you like boys around a veteran warrior, listening to battle sagas. The old one told me exactly what you did on Ondar." He glanced at her. "I did not reveal to him that I already knew."

She relaxed. "Thank you for understanding, sir. He didn't say that nobody was to know, but I felt uncomfortable letting you see it in my mind." She glanced at him. "I wouldn't have kept the secret if there had been any danger to you. Or to the Holconcom."

"I know that," he replied.

"Could you tell me exactly what they do?" she asked suddenly. "The *kehmatemer*?"

He hesitated, his eyes on the painting above the fireplace. She thought he was going to ignore the question. But then he spoke, slowly, as if choosing his words carefully. "They are an elite unit of my government, attached to the imperial Dectat itself," he said slowly. "The old fellow, as you call him, is the most prejudiced member of the high council. He has hated humans most of his life."

She was shocked. "He was very kind to me on Ondar," she pointed out.

He turned, his eyes turbulent, a mixing of colors that she couldn't decipher. "Surprising. Because he has the power to ask for your execution," he said bluntly. "When I attached you to the Holconcom, he did just that. I had to use every atom of influence I possessed to keep the Council from turning you over to the Dectat. The Tri-Galaxy Council is afraid of the old fellow, you see, and like the cowards who staff it, they would rather give in than risk his displeasure. The old one made other threats as well, but Admiral Jeffrye Lawson and I defended you, and prevailed. And you led his men into battle, at his own request," he said, shaking his head. "It is almost inconceivable to me."

She was beginning to feel very good about herself, although there was a minor skirl of sadness at what the kindly old Cehn-Tahr had tried to do to her before they met. She recalled his antagonism at their first meeting, before they got to know anything about each other, and felt chilled. "Is he really such a terrible person that he could order me, a woman, to be killed?"

"Oh, yes," he told her. His great eyes grew sad with memory. "When I was young, the finest military academy in the three galaxies was located on Dacerius. I was sent there to study."

Which, she thought silently, explained his affection for the Dacerian people. Somewhere in the back of her mind she recalled that, before the wars, Rojoks had also sent their finest command candidates to that military academy on Dacerius.

"I became attracted to a girl from one of the desert tribes," Dtimun continued. "We were intimate. I bonded with her, and she became pregnant with my child."

Madeline felt an odd emotion, a flash of jealousy that she was barely able to hide from him. She recalled seeing the woman in his mind, in the Dibella system.

"Your 'old fellow' found out about it, and with the Dectat's approval, he and his men came to Dacerius, kidnapped the girl and brought her to me. He killed her in front of my eyes, brutally, while I raged at him." His tall body stiffened with the memory. "I would have killed him, but his bodyguard kept me at bay. I had breached the interspecies edict. No child of mixed species has ever been created in my culture. It is our greatest taboo, and it still carries the death penalty."

She grimaced. It was hard to think that the kindly old man who'd taught her to call Meg-Ravens had been capable of such blatant cruelty. It must have hurt the commander in a way he'd never been hurt in his life. The scars were still there, in his emotions, as if all the years in between had done nothing to erase them. She recalled that flash of memory that she'd seen in Dtimun's mind on their away mission, and realized that it was this one. He was sharing it with her. Odd, for such a private person. But flattering.

"It must have been very painful."

"Painful." He sighed. "Yes. It was painful. I remained on Dacerius until I graduated from the military academy and accepted my commission," he said finally. "Although I retained my estates here, on Memcache, I have spent little time here in recent memory. The old soldier and I never spoke again face-to-face until the Holconcom was attached to the Tri-Galaxy Fleet, and duties of command required it." He turned toward her. "I studied on Dacerius sixty-five of your years ago," he told her, his tone wistful. "Long before you were born, warwoman," he added gently.

"It still hurts you," she said quietly.

His eyes narrowed on her face. "Of course. I loved her. I wanted the child very much. But she was Dacerian, you see—still Cularian, but different from the Cehn-Tahr. There has never been a child born of a Cehn-Tahr mating with a woman of another species." He smiled sadly. "It is said that the act of carrying a Cehn-Tahr child would kill an alien female. So if the old one had not intervened, perhaps she would have died in childbirth, or before, naturally and without terror."

She nodded slowly. "Some intervention would be necessary," she said. "And DNA modification would also be required. Though you and the Dacerians are both Cularian species, your physiology is just different enough from Dacerian to complicate what would be a natural process between genuine members of the same species. From what little we know of your obstetrical theory, and it isn't much, the ordinary birth weight of Cehn-Tahr children is far and away larger than that of a normal Dacerian fetus. Merely carrying the child would likely have killed her in a matter of weeks without close medical supervision. It would have been a very dangerous pregnancy." She tried very hard not to show the jealousy she felt.

He was watching her closely. "As dangerous as a Cehn-Tahr-human hybrid?"

Surely, he meant that hypothetically, she assured herself, but she recited multiplication tables in her head, just in case. "That would be far more dangerous," she said. "It would require intervention at the outset. If your women are like Rojok females, they have a gestation one-third the period of ours, and your babies weigh about two times as much. It would require constant monitoring."

His eyes, so sad, suddenly took on a faint green shimmer. "Indeed. We have genetic ties to Rojoks, as other members of the Cularian species. A Cehn-Tahr child, born of a human, is not even a remote possibility." He sighed. He smiled. "However, if it were possible, the monitoring would have to be done in the brig while you and I awaited summary execution."

She burst out laughing. It wasn't really funny. But it was. "Yes. There would be many problems."

He studied her quietly. "Many more than you know," he said, his voice very quiet.

He realized that he'd never shared these things with another living being, not even members of his own Clan. She invited confidences. And not just because of her professional integrity. "In between the instances when I am tempted to throw you in the brig for carrying weapons into battle and tearing up bars," he mused, "I find you very good company."

"Thank you, sir."

He looked around the great hall. "I love this fortress. I am bound to it by blood and tradition," he said. "But the memories are still too painful to allow me to live in it."

"At least you have some tender memories," she said wistfully. "Mine are colorless. I live in a gray world, without emotion."

He pursed his lips as he studied her. "During our confinement at Ahkmau in the Rojok concentration camp, you would have died for Stern, for Hahnson,

For Your Reading Pleasure...

The Editor's "Thank You" Free Gifts include:
- *2 FREE books!*
- *2 exciting mystery gifts!*

$Yes!$ I have placed my Editor's **"Free Gifts"** seal in the space provided at right. Please send me 2 free books and 2 fabulous mystery gifts. I understand I am under no obligation to purchase any books, as explained on the back of this card.

PLACE
FREE GIFTS
SEAL HERE

194/394 MDL GGGL

FIRST NAME	LAST NAME

ADDRESS

APT.#	CITY

STATE/PROV.	ZIP/POSTAL CODE

Thank You!

DETACH AND MAIL CARD TODAY

✦ HARLEQUIN™ READER SERVICE—Here's How It Works:

Accepting your 2 free Romance books and 2 free gifts (gifts valued at approximately $10.00) places you under no oblig
to buy anything. You may keep the books and gifts and return the shipping statement marked "cancel." If you do not c
about a month later we'll send you 4 additional books and bill you just $6.24 each in the U.S. or $6.74 each in Canada
is a savings of at least 22% off the cover price. It's quite a bargain! Shipping and handling is just 50¢ per book in th
and 75¢ per book in Canada.* You may cancel at any time, but if you choose to continue, every month we'll send you 4
books, which you may either purchase at the discount price or return to us and cancel your subscription. *Terms and
subject to change without notice. Prices do not include applicable taxes. Sales tax applicable in N.Y. Canadian residen
be charged applicable taxes. Offer not valid in Quebec. Books received may not be as shown. All orders subject to
approval. Credit or debit balances in a customer's account(s) may be offset by any other outstanding balance owed
to the customer. Please allow 4 to 6 weeks for delivery. Offer available while quantities last.

for Komak—even for me. Self-sacrifice springs from emotion."

"Yes, well, sometimes the neutering doesn't quite take."

"I overheard you speaking to Hahnson about it, on the *Morcai*," he replied, surprising her. "None of you are what your military intended. Even the clones who replaced Stern and Hahnson have emotional ties to you."

"I noticed," she said with a sigh. "As soldiers, we're flawed."

"I would call it a benefit," he told her. "Emotion is not evil."

"It distracts, they tell us."

He gave her a wry look. "I have not found that it distracts you from tearing holes in soldiers from the First Fleet during R&R," he replied.

She grimaced. "They insulted my commanding officer," she stated again.

He moved toward her, with his hands clasped behind his back, and looked down at her solemnly, frowning. "Have you never wanted a child?"

It was a benefit of her training that she didn't faint at his feet. The word produced a blinding wave of tangled emotions. She had never considered the possibility of it. She had only known children as a doctor knows a patient.

Her confusion seemed to make him less rigid. Aboard ship or on missions, he was tolerant and even amused by his human crewmen. But alone, with her, there was a distance that he kept between them. Now, it was slowly being closed.

He studied her face in its frame of long, waving red-gold hair quietly. "You have the courage of a galot," he said. "Your compassion equals it. You are loyal to your crewmates, and overly indulgent of Komak, who tests even my own patience to the limit. You are frequently the subject of praise from members of my government who would have gleefully attended your spacing when you first joined the unit. Yet, with all your attributes as a soldier and a doctor, it is your beauty which makes you stand out—a beauty of which you seem to be totally unaware."

She felt her cheeks burning. She wasn't used to comments on her appearance. Never having had them from any other source, she was ignorant of what her response should be.

"Your eyes always laugh," he said softly, searching them.

They were green. But unlike his, they didn't change shade to denote emotion. She was glad, at the moment.

The tension was suddenly explosive, full of promise, full of danger. He looked at her in a way he never had before, and her body seemed to recognize something in his expression that made it come alive with sensation.

He became aware of the sudden change as soon as she did, and the danger it presented. He clamped down on his emotions visibly and turned away from her. "We must go," he said. "We have tempted fate too often today already."

She didn't pretend to be unaware of what he meant. She felt odd. She followed behind him, silent, as he walked down the great hall to the front door.

He glanced back at her. "It is a greater irony than you know," he said.

"What is, sir?"

"The identity of the old fellow whose life you saved," he replied, with a faint glint of green in his elegant, elongated eyes.

"He must be a heck of a soldier," she remarked. "He was wearing more medals than Lawson."

He laughed aloud. "I assure you that he earned every one of them. One was awarded to him for thwarting a party of assassins who attempted to slit his throat while he was deploying his unit in the Great Galaxy War."

"Could I ask how he thwarted them?"

His eyes twinkled as he looked down at her. "He called a flock of Meg-Ravens to assist him. The assassins had to be led to their executions. Meg-Ravens always attack…"

"…the eyes," she finished for him, nodding. "Yes, I know."

"It was he who taught you how to communicate with them," he added, surprising her.

She chuckled. "Yes. We had very little time, which is why I only learned a few phrases. It was while we were in a stolen Rojok transport making our way back to our own lines. He managed to outmaneuver the skimmer chasing us and blew it up. He's a very good pilot."

"Yes," he agreed.

He opened the door for her.

She frowned, surprised.

"Another clash of cultures, Ruszel?" he mused, watching her expression.

"Well, I think it is," she replied slowly. "Nobody ever opened a door for me before. Since our military service renders us unisex, women don't think of themselves as women."

"Really?" He lifted an eyebrow and pursed his lips. His eyes went green. "If you have no feminine instincts, why are you so curious about Cehn-Tahr mating rituals?"

She rushed through the door without even looking at him. That slow, sensuous laugh made her walk faster.

BUT ONCE OUTSIDE, he made no move toward the skimmer. "Have you ever seen *canolithe* in bloom?" he asked abruptly.

Her eyes lit up. "No! They're legendary—the only species of plant known to any civilization which reacts visibly to emotion!"

He laughed. "Would you like to see them?"

"Oh, yes!"

"Come along."

He led the way down a small hill, through a stretch of forest with towering trees that reminded Madeline of a bamboo forest she'd seen once on Terravega during a rare visit to the human homeworld. The woods were cool and pleasant, their floor carpeted with lichens and thick green grass, with occasional growths of oddly shaped flowers in every sort of color.

The commander stopped in a clearing, and nodded toward a tiny mound of flowers that reminded Madeline forcefully of the neon lights that hallmarked the Silken Strip in Benaski Port.

They were on tall stalks. They were shaped like

tapering glasses, milky-white and glowing and then burnished with one vibrant color after another. A silvery murmur came from them as they moved gracefully in a light breeze that smelled of perfume.

"May I go closer?" Madeline asked him, so excited that her face was flushed with it.

He nodded.

She approached the beautiful flowers slowly, and with reverence. She didn't know a single soul, alien or human, who'd ever seen the plants, which were truly legendary.

Impulsively, as if she knew the correct protocol even though she'd never asked anyone or read about it, she bowed slowly to the plants.

She heard Dtimun's faint intake of breath. But before she could glance at him, the plants suddenly bowed back—all of them. And then they became the most beautiful, radiant red color that could be imagined.

She laughed. The sound echoed, and the plants suddenly glowed green, just like the commander's eyes when he laughed.

"How did you know?" he asked gently, joining her.

"Know what, sir?" she replied, lifting her eyes to his.

"You knew to bow to them."

"I have no idea," she replied. "It just seemed... proper, somehow."

He followed her lead, bowing also to the plants. For him, they also made a red flush, followed by the neon green, which lingered.

"I don't understand the colors, though," she added.

"Don't you?"

He looked down at her, and his own eyes mirrored the neon green.

She frowned. Odd thoughts were tugging at her mind. It couldn't be, of course, that there was some relationship between the emotional colors of the flowers and the ability of Cehn-Tahr eyes to change color to mirror mood…?

Everything went silver, and then gold—including Dtimun's graceful, elongated eyes.

"A mutation," she ventured.

He shook his head. He hesitated, for a few seconds. "A genetic combination was introduced into our DNA centuries ago, when our scientists were experimenting with gene enhancement. So you might conclude that we are 'related' to the canolithe."

She was fascinated. "Are they sentient?"

"At some level, I believe so," he replied, his attention returning to them. "They respond to language, and even to visible emotion. We protect them. Many were killed by visitors who broke them for bouquets."

"Barbarians," she snorted.

The plants turned a soft pink.

He laughed. "They agree," he told her. "They like you."

"I like them, too. Very much. I'll never forget seeing them."

The plants became blue, trimmed in gold.

Madeline was fascinated. "Those are the imperial colors of your government."

He moved away abruptly. "So they are. We must go."

"Goodbye," she called to the flowers.

They bowed, and she bowed back.

"I had heard they lived on Memcache," she told Dtimun on the way back to the skimmer, "but I never expected to actually see them."

"You must never divulge anything you have seen, or heard, here," he said curtly. "You know already how carefully we guard knowledge of our culture."

"You know that I would never say a word to anyone," she replied quietly. "I can keep a secret." She glanced behind them. "I saw rain!" she enthused suddenly. "Real rain!"

He paused in the edge of the bamboo forest to look down at her. "You danced in it," he murmured quietly.

She flushed. "I've very rarely felt rain in my life. On Terravega, where I was born, the vegetation was subtropical and beautiful. But I was kept in a state nursery and we were never allowed to venture outside the domes. I left when I was very small. Afterward there were terrible droughts and larger pressure domes had to be erected, like the ones they have on Trimerius. I never experienced a soft rain anywhere that I wasn't fighting to stay alive. It was…extraordinary. Real rain! I'll remember it all my life."

His hand reached out and touched her hair, the merest brush of his fingertips. Something dangerous flashed in his eyes as he looked down at her. "As I will remember this day."

Her full lips parted. She frowned, unsettled by the sensations she was feeling from that intent scrutiny.

Around them, the breeze increased in intensity, haloing her hair around her flushed face. She was more beautiful than ever, in the silence of the woods.

"Madeline, do you carry dravelzium in your drug banks?" he asked abruptly.

She stared at him without comprehension. "Well, I can manufacture it," she said hesitantly. "Veterinarians use it to sedate very large animals…."

He unfastened the collar of his uniform shirt. Visible in the opening was the thick, feathery black hair that covered his broad chest. "Two ccs, if you please. In the artery at my neck."

Her lips fell open. "Sir, that dosage is…" She tried to tell him how dangerous it was for a humanoid.

"…utterly necessary," he interrupted. "Obey me."

She sighed. "Okay, sir. But if you pass out, I don't want armed guards carrying me off to the brig."

He chuckled. "I can assure you, that won't happen here."

She drew up the dose and laserdotted it into the artery at his neck. It required her to go very close to him. And, as always, burst of pheromones saturated her body, and his senses. She closed the wrist scanner. "Sir, may I ask…?"

"Why?" he mused. "No."

He drew her forehead to his chest, drinking in the heady perfume of her hunger for him, secure in the knowledge that the dravelzium would protect her, temporarily, from his instincts—which would have been instantly fatal if he'd given rein to them.

He slid his arms around her and held her gently in the silence of the forest, while she stood in his embrace with rainbowing emotions, the foremost of which was a hunger unlike anything she'd ever experienced.

"I don't…understand," she whispered huskily.

He smoothed the hair at her temples. She felt his breath at her ear, at her throat. "This is a time out of time," he whispered. "It can never be repeated. Be still."

Her eyes closed and she let him take her weight. She shivered a little at the delicious, forbidden pleasure. In the back of her mind, she was gnawing on the implications of what she felt. What was most surprising was the lack of pain.

"Why?" he asked aloud.

"Well," she replied, "you see, we're mentally neutered for service. And part of the process is implanting of stimulus response mechanisms. It's supposed to cause excruciating pain if we permit ourselves to be touched in any, well, intimate fashion."

He smiled over her head. "I see."

Her hands spread out on his broad chest, aching to go under the fabric which was still splayed at his throat, to touch his bare, muscular flesh. It shocked her, to want that.

One big hand covered hers and flattened it over the fabric. "No," he said in her mind. "Even the dravelzium will not permit that."

She was surprised. She hadn't known about this use for dravelzium. She'd have to pump Hahnson.

"You will not speak of this, even to Hahnson," he replied shortly. "And you will give me your word."

She sighed. So many mysteries. "Yes, sir," she said. "It's very disconcerting, to have you in my mind."

Not for anything would he admit how often he visited it without her knowledge.

She sighed and closed her eyes again. Around them she heard wind chimes and felt the soft breeze on her warm face. It was the greatest peace, and pleasure, she'd ever known in her entire life.

"So odd," she murmured. "About the pain, I mean." She hesitated. "Perhaps something more intimate is required to trigger it."

That amused him and he laughed. He drew back slowly. The drug was already beginning to wear off. He couldn't risk keeping her close. "Ruszel," he said, reverting to the more formal usage of her name, "if you expect something more intimate here, in a religious preserve, I have grave doubts about your sanity."

She burst out laughing. She looked up at him, her green eyes bright with pleasure, her exquisite face flushed with it. She looked at him with her whole heart in her eyes and he ground his teeth together at the knowledge that this tiny space of time was all they could ever have together. Only this. And it must never happen again. He remembered the woman he had loved so much, on Dacerius. This was not love, he told himself. It was a purely physical need. Odd, though, the tenderness he felt with this human female. The thought disturbed him. His behavior disturbed him. The need must be playing with his mind.

He stepped back, letting her go. She felt empty, alone. Those thoughts mirrored his own, but he didn't voice them.

It was as if, in those few moments, a change had taken place in their relationship.

He searched her eyes. "As we have already agreed, tempting fate is unwise. We must go."

She followed him out of the woods, past the temple, past the robed figures who were smiling with something like amusement, and back to the skimmer.

She hesitated at her door and looked across at Dtimun. "It was a wonderful day. Thank you, sir."

His eyes sketched her face. "You have never used my name," he said suddenly.

She blinked. "It would be improper," she said. "Besides that," she added with twinkling eyes, "I have no idea of the proper pronunciation. I know that names are pronounced differently by each acquaintance, depending on the depth of kinship or affection or even enmity. Your language is still a puzzle to me. I had asked Komak for help, but as you might recall, his attempts to educate me were disastrous."

He chuckled. "So they were; some of the most offensive known to the Cehn-Tahr tongue!"

"I'm amazed that you haven't gone howling mad, having him as part of the bridge crew, sir," she replied, laughing, too.

The laughter animated her, made her even more beautiful. He drew his eyes away from her. "We must get moving."

She got in beside him.

She could not know, nor could he tell her, why there was no hope at all of anything physical between them. Ever. Just touching her had been dangerous. Exquisite. But deadly. He should never have allowed Caneese to tempt him into bringing her here. And she still had not divulged what Caneese had told her in secret. He only knew that she faced danger in the future. Hopefully, it wouldn't come from him. He would have to distance himself from her and hope that the mating cycle would diminish with that distance. If she had been Cehn-Tahr, it would have progressed naturally. But she was human, and fragile, and forbidden. There was no research extant on the behaviors in such a situation, because the Species Act forbade any intimacy with other races. He had to trust that Caneese would find some manner of stopping the cycle before he became a threat to Ruszel's life. As he had already told her, there was nothing in the universe as dangerous as a Cehn-Tahr male who was hunting.

All the way back to the *Morcai*, hardly a word passed between them. There was a new sense of comradeship, and something much deeper, that Madeline didn't dare spend too much time thinking about. But she knew that her life had changed forever in those few hours.

CHAPTER ELEVEN

MADELINE HAD THOUGHT that she could separate her professional identity from the woman who suddenly harbored feelings she couldn't control. But she couldn't. In the weeks since she and Dtimun had gone to Memcache, everything had changed. She found herself watching him, flushed and flustering when she was around him, nervous as a cat. In turn, he had begun to avoid her. Caneese had warned her, for reasons still not understood, to avoid being alone with him. But that was simple. He never permitted himself to be alone with her. Now, even when she had to consult him on assignments, the door to his office was always left open.

The distance between them was new and disturbing. She didn't challenge him, as she used to, or defy him. She had become quiet, intense, fascinated with the new emotion that was overwhelming her. Even as it grew, he became more elusive and his temper deteriorated even more. Things were bound to come to a head, and they did, at a called meeting of all Tri-Galaxy Fleet officers in the huge council chamber conference hall.

Lawson had called an informal briefing to update the officers of the various fleets on the newest Rojok technology being thrown at them on the battlefield. It came complete with holo images and tech specifications which were displayed on an enormous virtual screen, rather than on the implanted corneal screens worn by all personnel. Probably, Madeline thought wickedly, to give the admiral an opportunity to show off his new virtual toys. He did love high tech.

As they watched the information being screened, which had already been seen by the Holconcom, she found her thoughts wandering unintentionally toward her commanding officer.

Dtimun was leaning against one of the stone pillars, the epitome of relaxed elegance. She thought, and not for the first time, how regal he seemed in any pose he adopted. Ever since their outing on Memcache, her thoughts had been confused and disturbing. If it was a capital offense to have base desires for a comrade, it was twice damned for her to have them for an alien commander. Unwilling, her eyes went to his broad shoulders, to the hair as black as a Meg-Raven's wing, contrasting violently with the red of his uniform. She remembered falling from the cliff, when he caught her. She remembered their day on Memcache, with the rain falling as she stood with him near the canolithe. He shared things with her that she knew he'd never shared with any outsider. It was immensely flattering. The memory was the sweetest of her life. She had to stop thinking about it. She tried not to. But that one, unexpected day was the happiest she'd ever known...

Inevitably, she felt the probing of her mind, accompanied by a sense of irritation. Dtimun abruptly turned his head and she felt the impact of his eyes halfway across the room, dark with anger.

She turned away, flushed, and tried to camouflage her loss of control with mathematics. This time, it didn't work.

"I will see you in my office when the presentation concludes, madam," she heard in her mind. His tone was not pleasant.

She grimaced. Komak was watching her with an amused expression. Odd, she thought, how he seemed to know when she was communicating with their C.O. mentally. She must be hallucinating. She turned her eyes back to Lawson and tried very hard to pay attention to whatever it was that he was saying. Her heart was racing like a wild thing. What she felt was growing more painful by the day. She only wished she knew how to control it. Today's lapse was proof that she was losing her battle with her own feelings.

THE SILENCE IN Dtimun's office was freezing. She stood at parade rest, her eyes on the wall ahead of her, her hands locked behind her, her breath catching in her throat as she waited for him to speak.

Finally, he perched on the edge of his desk and pulled a small round white ball from the drawer. He activated it and placed it beside him. Its white glow would drown out any AVBDs that might be trying to eavesdrop. They were everywhere in the Tri-Galaxy Fleet, even in the offices of Admiral Lawson himself.

His eyes were still dark with anger as he stared at her. "I need not tell you how many protocols you have broken. It will suffice to tell you that it must stop."

She bit the inside of her lip. "Yes, sir."

"I should never have taken you to Memcache," he said stiffly. "It has encouraged you to dwell on matters which can never have a resolution, tempted you to indiscretion."

She started to speak, but a slice of his hand silenced her. His lips made a thin line. "I am not blameless. I agreed to take you to Caneese. I permitted an intimacy that should never have happened. But your lack of control over your...feelings for me," he bit off, "may provoke a tragedy. There is no future in this."

"Sir, I never...!" she exclaimed, shocked and humiliated by his blunt statement.

He stood up and moved toward her, stopping an arm's length away. "There are reasons why we never mate outside our own species," he said bluntly. "You will never repeat what I tell you here. Is that understood?"

She felt a cold chill. "Yes, sir."

He drew a harsh breath. "Ruszel, you know the old gossip, that the Cehn-Tahr are descended from Cashto, a pack leader of the great cats, the galots, of Eridanus Three."

"Yes," she replied, fascinated.

"In a sense, it is true. Our emperor, in the early days of his rule, decided to improve our race. He employed the best scientists in the three galaxies to that purpose."

She began to understand. "The canolithe," she said, recalling his comment about their DNA being used to give the Cehn-Tahr eyes that changed color.

He nodded. "But it goes much further than that. The galots are sentient, did you know?"

"No," she said, surprised. "That isn't in any of the scientific studies..."

"There are no genuine scientific studies, because

the galots tend to eat scientists who arrive to study them," he replied with faint amusement.

Her eyes widened. "Eat...them?" She gave him a speaking glance.

He glowered at her. "The Cehn-Tahr do not eat humans."

She cleared her throat. "I knew that. Sir."

"However, the combination of enhanced galot DNA and our own produced genetic anomalies," he continued quietly. "The mutations were encouraged when the scientists discovered that our latent *psiabilities* were so improved that we became telepaths, that our strength and speed increased exponentially, that we developed a third eyelid and additional cones in our optic makeup, so that we could see great distances in the dark. We could also hear and smell things that normal Cehn-Tahr could not." The odd remark went right over her head, she was so intent on what he was saying. His eyes searched hers. "Our genome was changed forever, mutated into something neither feline nor humanoid, but in between."

"That explains how you were able to rescue me from the cliff," she guessed.

He nodded. "We can leap like the great cats. The clones of the Holconcom have also been modified to produce metallic-strong claws in combat."

"Like yours."

"I am not a clone," he said. "My enhancements are far greater than those of your shipmates. The clones require microcyborgs to augment their physical abilities. I do not."

"But we used them on you at Ahkmau," she began.

"Yes, because I was unconscious and my control

over my own health was diminished," he agreed. His eyes narrowed. "But we digress. You recall what Ambassador Taylor said to you at the Altair reception some time ago, that if I attempted to mate with you, I would kill you."

"Yes, sir. You wouldn't explain why."

He reached out and picked up a metal ball sitting on a curved stand. He handed it to her. "Do you know what this is?" he asked.

It was very heavy. She nodded. "Yes, sir, it's drasteel. It's the hardest material known to current science. Not even a diamond drill can...pierce...it...."

Her voice slowed down because the commander took it in his hand and literally crushed it with his fingers. Their imprint was left in indentations that caused the ball to be grossly misshapen.

"Now imagine that this was a human body and I had no control over my strength," he concluded.

Madeline felt the blood drain out of her face. She couldn't take her eyes away from the misshapen ball.

"My normal strength is three times that of a human male," he explained. "I cannot control it under certain circumstances," he added delicately. "I injured you almost fatally on the planet in the Dibella system simply in the act of saving your life, and I was completely in control of myself."

She began to understand what he was implying. It was devastating. It meant that, even if the interspecies acts in her government and his were revoked, it would make no difference. It wasn't a cultural problem that separated them; it was a very physical one.

"During the Great Galaxy War," he said softly, "Hahnson became involved with a Cehn-Tahr female, an outcast. I tried to warn him, but he was infatuated and refused to listen." His face clenched. "She attempted to mate with him. When she realized what was happening, she called for assistance. If we had not been able to obtain an ambutube, he would have died. She broke his back in the first few seconds."

She thought she knew Strick Hahnson very well, but she'd never known that about him. Poor man! Poor, poor man!

She looked at Dtimun with new knowledge, with grief and loss.

He felt the intensity of her pain like a blow. He moved away. He went to the window and stared out it, fighting for control.

She understood now. Hahnson was a strong man. If a Cehn-Tahr female could snap his spine in the heat of passion, when she was out of control of herself, what could Dtimun, with his enhanced strength, do to Madeline in similar circumstances?

"Indeed," he said aloud, having seen the thoughts in her mind. He didn't turn. "My Clan was affected far more extensively than some of the others. Our… enhancements…make us extremely dangerous. Especially to humans. You have no idea of the modifications we have had to make to protect you. The microcyborgs used in the Holconcom clones had to be restructured to make them inactive when in contact with human flesh aboard the Morcai, and in battle."

She was feeling worse by the second. In all her imaginings, she'd never considered that their differences were so extreme.

"Your body exudes potent pheromones whenever you look at me," he said in a subdued tone.

She honestly hadn't known that it did. "But you shouldn't be able to smell those," she protested. "Your olfactory process…"

"My sense of smell is many times more developed than a human's," he said. "I have what you would call a vomeronasal organ, a Jacobson's organ, which processes scent into sensory information. Even from a distance, your pheromones provoke a response which is becoming far more unmanageable by the day. Eventually, it will be beyond my control, unless I can find a way to restrain it." He did turn now, and his eyes met hers across the room. "I told you once that nothing in the three galaxies is more dangerous than a Cehn-Tahr male when he is hunting. You have become prey. No other male is safe if he comes near you. I would kill Stern, Hahnson, even Komak just for touching you."

Her breath left her in a rush. It was far worse than she'd thought.

He moved back toward her, stopping an arm's length away with his hands locked behind his back. "The hunting instinct is involuntary, and purely physical, a shameful and painful legacy of the genetic tampering. It has little to do with emotion," he added bitterly, and her heart sank because she had hoped… but then she remembered the beautiful woman she'd once seen in his mind.

His eyes narrowed and his face hardened. "Yes," he said softly. "Deep emotion was involved there. It is not, with you. But make no mistake, a hunting male is capable of any deception to reach his goal. You understand?"

She nodded. She straightened into parade rest.

"Yes, sir." All of it, every tender moment, had been a means to an end.

"That is true," he said. And he was lying. He forced that thought to the back of his mind. "Perhaps now you can understand why I have tried to distance myself from you."

"Yes." She felt a sadness that permeated her very soul. She hadn't realized how deeply she was involved until now. She looked down, noting idly how very polished his black boots were. "Is there no chemical means of controlling the...behavior?"

"None that ever worked," he said flatly. "Caneese and I discussed this at length when we were on Memcache. She thinks the prophecy concerns you, but it also involves a child born of a human mother and a Cehn-Tahr father. That is impossible."

Her heart jumped at the remark. Hopeless yearning came, and went, in her mind. She nodded slowly. "Is it?"

"In four hundred years, no Cehn-Tahr has found a way to mate with a female of any species other than Cularian."

She looked up. "Four hundred...years?"

"The genetic tampering, and an unprecedented solar flare during the time of experimentation, mutated our life span as well. Our emperor is over four hundred years old," he told her. "He may live to be eight hundred years old. Our scientists think so."

She was astonished. Her eyes searched over his face. "Will you live so long?"

"I am two hundred and fifty years old, by your measure of time," he told her.

"You told us you were eighty-seven," she burst

out, and realized now that it was, like many things he had told the humans, a modicum of the truth. He could live to be hundreds of years old. A human life span was still a little over a hundred years, and many diseases and conditions of old age had not been eradicated. Dtimun would still be young, comparatively speaking, when she died naturally.

She had truly never realized how different their species were until now, when she knew the extent of it. A wave of grief washed over her and was reflected in the eyes that sought his face.

"So many differences," she said hesitantly.

"More than I can even tell you, some of which have nothing to do with physical dissimilarities," he returned flatly. "You must know that, under ordinary circumstances, I would never harm you. But my nature is savage, predatory."

"If Hahnson could do a short-term memory wipe on me," she began, "and take away the memory of Memcache…"

He touched her long hair, lightly, briefly, and withdrew his fingers at once. "The memory of that one day is all we can ever have of each other," he said bitterly, the words almost torn out of him. "And removing it would make no difference. Not now."

Her heart jumped at the unexpected admission. "But you said that the pheromones triggered the behavior," she said.

"It began because of a mistake I made." He held up his hand. "One day, perhaps, I can explain it. However, once the mating cycle begins, there is only one way to stop it," he said with subtle meaning.

She saw the traces of stress in his expression.

"Then, perhaps, if you…with a Cehn-Tahr woman." She tried to put it into words.

"You are the prey," he repeated simply. "It is not possible to make substitutions, if that is what you are suggesting."

She bit her lower lip. Talk about impossible situations. The atmosphere in his office was so thick with emotion that it was almost tangible. She didn't want to think about the loneliness of the years ahead, because her days with the Holconcom had to be numbered, now.

"At least temporarily, they are," he answered the silent thought. "In the close confinement of a ship in space," he added with a flash of faint green humor, "it would probably become noticeable quite rapidly if I began to murder male crewmembers who brushed against you in the corridor."

It took her a minute to realize that he was joking. She looked up and managed a smile. "Maybe I could take vitamins and work out," she suggested, tongue-in-cheek.

He chuckled softly, despite the gravity of the discussion. "An interesting thought, but it would make no difference."

"Microcyborgs and massive doses of dravelzium?" she persisted.

His eyes were a deep blue with sadness as he studied her lovely face in its frame of long, waving red-gold hair. "Our technology is not adequate to solve the problem," he replied. "Many scientists have spent whole careers, covertly, trying. I have kept cells from Hahnson's bonded consort all this time, in the event that a solution could be had." He shook his head. "It is unlikely."

"Edris Mallory will have to replace me on board," she commented.

He actually groaned aloud.

"Don't do that, sir. She's smart," Madeline protested, "and she knows her job. She just lacks self-confidence."

"I can never find her when I have a problem with a crewman."

"She hides. You scare her," she said. "If you could just temper your attitude a little..."

"My attitude is what it is," he gritted. "I have never modified it, not even for you."

She sighed. "How are we going to explain leaving me behind?"

He was wondering the same thing. It was going to be noticeable to the entire base. He hadn't considered that.

She brightened a little. "Altairian flu is going around," she said. "I'll inject myself with a mild case of it."

"A drastic solution, surely?"

"A mild case," she repeated. "And then what?"

"And then," he said heavily, studying her, "we will see if your absence alleviates my symptoms."

She was frowning, thinking. "Isn't there really any way to reduce them?"

"Yes," he said flatly. "Mating."

She flushed. "Oh."

He turned and moved around his desk to face her. "You must go back to your lab."

She met his eyes evenly and tried not to reveal that

her heart was breaking inside her body. "Thank you for telling me the truth, sir," she said. "You know that I won't repeat anything you told me."

He smiled gently. "I know. You have never spoken of the fact that I can read your mind in almost three years."

"It would be nice if I knew how to block that." She gave him an odd look. "I've had some...strange... dreams lately."

His expression was bland. "Have you?"

"Now, listen here...!"

He held up a hand. "I am not to blame. Perhaps you should refrain from drinking contraband coffee behind Lawson's back," he added.

She glared at him. "Coffee is the only pleasure I have in life. I refuse to give it up. He can throw me in the brig for a month. It won't stop me."

He chuckled at her determination. "Not much does," he commented. "I have enjoyed these years with you," he added, and the smile faded. "Perhaps Caneese can find a way to curtail the worst of the predatory behavior. At least you could return to the Holconcom."

Something that no scientist in four hundred years had managed, she recalled.

"Yes, but Caneese has a gift for biochemistry," he replied. "She likes you."

She smiles. "I like her, too." She frowned. "Sir, I'm not prying, but it seemed to me that she was closer to you than an acquaintance."

"She is," he said quietly, but he volunteered nothing more.

"Does she have a mate?"

"Yes. But she and her mate have been apart longer than you have lived," he said. "Her eldest son was killed in the Great Galaxy War," he said with quiet sadness. "She blamed her mate for that."

"I'm so sorry," she said gently. "She's such a nice person."

He searched her eyes. "It occurs to me that I have shared more of my private life with you than with anyone in recent memory."

She smiled. "It's because I'm a clam."

His eyebrows arched in query.

"A small crustacean with a shell that it closes under threat," she lectured. "A metaphor for the ability to keep secrets."

"I see."

She shrugged and her eyes twinkled. "Besides that, you trust me."

He smiled. "Perhaps I do." His eyes narrowed. "But you should not trust me. And this is the last time we must ever be alone." His hand moved to the mute sphere and deliberately deactivated it, at the same time he opened the door.

"Yes, sir." She gave him one last look and moved to the door. The weight of the sadness was growing.

"Life is not fair," she commented.

"No," he agreed. "It is not."

She wanted to wish him well, to say goodbye, to say anything. But she couldn't manage the words. She went out and closed the door behind her without looking back.

She walked away, oblivious to Komak's concerned gaze. He started toward the commander's office, but hesitated when he heard the crashing of ceramics and the muted, building growls coming from inside. What he had to say could wait a few hours, he decided, turning away. Or a few days.

He frowned as he considered the way Madeline looked. This part of her history was sad. He knew the monumental obstacles in the way of what she felt for her commanding officer. He wanted to comfort her. But things had to move at their own pace. He couldn't risk interference. Not yet, at least.

MADELINE WALKED OFF the *Morcai*, and caught a skimmer to the medical center. She walked blindly into her own office. She'd been able to keep her chin up in the commander's office, but the full weight of what he'd revealed to her was crushing.

"Oh, good, you're back," Edris Mallory said with a kind smile. The smile faded. "Dr. Ruszel...?" she added, worried.

"No calls for a few minutes, Edris," Madeline said huskily and with a wan, forced smile.

"Yes, ma'am." Mallory saluted and went back out.

She was nice, Madeline thought as she powered the door shut, and locked it. She pushed a button on her desk and activated her own white screen, to thwart any probing vids. Then she sat down behind her desk, laid her cheek down on her forearm and dissolved into tears for one of the few times in her entire life.

She wished she had someone to talk to about it. She didn't have a close friend. Well, Stern and Hahnson were close friends, but how could she talk to them about a situation that was potentially a death sentence if they let something slip?

She slid back the sleeve over her wrist scanner and

injected herself with a nonlethal form of Altairian flu. The symptoms, gratefully, presented immediately. She allowed herself to slump to the floor, buzzing Mallory on the way down. Unethical, she told herself. Necessary, her mind replied.

Edris came in and gasped when she saw her commanding officer on the floor. "Ma'am! What happened?" Lieutenant J.G. asked worriedly.

"Don't know. Some sort…of quick-acting virus, probably," she whispered. "We had that Altairian in here yesterday with flu…" She let her voice trail off suggestively. She was sicker than she ever remembered being. Lovely, lovely sickness that would save her from the ordeal of being around Dtimun, longing for something she now knew was impossible.

"I'll call Dr. Hahnson at once," Edris said, and scampered.

"ALTAIRIAN FLU," HAHNSON PRONOUNCED with a strange glance. "Funny how quickly you caught it."

"Isn't it?" she asked, so weak she could barely speak. "I felt fine earlier."

"I know. We're supposed to lift in two hours," he added quietly.

"Obviously, I won't be lifting with you, except in an ambutube," she said in a weak attempt at humor. "You'll have to take Edris."

"No!" he groaned.

"Mallory may be young, but she's good."

"She flunked out of combat school with the lowest grade in academy history," he exclaimed.

Madeline gave him a droll look. "She isn't going to be asked to shoot people. Just to treat them. Cehn-

Tahr people. Or if we get the opportunity, Rojok people. She won't get in your way. And it isn't as if it's the first time she's gone with you."

He grimaced. "The old man won't like having a substitute."

She closed her eyes. "Well, we don't have a choice—it's Mallory or nobody. Cularian specialists are thin on the ground. Our substitutes are on a training mission themselves. There is no one else."

"I suppose so."

She pushed the comm switch next to the examination table. "Mallory, in here on the double," she said in what she hoped was a commanding tone.

Mallory came in seconds later, flushed and worried. "Yes, ma'am?"

"You have to go with the Holconcom," she said.

Mallory flushed even more and started to argue.

"There's nobody else," Madeline interrupted her. "Get your uniform. Hahnson will keep an eye on you."

Mallory grimaced. "The Holconcom commander…" Mallory murmured, worrying her lip. "He scares me to death."

He'd once scared Madeline, too. "Scare him back," Madeline said weakly. "Go. It's an order. I'll handle any emergencies here, but with the Holconcom out of port, it isn't likely that I'll have patients except the recovering ones here. An orderly can handle those while I get well."

Mallory sighed. "Yes, ma'am," she said miserably.

"You can go to the ship with me," Hahnson told her with a kind smile. "It will be all right. Honest."

She brightened just a little. "Yes, sir. I'll try not to disappoint you, ma'am," she added, to Madeline.

She saluted and went back out.

"Were we ever that young?" Madeline asked her companion.

"Never," he said. He closed his wrist unit. "Something you might like to tell me?" he added, producing a portable white-out sphere. He activated it. Added to the fixed one on her desk, it guaranteed psychic privacy.

She stared at him, wanting to talk, afraid to.

He pursed his lips. "Come on. Tell Dr. Strick all about it. Your endorphins are screwed up like crazy. I won't even mention your blood pressure and your pulse, and it doesn't have a damned thing to do with the Altairian flu you just inoculated yourself with. Stern saw you coming out of the C.O.'s office. He said you looked as if you'd been skewered by a Rojok harpoon."

She let out a heavy breath. She really was sick. "I've been…out of line. Severely. I was staring at the C.O. in assembly and thinking things I shouldn't." She grimaced. "Somehow what I feel triggered a mating behavior in him," she explained. "I couldn't help it," she said huskily, her face contorting. "I've never felt like this…"

"He read your mind."

She stared at him.

"I served with him for two years during the Great Galaxy War," he said. "I know he's a telepath. I've never divulged it to anyone else. I never will."

"Yes," she said. "He read my mind. Called me into his office." She closed her eyes on the pain. "He told me everything." She opened her eyes and looked at her friend. "Including something about you."

He looked down at his hands. "I'm only a clone of the original Hahnson, but I have all his memories," he said. "That one is...poignant." He met her searching eyes. "I know how you feel, believe me."

"At least you lived through it," she said.

"I did. She didn't." He averted his gaze. "She killed herself. She couldn't live with the knowledge that we could never be together."

"Oh, Strick," she groaned. Now the commander's comment about keeping cells from Hahnson's consort made sense. Poor Strick.

"You see, once those behaviors begin, they don't end. The Cehn-Tahr pay a high price for their enhancements. The galot DNA made them into animals, in some respects. You've never seen them fight without restraint. I have." He shook his head. "No race that endured such predations would ever instigate a battle with them."

"I didn't realize how strong they really were, or that their senses and life spans were so enhanced," she replied. "I've been living in a dream. It was a beautiful dream."

"The reality is something less."

"Yes."

"I'm sorry."

She fought tears. "Oh, so am I."

"You can't be alone with him again. Ever," he told her gently. "He can't control it."

She nodded. "I may never be able to come back aboard ship. If only there was some way to stop it!"

"That's beyond my abilities as a researcher." He

pursed his lips. "You could do some experiments. You have research grants."

"Oh, sure, I know the admiral would be totally understanding if he knew I was using government grants to find a solution to my pheromone production or invest me with super strength."

He chuckled.

She did, too. "When I mess up, I do a good job of it. I did suggest a short-term memory wipe."

"Wouldn't help," he said. "He can't be memory-wiped, and it's his emotions that are causing the problem."

"Not emotions, exactly," she said sadly. "As he said himself, its more an animal response to stimulus on his part, one that he can't control." Despite the tenderness he'd shown her, his primary response to her was feral, physical, a need that drove him almost to madness. She knew that he had loved a woman in his past, that he still loved her. It was hard to accept that, but she had to rid herself of illusions about the future.

"There isn't much difference."

"We can agree to disagree," she said. She swallowed a bout of nausea. "I feel awful."

"Next time, call me. I can give you something incapacitating that's much nicer than what you injected."

"I was desperate and didn't have much time," she said defensively. She drew in a long breath. "Take care of Mallory. Try not to let her get eaten alive."

"I'll do my best."

She looked at the white-noise generator. "Can that block a telepath?"

"Most of the time, depending on the distance

involved. Not formidable telepaths, however. Old Tnurat, the Cehn-Tahr emperor, can do it across parsecs of space. I heard about it during the Great Galaxy War. They said he could heal the dying just with the power of his mind. He has incredible gifts."

"The Royal Clan," she said absently, her mind still on blocking Dtimun's mental probing, not really on what Hahnson was saying. "They're very different from other members of their species."

"Some even more powerful genetic engineering there, unless I miss my guess, but I wouldn't want to say it without a noise screen running."

She remembered what Dtimun had told her, in confidence. Maybe it explained why modern Cehn-Tahr were so rigid about no interference with natural rhythms. They didn't allow any sort of genetic modification now.

But she didn't say any of that. She just nodded. "How about getting me a portable white-noise generator for my quarters, so I don't get spaced for mooning over my C.O.?" she asked heavily. "And don't put it on the books," she added.

He whistled softly. "Dangerous."

"It will be more dangerous if I can't get a handle on what I'm feeling. If he couldn't read minds, I could probably manage."

"I'll keep your secrets. Meanwhile, don't give yourself any more injections."

She smiled at him. "I'm so glad we got you back after Ahkmau."

He smiled, too. "At least I get to serve with the one bunch in the galaxy who respect clones."

"The best bunch of fighters in the three galaxies," she replied.

"We are. Get well."

"I will. Come back alive. And take care of Mallory."

He grinned. "I'll do both. See you, Maddie."

He handed her the white-noise sphere. "I lost it somewhere," he mused. "Damned if I know where. I'll have to requisition another."

"Thanks," she said huskily.

He patted her shoulder. "No need for that."

She needed time, she thought, to find a way to get her unwanted feelings under control. She had to hope she could do it, or she might never be allowed back aboard the *Morcai*. Now that was a horrifying thought, indeed. She gave herself an injection to make her sleep. Being a doctor had its advantages, she thought as she drifted away.

CHAPTER TWELVE

MADELINE SPENT HER R&R in the base gym, trying to make up for all the missed practice in combat techniques. If she did have to leave the Holconcom and join an SSC unit, she'd never cut it without some remedial combat practice. Dtimun wouldn't permit her to carry a weapon and he insisted that she remain behind the lines in any forward mission. Combat wasn't really required of her aboard the *Morcai*. In a forward division of troops, it would be. The Amazon Division would be the only place she could go, if it came down to it. Maybe that wouldn't happen. Maybe the absence would relieve Dtimun's symptoms. She hoped so.

Flannegan, of the First Fleet, helped her with the workouts. For all his bluster and insults in bar brawls, he was a formidable fighter on the mats. He'd been in combat even more than Madeline, and he knew moves that she didn't, handy for close-in fighting, which Rojoks loved. He was a master trainer in hand-to-hand for the First Fleet, to which he belonged. He wasn't bad-looking, either, she had to admit, with that shiny pale blond hair down to his waist in a ponytail and his light brown eyes that twinkled when he teased her.

"Not like that, you rimscout reject," he chided when she led with a right and walked into his elbow. "Hit and duck. Like this, see?"

She laughed. She'd been doing a lot of that just recently, in his company. She realized with a start that it had been a very long time since she'd felt like laughing. Her helpless, unrequited passion for her C.O. had beaten her down. But here, with her former brawling adversary, she was coming back into the light.

She followed his instructions and punched him with the cushioned glove, then ducked to the side and hit him in the diaphragm.

"Oofff!" he exclaimed, laughing, because she hadn't pulled that punch.

She grinned at him. "Of course, if you were a Rojok, I'd have made that hit a couple of inches lower."

He ruffled her hair with some familiarity. "Reprobate," he teased.

A long, low, building growl fell deep and threatening on the silence, reminiscent of the *decaliphe,* the death cry of the Holconcom. They both whirled, to find Dtimun, with a worried Hahnson at his side. The Cehn-Tahr was glaring at them with dark brown eyes and he didn't speak. The growl hadn't abated. His posture, although barely altered, was threatening. Chilling. Madeline knew what was happening at once. She hadn't known Dtimun was anywhere on the base. Beside Dtimun, Hahnson tensed.

Flannegan felt the chill. "Sir," he said, standing at rigid attention. Madeline, close beside him, followed suit.

The growl grew louder. All at once, every ABVD in the small gym cubicle exploded in a blinding flash of light and sound.

Hahnson, standing beside Dtimun, was working

frantically with his wrist scanner. Not two seconds later, Dtimun was in front of Madeline, facing Flannegan, having moved so fast that the human didn't even see him coming.

Flannegan, flustered, backed up a step and gaped at the tall alien. A low, threatening growl came up from Dtimun's throat and his eyes began to turn black. The genetically engineered claws began to slip out from under his clean, manicured fingernails.

Hahnson moved to Dtimun's side. "Divert him!" he shot at Madeline in Old High Martian.

Not knowing what else to do, she reached out cautiously and caught at the sleeve of Dtimun's uniform.

His head turned toward her. He was scowling. His posture, like his expression, was dangerous. But the feel of her fingers on his arm apparently calmed him.

"Dismissed, Flannegan!" Hahnson called. At his side, unseen by his commanding officer, he was gesturing the spacer toward the exit, urgently.

"Yes, sir!" Flannegan grabbed his gear. He didn't even take time to send a smile in Madeline's direction.

Madeline wanted to thank him for the lesson, but she kept her mouth shut. Dtimun had blown out all the surveillance equipment with just his mind.

Hahnson went with Flannegan, closing the door, locking it and then moving as rapidly as he could back to Dtimun.

"He touched you," Dtimun told Madeline in a voice that sounded odd, like the sound a cat would make in anger. For a second he seemed bigger, broader, altogether different in appearance. But she blinked and he was the same commander he had always been. She must be seeing things.

"Sir, we were…sparring," she faltered, because he'd moved close to her. His lean hand shot out and caught the ponytail at the back of her head. He gripped it to force her close to his hard, powerful body.

He spoke to her in the Holy Tongue, words that even Hahnson, with his greater command of Cehn-Tahr, couldn't translate. He was only half listening anyway. He was drawing fluid into a laserdot.

"He will never touch you again," he growled as his gaze fell to Madeline's body. She was wearing a sleeveless T-shirt. Her soft, creamy skin was visible. His eyes fell to the flesh just below her collarbone. He wanted to mark her. He wanted to make a visible statement, one that no other male could mistake, that she was forbidden to any male except himself. His head started to bend toward her.

"Sir!" Hahnson groaned when he realized what his commanding officer was about to do. He rushed forward, reached up, unfastened the collar of Dtimun's uniform shirt and started pumping dravelzium into the artery at Dtimun's throat. He was barely going to have enough. He hadn't resupplied his wrist scanner's drug banks, damn the luck!

"Hahnson!" Dtimun growled, disoriented.

"It's okay, sir. It's okay. Just a little more…sorry, sir," he murmured, still pumping. "Sorry again, sir."

Dtimun's hand in Madeline's hair lost its tautness and began, ever so slowly, to relax. He drew in harsh breaths, as if he'd been running. She felt him release the long hair at her nape. It felt as if it had almost been detached. She grimaced.

"Thank goodness," Hahnson said at last, nodding as he read his monitor. "I think that will do it."

Dtimun lifted his head, as if he was feeling cool air on his face. "Another cc, if you please, Doctor," he said heavily.

Hahnson hesitated. "Are you sure, sir?"

Dtimun nodded.

Hahnson shot one more dose home into the artery and moved back.

Dtimun let out the breath he'd been holding. He looked down at Madeline with strange, golden eyes. She was spellbound. It was a forbidden look into Cehn-Tahr mating behaviors. One which, if she read it right, had almost cost Flannegan his life.

"An excellent point," Dtimun said in a strained tone. He pulled up Btnu's image on his communicator ring and spoke again, but this time in a dialect of Cehn-Tahr that Madeline and Hahnson could both understand. Btnu nodded and saluted, and the image faded.

"You're sending your bodyguard after Flannegan?" Madeline exclaimed. "But, sir…!"

He held up a hand. "They aren't going to harm him," he assured her. "They're going to prevent me from killing him, in case the dravelzium wears off before I can get back to the *Morcai*." He glanced at Hahnson and gave an order mentally.

"Yes, sir," Hahnson replied. "I'll, uh, make a few adjustments to the wiring so that it will look as if the AVBDs malfunctioned due to a faulty connector."

Dtimun nodded. He managed a faint smile.

Hahnson pulled out two laserdots and handed them to Madeline. "Just in case," he added, and went to perform his task. He closed the door behind him.

Madeline's misery was visible. She knew that she would never be able to return to the Holconcom. If what had just happened was any indication, leaving her behind had only whetted Dtimun's appetite, not diminished it.

He nodded. His face was hard, grim. "The behavior escalates, as I told you once."

She ground her teeth together. "It's my fault. I'm so sorry!"

"How is it your fault?" he asked quietly. "I know your mind as well as I know my own. The...feelings you have for me are not assumed or pretended. You are as incapable of controlling them as I am of controlling my need."

"Will it stop if I stay here?" she asked.

"We find ourselves in uncharted space, so to speak," he replied. "The only real cure is mating, which is impossible. I have no experience of this situation. There is no literature which addresses it."

"I have even less experience than you do," she began.

"Yes, your knowledge of male behavior is oddly lacking, for a physician," he mused. "Flannegan wants you. How can you not be aware of it?"

"He...what?" she stammered.

He shook his head. "Another example of the inefficiency of your so-called neutering drugs." His face hardened. He lifted his chin, and his whole expression was arrogant, possessive. "You will not spar with him again."

It was a command. There was a time when she would have resisted it, argued with him, defied him, dared him to dictate her private life. But the sensation his possessive attitude provoked was…strange. She felt heat rush through her body, because of the way he was looking at her. As she had noted once before in their turbulent relationship, he looked at her as if she belonged to him.

"Yes," he said softly. "You like it."

The color grew redder. "Sir," she protested. "That is a very unmilitary attitude to take…"

His breathing was heavier. His eyes began to darken. He grimaced. "Madeline, that dravelzium Hahnson gave you," he said in a strained tone. "This would be a good time to use it."

She grimaced. "These are very heavy, dangerous doses, sir," she protested as she lifted the laserdot.

"What I would do to you," he said in a tone that almost purred, "would be even more dangerous."

And in that instant, in her mind, she felt a rush of pleasure so intense that she gasped and almost lost her balance.

He caught her arms to steady her. She felt muscles straining in her arms at the painful grip. "Hurry," he whispered.

She reached up quickly, shivery at the contact, and shot home the laserdot in his strong neck while he watched her with hunger consuming him.

He was bending toward her when the dravelzium took effect. He drew in a sharp breath and suddenly let her go and stepped back. "I injured you," he bit off.

She swallowed hard. "Just a little bruising," she

lied, as she ran a mender over her arms and repaired the muscle tissue.

"Lies," he murmured. "I am truly sorry."

"I know. It isn't something you can help." She studied him curiously. "Sir, what was…?" She wanted to ask him about the sudden sharp pleasure.

"Forbidden knowledge," he said curtly. His eyes narrowed and became an opaque blue. "You will forget it."

She blinked. She frowned. Hadn't she just asked him a question?

"Hahnson!" Dtimun called, to prevent any more questions. He had effectively blocked the memory of what he had involuntarily shared with her.

Hahnson came back in. He glanced from Dtimun to Madeline and relief claimed his features.

"I rigged the wiring," he said with a grin. "Not bad for a physician, either. I doubt Higgins himself could have done better."

Dtimun managed a tight smile. "Thank you. And not only for providing a logical reason for the AVBDs to malfunction."

Hahnson nodded and smiled. "You're quite welcome."

Dtimun turned back to Madeline. "We must go, before the dravelzium wears off. Fare well, Dr. Ruszel," he said formally.

"And you, sir," she replied, saluting him smartly. She glanced at Hahnson with a sad smile. "I'll miss you, Doc."

"I'll miss you, too," he began, smiling back.

A low, threatening growl stopped him at once.

"We have to leave, right now," Hahnson told Dtimun. "That dravelzium has a short life and it isn't as effective when it's given in successive doses."

"I agree," Dtimun said, regretting the behavior he couldn't control. He grimaced. Even Hahnson, his friend, wasn't safe.

"See you, Maddie," Hahnson said to her, but he didn't dare approach her.

"See you, Doc," she replied softly.

Dtimun paused when Hahnson was out of earshot.

"That white noise ball that Hahnson gave you when you left the ship," he began, laughing softly at her guilty flush. "You must activate it when I leave," he added more seriously, "and never turn it off. You must deny me access to your thoughts."

She didn't question why. She was certain that her hopeless feelings for him might trigger disaster.

He nodded. "You are correct. I can invade your dreams, influence them," he added surprisingly, his voice hard. "Enough stimulation, even of a mental kind, could bring me here unannounced. The behavior is uncontrollable when it reaches a certain point." His face grew taut. "I would kill you. I could never live with the shame of it."

She drew in a slow breath and looked up at him with hopeless longing. She bit her lower lip, hard. "I'll turn it on the minute I get to my quarters," she promised.

He searched her pale eyes quietly. It would feel strange not to hear her thoughts. He was in her mind a great deal more than she realized.

His eyes narrowed as he sketched her delicate, beautiful features for the last time.

"What might have been," she heard in her mind— or thought she heard—in a tender, wistful tone, "if you had been Cehn-Tahr, or I human." He turned, then, and left her.

He didn't look back as he walked out the door.

She went back to her quarters and activated the small white ball Hahnson had given her. A second later, her vid player buzzed. She answered it. Hahnson smiled at her.

"Something I forgot to mention," he told her. "There's going to be an attempt by Ambassador Taylor to grab your research grants. But don't worry. We'll find a way to stop him."

She was still absorbing what she'd learned about Cehn-Tahr behavior in one day. She shook her head. "It's been a hell of a day," she said heavily.

"I don't doubt it. We're leaving port, so Flannegan is safe, in case you wondered."

"I hope he doesn't discuss what happened," she worried.

"That makes two of us. One other thing. Your Holconcom assignment has been revoked by the commander," he added gently. "There may be some gossip about why. He had to do something to explain your continued presence here at HQ."

"I'm not surprised," she said gently. Dtimun had done what was necessary. She didn't blame him. He'd said already that her future would have to be here, in the medical center on Trimerius. "I'll deal with it, don't worry."

Then she remembered what else Hahnson had said. "The ambassador is going to try to take my grants away?" she asked suddenly. "I won them in competition, fair and square. Is he holding a grudge because I knocked him on his butt at the Altair reception?"

"You did what?" he exclaimed, laughing.

"He made a nasty remark to me and put his arm around me, and the C.O. growled..." She stopped. That had been the beginning. Dtimun had been ready to attack the ambassador because he had insulted her. "So Taylor's getting even."

Hahnson just smiled. "He won't succeed. No worries. Komak knows things, I don't know how. He says it's not going to be a long separation. And that you'll be back with us in no time."

Would she? She wondered. In just over two and a half years, Madeline had come to call the Holconcom home. She loved the *Morcai* and its crew. She loved the camaraderie of her fellow soldiers. She was accustomed to the pace aboard ship, the Cehn-Tahr fare in the canteen, the odd sounds and smells, the sometimes outrageous playfulness of Komak when the crew went together to the officers' club. There was also the daily sight of Dtimun, which gave meaning to life. All those things would be gone forever.

"Don't borrow trouble," Hahnson advised. "I'll shepherd Mallory. Maybe," he added hesitantly, "things will work out."

She nodded, but she was recalling Dtimun's violent anger at Flannegan when he touched her and the abrupt, violent move he made toward her. Obviously, absence hadn't helped his situation. If anything, it had made him hungrier. No, things were not going to work out. She was sure of it.

DURING THE NEXT WEEK, she worked out in the gym, alone, reworked medical filing systems, went through the motions of seeing patients and writing up reports.

But her heart felt like lead in her chest. The joy of that incredible day on Memcache, the memory of what she thought she heard Dtimun say in her mind, in the gym, seemed as distant now as the three moons of Enmehkmehk when the crew was transported to the horror of Akhmau. And about as hopeless. His remarks had been tender, but beneath them had been the furious hunger that was consuming him, driving him mad. That hunger had separated her from the Holconcom, probably forever. She felt the separation like a wound.

Her misery was made complete by a visit from Aubrey Taylor, the Terravegan ambassador to the Tri-Galaxy Council. He'd replaced the former one; a kind and sympathetic man who frequently played vid games with Madeline's father, Paraguard Colonel Clinton Ruszel. Taylor looked as if he'd never played a game in his life. He was cold, unyielding and as friendly as a Nagaashe serpent in a fever.

"If you're attached to the Holconcom, Lieutenant, why are you here on the base?" he asked curtly.

A good question. She wished she had a decent answer. "I had a bad case of Altairian flu, sir," she replied courteously.

"Flu. You're a doctor and you couldn't inoculate yourself against it?" he asked.

Her face colored. She didn't dare argue.

He glanced at her. "They say your commander values you."

"I've heard that myself," she said, trying to sound amused.

He didn't laugh. He paced around her medical ward, inspecting things. "You have two classified military research grants coming up for renewal, I believe."

Her heart felt cold. "Yes, sir."

He glanced at her. "And how do you conduct research as a battlefield medic?" he asked.

"I do the research in my downtime, sir," she replied.

He scoffed. "Downtime. This is your first downtime of any length in over two years, I believe?"

She felt her teeth clench. She didn't reply. She hadn't wanted to be away from the Holconcom even for the small space of time required to do intensive research. That was a failing she couldn't deny. Adventuring in space was far more suited to her taste than bending over beakers and test tubes—or the modern equivalent.

"There's a young Jebob woman in the Terravegan unit who has excellent grades in graduate school and has asked for your grants. She's already won prizes in molecular biology. I favor transferring the grants to her."

Madeline was winded, as if he'd punched her in the stomach. So Strick had been right. It had never occurred to her that she could lose her grants. There had been no deadline on her research into a new strain of bacterial parasite that infected Cularian bronchial passages—linked to Rojok DNA—and was almost always fatal. She couldn't say that she was reluctant to develop it, remembering how noble Chacon was, and that she owed her life to him.

Taylor waited for her reaction and seemed irritated when she didn't reply. "No comment?"

"Sir," she said politely, "the grants aren't mine by right. I won them through hard work and debate."

"You're welcome to debate my Jebob candidate," he said easily. "You'll lose, of course."

She could have kicked him. The obnoxious little worm!

He picked up an antique beaker and studied it through the light. "It also seems unacceptable to me that a human female, a Terravegan national, has been transferred to an all-male battle group across racial lines. My predecessor approved the transfer, but I've had second thoughts. I think it looks bad. One woman, among all those men."

"Sir, the military are mentally neutered…" she began.

"Oh, don't hand me that bull," he muttered. "The process can be reversed, and many times, it doesn't even work. We've got a pregnant supply sergeant right now who's being dishonorably discharged and sent to a breeder colony. Once the child is removed, she'll be spaced for her actions." He stared at her. "Some of your colleagues say you'd die for your commanding officer."

"We all would, sir," she replied smartly, although the reference to the misbehaving supply sergeant's fate made her feel even sicker. She didn't let it show. Not that she herself would ever experience that particular fate.

Taylor gave Madeline an irritated glance. He moved around her, his hands on his hips, and the way he looked at her made her uneasy.

"Your pal Flannegan is talking about an incident in the gym a few days ago. It seems your commander threatened to attack him when he found you sparring with him. Does the Holconcom C.O. have an interest in you that isn't professional, Ruszel? Pity, considering that he'd kill you if he acted on it. His military authority at the Cehn-Tahr Dectat would be very interested to know about that, wouldn't they, Ruszel? I mean, you're a human. It's against his law for him to even touch you."

His comments made tragic sense. He couldn't get at her directly, so he was going after Dtimun, to get at her that way. He was going to dig until he discovered that her commanding officer had an involuntary attraction to her. It would mean the end of Dtimun's career, perhaps his life, if Taylor persisted.

She had to think fast. This was dangerous territory. She had to protect Dtimun, whatever the cost. "Sir, Flannegan called my C.O. a 'cat-eyed bennywhammer' in the officers' club not too long ago," she said, improvising. "I got in trouble for slugging him, and I had to tell the C.O. what prompted me to get into a brawl. That was why he threatened Flannegan."

Taylor looked disappointed. He paced some more. He brightened. "I notice that the Holconcom commander has replaced you with your assistant, Mallory," he said. "In fact, you haven't been on missions with the *Morcai* for some weeks now and your Holconcom assignment was recently revoked." He smiled coldly. "Are you incompetent, or is your commander leaving you behind for some other reason? Some... unmilitary reason?"

She bit her lip, hard. She would have to act. Dtimun couldn't be sacrificed because she couldn't control her own feelings. Her behavior had prompted his.

He couldn't help it, either. This was going to hurt. But it had to be done. There was only one way she could think of to save the situation.

"Sir," she said in a hopefully conspiratorial tone, "I'm not happy in medicine. Not the way I thought I would be." She averted her eyes, as if shamed by what she was admitting. "I was better suited as an Amazon captain. I asked to be relieved from duty with the Holconcom, to have time to review my options." She glanced at him covertly. "There's not much hope of a transfer. Admiral Lawson says it gives our services a boost to have an SSC medic, a human female at that, posted with a crack Cehn-Tahr commando unit."

Taylor pursed his lips and looked elated. "I can manage that transfer, with or without Lawson. That what you want, Ruszel, to serve with humans again?" He emphasized the word "humans."

She wanted to slug him, but she couldn't afford to. She needed the transfer. It might spare Dtimun his career and his life. He stood to lose both if he had to be around her for any length of time.

"Yes, sir," she lied. "I want to serve with a human division again."

He smiled. It was a chilling smile. "I'll get the paperwork through. Since you're going into a forward division, you won't need those grants or your research. I'll give them to my Jebob candidate. Have a good day, Ruszel."

He left. She waited until he was out of earshot, behind the closed door, before she let loose with a barrage of Cehn-Tahr curses, learned from Komak, which would have incensed the commander.

"An apt description of Ambassador Taylor, indeed," came an amused, deep voice into her mind. "This is a sacrifice of some proportion, Ruszel," the voice continued quietly. "Why are you making it?"

"You're invading, sir," she said, recalling the grizzled old face and snow-white hair that went with the voice even while she marveled at the reach of his mind through the distance between them. And his ability to pierce the white-noise generator. "It isn't ethical."

"Many things are not. Taylor wants your research because it threatens the Rojoks."

"I suspected that."

"Yet you are playing into his hands. Why?"

She closed her mind with mathematical formulae. The old voice chuckled.

"I see more than you realize," he said gently. "Your commander will not understand your decision. It will enrage him."

"Better enraged than dead, sir," she said, and then could have bitten her tongue for the slip.

"I would never let them harm him," he replied. "Or you."

She recalled what Dtimun had told her, about the old one's attempts to have her spaced when she was added to the Holconcom.

"I did not know you then, warwoman. I deeply regret my actions," he said quietly. "I lived in bitterness, with my grief and my guilt. Dtimun and I have been at odds for many decades. He goes out of his way to enrage me."

"You and the emperor, sir," she said with a smile in her voice.

He chuckled. "As you say. I am in good company,

am I not?" He became serious. "You may think your assignment will profit you both, but Taylor has an agenda. He will seek to harm you."

"He'll have to go through Admiral Mashita, sir," she said, "and she knows me a great deal better than the ambassador does."

He sighed. "Very well. But be wary of any dangerous assignments. Things are progressing at a pace I had not anticipated," he added. "I must double my efforts to effect research progress, and also change in my own government."

"Sir?"

"Never mind, Ruszel." He hesitated. "Your feelings for the Holconcom commander—you do not understand the obstacles."

"I do, sir," she said stiffly. "Better than you realize."

There was another hesitation. He saw her last conversation with Dtimun, in his office, in her mind. It saddened him. "I have committed many crimes in my long life, warwoman. Now I begin to pay for them. I will not interfere further. But there is a danger in being near your commanding officer, a grave one."

"He would never hurt me," she began defensively.

"He would never intend to hurt you," he corrected.

She frowned. "Sir, I have a white-noise ball and it's activated," she began. "It blocks telepaths…"

He chuckled. "Some telepaths."

She laughed. "Okay."

There was a brief pause, as if he was speaking to someone. His voice came back into her mind. "I must go. Keep well. I must now attempt to find solutions for problems I, myself, created." He hesitated.

"One more thing, Ruszel," he added quietly. "If Ambassador Taylor attempts to put you in harm's way, contact me. I will hear your thoughts, and I promise you, I will stop him." His tone was as unyielding as the commander's on a bad day.

"Thank you, sir."

"It is little enough to do, considering the trouble I have already caused. Farewell."

And he was gone. Well, at least she had a way out, for Dtimun and for herself. It would mean giving up everything she loved. But at least Dtimun wouldn't have to give up his career, or his life, if she left. It was her fault that he'd had to sideline her, because of her helpless attraction to him, which had caused him to react in that violent way with Flannegan. Now she had to provide a solution, however she could.

Ambassador Taylor was a sick little man. He was already notorious for his racist views about the Cehn-Tahr Empire and aliens in general. He was also an advocate of family rights groups who felt that the government's policy of neutering was a detriment to the human genome. The groups were trying to do away with the mental neutering of the military and even the breeder colonies. They had some radical idea that humans should choose their own mates and breed when they chose. It was a revolutionary attitude that was gaining strength.

But Taylor himself had no real agenda that could be discovered. He attached himself to whatever cause brought him the most prestige. He was a radical with power, one of the most fearsome of opponents. Madeline couldn't fight him, and she couldn't afford to let the commander become involved, for his own sake.

Pretty soon, she was going to be out with a combat unit and her stint with the Holconcom would be a warm memory to take out on cold nights during deployment. She wondered at her own docility. The human medic who'd dared Dtimun's hot temper on Terramer had let the Terravegan ambassador walk all over her. It was out of character; but, then, she'd had a hard few weeks. She had no more heart left for a fight. Dtimun had said that distance might provide a solution. They could see if he was correct, when the distance was far greater than Trimerius. She had already decided not to ask the old fellow for help. He, like Madeline and Dtimun, was a soldier, and he probably had a great deal more to lose than either of them, considering his age. She would soldier on, as she always had, and take the blows as they came.

As she thought it, she suddenly remembered Caneese's words, that she would face a grave danger and make a decision that she didn't want to make, a sacrifice. Was this it?

For an instant she recalled the old fellow's invasion into her thoughts and was afraid that he might mention the tangle of problems her involuntarily emotions had created for Dtimun. It was a violation of the Species Act for Dtimun to even touch her, must less react to her the way he did. But if the old one had meant to cause trouble, he would have already done it, surely, and he wouldn't have offered to help her. She had to trust that he wouldn't betray her commanding officer.

At least she had sidelined Ambassador Taylor by misdirecting him about Flannegan's comments. The commander would be safe enough, for now. She really would have to plant her fist in Flannegan's face one day, to pay him back for his gossiping. The thought gave her real pleasure.

Two days later, her orders came through. She was to report within the week to Admiral Mashita in the forward lines of the Amazon Division for reassignment. She donned her copper-colored Amazon armor, settled her Reina—or short ceremonial sword—in its sheath at her trim waist and went to war.

CHAPTER THIRTEEN

Two weeks later, Madeline was in charge of a company of girls in the forward division, charged with search and rescue of a downed Jebob ship on one of the planets in the Meg-Warren sector, which was several parsecs' distance from the front. It wasn't a choice assignment. The planet on which the ship went down was Akaashe, as the Cehn-Tahr called it, the home planet of the fearsome Nagaashe, the giant serpents who had once been the terror of the three galaxies. Their numbers were reduced now, and no one believed that any were left even on their home world. Madeline, who had seen both adult and child of the species, and knew of the Cehn-Tahr hopes for a treaty with them, knew better.

"No one's seen a Nagaashe in decades," Madeline's EXO, Darmila, mused. "They're probably extinct. This is just a milk run, ma'am, something to get you back into the rhythm of the job."

"I've seen a Nagaashe in the past six standard months," Madeline said solemnly. "And you have no idea of the size or ferocity of the adult of the species."

"Where did you see one?" she asked, excited.

Madeline almost bit her tongue. On Memcache, but she couldn't admit that. It had been a dangerous slip. She struggled for a reply that wouldn't get her in more trouble. "That's classified, sorry," she said, and smiled.

Darmila bought it. "Oh. Sorry." She frowned. "Then, what if they're not extinct after all? You know, a shipload of children went down on Akaashe during the Great Galaxy War," she added. "They were survivors of an attack by the Rojok/Jebob Alliance, pitifully crippled. They were never heard from again." She shuddered. "Nobody high up ever commented, but gossip was that the giant serpents killed them all, every one."

Madeline had to repress a shudder of her own. She was familiar with the giant serpents from Memcache, but she'd been terrified when the parents of the small Nagaashe she'd rescued had coiled and spread their great hoods and hissed at her. Imagine a whole planet of them, and a shipload of children at their mercy. It was a sickening thought.

"Maybe there aren't any on this continent," Madeline said. She smiled. "But even if there are, we're still going down to investigate. We have a fix on their last known position."

"How are we going in?"

"It's a standard S&R until we know it isn't," she replied. She moved to the navigation console occupied by a blonde Terravegan ensign. "Position?"

"We're one A.U. and closing, Captain," she replied. "I've got a grid with the position enhanced over a holotope. It's lush, there. Green and subtropical. Lots of water."

"We should take some vids of it for the files," Darmila said.

"We'll reconnoiter first," Madeline said firmly.

"Then we'll do recordings and sensor logs." She frowned as she looked at the interpretive overlays. There were no files of vids on this planet. Odd, she thought, because the history textdiscs referred to a surveying party sent here centuries earlier. Only one adventurer actually returned, but he had the vids in his possession when he was rescued in space. Yet, the vids were now nonexistent. Rumor was that they'd disappeared out of a top secret vault.

"How do we deploy?" asked one of the new women, still in her teens.

"We'll send out a single recon unit." She glanced at the woman, who was eagerly watching her. "I suppose we can use Rema One Platoon on the reconnoiter," she added.

"Yes!" the woman enthused. She caught herself and stood at attention. "Yes, ma'am, I mean."

Madeline chuckled. She was beginning to feel at home with her unit. It was like old times. Almost. She forced a memory of the commander, as he'd been the last time she saw him, to the back of her mind.

"That's odd," Darmila said aloud as she pored over the screen.

"What is?"

"There's something ahead, some sort of distortion. See it?" She indicated a broad area of sensor verga on the screen, wavering like a white ripple in front of the ship.

"It can't be a storm," the pilot murmured. "Not this high in orbit. And we're…hang on!"

The warning came too late. The whole ship was stopped as if it had slammed into a wall. There were explosions aft, toward the main engines. Smoke began to fill the cabin.

"All hands, abandon ship!" Madeline called over intership comms. She dragged the pilot out of her chair and herded her and Darmila out of the compartment toward the little drop ships affixed to the fuselage to port and starboard of the swept-back wings.

"We won't make it," Darmila shouted. "There's no time…!"

An explosion like red death washed over them with a sound as final as an emerillium blast in a hydrogen field. Madeline felt the ship shudder and start to go down, but she was too badly injured to react. The pain was excruciating, and soon she lost consciousness. Just before she blacked out, she felt the ship, incredibly, slow down as it entered the planet's atmosphere. She must be hallucinating, she decided. She remembered whispering Dtimun's name, a facsimile of its pronunciation, as the darkness overtook her.

SHE CAME TO in waves of pain, so excruciating that she couldn't move at all. She was lying on the ground. The smell of acrid smoke was in her nostrils. It was hard to breathe. Something was broken inside her. It was bad.

She opened her eyes and caught her breath. Standing, coiled, around her were several towering Nagaashe, the intelligent white serpents with blue eyes who populated this remote planet. They were watching her. Not moving. Not threatening. Just observing.

Her chest rose and fell painfully. "We were sent…

to rescue…Jebob nationals…who crashed here," she managed weakly.

The Nagaashe looked at each other.

She smiled faintly. The Nagaashe on Memcache didn't speak to her; they'd only hummed and rubbed up against her after she'd saved their child from the galot. They probably couldn't speak…

"On Memcache…It was you?" came an odd sound into her mind. "You saved the infant?"

It wasn't exactly Standard, but it was understandable. "Yes," she thought back.

The tallest, and apparently the eldest, of the serpents undulated forward and bent his neck down so that his huge, bright blue eyes were looking right into hers. Oddly, they had rounded pupils, instead of the slit ones of most reptiles. "You called Meg-Ravens to chase the galot away," he said in her mind.

"Yes."

The bright blue eyes searched hers. There was a smile in the voice that came into her head. "A novel solution. You can speak to Meg-Ravens?"

"Yes. An elderly Cehn-Tahr taught me, after I rescued him from a Rojok on Ondar." She had the picture of the old fellow in her mind.

There was a pause. The giant serpents swayed and hummed to each other uneasily. "That one is more dangerous than all the other Cehn-Tahr put together," the eldest thought to her. "We have great fear of the Cehn-Tahr. We will not trade with them. They are animals."

Madeline was shocked. She thought of Dtimun saving the Altairian child, rescuing Madeline from the cliff when the Rojok was ready to throw her over it. She thought of him with Caneese, that gentle touching of foreheads. She thought of him holding her in the rain…

The serpent's head turned to one side as he saw those thoughts. "The younger Cehn-Tahr. He leads the Holconcom."

"Yes," she thought back.

"You were his medic. Why are you here, in battle armor?"

She managed a sigh. It hurt. "It's a very long story."

The serpent settled down into its coils with grace. "May I hear it?"

What the hell, she thought. She was certainly going to die. She might as well spend her last minutes reliving her happiest moments. After all, who would the serpent tell? These Nagaashe, if memory served, had never left their own planet. And nobody would come after them in a rescue attempt. A small ship carrying crippled children had gone down here during the lengthy Great Galaxy War, and they were never recovered.

"They lived happily here," the giant serpent thought to her. "We healed them as best we could. They were very afraid of us at first, but we brought them food and water and mended the injuries that we could. Many injuries we could not heal. Eventually, they welcomed us. We gave them…" He turned his head and hummed to the others in tones that sounded almost musical. One of the others hummed back in different tones. The elder serpent turned back to Madeline. "We gave them fantasy which was like reality. They could walk again. They could run. They could fly. In their minds, they could live as never before."

She was impressed. "Are any of them still here?"

"No. All dead now. Could not reproduce. But died happy."

Madeline shifted. She blinked. "My girls," she said suddenly. "My command crew...?"

The serpent bent its head. "We thought it was invaders. We caused the engines to overload. We are sorry. We did not know."

She bit her lip. "All...all dead?"

"Not all. Two others live. They have injuries. But not as bad as yours." He paused. "We protected the ship when it came down, so that it would not crash. We wanted survivors because we were curious about the creatures inside." He felt her pain. "You are injured. Can you treat the injuries?"

"I could, if my wrist unit still functioned." She had tried it, but the unit was dead. Dead, like me, she thought blackly, with nothing to treat what felt like catastrophic injuries.

"Others like you will come. Will find you."

"Not in time," she whispered.

"We will bring them," he returned. "Tell me about the Cehn-Tahr. The one who commands the Holconcom."

She hesitated, but only for a minute. It was nice, remembering. She told him about Memcache. It didn't matter now, if someone else knew, too.

A COUPLE OF hours later, Madeline was fading in and out of consciousness. Going into shock, she thought. Talking about the past, keeping her mind alert, had helped keep the shock at bay, for a time.

"We must take you to shelter," the serpent thought

to her. "It is very cold here at night. But we have no hands. We must carry you in our mouths. This will frighten?"

"No," she said gently. "It will not."

There was more humming. Some of the serpents departed. The big one slid down onto his belly, up to Madeline. Heavens, he was huge! She would fit in his mouth like a fish in a barrel.

"A little discomfort," he thought to her.

His mouth opened and he slid closer, scooping her up sideways, careful of his fangs, so that they didn't threaten her skin. She relaxed, to make the process easier. It was so painful. She knew then that her injuries were extensive. The possibility of death loomed ever closer. His tongue was soft, she noted with some fascination, and it was warm. Because he was endothermic, like humans? Not a reptilian trait. Reptiles were ectothermic; they needed an outside source of heat to warm them up. Well, the Rojoks had traces of reptilian DNA, but they were also endothermic. Her mind rambled on.

The serpent rose up gently, with Madeline in his mouth. Two smaller Nagaashe had the other, unconscious, women in their mouths. The eldest serpent turned and undulated toward the base of the mountains the ship had flown over on its way here. In a matter of minutes, he deposited Madeline on a bed of soft, fresh grass inside a cave.

She had been surprised that the serpent's breath smelled not of carrion or meat, but of pleasant herbs and legumes.

Laughter filled her mind. "We are vegetarians," he thought to her. "We eat no carrion."

"But the legends say that you are deadly poison-ous."

"Ah, yes, that is also true," he said. "But we rarely bite. We have not needed to, for centuries."

She turned her head and saw two of her girls, one of whom was Darmila. Madeline was glad that she'd survived. But only the three of them, out of so many. Her heart ached.

The serpent apologized yet again. This time she was in too much pain to answer. He settled her. Other serpents brought bags of water and strange smelling vegetables. Madeline was too sick to eat, but she was grateful for the water. She wondered how the bags had been made.

"We can discuss this at a later time. You must rest now."

She felt sleepy suddenly. Amazingly, the excruci-ating pain diminished and her eyes closed.

THE OLDEST NAGAASHE tossed his mind far into space, all the way to Memcache, to the Imperial Dectat itself.

The old fellow was shocked when he heard the oddly accented voice in his head. And then he knew to whom it belonged.

"Ruszel is here," the serpent said. "She is gravely injured. She does not know. Her medical device is broken. If she is not assisted, very soon, she will die. We can kill with thought, but healing one so delicate is another matter. Her injuries are extensive. It is be-yond our abilities to save her."

The old fellow felt a jolt of sorrow all the way to his feet.

"She is…of value to you," the serpent tried to communicate the emotion.

"Of great value, and not only to me," came the reply. There was a pause. He read the serpent's thoughts. "You blew up her ship."

"We thought it was invasion," the serpent thought back. "We were told so, by a human comm beam, from the Terravegan embassy. Said invasion force was coming."

"Who?" the old fellow demanded.

"Taylor."

"I will kill him with my bare hands!"

The serpent was curious. "Not your ally, that one?"

"Not anyone's ally."

"I see." There was a pause. "Red-haired female has feelings for Holconcom commander," he said. "She told me much of him. I have…we all have…feared Cehn-Tahr since end of Great Galaxy War."

"That was a fault of ours," the old fellow said sadly. "We were given false information when we invaded your continent."

"Yes. By same man who is now ambassador."

The old fellow caught his breath. Yes. That was true, and he'd just now realized it.

"We have been wrong about you," the serpent said. He paused. "You may send embassy to us. We will send representative to you. We may fix treaty."

The old fellow's surprise, and pleasure, was evident in his thoughts. "This is an honor."

"For which you may thank Ruszel," came the reply. "We know of prophecy, now. I found old woman at Mahkmannah on Memcache with my mind and read hers. She is right. Red-haired healer has made friends with serpent. But not ones the old woman thought of. Not little serpent on Memcache, but whole race of Nagaashe, for treaty."

The old fellow smiled. "It must be the prophecy."

"You must come quickly," the serpent said. "No Ruszel, no prophecy."

"I will have a ship come and bring me to you."

There was a hesitation. "This would be great risk."

"For Ruszel, I will take the risk."

DTIMUN WAS READY to return to base. His scouting mission had gone badly. Mallory had accompanied the landing party and thrown up on the way down again. She couldn't get used to the C.O.'s high-grav landings. The C.O. was coldly furious. Nobody said a word. Just lately, the commander had been more unapproachable even than he usually was. Even Komak was avoiding him.

Their quarry had flown the coop minutes before the Morcai's scout ship put down on the planet. That hadn't improved Dtimun's mood, which was black already.

He had forced himself not to try to access Madeline's mind across the vast parsecs of space that separated them. She had the white noise ball activated, he could tell. He hadn't told her that he had the ability, just as his father had it, to bypass the interference if he concentrated intensely. But he considered that it would only aggravate the discomfort he already felt when he remembered their last encounter and her proximity to Flannegan. It was worse when he remembered their day on Memcache.

But suddenly he felt a burst of anguish, a melting of thought into chaos. He heard his name whispered, in a mangled pronunciation that would have amused him under different circumstances. But then there was silence. He knew it was her mind reaching out to him. Then, when he tried to link with her, he could not. The distance would not have mattered. The white ball would not have stopped him if he concentrated. No, it was something else, something wrong. But what? He went about his duties with a feeling of disruption. The experience was disturbing. Nothing could have happened to her on Trimerius, surely. Or could it? He ordered the ship into a faster mode of travel.

THE INSTANT THE *Morcai* touched down on Trimerius, Dtimun went to Lawson's office, so quickly that he seemed a red blur. He made it to Lawson's office in a matter of seconds. He didn't even wait to be announced by the adjutant.

Lawson glanced at him and grimaced. He was speaking to an older man, a tall Paraguard colonel. He paused as Dtimun joined them.

"I'm so sorry," Lawson repeated to the old man.

Lieutenant Colonel Clinton Ruszel had wet green eyes. He wasn't hiding them. He turned, stared at Dtimun as if he didn't recognize him. Finally, he nodded absently, and walked out of the cubicle. The door powered shut behind him. Dtimun had a cold premonition. He'd known Clinton Ruszel for years. He'd never seen him shed a tear.

He stared at Lawson with a cold chill in his heart.

Lawson winced at his expression. "I shouldn't have to tell you, too, in the space of ten minutes," he said angrily. "It's killing me! After she took up her new assignment, Taylor sent secret orders, which had Ruszel attached to a special operation force in the front lines for a covert rescue mission. Clinton Ruszel and I tried every way we knew to stop it, but we found out too late." He indicated the white static ball on the desk that permitted private conversations. "We couldn't stop it without exposing Taylor. You know what that would mean. It wasn't even an option, not at this stage of the war."

"What new assignment?" Dtimun demanded. "And what covert mission?" Dtimun added in a voice so cold that it made Lawson shiver.

Lawson took a deep breath and told him what had happened in his absence.

"Where is she?" the alien asked icily.

Lawson looked as if he wanted to get under something heavy. He linked his hands behind him, tight. "She was sent, with a platoon, to find a downed Jebob ship on…on Akaashe."

Dtimun seemed to stiffen. "The Nagaashe home planet."

"Yes."

"No Jebob ship would go near it! The Jebob are terrified of serpents!"

"I know that, but Madeline's C.O. didn't." He closed his eyes. "The minute they inserted into orbit, there was…there was an explosion. Sensors read nothing more except catastrophic failure of the engines."

Dtimun might have been cut out of stone. He hadn't been able to read Madeline's thoughts. Not because she was blocking him out, but because her ship had crashed and she was...

"No!" he exclaimed. His tone was anguish verbalized. "Sensors can lie," he said, quickly collecting himself. "She and her unit could have survived. Have they sent a search team in?"

"Dtimun, Taylor won't permit us to withdraw resources from the war effort to, as he put it, waste on a futile search for dead women. I'm sorry."

"You can override him," he said.

"I can't override him, and you know why!"

"She is not dead!" Dtimun exploded.

Lawson felt the pain as if it were tangible. He'd never seen the alien so out of control, so enraged and wounded. Ruszel obviously meant more to him than he'd ever permitted himself to express. Too late now. Far too late.

He put his hand on the alien's shoulder. "I can't do anything about sending men in to reconnoiter. But we both know someone who can," he added quietly.

Yes, Dtimun knew. There was one other person who valued Ruszel almost as much as he did. It was time to put aside old vendettas and go to the one hope Ruszel had of being rescued. If she was still alive.

"There's just one thing," Lawson added. "Taylor has forbidden any Tri-Galaxy Fleet units from searching for her. Worse, all Terravegan units assigned to other Tri-Fleet units have been ordered to report back to Trimerius at once for reassignment to Terravegan commands." He grimaced. "I'm sorry. You've had those guys for going on three years. None of them is going to want to leave. Especially Stern and Hahnson, once they know about Madeline."

"I will detach the Holconcom from the Tri-Fleet and go after her myself," he said shortly.

"That's what I expected you to do. It will cause problems. But it's the only way." Lawson managed a smile. "Bring her home," he said, almost choking on the words.

Dtimun couldn't answer. He wasn't certain of his own ability to speak normally.

HE MOVED QUICKLY. He sent the Cehn-Tahr ambassador to the Tri-Galaxy Council with the formal announcement of the Holconcom's removal from the Tri-Galaxy Fleet. He contacted the Dectat and told them the situation. But the president of the Dectat refused permission for a rescue attempt. No person could land on Akaashe in violation of the Nagaashe dictate. That could jeopardize the ongoing diplomatic attempts to forge a treaty with the reptilian species. Ruszel's loss was regrettable. But, then, she and her human—he had used the word as if it was distasteful to him—crew had most likely perished, anyway.

Dtimun cut the connection and let out a barrage of curses that would have shocked even Btnu. Well, let them court-martial him. He was not going to abandon Ruszel.

He called a shipwide meeting in the main mess hall. Once every crewman was in place, he spoke.

"The Terravegan ambassador has issued an immediate recall for all Terravegan personnel to report to Lawson for reassignment."

There were shocked murmurs.

"I must ask you to pack your gear and leave as quickly as possible, just for the time being. I'll find a way to get you back in the Holconcom once this emergency is past. Dr. Madeline Ruszel was reassigned to the Amazon front lines without my knowledge. Now her ship has gone down behind enemy lines and Ambassador Taylor has refused Tri-Fleet permission to mount a rescue. I've just formally detached the Holconcom from the Tri-Galaxy Fleet and I am going after Ruszel myself, with my Holconcom…"

"Begging the hell your pardon, sir, but we are Holconcom, too, and we're not leaving the ship," Holt Stern said curtly.

"You can pour syrup on that," Hahnson agreed, stepping up beside his friend.

"My men and I are not leaving," engineering officer Higgins said curtly.

"My men and I are absolutely the hell not leaving," communications officer Jennings added firmly.

"Neither am I," Edris Mallory chimed in with unusual firmness, her blue eyes flashing. "Dr. Ruszel is my colleague, and my friend. They can court-martial me if they like."

"Our whole departments are at your command, sir," Higgins, the engineering officer said shortly.

"Both our whole damned departments, sir," Jennings seconded.

"Ambassador Taylor can hang us—we're going with you!" another officer called out.

"Every man!"

"And woman!" Mallory ventured, a little shyly because she was the only female aboard.

"You bet!" Strick Hahnson chuckled, smiling reassuringly at her.

"Ruszel is Holconcom," Abemon, another of the

Cehn-Tahr, spoke up. "We will not leave her to be killed because the politicians deem her expendable."

There were loud murmurs of agreement, from both human and Cehn-Tahr.

Dtimun relaxed a little. "It could mean court-martial, even execution, for all of you Terravegans," he said gently.

"In that case, sir, wouldn't you just have to bring the Holconcom and break us out of the brig in the nick of time?" Stern asked with a grin.

"Hear, hear!" Hahnson seconded.

Dtimun managed a smile. "Yes, I would. Very well, then. Battle stations! I expect to find a squadron of Lawson's best fighters facing us down the minute we lift. Ambassador Taylor will not take the loss of his nationals lightly."

"We can shoot better than his guys, sir," Higgins assured him.

"And straighter," Jennings agreed.

"Posts, then."

Everybody scrambled for positions.

Komak glanced at Dtimun. The C.O. was putting on a front. He was uncertain about Ruszel, and worried sick for her.

Komak placed a hand on his arm. "I am still here."

Dtimun nodded and started to turn.

Komak detained him. "You do not understand. I am still here. If she were dead," he added enigmatically, "I would not be."

Dtimun scowled in confusion.

"It does not matter. We must hurry."

"I agree."

They ran side by side for the access ladder.

THE OLD ONE made contact with Dtimun's mind.

Dtimun was in his quarters, brooding in front of a bust of Cashto, the galot pack leader from whose DNA the Cehn-Tahr were transformed. The great black head sat on a table with holocandles, its huge green eyes gleaming in the subdued light. He was still debating his next move. He had detached the Holconcom without the authorization of the Dectat. He was going to be in real trouble for that, regardless of his Clan status. There was another communication, from the president of the Dectat, which he read and didn't answer, that his decision was going to be debated and there might be repercussions. He was also headed for Akaashe in direct violation of a verbal order from the Dectat not to proceed. He was uncertain about contacting the old one for help. It might result in the *kehmatemer* being sent to apprehend him. He couldn't risk that; the loss of time might cost Ruszel her life. If she wasn't already dead…

The *Morcai* was en route to Akaashe, but although he knew that Madeline's ship had gone down there, he didn't know where. The Nagaashe planet was large and had many continents. Nor did they have diplomatic ties with the Nagaashe, which could cause grave problems if they landed there without permission, as the Dectat leader had already informed Dtimun when he refused permission for him to go to the Nagaashe homeworld. There was also the question of Madeline's survival. Even with their best sensors, it would take time to locate her. In that time, she could die. If she wasn't already dead.

He felt a burst of anguish, a darkening. He did not want to be vulnerable again. He thought his reaction to Ruszel wasa purely physical need. His mind was telling him something quite different, and he did not want to listen.

Could she be dead? Lawson thought so. Her father thought so. He closed his eyes on the anguish of that thought. Komak seemed to believe she was alive, but Dtimun had known too many disappointments to feel much hope. He pictured the rest of his long life without the occasional sight of Ruszel's laughing green eyes to sustain it. The light would go out of the galaxies...

Suddenly, he was aware of an intrusion on his thoughts. He felt the old one there, in his mind. "Why are you here?" he asked abruptly.

"I have found Ruszel," he replied solemnly. "You must come to Memcache, at once."

His heart jumped. "Is she alive?"

"She is gravely wounded, on the island colony of Kanah, on Akaashe," the old one told him. "The Nagaashe cannot heal her."

Dtimun's chest rose and fell heavily. The depression he had felt since he spoke with Lawson had worsened. The old one would see that, and he no longer cared.

"Lawson said she had asked for reassignment to the Amazon Division," Dtimun said harshly.

"Yes. I found the reason, in Ambassador Taylor's mind. She asked the Terravegan ambassador to reassign her to the Amazon Division, to spare you."

"From what?" Dtimun demanded.

"Taylor knows that you attempted to attack a crewman who touched Ruszel," he said. "He said this to Ruszel. In order to allay his suspicions, Ruszel told him that an insult Flannegan made was responsible for your anger, and that she was tired of serving in an alien unit. She asked for reassignment, to protect you."

The enormity of her sacrifice made him feel humble. "Can you give me coordinates to her position?" he asked curtly.

"Yes."

"Why was she sent to Akaashe?" Dtimun persisted.

"The Nagaashe were contacted by Taylor and told that an attack on their settlement was imminent. The Amazon unit, commanded by Ruszel, was sent on a false mission to rescue a downed Jebob ship. He hoped to kill her that way, in revenge for the loss of Ruszel's grants to his Jebob candidate."

"The Jebob would never go near Akaashe," Dtimun said angrily. "They are terrified of serpents."

"Ruszel did as she was ordered. The Nagaashe caused the ship's engines to overload. All were killed, except for Ruszel and two women under her command, although the Nagaashe levitated the ship to ground so that there were survivors whom they could question about the intrusion. The explosion did… much damage."

"I have already set course for Akaashe. Hahnson can heal her…"

"You will take me to Akaashe," the old one commanded imperiously. "Memcache is on the way, you will lose very little time. The *kehmatemer* and I are coming with you."

"You take a great risk," Dtimun said.

"I have been known to do that," the old one said

with faint humor. "It is possible that Hahnson can mend her. But if he cannot, I can."

The younger alien didn't ask how. He knew from years past the power in that old mind. It had healed many Cehn-Tahr on the point of death. The old one might be Ruszel's only chance to live. It would never be possible for Dtimun to have a life with the red-haired medic, but he could not face the possibility of a life without her presence somewhere in the galaxies.

"Komak is still there, is he not?" the old one asked gently. "If he lives, so does Ruszel."

"Komak said the same thing. What does this mean?" Dtimun asked.

"There are things I must not yet reveal to you. I have contacted a negotiator who can bargain for Ruszel with the Nagaashe. They have diplomatic re-lations with them. A Dacerian is bringing him to rendezvous with us. Throw all the lightsteds," the old one commanded. "It does not matter now if the humans of the Holconcom see our true tech. They are part of us."

Dtimun was amused, and pleased, at the old one's comment. "Yes. They are." He hesitated. "I have caused grave problems for the Dectat," he said, an edge in his voice. "The President and I had words. He refused permission for the rescue, with some pointed comments about the lack of urgency to save 'humans,'" he added coldly. "He was equally upset that I removed the Holconcom from the Tri-Fleet in order to save Ruszel without permission. He seems to forget that I have the authority to make such a de-cision under Holconcom statute."

The old one saw the discussion in his mind. "Let

me worry about the Dectat, and its president," he said shortly. "There will be no problem there, I assure you." There was a sudden smile in the old, gravelly voice. "A former leader of the Holconcom made equally unpopular decisions, in the years before the Great Galaxy War, and once came to blows with the president of the Dectat when his orders were questioned. He will regret his words, I promise you!" he added smugly.

Dtimun's eyes made a faint green laugh.

The old one left him.

DTIMUN MADE THE announcement to a packed audience in the galley. "We are en route to Memcache to pick up a...representative of our government, to assist in negotiations for Ruszel and her crew. This will require me to disclose secret tech, which we have not before used in connection with our missions. If any of you have second thoughts about defying your military, you may have access to skimmers to return you to Trimerius before we employ acceleration."

"I'm still not leaving," Lieutenant Mallory said. Hahnson and Stern only nodded, agreeing.

"My whole department is still staying here," Lieutenant Higgins said.

"So is my whole damned department, sir," Lieutenant Jennings seconded.

"Shouldn't we get going?" Hahnson spoke for all of them.

Dtimun nodded. "Combining you humans with my command was one of the wisest moves of my career. You will see more things that we have not revealed to you before. You will not speak of them to outworlders."

Several of the humans grinned, because the C.O. apparently now thought of them all as Cehn-Tahr.

"Stations," he said. "And if Taylor attempts to court-martial any of you, he will have to go through me."

That brought laughter, and more smiles, as his crew rushed to their posts.

"Throw all lightsteds," Dtimun commanded the bridge crew. He looked around at the remaining crewmen. "Hold on to something," he advised.

Even as he spoke, the great ship wavered, wobbled and suddenly accelerated in a burst of speed that left the humans gasping.

Edris Mallory was sick all over the deck. But this time Dtimun didn't say a word.

THE OLD ONE and the *kehmatemer* came aboard the *Morcai* in tight formation. Several of the human members of the crew, including Edris Mallory, were present when they entered the airlock.

Dtimun and Komak met them, with Holt Stern. The old one gave the humans a curious appraisal from amused green eyes.

"It has been many decades since I saw so many humans," the old one remarked.

Rhemun, captain of the *kehmatemer*, glared at Edris Mallory. "Is this the one who took Ruszel's place?" he asked haughtily.

Edris, the mild-mannered, gave him back the glare, her blue eyes sparking. "I am Dr. Edris Mallory," she said coldly.

"Another warwoman?" the old one mused.

"A Cularian combat surgeon," Dtimun corrected. "Like Ruszel."

"There is no other female like Ruszel," Rhemun said shortly. "She is a warwoman. We have no need of physicians." He made of the word an insult.

Mallory drew herself up to her full height, which was far shy of the captain's. "If you ever have need of one, sir," she said in a biting tone, "pray that it isn't me."

"Mallory," Dtimun said shortly. "Captain Rhemun is a visitor. We do not insult visitors."

She saluted Dtimun. "Sorry, sir, he looked like a Rojok to me, sir." She turned and beat a path out of the sector before she could be reprimanded.

Stern and Hahnson were struggling not to laugh. They saluted and followed her.

"At ease, Captain," the old one told the ruffled captain of his guard. "We are fighting one war already. Settle your men."

"Yes, sir!" He saluted. So did his squad. He dismissed them.

Dtimun and Komak and the old one dashed up the ladders to the bridge.

The Cehn-Tahr in bridge crew bowed to the old one reverently before they went back to their positions.

"It is a great honor to have you here, sir," Komak told the old one with something like awe.

The elderly alien gave him a penetrating opaque blue stare. His eyes suddenly went green. Dtimun, watching, was blocked out by both their minds at once. His surprise was visible.

"One day, we will explain it to you," the old one said. He sobered. "But for now, Ruszel is our priority. Leave orbit at once."

Dtimun nodded and gave the command. For the first time, he felt a flutter of hope.

THE NAGAASHE PLANET was a contrast in colors and climate. The island continent on which the *Morcai* put down was lush and green. Under other circumstances, Dtimun might have taken the opportunity to enjoy it. Now, his only thought was to find Ruszel in time.

CHAPTER FOURTEEN

DTIMUN WAS OUT the airlock of the *Morcai* ahead of the old one and the *kehmatemer* as soon as the ship's massive engines whispered to a stop. His mind searched for Madeline's and could not find it. Anguish washed over him.

The Nagaashe approached the Cehn-Tahr warily. The humans in the Holconcom started backing up at just the sight of the giant serpents. Weapons Specialist Jones raised the barrel of his nanomissile launcher. Dtimun caught the barrel and threw it up without even looking at him.

"Put yourself on report, Jones," he said.

"Yes, sir," Jones groaned. "Sorry, sir."

The old one came outside with two robed figures, both of whom had joined the ship from a skimmer as they passed Dacerius. Everyone stood back to let the robed figures approach the giant serpents. They bowed and hissed. The robed figures hissed back.

So began the long and arduous process of negotiation for Ruszel's release. But Dtimun was losing his mind as he stood beside the Cehn-Tahr contingent, tormented by the slowness of the process.

The eldest of the Nagaashe, who had spoken with Madeline, approached him. "You fear for her, so you are impatient," he thought to Dtimun. "Go to her, with your medics. It will be proper. We will continue the negotiations in your absence."

"Thank you," Dtimun thought back.

"She is just inside the cave there. She is quite unique," the serpent replied. He turned and undulated back to the others.

Dtimun motioned to Hahnson and they darted toward the cave. Madeline was just coming around, swamped with pain and barely lucid. When she saw the commander, her eyes burst with helpless delight. He rushed to her and made an odd sound when Hahnson bent over her.

Hahnson sent the medic to check the two survivors of Madeline's company. "I wasn't going to touch her," he assured Dtimun, tongue-in-cheek, as he pressed a sensor from his wrist unit against Madeline's abdomen. "Death was very unpleasant and I have no wish to repeat it."

Dtimun didn't look at him. He was watching Madeline, whose own eyes were open and staring at him.

"You came…after us," she whispered, astonished.

"Yes." He fought to keep emotion from escaping his control. His big hand slid to her cheek. She caught it and cradled it against her face. Dtimun leaned toward her with a low growl. "Hahnson," he said huskily, his eyes troubled as they met the physician's. He could barely contain the hunger at all.

Hahnson hit him with a laserdot of dravelzium in his neck artery.

Dtimun looked at Madeline, whose soft hand he still held. "Again," he whispered.

"Too much…" Hahnson began to protest.

"I would rather die than harm her," he told the

husky physician, and his elongated eyes echoed the words.

Hahnson added another large dose, checked the monitor and nodded.

"What happened here?" Dtimun asked after a minute, slowly calming from the effects of the sedative he'd been given.

Madeline caught a breath. It hurt, but not as much. "We were sent here on a rescue mission." She nodded toward the outside of the smooth rock cavern. "They," she said, meaning the Nagaashe, "were told that an invasion force was coming. We...didn't know. Message said...a Tri-Fleet ship, a Jebob ship, went down here. We were sent in...to rescue them." She managed a laugh. "No crashed ship. Just furious Nagaashe."

"They didn't kill you," Hahnson said as he examined his instruments, shaking his head. "Amazing. They have a reputation for aggression."

She drew in another painful breath, aware of Dtimun's stillness. "They're telepaths," she said. "Knew...I saved one of them...on Memcache."

Hahnson's eyebrows rose. He stared at her expectantly.

Dtimun laughed lightheartedly for the first time since the ordeal began. "She called a flock of Meg-Ravens to deter a galot who was pursuing a Nagaashe child."

Hahnson let out a laugh. "You can communicate with Meg-Ravens?" he exclaimed. "You should be teaching bird speech at the medical academy! Better yet, at the military academy!"

"I'd love to know how you...got around Ambassador Taylor to come and get us," Madeline said to Dtimun.

He studied her smudged, weary face, her tangle of red-gold hair, her cracked and missing copper-hued armor plate. "I broke a few laws."

She managed a weak laugh. "Typical." She drew in a quick breath. "Thanks."

"You are still Holconcom," Dtimun said curtly. "I put you on reserve status to protect you from your military."

"Oh," she faltered. "I didn't realize…"

"We do not desert our own," he added softly.

She blinked. Hahnson had given her something for pain and she was suddenly drowsy. "How bad?" she asked him. "I can't diagnose—my wrist unit is in need of repair." She laughed and thought to Dtimun, "So is that white noise ball."

He only smiled. She was alive, at least. The need still ached in him, but his reactions to her were… more than that. He dismissed the thought. Surely it was just his relief at her survival.

Hahnson looked at his readouts. He wasn't smiling anymore. He looked at Dtimun, who seemed to pale as he read the medic's mind. "Nothing major," he told Madeline. He gave her a dose of sedative. "Rest now." Her head leaned back against the wall. Her eyes closed.

Hahnson tugged Dtimun to one side. He was solemn. "I can't fix her," he said stiffly.

"The ship has more resources…"

"You don't understand." He looked anguished. "She has catastrophic damage to her internal organs. I don't know how she's managed to stay alive this long. Nothing in my medical background prepares me to mend this sort of thing," he added miserably. "Her liver, and her kidneys are failing, she's bleeding internally..." His voice broke.

Dtimun stared at him uncomprehending. The drug made his thought processes slower. Then, all at once, he realized what Hahnson was saying. Madeline was going to die. Hahnson couldn't repair the damage. She was going to die...!

"She is not!" came a firm, authoritative voice from behind him.

The old one, trying to restrain the *kehmatemer*, strode into the cave and paused next to Madeline. "I will deal with the warwoman," he said. He grimaced. "Hahnson, your skills are needed outside. Three of the human Holconcom attempted to stop my men from entering the cave. There are a few assorted fractures," he added with a grimace.

"Yes, sir," Hahnson said. He hesitated. "Can you...?" He couldn't put it into words.

The old one knew more about Hahnson than he realized. He put a comforting hand on Hahnson's shoulder. "Yes, I can heal her," he said gently. "She will not die. Go to work."

Hahnson grinned from ear to ear. "Yes, sir!"

He left, plowing through a squad of *kehmatemer* who were just barely kept at bay by an impatient gesture from their leader. Outside, Edris Mallory had approached one of the injured Cehn-Tahr and was stopped abruptly by Captain Rhemun.

"Attend to the humans," he said bitingly. "We take care of our own."

"As you well know, Captain, we don't carry medics

of your race," Edris shot back, her blond hair wisping around her soft oval face. "I'm a Cularian medical specialist, just like Dr. Ruszel. And if you don't let me treat these patients," she added bitingly, "I will refer you to the commander of the Holconcom!"

Rhemun's dark eyebrows levered up under his helmet. He glowered at her, but he did step aside. "Very well," he said with cold courtesy.

Hahnson appeared beside her, moving toward the human casualties among the Holconcom. "Way to go, Mallory," he said under his breath, with tacit approval. "That's how we do things in medical service."

She was still flushed with anger from the encounter, but she tossed him a grin as she bent over the first casualty and, following protocol to the letter, formally asked permission to treat him.

THE OLD ONE sat down beside Madeline and took her face in his hands. Dtimun couldn't repress a low warning growl, despite the tranquillizer. The older alien looked at the younger one. "You might as well subside," he told him with an amused smile. "I have no fear of you, and I am too old to be a rival."

Dtimun cleared his throat and straightened. "Reflex."

"Understandable," the old one said. He turned his attention back to Ruszel. "Ruszel," he called softly. "You must awaken now."

She opened her soft green eyes and looked at him with awe. "Sir," she said, grimacing, because the pain had returned full force. "You came…with them?"

"You are valued by all of us who are Cehn-Tahr," he said solemnly. "Not just by the Holconcom. Ruszel, you have shattered organs. Hahnson cannot mend you. I can. But it will require an intimate contact between our minds. You will not be able to hide anything from me."

Madeline thought at once of that one, almost fantasy-perfect day on Memcache and she knew she couldn't allow the contact; not even to save her life. She could condemn her commanding officer to death if this high-ranking member of the Dectat had access to her thoughts and knew how close the two of them had been that day. Not to mention, if he was able to read her memory of the encounter with Dtimun on Lagana, which was far more intimate.

"I cannot allow it, sir," she said in a rough whisper. "You must…let me go."

Incredibly, the old one's eyes misted. He made a rough sound in his throat as he lifted his gaze to Dtimun, standing tortured a few steps away.

"Let him mend you," Dtimun said sternly. "It will not matter."

"It will," she whispered. Her eyes, her tormented eyes, met his and went liquid with feelings she couldn't hide, even now. "I am expendable."

"No!" Dtimun raged, the word dragged out of him in anguish.

"*Comcaashe*," the old one told him, gently, involuntarily using the familiar tense of the word. "I know a great deal more than either of you realize. And your commander is right, Ruszel, it does not matter. You must permit me to mend you. Otherwise," he added with a faint smile, "the *kehmatemer* will murder both your commander and me for letting you expire."

"Not true," she whispered, but she was beginning to realize that her old fellow was not the enemy.

"Hahnson even now is mending three humans who tried to stop my men from entering the cave where you were," came the droll reply. "There were many fractures, and you can see the outcome." He gestured where his men were standing frozen, worried, just inside the cave.

"Nice," she managed, "to have friends. Oh!" The pain convulsed her. She could feel her organs starting to shut down.

"You must remain conscious. You must concentrate as I tell you to." The old fellow took her face in his hands again and looked straight into her eyes. "You must instruct your body to mend itself. I will show you how."

It was the most intriguing few minutes of her medical career. She felt the power of the Cehn-Tahr's mind with wonder. This wasn't any ability boosted by microcyborgs. This was pure, raw, power, beyond explanation. She could actually feel the cells of her body reforming in response to his mental commands. It was centuries beyond anything she'd been taught, far beyond the highest medtech interventions known to common science. She felt the old fellow's mind and could not hide her thoughts from him. Nor could he hide his, from her.

She saw great battles. She saw him as a young man, proud and tall and muscular, leading armies. Leading the Holconcom!

"Be still, Ruszel, you are not supposed to see that," he thought to her.

"You were very impressive," she replied silently.

He laughed in her mind. "Yes. She who bonded with me also thought this."

Madeline could see her—a proud, tall, elegant young woman with black hair to her waist and pale blue eyes that suddenly sparked with green laughter as the proud warrior presented her with a single shaft of *canolithe* nestled in an elegant pot. Strange, how familiar that woman looked…

The old fellow's sadness erased the image. "I was arrogant and made bad choices in my life. I lost her, and many of my children. We have been apart for longer than you have lived, but my heart is still owned by her."

"I am sorry for you," she thought back. "I…understand."

"Yes," he replied silently. "You understand all too well, do you not? You could have refused the reassignment, Ruszel. Even Taylor would have been forced to pursue his command through channels."

She conceded the point.

"You could not control your feelings, nor could Dtimun contain his own. So you found a more reckless way to protect Dtimun from contact with you."

She wondered at the pronunciation, because it sounded far different than the way she'd always heard her commander's name used.

The old one ignored the stray thought. "You think that he will die if you live."

"Sir, you must not save me, at the expense of his life," she began miserably.

"That will not happen," he replied firmly. "I will not permit either of you to die."

She drew in a long breath. It didn't hurt.

"You see?" he told her. "Your own mind can control your physical integrity."

"This is centuries advanced from anything I know," she confessed.

"It exists alongside telepathy. You know already that your commander has the gift."

She wasn't going to speculate why he had it. Perhaps the rumors that only the Royal Clan was so gifted was a myth, like so many others.

"Why couldn't he do what you just did?" she wondered.

"Because his attachment to you is too deep," he said simply.

She shook her head. "He feels nothing for me, really, sir," she said gently. "It's a behavior he can't control. It's just a physical response to stimulus, that's all."

He pursed his lips. "You have no idea what methods he used to come to your rescue. It will open your eyes, I think." He thought it with a smile as he got to his feet. "You still have injuries, but Hahnson can deal with those. I must rest. At my age, even such mental exertion has consequences."

"Thank you, sir," she said with gratitude evident in her face.

He studied her silently. "Saving life is an obligation, not a kindness," he said quietly.

She recalled those words spoken almost identically by her C.O. aboard the *Morcai* almost three years ago, when he saved a young alien clone from death.

Dtimun moved forward, almost as if he wanted to interrupt her revealing thoughts. "We must get her aboard ship, where there are more resources for Hahnson to use," he said.

"My thoughts exactly," Hahnson said, rejoining them. "Don't worry, sir, they didn't kill anybody," he added, with a rueful glance at the *kehmatemer*. "What a formidable bunch! I'd hate to see even the Cehn-Tahr members of our unit try them."

"So would I," the old one chuckled. "I will see you later, warwoman." He left, motioning the reluctant members of his unit out with him, reassuring them all the way.

Hahnson read his medcom to her. "Now you only have a pierced lung and concussion, not to mention numerous contusions and lacerations." He shrugged. "A few hours' work and you'll be dancing in the corridor. Well, limping in the corridor. You'll need a couple of weeks of R&R before you return to duty."

She smiled. "Thanks, Strick."

He glanced at Dtimun. "She can't walk."

"Strick can carry me," she said.

"Strick isn't in a rush to die again," the doctor corrected with a meaningful glance at Dtimun, whose eyes were threatening violence, despite the sedative.

Madeline was drowsy. She frowned at the byplay, not understanding.

"If you'll carry her inside, I'll treat her," Hahnson invited.

Dtimun hesitated just for an instant.

"The tranquillizer will keep you from going over the edge for that long," Hahnson told him solemnly. "It's safe."

Dtimun nodded. He bent, slid his arms gently

under Madeline and lifted her, standing up in a graceful, fluid motion as if she weighed nothing at all.

"You can't...they'll court-martial you, they'll space you if they see this!" she protested, struggling.

"Everyone here is Holconcom," Dtimun told her. "Your surviving comrades are unconscious. It does not matter."

"But...!"

"Cease and desist," Dtimun said curtly, turning toward the cave entrance. He folded her even closer, feeling her warm body relax. He was very careful not to contract his arms. It would kill him to injure her even more. "Even the strictest protocols make allowances for extreme circumstances." He strode out into the clearing. Komak and Stern smiled at him.

They moved closer. "Hey, Ladybones," Stern said gently. "How you doing?"

She managed a smile. "Poorly. But I'll heal. Thanks for the mutiny on my behalf," she chuckled, grimacing when it hurt.

Dtimun stiffened. Involuntarily, a faint growl came from him.

Komak moved closer. He said something to Dtimun in the Holy Tongue, that the others couldn't translate.

Dtimun took a deep breath. He nodded. The anger seemed to drain out of him, but Stern moved cautiously back to the others.

The largest of the Nagaashe moved close.

"We know who you are," it thought to Dtimun. "We will keep your secret. We know of the Nagaashe whom you protect on your estates on Memcache, and the child the red-haired female saved. We are in your debt. Our numbers are decimated."

"I understand," he thought back.

"You have risked much to rescue this one. The female is important to you," the serpent added. "Not as a comrade. And she did not come here voluntarily on a military ship."

Dtimun scowled. "No. She was sent here deliberately to provoke a response. We know who, and why."

The serpent's blue eyes closed and opened. "We will not retaliate. But this must not be allowed to happen again." He cocked his great head and his hood vibrated. "You know what we can do. We have no ships, no weapons. But thought can kill. Can destroy. You know this better than any of your crew."

"I do," he replied grimly. "We will not allow another incursion into your planetary system by any Tri-Fleet personnel."

The serpent nodded. "We are sorry for the destruction of the other females. It was not intentional. Their ship was fragile."

"I understand."

"We have told your...old one...that your Dectat may send an ambassador to us, and we will make a treaty with you," the serpent said. "And then we may negotiate for inclusion in your Tri-Galaxy Council."

"The Dectat will be gratified," he thought in reply. The liaison had long been hoped for by the Cehn-Tahr, because the Nagaashe had resources on their planet that no other system offered, especially vast Helium 3 deposits. "And the president of the Council will be gratified as well. I will inform them."

The serpent bowed. So did Dtimun.

The serpent went back to the translator and began to hiss again.

"A whole conversation took place that we missed, right?" Stern whispered to Dtimun.

The alien smiled. "Yes. Pay attention to the negotiations. I may require you to learn Nagaashe."

Stern groaned.

Dtimun carried Ruszel into the ship and down the long corridor to Hahnson's medical unit.

She curled close, drowsy and content, her arm going naturally around his neck. "I was so happy to see you. All of you," she corrected at once, flushing.

"As were we, to see you. We thought you dead."

There was a note in his deep voice, heavily accented all of a sudden.

She opened her eyes and looked up at him, frowning.

"I could not access your mind after the explosion," he said, without looking at her.

"I could have been dead. But you still came?"

He looked down at her with an odd, golden shade in his cat-eyes, one she'd seen before. "I knew you were not dead."

"How?"

"The old one knew. Because Komak was still here," he answered enigmatically. He lifted his eyes back to the corridor and kept walking.

He put her down on an examination table. Komak joined them, his face oddly flushed. "Incredible," he said, staring down at her. "I never believed it possible to land on the Nagaashe planet at all. The treaty is history, but I thought the rest, including this rescue, was only an inflating of the legend. And the identity of those who came with the commander to rescue you…!"

"Excuse me?" Madeline said blankly.

Dtimun glared at the younger alien. But Komak's attention was only on Madeline.

"The identity of your rescuers was also supposed to be part of the legend…!"

"Shut up, Komak," Dtimun said sharply.

"Yes," came a deep voice from the doorway. "Shut up, Komak."

The younger alien tried to bow and salute at the same time as the old fellow marched into the room. Dtimun kicked his boot. Hard.

"You have duties," Dtimun told him.

Komak saluted. "Yes, sir." He grinned, at Dtimun and then the old fellow on his way out. He paused at the door and actually laughed as he went on his way.

"Ruszel," the old fellow greeted her with a smile.

"Sir!" She tried to salute and grimaced. "Sorry, sir, I can't lift my arm."

"There is no need for protocol between us," he replied.

There was a commotion in the hall. The old fellow muttered. "My men will not rest until they see for themselves that you are alive. We shall have to let them in," he said curtly, "or there will be bloodshed. Again." He glanced at Dtimun. "Even your best Holconcom would be hard-pressed to overcome my bodyguard."

"Indeed," Dtimun said with a sigh. He nodded to the Holconcom guard, who stepped back with what looked like relief.

The *kehmatemer* filed in quickly, in formation,

their royal blue uniforms bright in the cubicle's stark lights. They gathered around the examination table, all talking at once. Their captain, Rhemun, silenced them.

"Ruszel, we are happy that you survived," he spoke for them. "We were prepared to give our own blood to recover you! We swore a blood oath!"

She laughed and winced. It hurt. "Thanks, Captain. Hi, guys! I'm so glad to see you. I thought my girls and I would die here."

"Never while there was a breath in my body," Dtimun thought grimly. Madeline and the old fellow both stared at him, Madeline with surprise, as she heard the words in her mind.

"I don't have the words," she said, almost choking on emotion.

The Cehn-Tahr, as a unit, smiled at her with green eyes.

"Come. She needs rest," the old fellow told his unit. "We will speak again, Ruszel. But in the interests of interplanetary relations, you must forget that you have seen us aboard the *Morcai*."

"Seen whom, sir?" she asked with a grin. "It was only the Holconcom here."

He chuckled. The *kehmatemer* tried to bow to Dtimun but he growled at them. They rushed out after the old one.

Madeline eyed him strangely.

He straightened. "I outrank them," he said abruptly.

"Oh. Okay." She glanced at Hahnson, who was placing a healer on her bare stomach and activating it. "How are my girls?" she asked.

"They're still unconscious." The way he said it was odd.

She frowned. "And...?"

He shrugged. "It's better if they don't know the particulars of this expedition," he replied. "They aren't Holconcom, so they don't owe us silence. I knocked them out and I'll keep them that way until we get home. We'll have our story straight by then. They're going to be fine," he added.

She was solemn. "I lost my whole unit except for Darmila and Rayson. It's all Ambassador Taylor's fault!" She looked up at Dtimun. "Sir, if you'll loan me a novapen and turn your back for five minutes when we return to Trimerius, I'll...!"

"Your indignation is understandable," Dtimun interrupted. "But we need him where he is. As a conduit of intel, he is invaluable. We have access to his private communications with the Rojoks. However, a day of reckoning will come. Soon."

"I, uh, have work to do," Hahnson said, smiling as he moved away.

"Thanks, Strick," she replied gently.

"You're very welcome." He gave the C.O. a reassuring look and went to his patients.

Dtimun stared at Madeline for a long moment. His expression was strange.

"Thank you for coming to rescue us. And please thank Lawson and the Council..."

"That...pacifistic...glutted...posturing conglomeration of fools and their prehistoric attitudes!" he growled, whirling. His eyes were dark brown with anger. "The Terravegan ambassador convinced the Council that a rescue mission was not only impossible, but economically hopeless. He demanded the recall of all Terravegan troops from the Holconcom and dared them to refuse under threat of court-martial or spacing! Lawson's hands were tied."

She didn't speak. She didn't know what to say. "Then how...?"

"Your old fellow," he explained, calming a little. "He was contacted by the Nagaashe and led here. I pulled the Holconcom out of the Tri-Galaxy Fleet, with his...and the Dectat's," he corrected abruptly, "permission." He'd heard that from the old one aboard the ship on the way here. From what he learned, the president of the Dectat was apologizing in several dialects for what he'd said. Dtimun chuckled silently. The old one was formidable in council. His presence here alone would ensure that the Dectat couldn't act against Dtimun without implicating the older Cehn-Tahr. And that the Dectat would never dare to do.

She felt warm affection for the old fellow, but shock for the unexpected diplomatic upheaval Dtimun's decision would have had on the Council and even the Tri-Fleet. All that, for a mere woman?

"You are still Holconcom," Dtimun explained solemnly. "We would not leave you to your fate."

She frowned. "If Taylor forbade a rescue attempt—I mean, half the crew is Terravegan...?" She left the question hanging.

"Because of the Terravegan ambassador's threat, I attempted to leave the Terravegans behind, but they mutinied and refused to leave the ship. Then the old fellow and his *kehmatemer* came aboard and also refused to leave," he added with a flash of laughing green eyes.

She began to smile. She'd never felt more valued. It was surprising, but touching. She studied his hard face. The strain of the past few days showed there. "But how did you negotiate for our release? The Cehn-Tahr have no embassy here."

"We picked up a…diplomat, of sorts, who negotiated with the Nagaashe for us. His race has a treaty with the Nagaashe. We are at war with him, but he came with a friend who provided him with a disguise."

He turned toward the open door, and motioned to two figures standing there. One was dressed in the robes of a desert chieftain. He looked quite human-oid, with black hair and eyes and a dark complexion. He smiled, and white teeth flashed at her. His tall, muscular companion was wearing robes like a Ter-ravegan monk, his features obscured, but Madeline was fairly certain that he was a Rojok.

"Ruszel," the chieftain said, still smiling. "With the heart and courage of a galot! Do you remember me?"

She caught her breath. "You're Dacerian," she exclaimed. "Hazheen Kamon, if I recall. The chief of one of the bigger tribes on the planet. The commander offered to trade me to you for a yomuth, as I recall," she added and laughed.

Dtimun's eyes made a green, shimmering smile at the memory.

"That is true," he chuckled, "but I am certain that he didn't mean it. I am, indeed, Hazheen Kamon. Your commander lived with my tribe many decades past, when he was a cadet at the military academy on my world."

"It was the finest military academy in the galaxy," the Rojok added. There was a smile in his voice, which seemed oddly familiar.

"Indeed," Dtimun replied easily, "and friendships made there have outlasted alliances and even wars."

Hazheen Kamon chuckled. "So it seems. It is an honor to aid in your rescue, warwoman," he told Madeline.

"Thank you for your help, sir," Madeline said with genuine gratitude.

"You are welcome." He bowed and nodded to the other two before he left the compartment.

The Rojok moved his hood back and Madeline's gasp of recognition was audible. The "monk" was Chacon himself.

"Sir, the risk…!" she exclaimed.

He shrugged and smiled. "I owe your commander my life. It was little enough to do in return." He wagged a long finger at her. "However, Ruszel, I will expect you to behave with better judgment in the future. You should never have left the Holconcom. Specialists in Cularian medicine are thin on the ground, even in these times."

She managed a wan smile. She couldn't tell him why she'd left. "That's twice I owe you my life, sir," she said.

"One day, you may save mine," he chuckled. He turned and clasped forearms with Dtimun. "Hazheen and I will transfer to the scout ship in your hangar and return to Dacerius before any of your complement and crew recognize me and ask awkward questions. Keep well, Dtimun."

"And you. We owe you a great debt of gratitude for your help."

Chacon replaced his hood and moved back out into the corridor.

"One must say that you collect unique friendships," she told Dtimun. Now she understood Dtimun's relationship with Chacon. Long before the war, the two had been friends at military school.

He clasped his hands behind him as he studied her. "One could say the same for you."

"How is Mallory working out?" she asked.

He sighed. "It would be better not to ask."

"That bad?" she murmured.

"She is terrified of me."

"Imagine that," she murmured dryly. She moved and grimaced. The pain had eased, but there was a lot of discomfort. But she looked at him and helpless delight flooded her.

He stiffened, his lips making a thin line, as the bombardment of pheromones engulfed him in tension. "And here we are again," he muttered. "I shall have to leave or call Hahnson back with more sedative."

She grimaced. "I'm sorry, sir. Really I am."

He drew in a harsh breath. "It's not your fault."

She felt the powerful hum of the ship's engines as it left orbit. "Are we headed back to Trimerius now?" she asked, anticipating that she would be returned almost at once to Admiral Mashita's unit for recuperation.

"No," he said shortly. "We are taking you to Memcache. Caneese has already contacted Admiral Lawson about this. You will stay at Mahkmannah. Lieutenant Mallory and Hahnson will remain, to oversee your care. I have duties that will require a few days in the capital. The Holconcom will be allowed R&R during my absence."

She managed a smile. "They'd probably prefer to go with you. Mahkmannah is rather serene for our crew."

He smiled, too. "I agree. I will take the majority of them with me to the capital and allow them the use of scout ships for their leave."

She settled back down, shifting restlessly. "Thank you for coming after us, sir," she said quietly. "I expected to die, especially when I came to and found myself surrounded by Nagaashe." She frowned. "They really hated the Cehn-Tahr."

His eyes narrowed. "There was something more, was there not? A reason that they contacted the old fellow instead of letting you die?"

She nodded. She hesitated. "I showed them the memory I had, when you saved the little Altairian child aboard ship, just after you rescued us from the Rojoks near Terramer."

He didn't say anything for a few seconds. She knew he was reading, also, her helpless disclosure of that one day with him on Memcache. She had been forced, unwilling, to allow the old fellow access to it as well.

"You wanted to refuse the old one access to your thoughts," he said. "It would have meant your death."

"He belongs to the Dectat," she said softly. "I was afraid that he might put duty above comradeship."

"Once, long ago, that might have been true. He and I have been adversaries for longer than you have lived," he added. "But because of you, wounds have been mended. Many wounds."

"I haven't done much lately, except mess things up," she sighed.

He cocked his head and studied her with faint green eyes. "You have made possible a treaty with the Nagaashe which none of our best diplomats could manage in over a century of negotiation."

"Well, that was an accident."

"For our people, a very good accident." He frowned quizzically. "It is curious to me to consider that one human female, fragile and quite frankly insubordinate, is responsible for so many changes in my society in such a short time."

"I could be responsible for a good one in my society if you'd give me a weapon and five minutes alone with Ambassador Taylor."

He laughed. "Not possible."

"Darn."

"You must rest," he said. "The old fellow is also recovering. His mental gifts are formidable. Perhaps that is one of the few benefits of all the DNA tampering."

"There are others," she replied. "The Cehn-Tahr have protected many races from extinction by madmen like Mangus Lo and Chan Ho. Your altered genome is responsible for the abilities that made that possible."

"Yes, but the burden of those abilities is also ever present." His eyes narrowed on her face, and she understood what he meant.

She sighed and closed her eyes. "I've already said that I could take megavitamins and work out with weights," she said drowsily. "Maybe have a few injections of whatever they put in Stern's bones to make them hard as steel..."

She drifted off. His eyes flashed green at the insinuations, and then became a somber blue as he realized what a dream that was. She would never be able to withstand a Cehn-Tahr bonding.

CHAPTER FIFTEEN

MADELINE WAS TAKEN to the fortress near which she had first met Caneese, in the religious compound at Mahkmannah on Memcache. The older woman was there to meet the ambutube, tossing out instructions as if the fortress were as familiar to her as her own home.

Madeline noticed it. Dtimun only smiled.

Lieutenant Edris Mallory and Dr. Strick Hahnson were guiding the ambutube into the bedroom that Caneese signified. It was bigger than the entire barracks where Madeline had lived for most of her career as a medical practitioner.

"Here?" she asked weakly as two strong attendants eased her out of the ambutube and onto a bed which seemed big enough for six people.

"Here," Caneese said gently, and with a smile. "You are an honored guest."

"Why?" Madeline asked bluntly. "All I did was get blown up by some angry serpents."

Caneese laughed. "You made peace with the serpents, who have been our adversaries since the Great Galaxy War. The Dectat is in an uproar. Our finest diplomats have tried for decades to bring about a treaty with the Nagaashe, who have abundant stores of Helium 3. You accomplished this in less than a solar week."

"It was an accident, I assure you," she said with a wan smile. "And not due to any diplomatic skills I possess. They were impressed because I saved the little serpent here..." She stopped because Mallory was giving her an odd look.

Caneese laughed. "She called a flock of Meg-Ravens to save the little Nagaashe. It lives here on our...on the estate, with its parents." The slip was so smoothly covered that only Madeline noted that it had been made. If Madeline had been less nauseated by the trip, she might have realized more than she did.

She wanted to tell her fellow humans that the Nagaashe could travel through time, but she didn't. That was a private matter.

Caneese nodded; she heard the thought. She turned at an odd, uneven step coming closer. "Oh, dear," she said softly. "Madeline, I fear that your presence here may attract consequences."

Madeline's first thought was that the emperor might send a squad to evict her from his planet.

Caneese laughed. "Certainly not!" she exclaimed. "He has made a public announcement of your achievement and means to honor you in the Dectat. No, I meant Rognan."

Edris Mallory blinked. "Who is Rognan?"

Caneese nodded toward the doorway with a re-signed sigh.

Rognan, the Meg-Raven, clomped toward them on his bad leg, making a horrible screeching sound. "Rus...zel," he wailed. "Rus...zel not dead?"

"Ruszel is not dead," Caneese assured him, moving back quickly, as if she were afraid of him.

The huge bird moved to Ruszel's side. He laid his huge head against her arm. "Scared," he croaked. His feathered body shivered.

Madeline put an arm around him, and then lifted her hand to stroke the silky feathers. "No need," she said softly, touched by the bird's obvious concern and affection. "I'm going to be fine. Just fine. There, there, it's all right."

Edris was staring, mesmerized, at the enormous avian. "He can speak Standard," she exclaimed. "Does he know you?" she asked her comrade.

"Yes. I came here once, with the commander," Ruszel said. "It was when I rescued the little Nagaashe."

"Rognan has been fascinated with her, because she can speak in his language," Caneese explained. "Very few humanoids can master the bird speech. It is extremely complicated…"

A burst of Meg-Raven speech came from the doorway, where Komak was just entering. His eyes were a mischievous green as he communicated something to the bird, which no one else in the room understood.

Rognan turned and clomped over to him, enveloping him with one huge wing. He spoke in his own tongue in return, and laid his head against Komak's chest.

"How very strange," Caneese exclaimed. "He does not like strangers, even if they are Cehn-Tahr. And how is it that you can manage his language so easily?"

Komak moved to the older woman and touched her cheek before he bent to lay his forehead against hers, as Madeline had seen Dtimun do. "It is a long story," he chuckled.

Caneese returned the gesture. Her eyes went an opaque blue as they searched his. "But, it is not possible," she stammered in Cehn-Tahr.

"It will be," he replied in the same tongue, smiling. "We have much to discuss. You are about to make an astounding discovery."

"I am?" Caneese queried.

"Could the two of you possibly speak in Standard?" Madeline asked.

They turned and stared at her, and she had a sudden shock of recognition. They looked very much alike.

They looked at each other and Komak pursed his lips. "Well, not so very much," he commented. "She is female." He frowned and turned back to Madeline. "I do not look like a female?" he asked with such horror that everyone laughed.

The question diverted them, which had been its purpose. No one seemed to realize that Komak had answered a question which Ruszel had not voiced.

"We should leave Madelineruszel alone, so that she can have peace and quiet in which to heal," Komak commented.

"Yes, we should," Hahnson agreed. He checked her over with his wrist unit one more time and nodded, satisfied.

"I can stay with you, if you like," Edris offered, and in a very enthusiastic manner.

Caneese gave her a wry glance, as if she understood something the rest did not. "Captain Rhemun will only be here for two days," she said. "I promise."

Edris made a face. "Very well, ma'am." She smiled at Madeline. "I'll see you later. We're not lifting for a few more days, either. The commander says he has duties in the capital, so we might as well be on hand here if you need us." Her lips thinned as she pressed them together. "He didn't mention that the captain of the *kehmatemer* would be around, also. Captain Rhemun absolutely hates humans," she informed Caneese. "But he likes Dr. Ruszel, and she's human!" she added.

"It is a long story, and this is not the time," Caneese said, but smiled to lessen the sting of the remark. "I will tell it to you one day."

Edris nodded. "If you need us," she told Madeline, and placed a synthcomm on Madeline's wrist, which, if pressed, would alert the medics that they were required.

"I'll call," Madeline promised. "Thanks, Edris. And thank you, Strick," she added.

He chuckled. "I didn't do much. Your 'old fellow' saved you," he reminded her.

"He did," she recalled, "with some of the most astounding methods I've ever known. I could do a dissertation on what he taught me."

"Not a bad idea, to revisit your doctoral studies."

"I'll think about that."

He and Edris left with the attendants, Komak and Rognan. Caneese remained. She sat down gracefully in a chair beside the huge bed.

"This 'old fellow' of yours," she began. "How did you meet him?"

Madeline sank back into the pillows and related the events that had happened on Ondar.

"If your colleague Mallory thinks that Captain Rhemun hates humans," she began, "she knows nothing of the prejudice that has existed against humans here. Your 'old fellow' leads the *kehmatemer*, and he has been the single most adversarial member of the Dectat on racial policy."

"Yes. He tried to order my execution when the commander added me to the Holconcom," Madeline recalled. She smiled gently. "But his attitude changed when we went into battle together."

"You and his men went into battle," came the soft correction, and a laugh. "You could not mend him completely, although you saved his life. And now he has saved yours." She tilted her head. "Is it not amazing, the reciprocity of existence?"

"One event links to another event, like links in a chain," Madeline agreed. "You and Komak favor each other very much."

The older woman caught her breath at the sudden change of topic. She averted her eyes. "We Cehn-Tahr all resemble each other. We do not have the variations in color that you humans do. We all have pale golden skin and black hair."

"You aren't going to tell me, are you, ma'am?" Madeline asked.

Caneese laughed. "I would not dare. Komak has knowledge of a plot," she added more solemnly, "that may involve some risk to you and Dtimun."

She noted again that odd pronunciation of the commander's name which the old fellow had given it. Perhaps it was some pronunciation that outworlders weren't privy to; due to relationships or social status names were pronounced in different ways by different members of the society.

"But we can speak of this later. Your 'old fellow' has a voice in the making of policy. He now favors great changes. Your influence is being felt in the very heart of the Dectat. It is the prophecy, Madeline. You carry the future inside you."

"You were right, about the danger, and the sacrifice," Madeline said, almost awed by the prophecy that had been so accurate.

Caneese nodded sadly. "I had hoped to see the future well enough to warn you. If I had, this would not have happened to you."

"Such gifts are not always perfect," Madeline said gently. "And I was rescued, against impossible odds."

"Indeed you were."

Madeline blinked. She felt very tired.

"Yes, you are tired. You have been through a traumatic ordeal, and you should rest." Caneese got to her feet. She paused beside the bed to smooth back Madeline's hair. "It is the most incredible color," she commented. "I have never seen anything like it."

Her touch was gentle, like her voice. Madeline had never known a woman's influence, having been raised in a military fashion. It was comforting.

She hesitated. "You would have sacrificed your life, to prevent the authorities from seeing how your commander reacted to you. It was a noble thing to do."

So much for hiding her relationship with Dtimun, if it could be called that. Her eyes met the other woman's and she sighed. "I lived on dreams, after we came here that day. Then he told me the truth." Her eyes lowered. "Something died in me. I went back to the only other life I knew, when Ambassador Taylor threatened to reveal what had happened in the gym. A crewmate was teaching me hand-to-hand combat techniques, touching me. The commander saw. He reacted violently."

Caneese sat down on the bed at Madeline's side. "It is of great sadness to us, that the addition of galot DNA produced such negative characteristics in us, especially in our men. We have feline traits which are never revealed to outworlders. The mating cycle is one of them. Once initiated, it escalates in violence until the very life of the female partner is threatened. We have tried for decades to find a method to diminish the violence, without success."

Madeline nodded. She knew, too, that the uncanny strength of the Cehn-Tahr male would make mating with a human impossible. Hahnson's example was proof of it.

Caneese's face was sad, but her eyes began to twinkle. "Your friend Komak has access to tech which is of an odd and inexplicable source."

"Rojok tech?" Madeline wondered worriedly.

Caneese sighed. "Not that. The 'old fellow' told Dtimun that he thinks Komak comes from the future. He knows the pattern of things that happen, but not the details. It is as if," she pondered, "he read about this epoch in a book which provided only highlighted episodes and not explicit passages." She didn't dare add what she herself had seen in Komak's mind. Not yet.

Madeline frowned. Now that she thought about it, Komak always seemed to know what was coming.

She had put it down to intuition. But what if he really did come from the future? Did he have relatives here? Did he know any of the crew in the future? Did he know Madeline in the future? And if he was out of place and time, why had he stayed so long? Perhaps he was unable to return to his own time.

"I do not think so," Caneese interrupted her thoughts.

"But he's been here a very long time," Madeline commented.

"Time is fluid, like water, and has currents. Perhaps in his own time, he has only been gone for seconds." She smiled. "I did study theoretical physics, in my youth."

"Has your hair always been silver?" Madeline asked.

"No. It was black when I was a young female, and very long. He with whom I bonded found it fascinating." She laughed. "He brought me a pot of canolithe…" She stopped suddenly at Madeline's gasp. "You saw that, in his mind, when he saved your life. You must never say it to another living soul!"

Madeline was puzzled, but she agreed. "I have never told anything that I know. The commander is a telepath. So is the old fellow, and you. And Komak, too." She frowned. "But I was taught that only the Royal Clan had such abilities."

Caneese toyed with the bedspread. "Yes, such misrepresentations are common, because we seem mysterious to outworlders."

"The old fellow said that he had lost his family," Madeline said delicately.

Caneese nodded. "My mate and I had a furious ar-

gument when my eldest son was killed, in the Great
Galaxy War. I swore that I would never forgive him.
I came here, to Mahkmannah, and became a religious. I was so certain that I was right. But over the
decades, I have started to doubt my certainties. Perhaps I was wrong, too."

"You and the old fellow," Madeline began. "Are
you...?"

"Did the others not leave, so that Madeline could
rest?" Dtimun asked from the doorway, deliberately
interrupting the conversation.

Caneese laughed and got up. "Yes. I have been
bombarding her with questions. I am sorry," she told
Madeline. "You may not know that you are becoming well-known here, and many of us are curious
about you."

Madeline smiled. Her eyelids were drooping.
"Flattering," she said in a flyaway voice. She was
drifting off.

"It is not flattery," Caneese denied. "You are unlike anyone I have ever met, of any species."

But Madeline didn't hear her. The stress and pain
had combined with Hahnson's painkiller to knock
her out. She didn't want to sleep. She wanted to look
at the commander. It was impossible. She was already asleep.

Dtimun stood at the edge of the bed and studied
her with barely controlled instincts raging.

Caneese laid a gentle hand on his arm, calming
him. "Many things are happening that I would not
have believed possible, even though I was certain that
the prophecy was a true one."

He nodded, his hands behind his back. "Komak

will not tell me what he knows." He turned to her. "But he says that events are in motion that will require a great sacrifice from Madeline and from me. He intends to speak to us about it later, when she is better."

She nodded. "I have also seen this turbulent future, but not with his clarity."

"Who is he?"

"A traveler in the wastelands of the galaxies," she said. "And do not attempt to read my mind. I can shield it, as you well know."

He smiled. "Forgive me."

She reached up and touched his cheek. "Of course. As I always have."

He felt a sense of guilt from his long absence. His anger at the old fellow had also alienated him from Caneese. His regrets lay on the surface, easily read.

"We must not dwell on the past," Caneese said softly. "But we must look to the future now." She sighed. "You know that Lyceria maintains contact with Chacon, despite the war and her possible prosecution. Even her rank would not save her."

"He cares for her as well," Dtimun replied, remembering the Rojok warlord's urgent help to rescue Lyceria from the horrors of the Rojok prison, Ahkmau, during the Holconcon's imprisonment there.

"She would do anything to save Chacon." She looked at the bed. "Just as Ruszel was willing to sacrifice her career, even her life, to save yours."

His face revealed nothing.

"She is quite beautiful," Caneese commented when she noticed Dtimun staring at Ruszel.

Hahnson had given him another dose of tranquillizer to keep his emotions in check. What he felt, he would not disclose.

Caneese attempted to probe his mind, but met a wall. She laughed. "You could always block me."

"I could return the compliment."

"What will happen to her?" she asked him, nodding toward Madeline. "Will the human ambassador try to send her again into combat when she returns to duty?"

"I think this is possible. I could transfer her back to the Holconcom, override him. But that would threaten her more than remaining in the Amazon Division."

Caneese turned to him, her face solemn. "What if it were possible for you to mate with her, without harming her?"

A tiny hint of expression escaped his iron control. "That is not possible by any means we know."

"Komak has found a way."

"You have dared to discuss this with Komak?" he demanded imperiously.

She drew herself up to her full height, which was formidable. "Remember to whom you speak!" she said shortly.

He straightened his posture. "Excuse me."

She nodded, placated. "I saw it in his mind. Komak has some stake in this, I know not what. He has secret tech which he is employing with viruses as a medium."

"Tech?"

"A way to increase Ruszel's strength, improve her genome."

"Genetic engineering," he said coldly. "Think of what the same modifications did to us, as a species.

Once the matrix is replaced, it would be impossible for her to return to what she was. There could be terrible consequences."

Caneese read the concern in him. "There could," she agreed. "But Komak is from the future," she reminded him. "If there were consequences from this, he would know."

That was true. But he was still uneasy.

"When he speaks to both of you, ask him," Caneese advised. "It might quiet your mind. He can tell you what he knows about Chacon and Lyceria as well," she added enigmatically. "What he will ask concerns you. And her."

He was looking at Madelinc. He was stiff with reserve and control. She was so beautiful. He forced himself to turn away.

"You know already what he proposes," he guessed.

She smiled gently. "I know. But it is for him to tell you. Let us go," she added, glanced at Madeline. "She needs rest."

He nodded and followed her out of the room, his mind in turmoil.

HE STOPPED BY Caneese's lab, which was in an adjacent building on the estate. Komak was there, surrounded by exotic technology in the lab, so deep in thought that he didn't hear the approach of the commander.

"What sort of tech is this that you are developing?" Dtimun asked curtly.

Surprised, Komak turned. For an instant, there was something oddly human in his expression. "A revolutionary discovery," he told the other alien with sparkling green eyes. "Caneese was given the Dectat's highest civilian medal for it…that is, she will be given it."

Dtimun paused beside him, his eyes on the array of virtual comps and accelerated microscopes. On the screen was a genetic matrix that was strangely familiar. Before he could study it, Komak discreetly made it vanish.

"There are some things that you must not know," Komak explained, and now he was solemn. "In the future, string theory has been proven by time travel. We now know that all possibilities have a physical expression. This timeline," he said, waving his hand around, "is the best of many. But it cannot happen without intervention. Madelineruszel is the key to the future. She is the mother of change."

Dtimun frowned. "What sort of change?"

"Peace," the younger alien said flatly.

"That would be a change, indeed," came the quiet reply.

"However," Komak continued, "it is a choice she must make for herself. We cannot interfere, except to make the future possible."

Dtimun scowled at the materials Komak had assembled. "What do you know about the future?" he asked bluntly.

Komak got up and stared into the older man's eyes. "I will explain that to you and to Madelineruszel when she is a little more healed. But it will involve travel, and covert activity. " He stopped, his lips thinning. "I will say no more, for the moment. But the future is in grave peril. You and Madelineruszel, Chacon and Lyceria form a link that will affect the fate of three galaxies."

"This travel you infer. If I travel with Ruszel, she will die," Dtimun said icily. "She is prey. Do you understand?"

Komak nodded solemnly. "That is why I have been working here." He indicated the paraphernalia around him. "I brought a formula back with me. I have synthesized a chemical catalyst which will effect the same change in Madelineruszel's anatomy which was produced in Stern's by the Rojok cloning process."

"This would make it possible for her to bond with me," he said without any expression in his tone.

"Yes," Komak said. "But not for the reason you think. It will make it possible for the two of you to save the Rojok warlord Chacon. If you do not," he added quietly, "things will happen that will tear the galaxies apart."

Dtimun scowled at him. "What things?"

Komak groaned. "I cannot tell you."

Dtimun's eyes narrowed. "You are a descendant of someone living here, now."

Komak nodded.

"Can you tell me who?"

Komak shook his head. "Some things I am not allowed to mention. I am a scientist, but I am also a historian. Records of this time period were destroyed in the worst solar flare our world has ever experienced. No hard copy had been kept, owing to a mistake in archiving, so everything was lost. Elders were questioned, especially the emperor, about the missing time. The emperor was not forthcoming about some areas, so I thought it best to investigate for myself and make vids of the time period." He pursed his lips. "Some of them will entertain you in the future."

"You have been here for almost three years," Dtimun began.

Komak laughed. "When I return, it will be more like one standard hour since I jumped here through time. Time is fluid and there are currents, which must be maneuvered. I am quite good at it by now. I have visited many epochs in our civilization, and in other civilizations."

Dtimun shook his head. "It is a difficult concept."

"Yes, I know." Komak was serious now. "I must leave soon, and go back to my own time," he said sadly. "I have enjoyed this visit more than you can know. To me, this time period was only history, and fragmented at that. To have known you and Madelineruszel as comrades..." He stopped, swallowed and averted his eyes. "It has been an honor to serve with you both. I will...miss you."

Emotion was hard for Dtimun. Since childhood, he had been taught to contain his emotions, to behave as a person of his station was expected to behave. That rigidity was difficult to relax, especially when the confusion of his need for Ruszel was shaking his control as well.

"I will miss the irritation," he replied with faint humor, and his eyes flashed green as they met Komak's. He frowned. "Why leave now? Is there some urgency that requires your departure?"

Komak's green eyes twinkled. "A great urgency."

"Will we meet again?" Dtimun asked curiously.

"Yes, we will. Although," he added softly, "you may not recognize me."

"And now you speak in riddles."

"I must," Komak said gently. He indicated the experiment. "I have given Caneese a formula for another drug, which will be needed as time goes by. Since she is credited with creating both substances, I am not interfering in the timeline." He was somber. "There is a great risk for Madelineruszel if she carries your child. I need not tell you the dangers."

Dtimun frowned. "This will be possible?"

"Yes," Komak assured him. "The catalyst guarantees it. She will still have frailties, despite her increased strength. The pregnancy will be dangerous. It could kill her. I do not think it will. But there is still a possibility."

Having so recently retrieved her from certain death, he felt great concern at putting her again at risk while she was still recovering from her ordeal.

"That is a decision she must make," Komak reiterated. "I will speak to you both soon. Let her decide. You cannot decide for her."

Dtimun's jaw tautened. "In your future," he asked, "is she still alive?"

Komak brightened. "In this timeline? Yes. She commands a whole division of female troops and sneaks out with them on missions," he chuckled. "She is a brigadier general," he added. "And before you ask, yes, Caneese and the old fellow are also still around."

"In this timeline."

Komak nodded. "There are others. Less desirable. If Chacon dies."

"Then, he must not," Dtimun replied. "When do you leave?"

"Not just yet," Komak mused. "There are still a few things I wish to know." What they were, he didn't say.

Dtimun left him to his work. He smiled at the thought of Madeline as a brigadier general. He hadn't wanted to know more. Even if by some miracle it was possible for him to bond with her, to save Chacon, there were political considerations which would make a future with her impossible. He was not sure about the child; he personally thought it unlikely that two such different species could breed. It would at least end his own torment. But what about Madeline? And what of the child they created? He hoped Komak was right, about the future, about the fact that it could be saved

Komak, watching him leave, hoped with all his heart that this precious timeline would survive. Everything would depend on Madeline's decision. But the chemical catalyst that would make her as strong as a Cehn-Tahr woman, that would give her the choice of bonding with Dtimun, to save Chacon and the princess, was already complete.

All that now remained was for Madeline to agree to its use. If she refused, for any reason, disaster would ensue. Komak felt a shiver of cold at the alternate reality which he had already seen. If Madeline Ruszel made the wrong decision, the future would be a nightmare.

CHAPTER SIXTEEN

MADELINE WAS FEELING much better. Caneese had the staff of the fortress, as Madeline thought of it, concoct recipes with tastes that appealed to a human palate.

The room had been filled with pots of wonderful flowers that emitted a subtle perfume, one that didn't cause the head stuffiness that some plants did. The window was open, so that Madeline could look out on the formal gardens behind the structure. Imagine a simple soldier in a place like this, she thought, and was more aware than ever of the differences between herself and the Holconcom commander. He was obviously an aristocrat, important in his society far beyond his abilities to command a crack military unit. The hopelessness of her situation didn't improve with that thought. Soon, when she healed, she must return to the Amazon Division, to war and more war until the conflict with the Rojoks was resolved, one way or another. And that didn't appear to be an event that would occur soon.

She pulled her aching body out of bed, in its silky blue gown, and she made her way to the stone casement of the window. Below was the panorama of distant mountains and green hills and plains. Closer was the garden with its mix of color and scent, with stone benches all around, so that visitors could sit and admire the scenery. Huge insects, like butterflies, were landing delicately on the blossoms. She sighed with appreciation of the sight.

"You should not be out of bed," Dtimun commented as he entered.

Her heart hammered, as it always did when he was in the vicinity. His face tautened as the flood of pheromones washed over him. Despite Hahnson's tranquillizer, he had to fight his instincts.

She grimaced at his taut expression and climbed back into bed, pulling the covers up. She still wasn't used to a male who saw her in a nonmilitary way. She only wished that she could control her reaction to him.

"Sorry, sir," she said formally.

He relaxed, but only a little. "You are feeling better?"

"Much," she said. "I'm still a little weak but most of the damage has already healed." She frowned. "Something has upset you."

He glared at her.

"Hey," she said, holding up both hands, "you walk in and out of my mind all the time. It was my turn."

"Komak wants to speak to you. To both of us," he corrected. He turned to the door and nodded.

Komak came into the room. He locked the door and disabled all the ABVDs and sensors. He was oddly somber, not the high-spirited comrade Madeline had come to know, at all.

"You are wondering what I have to say," he said. He smiled at the commander. "But I think you, at least, already have some idea from when we last spoke together."

Dtimun moved to Madeline's side. His posture, his eyes, were threatening. Komak was careful to keep his distance. He knew the dangers, when a Cehn-Tahr male was in hunting mode. Any threat would be met by deadly force.

"Yes," Dtimun replied. "Caneese says that you know the future, even better than she can discern, with her gifts." His eyes grew opaque, but he couldn't penetrate the other alien's mind. "It disturbs me that you can block me," he added.

Komak smiled. "Necessary, I'm afraid," he replied. "There are things I dare not tell either of you." He folded his hands behind him. "I come from the future. From a future," he qualified, taking in Madeline's surprised look, "that is the best of several timelines, for all of us." His face grew hard. "You have both studied theoretical physics. You know about string theory, multiple universes based on each version of a pivotal choice made at a certain time in a person's life, yes?"

They both nodded.

"In this timeline," he continued, "there will be an attempt on Chacon's life. It will come from a trusted source, unexpectedly. If it succeeds," he added, "the three galaxies will be plunged into a war which will decimate our people, and the humans..."

"Komak, we're already at war, and Chacon is the enemy," Madeline pointed out.

"Yes. But you do not know the future, Madelineruszel."

She sat up straighter, tugging the cover up to her neck. Dtimun seemed to relax when she did that. He perceived any other male as a threat, she thought.

He gave her a glance with amused green eyes. "Precisely," he thought to her.

He turned his attention back to Komak. "What will happen, if Chacon dies?" he asked.

Komak's eyes were haunted. He hadn't wanted to say. But he had to convince them of the necessity to act. "What I have seen," he said, "is shattering. Memcache, Trimerius, the Terravegan colonies, all gone, decimated by a weapon of extreme power."

"Gone?" Dtimun exclaimed. "There is no such weapon in existence."

"Yet," Komak qualified. "And if we act now, there will never be. There is an alternate timeline, in which Chacon is assassinated." He swallowed. "Chacon has been the only barrier to Mangus Lo, and then Chan Ho's, imperialist madness. He opposed them in council, and his great popularity as a war leader curbed their ambitions. They could not kill him openly because they would be suspected, and deposed. However, his death permits Chan Ho to put his best scientists to work to devise a new and powerful emerillium plasma weapon the like of which the universe has never seen, using stolen tech acquired from the capture of one of your *kelekom* operators," he told Dtimun. "Neither the Cehn-Tahr Empire nor the Terravegan government will have any knowledge of its existence until it is used, and the weapon is a planet killer. The first blow will be unexpected, and so powerful that none of the governments will be able to recover from it. Chan Ho will put himself at the head of the Tri-Galaxy Council, without protest once the power of his weapon is demonstrated. He will become dictator of the three galaxies. The result will be...horrible."

Dtimun just stared at him. "It is a possibility, not a certainty."

Komak smiled sadly. "It is a certainty," he corrected. "Even allowing for small modifications of decisions, protests, intervention, the outcome is predictable. I have traveled back many times, to many worlds. I have seen this result over and over again in all of them. Chacon's death is the catalyst, the common denominator. If he survives, so do all of us." He hadn't meant to say that, but his face didn't reveal it, and they were too intent on his prediction to notice, thankfully.

"Do you know when, and how, the assassin will strike?" Madeline asked.

Komak drew in a long breath. "Not exactly," he confessed. "You see, I know the overall pattern of this future, but I have been unable to chart specific events. It is like a skeleton with no flesh. I must extrapolate from historical certainties."

"Coming here must affect the timeline," Dtimun pointed out.

Komak shook his head. "Not if it is done correctly, and I am quite efficient." He cocked his head, studying the two of them. "Caneese has also seen the result that I see, although her methods are less scientific than mine. We are both concerned."

"Is there a way to prevent the assassination?" Dtimun asked finally.

"I think so. But it will involve some difficult decisions, for both of you."

"For us?" Madeline asked, glancing at the commander, whose face was unreadable.

Komak nodded. "I am 95 percent certain that the attempt will take place at Benaski Port. The Princess Lyceria will be involved, in some fashion, as will a certain member of your Clan's household," he told Dtimun with a mysterious smile.

Dtimun glared at him. He didn't like being reminded of his household.

"Lyceria, will she be hurt?" Dtimun asked.

Komak shook his head. "I do not think so. If my calculations are correct, she is the reason that Chacon will go to Benaski Port."

"Why?" Dtimun asked irritably.

"Because she will ask Chacon to meet her there. She has knowledge of the plot and has been unable to reach him with her comms."

"Then we can stop it now," Dtimun said, rubbing his communicator ring to bring up the interface.

"I do not think so," Komak said, stopping him. "It is already too late. She has left Memcache. You can verify this later. You must listen to me. I have little time left here."

"You're leaving?" Madeline asked.

"I must," he said, and regret was in his expression. He went closer to Dtimun. They were of a similar height, and Madeline found it odd that they resembled each other when they stood together. She'd never noticed that before.

"Benaski Port is the haunt of outlaws and thieves," Komak continued. "The pirate who controls it has sensors in place to guarantee that no Tri-Fleet military personnel will set foot there, even though it is a neutral port. He has an arrangement with the Rojok Empire and I can assure you that no covert infiltrator with a sensor net has ever been able to make port there."

"I see," Dtimun replied. He was concerned, and it showed.

"Chacon will land on Benaski Port because of Princess Lyceria. While he is there, a trusted colleague will arrange his assassination, or his kidnapping, that is not precisely clear in my calculations. But the princess has covert knowledge of the attempt and wants to warn him of a threat. She has no real knowledge of what the threat may be."

"Then why go?" Dtimun asked angrily.

"Because she loves him."

"Love," Dtimun said, and his expression made Madeline's heart fall. "A primitive, ridiculous emotion which has no place in the scheme of things." He shifted uncomfortably, his need of Madeline making him more irritable, and the dravelzium Hahnson had given him was beginning to work out of his system.

Komak's elongated eyes turned green, signifying that he was, oddly, amused.

"Then what do you suggest?" Dtimun continued.

"This will be difficult, for both of you." Komak hesitated. "It is known in the galaxies that our people permit no bonding with other species, and that no artificial means of conception are permitted, and that the Terravegan military punishes its members for intimate contact with the other sex. It is also a fact that any Cehn-Tahr who mates with a human, if that were possible, would be immediately put to death for violation of the Species Act. These factors would give you a disguise that even the best sensors on Benaski Port would not be able to question. As renegades, outcasts facing death from two governments, you would be accepted as residents without question—the fact of the child would certainly give you a perfect reason for being there. You would blend in perfectly, a Cehn-Tahr aristocrat and his human mate, hiding from the authorities."

Dtimun studied Madeline with barely concealed hunger. He glanced at Komak. "You have already stated the impossibility of such a liaison."

"Yes, but as I explained to you earlier, I have a solution. I brought from the future a method which will make conception possible, and, hopefully, give the pregnancy a great chance of success. Caneese is already credited with both scientific accomplishments, so I am not changing the timeline." He smiled. "Her skills in biochemistry are truly unsurpassed."

Madeline was fighting a hunger of her own. She'd never wanted a child. But now... She swallowed. "Komak, how would you accomplish this? The differences in our species..."

"The first drug is used in genetic modification," he told Madeline. "It would change your genome, give you both equal strength and permit you to mate with the commander."

Her heart jumped.

"No," Dtimun said coldly. "I forbid it."

She glanced up at him. "Sir, you can't forbid it if I decide to agree," she pointed out. She glowered at him. "I know that you can't help being possessive, under the circumstances. However, I do mind if you try to make decisions for me. Sir." She pursed her lips and her eyes twinkled.

He shook his head. "Never in my life," he began.

"Yes," she agreed. She grinned. "See what you've been missing?"

His eyes flared green before he could contain the humor. But he quickly corrected it and his attention went back to Komak. "You see what genetic modification has done to my Clan, and others related to it," he told Komak quietly. "It has destroyed the basic genetic identity of our people, changed us into beings that are more galot than humanoid."

An odd statement, Madeline thought. He didn't in any way resemble a cat.

He glanced at her. He was keeping so many secrets from her. Was it fair to let her genome be altered before she knew the whole truth of what the Cehn-Tahr were?

"It will be all right," Komak told him gently. "You must trust me. I see farther than you can." He moved to face both of them. "More depends on this than I can tell you. The two of you must discuss it. But it must be a mutual decision, or I will not intervene, regardless of the outcome. It is dangerous. The genetic modification will not be a threat, but the pregnancy will." His face hardened. "In the history of our species, there has never been a Cehn-Tahr/human hybrid."

"The child," Madeline asked, her voice strangely gentle, "he would be…he would not be able to breed."

Komak raised an eyebrow and his eyes twinkled green. "I assure you, that is not, will not, be the case. Our methods of genetic modification are, well, advanced."

"We allow no modification of conception, or termination," Dtimun began.

"The Dectat has brainwashed you," Komak accused with howling green eyes. "Do you honestly believe that all Cehn-Tahr are intimate only for the creation of children? Do you believe that no artificial means of conception are used? Because I can quote future statistics of this era which will raise your hair. Sir."

Dtimun was torn between amusement and ruffled dignity. Amusement won. His eyes flashed green. "I must admit that life without you in the Holconcom will be far less eventful," he said, hiding a sadness that the younger alien must leave. "You have been a fine officer."

"Thank you," Komak said. "It has been an honor, and a privilege to serve with you both, to know you as comrades," he added, implying that he might know them as something else in his own time.

"There is the matter of the pregnancy," Dtimun said, his eyes quiet for a minute on Madeline's flushed face. "Both our governments set the death penalty for such interaction. And there is the matter of the child, if conceived," he added. "Termination is not possible, in our culture. Especially for me."

Komak nodded. "The solution is not yet apparent. You must trust me. Things are in motion that will make this conversation quite irrevelent in the near future."

"Trust you." Dtimun glowered at him. "I recall hearing this many times, one of which preceded an enemy agent being stuffed alive into a plasma oven for interrogation."

Komak's eyebrows arched. "I did not kill him," he reminded Dtimun. He grinned. "And he was quite talkative when I took him out."

Dtimun actually chuckled. Madeline was laughing openly. Komak was incorrigible. She would miss him.

"You must not be concerned about your military," Komak told Madeline gently. "Or the child. It will happen as fate decides. And as things now stand, there will be a gentle and good resolution."

Madeline didn't quite believe that. She was a combat officer now. She couldn't keep a child or terminate it, and that only left…regression; returning the fetus to its individual components in a gentle process that simply unmade it. She'd seen it done, once. The fetus registered no discomfort at all. Still, it had been traumatic for Madeline, for reasons she didn't understand.

"You must not think of it," Dtimun told her at once, his eyes solemn. "We must trust that Komak knows more than we do." He glanced at the other alien and his eyes narrowed. "You are certain that I will not kill her in the process? You know more than she does about the first mating, about the violence of it."

Komak nodded. "She will not be quite as strong as you are. Her human makeup will not make that possible. But she will be able to endure it, with some help from dravelzium and medical care afterwards."

Madeline was looking worried. Komak smiled. "It is only the first mating that presents such problems…"

"Bataashe!" Dtimun snapped at him, and his posture became menacing.

Komak held up both hands. "I forget, that in your time, these things are taboo to discuss, even with Clan intimates," he said. "I apologize. I meant no offense."

"It's all right," Madeline said in a soft tone. "These are things I really need to know. Okay?"

Her tone calmed him. He took a long breath and straightened, but the strain was showing. "Can you make dravelzium?" he asked her tautly.

She nodded. She opened the wrist scanner and went through the combinations, producing a laserdot with the usual amount. "I do worry about using such heavy doses of this drug," she said.

"It will not be required for much longer," Komak assured her.

Dtimun sat beside her on the bed. His features were strained, his eyes dark with hunger. He opened the uniform shirt at the throat, enjoying her burst of phermones when she saw the thick hair over the hard muscles of his chest as she shot the laserdot into his artery. She wanted to touch him...

"Soon," he whispered in her mind, and the tone was intimate enough to make her flush.

The dravelzium took effect and he rose again, fastening his shirt. He turned to Komak. "When?"

"When Madelineruszel agrees," he replied gently.

She laughed. "I already have," she replied. "Breaking laws is what he does best." She indicated Dtimun. She grinned at his irritated expression. "And we all know that I've been breaking them for years."

Komak chuckled. "Very well, then. I will have the drugs ready tomorrow morning."

"Tomorrow?" she asked, curious.

Komak straightened. "It is a decision you must not make in haste," he replied. "You must think about it overnight."

"I agree," Dtimun said. He turned to Madeline,

drinking in her beauty. "Your entire genome will be reconstructed. You will never be able to go back to what you were, because the matrix will be destroyed."

"He means," Komak added, risking his temper, "that you would never again be able to mate with any human male."

Dtimun looked impossibly arrogant when he said that. He looked at Madeline with that same expression that had haunted her from their conversation on Trimerius, before her return to the Amazon Division. He looked at her as if she belonged to him.

His expression was eloquent. Smug. Outrageously smug.

She glared at him. She turned her attention back to Komak. Images in her mind were confusing her. "Tomorrow, then, Komak."

"Tomorrow," he replied. He smiled. "You should rest until then."

She nodded. "Okay."

Komak smiled at her, and a flash of an image in his mind was briefly noted by Dtimun.

"You have a stake in this, beyond the saving of our species," he told Komak. "You said that you have family in this timeline."

"You do?" Madeline asked, fascinated.

Komak groaned. "Well, yes," he confessed softly. "It is one reason I interfered." He averted his eyes. "I do not wish my family to die."

Which explained his urgent efforts to secure this timeline, Madeline thought.

"Exactly," Dtimun replied in her mind.

"I will see you in the morning," Komak said. "I will continue my work in Caneese's lab." He bowed formally to Dtimun and smiled at Madeline. He left the room.

Dtimun didn't enable the security protocols. He moved to the bed and looked down at Madeline with conflicting emotions.

"I know," she sighed. "You'd rather mate with a yomuth."

He glared at her with silent outrage.

"Figure of speech," she added, not wanting to set him off again. She knew that his control was perilous, even with the drug she'd given him.

"This mission could be suicide," he pointed out. "Even with your…modifications."

She sighed. "Well, sir, do you want to live forever?" she asked blithely.

He burst out laughing. "Immortality, they say, is boring." His face grew somber. "We have discussed gestation. But not in detail. You were right in your assumptions. Our babies have twice the size of yours and our reproductive cycle is a third of yours. The baby would grow rapidly, perhaps too rapidly for even a modified human body. There is another problem, one of which you are unaware." He hesitated. "I am not exactly as I appear."

She nodded. "Your weight is uncanny for your size and build," she said. "I remember it…" She cleared her throat and flushed slightly. She was remembering her fall from the cliff, when he'd caught her in midair and took her to the ground. It had been a very intimate position, and the beginning of her helpless attraction to him. "You're far heavier than your physical appearance denotes," she concluded.

"That is true."

"You don't really look like this, do you?" she asked with open curiosity.

"The mating is another issue." He moved closer to the bed. "I told you once that passion is always violent. That applies to the first mating. It is brutal, savage, like that of the great galots. We have tried, in vain, for centuries to counteract the instinct. We cannot. It is one of the residual traits that comes from our genetic manipulation. If Komak uses this manipulation on you, the results could be more devastating than you realize. Even worse, they are irreversible. You understand?"

"Yes, sir, I do." She drew in a breath. It was still a bit uncomfortable to breathe. Her injuries in the crash had been severe, although she had recovered almost completely. "But if Komak is right, and the future will die with Chacon, can we live with the knowledge that we could have prevented the loss of everything we know?"

"A good point."

"It's just…the child," she faltered.

"I, too, have issues with termination. It is unheard of in my culture."

She managed a smile. "Maybe we could hide him somewhere?" she asked.

He actually laughed. "In your quarters aboard the Morcai? I think he might be noticed."

She rested her hand on her flat stomach. It surprised her how badly she wanted a child. Not just a child. His child. She tried working trig in her head to disguise the thought, but it was too late.

He looked down at her oddly. "You want the child."

She grimaced and averted her eyes.

"This is no cause for shame," he pointed out.

She looked up at him. "It is, sort of," she said. "We're doing a noble thing. But a child should be born of..."

"If you say 'love,' I intend to leave the room," he gritted.

"Go ahead, because that's what I think," she shot back. "We're creating a child as a sort of sensor shield, a child we can't even keep, who will most likely have to be regressed afterward. It's shameful, however you look at it."

He conceded that. "Madeline, I have ordered men to their deaths," he said softly. "I live with that every day. I remember their faces, their personalities, every one of them. It is a burden I carry, because it goes with command. Sacrifices are sometimes necessary for the greater good."

"Yes, and I'd sacrifice myself in a heartbeat for that," she said. "But this is a child." She hesitated. "And besides that, I've ruined your life."

His eyebrows arched.

"Well, I have," she muttered. "I tried so hard not to feel these things..."

He sat down beside her and put a long forefinger across her lips. "I took you to the remembrance ceremony on Trimerius, in what was a very unmilitary act," he reminded her, "and then, I took you to Memcache, to show you my home, my past." He withdrew his hand. "I share things with you that I could never share with another person, not even a member of my Clan."

That was flattering. She wondered why. In fact, she wondered what had changed a military relation-

ship of three years into something so suddenly intimate. She searched his face, but his expression was
closed. She sighed. "What should we do?"

"You already know."

"Yes." She managed a faint smile. "Komak uses
that word, *karamesh*, fate."

"Everything is already written. Or so we believe."
His face became solemn. "There will be risks."

"Sir, I've taken risks my whole life," she pointed
out. Her lips pursed. "My biggest one, of course, was
when I was hijacked by this Cehn-Tahr commander
and became the first human female ever to serve in
the Holconcom." She shook her head. "You can be a
real pain sometimes, sir, begging your pardon."

A laugh escaped him. "May I return the compliment? Wrecking bars. Sparring with human
males...." His expression grew dark and dangerous.

"All you have to do is see into my mind to know
how I felt about Flannegan," she invited.

His expression relaxed. It grew possessive. Arrogant. Then he glared at her.

She laughed. "I know. It's just a gnawing hunger for you, one that you can't control, and that irri-
tates you even more." The laugh faded. "I know that
you have no...feelings for me. It's okay," she added
quickly. "I can't help mine, but I don't blame you for
yours. I know what happened to you on Dacerius,
how much you...loved the female with whom you
bonded there."

He averted his eyes. He would never have told her
about the Dacerian woman, but she'd seen it, somehow, in his mind when they went to Lagana and he

saved her from the deadly fall. "It still perplexes me, how you knew about her," he said quietly.

"I don't know," she replied. "I just…saw it, in my mind."

Mind links were common between Cehn-Tahr mates. But she was human. And he did not love her. He only wanted her. It should not have been possible. He looked troubled.

"Not to worry, sir, I won't tell anyone," she assured him. "I never should have blurted it out in the first place. It's just…her death was so violent…"

"Yes. Violent." His eyes narrowed. "You have no idea what you may be walking into."

She studied his hard face quietly, loving its strength, its utter perfection. "We can save our way of life. We can save the people we care about. That's worth the risk."

He sighed. "Yes. It is."

His expression changed. He pulled up his communicator ring and brought up an image of an officer. He spoke to him in the Holy Tongue. The officer was respectful and kept bowing. It amused Madeline, but she didn't let it show and he was too occupied to see it in her mind. He nodded, spoke curtly and broke the connection. The image faded.

"It seems that Komak was correct. Princess Lyceria has gone missing."

"What?" she exclaimed, picturing the beautiful Cehn-Tahr she'd first met on Ahkmau.

"She took a flight to the largest of our moons with a complement of *kehmatemer*, apparently to shop at the duty-free market. She did not return, and flashes sent to her module do not reach her."

"You think she was kidnapped?" she asked.

"With the *kehmatemer* watching her?" he replied, astounded.

She recalled fighting alongside them on Ondar. They were as formidable as the Holconcom.

"They are more developed," he said, reading the thought, "and they also have enhancements which we have never revealed to outworlders."

She recalled their ability to scale walls and move so fast they couldn't be seen. She'd had a taste of that when the commander had rescued her in the Dibella system.

He nodded. "You begin to understand," he said. "We have many sorts of tech that we have kept hidden even from the humans who serve with us on the *Morcai*." He studied her lovely face. "The 'old fellow' permitted us to travel as we usually do, to let the humans see. He has changed a great deal since the Great Galaxy War. You are responsible for that."

Her eyebrows lifted. "But I haven't done anything..."

"You underestimate your gifts for charming stoic and dangerous males."

She pursed her lips. "Including you? Sir?"

He glowered at her. "The tranquillizer has a finite time limit," he said deliberately.

She cleared her throat. "Sorry. You were saying?"

"Princess Lyceria eluded her escort in a shop by going out the back door while she was supposed to be conferring with a tailor. She vanished. There is more," he added grimly. "While Hazheen Kamon made it back to Dacerius, Chacon did not report back to Enmehkmehk, the Rojok capital. He, also, has gone missing."

Madeline sat up straighter against her pillows. "That is more than a coincidence. They very likely arranged a rendezvous," she added, because she knew how the Rojok felt about Lyceria. It was possible that Lyceria returned his affections.

Dtimun sighed and locked his hands behind his back as he paced. "This thought had also occurred to me."

"Could they have met on your planet's moon?" she asked.

He shook his head. "Regardless of my friendship for Chacon, he would have been arrested the moment he was seen. He would not dare risk it, nor would Lyceria. No, if they planned a meeting, it would be far from here, in someplace where neither of our military had jurisdiction."

"Someplace like Benaski Port," she suggested thoughtfully. "Just as Komak said."

His lips made a thin line. "An astute conclusion."

"Thank you, sir. Among my many attributes, I consider my astuteness is my best one."

"Ruszel…" he muttered.

"Can't the Dectat track the princess?"

"Yes," he said. "Unknown to her, she always carries a homing membrane. The thing is, we can find no trace of a signal."

She gave him a wry look. "Obviously, you don't give her credit for much intelligent thought."

He was shocked. "I did not say such a thing."

"Females are wily, especially when they're pursuing males. Or so I'm told," she sighed. "Komak knew they were going to Benaski Port. He quoted a percentage of certainty, at least…" He hesitated.

He frowned. "Komak is not what he seems," he began.

"No, he isn't," she agreed, diverted from the subject at hand. "When I was operating on you, at Ahkmau, I thought I saw traces of human DNA in his matrix…why do you look like that?" She stopped, puzzled.

Incredible possibilities claimed his mind, but only for an instant. Anyone looking at Komak could see that he had no human attributes.

"Human DNA," he said hesitantly. "It is unlikely."

She nodded. "It wasn't there when I rechecked. He does have some very human characteristics, though." She hesitated. "Do you think he's a descendant of someone in the Holconcom?"

"I think this very possible."

"He couldn't really have human DNA. And he doesn't look human."

"If he did, it is possible that he disguises himself in some way. With a sensor net that distorts his true image, perhaps. Yet I agree—he does not look human."

"If we could get one hair from his head," she murmured thoughtfully.

He chuckled. "I will make that a priority, before he leaves."

"I know he's leaving," she said. "But when? And why?"

"He says little," he replied. "I do not know. But soon."

She frowned. "Everything is changing so quickly," she said.

Dtimun was still thinking about Komak. He shielded his mind far too well for a regular Cehn-Tahr, and he was a telepath. But human DNA? A child born of a Cehn-Tahr and a human would be put to death instantly, with its parents, if it were even possible.

"Why wouldn't Chan Ho just have Chacon killed?" Madeline wondered aloud.

He moved closer. "If he were to be assassinated, his death would be laid at the door of Chan Ho, who has a precarious hold on his power," he replied. "The Rojok commoners love Chacon. They do not love Chan Ho, who lacks the ability, because of Chacon's opposition, to create terror as his late uncle, Mangus Lo, did. If Chacon simply disappears, people will wonder, but there will be no proof. Certainly, there will be no body." His lips compressed. "Chacon and I attended the military academy on Dacerius together. We were friends. It has been a great sorrow to me that we found ourselves adversaries in this conflict."

"He is a noble adversary," she agreed. "I owe him my life."

"I owe him mine as well."

She tried to imagine Chacon in the same position she and Dtimun and the Holconcom had been in at Ahkmau. It was distasteful.

"Komak believes that Lyceria's spies found out something about the kidnapping and that she has gone in person to warn him," he said grimly. "Chacon would not have dared meet her near Memcache, but if they decided to meet at Benaski Port…that den of thieves is far removed from here. It would take at least two or three standard weeks for them to arrive there, and they would have to travel covertly, which would also take more time." He seemed unusually worried. "They say that the emperor is frantic."

"Well, of course he is. She's his only surviving child."

He nodded, but he didn't meet her eyes.

"You and I would go to Benaski Port and save her and Chacon, then?" Madeline asked.

Dtimun's eyes flashed green. "As you are now, your own life would be in greater danger than Chacon's."

She flushed. "Oops."

He frowned. "We know that Komak has a way to alter your DNA, to make you far stronger than you are. But the process is dangerous. Any DNA manipulation has consequences. As you have already seen," he added bitterly, alluding to his own negative qualities.

"Not all tampering is bad," she argued as a scientist. "I've seen lethal viruses displaced by scientific method, genetic malformations cured with gene therapy. It has benefits, as well as consequences." Her eyes twinkled. "My, my, think of the possibilities, if there's a breakthrough in nanotech that would make me the equal of a Cehn-Tahr woman in strength and fortitude." She cocked her head. "I could get into even better brawls with my comrades aboard the *Morcai*."

He gave her a speaking look.

"Sorry," she said. "Just a stray thought." Her eyes twinkled even more. "I could put Komak over a table," she considered. "Wouldn't he be surprised?"

"Very surprised, when I threw him off the roof for touching you," he returned and he wasn't smiling.

She let out a breath. "I miss the Holconcom," she confessed and averted her eyes. "I love duty with the Amazon Division, but I miss the *Morcai* and her crew."

"Stern and Hahnson and Komak," he interpreted coldly.

"And, of course, you, sir," she added with dry humor. "Nobody dresses me down twice a day for behaving in a nonmilitary fashion." She sighed sadly. "I've become like you, sir, somber and duty-minded. Imagine that."

His eyes went green for just an instant. "I cannot."

She studied him curiously. She wanted to ask a question, but she was too wary of him to put it into words.

He anticipated it and changed the subject abruptly. "There is another matter. The Dectat wishes to honor you for the treaty with the Nagaashe. They are debating the means."

Her heart jumped. "My goodness! But I didn't really do anything."

"Your 'old fellow' would certainly debate that opinion," he said, and he laughed gently. "The worst of your enemies in the days before Ondar has become your greatest advocate. The irony is incredible."

"Irony, sir?"

"The soldier who would gladly have ordered your death in your first days with the Holconcom is the one who suggested the honor."

She laughed. "The Nagaashe said that he was the worst of all the Cehn-Tahr." She frowned introspectively. "I don't understand how they even knew him. Anyway," she continued, "the Nagaashe were afraid of the Cehn-Tahr. They thought of you as animals. They saw you through my eyes. It changed them."

He smiled. "For which the Dectat is more delighted than you realize. Our stores of Helium 3 have been greatly diminished during the war, and our supply lines fragmented. The Nagaashe planet is close to us, and they have almost unlimited concentrations of it on their world. Our supplies were dwindling to a critical level because of the war."

"The Nagaashe were kind to me."

He looked at her with growing unrest. The sedative was just beginning to wear off. He straightened with regal grace from his perch against the window. "Later, we must let the *kehmatemer* in to see you, or face a riot…!"

His sudden sharp pause was due to the entrance of a flaming mad Dr. Edris Mallory, soaked in some interesting and colorful substance, with a furious Captain Rhemun of the *kehmatemer* right on her heels.

She saluted Dtimun at once, dripping on the smooth stone floor. "Sir."

Rhemun followed suit. Odd, Madeline thought, for an officer of another service to salute Dtimun like that, as if he were Rhemun's superior. Perhaps it was military protocol here. Dtimun had said that he outranked the *kehmatemer*.

"Mallory, why are you dripping on the floor?" Dtimun asked curtly.

"Sir, he—" she pointed to Rhemun with her saluting hand and put it quickly back in place "—poured a pot of vegetable soup over my head!"

"I can see that. Why did he pour a pot of vegetable soup over your head?" he asked, glancing toward Rhemun.

"Permission to speak, sir?" Rhemun asked formally.

Dtimun sighed. "Very well."

"We feel that Ruszel needs protein to mend her body," Rhemun said curtly.

"She—" he indicated her with his helmeted head "—insisted that a vegetarian concoction would be better for Ruszel. The disagreement became…physical. She threw a serving spoon at me. I…reciprocated."

"I threw something small!" Edris raged.

"Soup is small," Rhemun muttered. "At least, parts of it are."

Dtimun looked as exasperated as he felt. The diminished effect of the tranquillizer didn't help his temper.

"Get yourself cleaned up, Lieutenant," he told Mallory sharply. "As for you—" he turned to Rhemun "—another breach of protocol in this house will produce unpleasant consequences. If I report you to the…old fellow—" he used Ruszel's terminology "—I doubt that he will be pleased to learn that the captain of his guard resorts to physical means to terminate an argument. Especially with a female."

Rhemun's lips were tight. "Yes, sir," he said smartly. He glanced at Madeline and grimaced. "I apologize for the altercation, Ruszel. It was not deliberate…"

Dtimun made a sound that brought Rhemun to instant attention, his eyes elsewhere, rather than on

Ruszel. Obviously, he understood immediately what was wrong with his superior officer. "Forgive me, sir," he said smartly. "I meant no offense."

Dtimun didn't excuse him. His eyes were dark and angry. "Dismissed!"

"Yes, sir!"

Rhemun bowed deeply and then saluted. Mallory followed suit with the salute, shot Rhemun a speaking glance as she turned and marched soggily out of the room, with the *kehmatemer* officer at her heels.

"Just when I thought there was a possibility of peace," Madeline sighed.

Dtimun shifted uncomfortably. He was still bristling, in a subtle sense of the word.

"He was only being polite, you know," she said softly. "He thinks of me as a fellow soldier. We fought a battle together, as comrades."

That didn't help. He turned, his eyes blazing as they met hers. He didn't speak.

She studied him with open curiosity. "I don't understand why it happened like this," she said. "I mean, with me, a soldier of another species. The women on your planet are lovely, if Princess Lyceria is any example of them. I'm a woman, and she even fascinated me!"

He tried to relax. "Nor do I understand it," he replied. His eyes slid over her slowly, intently. "Having considered the matter, I think it has less to do with beauty than with courage and honor and integrity."

Her breath caught.

"You have qualities which I admired, from the moment I saw you again, as a physician, on Terramer," he commented. He smiled. "You made an impression the first time we met, when you were a child, and you bit me when I attempted to separate you from a bush during the last battle of the Great Galaxy War."

"I was frightened," she confessed. "You and my father made a formidable team."

"We digress," he said. "When the *Morcai* leaves orbit, Mallory must replace you as our Cularian expert for the time being. While we are detached to pursue the princess, Rhemun, as next in the chain of command, will have to lead the Holconcom in my absence if any mission presents itself. The antagonism she and Rhemun share will not make for cordial relations aboard ship." His eyes twinkled green. "She may become the first human to be eaten by a Cehn-Tahr."

She laughed. The sound was soft and pleasant in the airy room.

"You laugh. But we are carnivores."

"Similar to carnivores," she said. "You have bunodont teeth, like humans, not carnassial teeth like the great felines. You do have the micturtating membrane that allows you to see in the dark, but unlike felines, you can see color." She hesitated. "You also have an odd structure in your esophagus—more striated muscle than humans."

"Like the great cats, we can eat live prey," he told her quietly. "The whole prey, and regurgitate the parts that do not digest." He didn't add that some details of Cehn-Tahr anatomy were still hidden from the human medical corps' computers.

She was fascinated. "I did wonder, but it seemed impolite to ask."

His eyes narrowed on her face. "We share many

traits with felines. As Caneese told you, they are never shared with outworlders. You may not like what you learn about us if you permit the genetic restructuring of your body," he added quietly. "But, it will be too late. You will never be able to return to the way you were."

They were still dancing around the main issue: Dtimun's uncontrollable response to her.

"If you are...restructured," he said stiffly, "it would permit us to...bond."

She narrowed her eyes on his rigid expression. "Will that reduce your aggression?"

He nodded. "It will reduce the threat to other males at once. However," he mused, "if you become pregnant, the behavior will return. We become protective."

She sighed. "So we start all over again with men running out doors if I get too close to them...?" she said with a grin.

He glowered at her. "Will you permit me to finish what I was saying, madam?"

She held out a hand, palm up.

He clasped his hands behind him. He was worried. "We have only two or three weeks to act. It will take Chacon that long to get to Benaski Port. The princess will also be confined to covert methods of travel, and they take longer." He hesitated. "It is an insane risk. I have no idea why Chacon would undertake it."

"I do," she said solemnly. "If he's going there to meet Princess Lyceria, it would explain why. She might not have been able to tell him why she wanted him to meet her. But he would go, because he loves her," she said simply.

"An insane state of mind," he muttered.

She almost bit her tongue off trying not to reply. She was thinking of Dtimun defying the whole council, withdrawing the Holconcom, lifting with a renegade force of humans under threat of court-martial, just to rescue Madeline.

He glowered at her. "That was a different matter. I cannot control the need to be with you," he said curtly. "But the behavior is primitive. It has nothing to do with emotion."

What a harsh thing to say, she thought. Harsh and cold and unfeeling. As she looked back at him, she wondered what a female's life would be like, bonded to such a being, living year after year in the shadow of his indifference. What he felt was a primal urge to reproduce, nothing more, and she had better remember it.

Something occurred to her. "There has to be a child...?"

"Yes," he said. "If you and I went to Benaski Port, as a Cehn-Tahr aristocrat, with a pregnant human female as consort, it would put us out of reach of any suspicion. The fact of our bonding would confound anyone who saw us, but it would also put both of us at risk of death by each of our military authorities. We would blend quite well in that den of iniquity. We could find Chacon and prevent his capture, or assassination, and save the princess as well. Komak reveals little, but he has intimated that this is the future, if you decide to go with me. It will be a risk for both of us. A great one."

She was dubious about the whole thing, for a number of reasons. "I'm not sure there isn't a better way to do it. You could take Mallory along and pretend that she's pregnant. I could go back to my unit once I'm certified fit for duty."

He seemed to clench from head to toe. "There is another aspect of this behavior," he said. "A male who is hunting will follow a female, regardless of the distance, until he can coax her into reciprocating his interest."

"Oh, that's just great," she muttered. "I go away to forget you, and you come along for the ride."

The comment amused him. He laughed out loud. His eyes flared green. "I rarely laughed, until you came aboard my vessel," he confessed. "Even Komak was hard-pressed to provoke me to it."

She cocked her head and smiled back. "I'm beginning to wonder if life with you, even for a few standard weeks, wouldn't be more of a punishment than a blessing," she said glibly. "Sir," she added as an afterthought.

He lifted an eyebrow and smiled. "You will not find out by rejoining Admiral Mashita's crew, madam."

She had a sudden, unpleasant thought. "Sir, the law is still the law. Your government would put you to death if they discovered what we plan to do. I'm not sure that saving the princess would be enough incentive to excuse it to them. My government, especially Ambassador Taylor, would space me in a heartbeat just for being with you in a notorious spaceport like Benaski."

"I am aware of this," he said quietly. "But if Chacon dies, the Rojok homeworld will revert to Chan Ho's madness. They will begin to build ovens again. Along with the planet killer that Komak has seen in this future."

Madeline shuddered. "A horrible thought."

"Komak hints at a future even more horrible, with Chacon gone."

"But he's still the enemy," she pointed out.

"He is my friend," he said simply. "He always has been. I cannot stand by and let Chan Ho kill him, not in such a merciless way. Can you imagine Chacon reduced to serving as a digger in the mines?"

"No," she replied. "I can't."

"Such would surely be his fate."

She grimaced. "Then I guess I need to consider my options very quickly."

He nodded. "By tomorrow, as Komak has said," he repeated curtly. "You must decide carefully. It will not be reversible. As you have seen, DNA manipulation has side effects."

"If I decide to take the risk," she said, "will you tell the Dectat what we're doing?"

"I would not dare," he confessed. He didn't add that the Dectat's president would probably send off fireworks if Dtimun was caught consorting with a human female, despite his apologies. "The Species Act is still in place. Of all aristocrats on Memcache, I am the last who should be accused publicly of breaking it," he added enigmatically. He didn't add that his first offense, with the Dacerian woman, had not been prosecuted. He was still uncertain why. "If we are caught in the deception, even to aid the princess, my time with the Holconcom will come to an end."

That disturbed her. "It would be a great sacrifice

for you, if you had to give up command of the Hol-concom."

He searched her eyes. "It would mean a great change." He shifted. "I had never thought to become a diplomat, even though my early education was modified to make me into one. I always sought great battles, and command. My years with the Holconcom have been satisfying ones."

"If I went back to the Amazon Division," she began slowly.

"Nothing would change," he said flatly. "The behavior would only mutate until I was a threat to you, wherever you went. I cannot...control it."

And that was galling; he didn't even have to say it. He hated his condition. Maybe he blamed her for it.

"I do not," he said, answering the thought. "As we once discussed, it could have been any female."

"I suppose so."

His eyes narrowed. "There is something else. Something you seek to hide from me. What?"

It was like telling someone not to think of a yo-muth. Immediately, her greatest fear rushed to the surface of her thoughts, the fear that he would never feel anything for her past the relief of a gnawing hunger.

His brows drew together. "When my bonded companion was killed by your 'old fellow' on Dacerius, I made a vow that I would never feel such emotions again. I swore that I would never breed again, never produce a child. This was a source of great anguish in my Clan. At that time, there were two sons left alive. Now, there is only one." He sighed. "I am the last of my line. It is a grave responsibility. There must be heirs. But this emotion you call love…I no longer believe in it." He said the words. They were a defense. He recalled with faint anguish his reaction to Madeline's crash on Akaashe. No purely physical need could explain his desperation to get to her.

Her sadness was almost palpable. She'd mistaken his headlong rush to save her as emotion, when it was involuntary. Long, lonely years faced her, after he was "cured" of his obsession. Would he expect her to go back to the Amazon Division, as if nothing had happened? Surely it would be a continuing embarrassment to him to have her in the Holconcom, even if his hunger for her was cured, because he would still have his memory of her. And what about the child, if there was one and it didn't kill her to carry it? His people—most of them—did not like humans. He was the last of his line. He would have to have a Cehn-Tahr child to inherit his position. A half and half child would be an actual embarrassment to him if it wasn't regressed. But that wasn't part of the problem. Chacon's fate was.

And was there really a choice? "If we do…produce a child, once we save Chacon, it could be regressed, gently absorbed back into the tissues of my body."

He started to protest, but she held up a hand. Her heart was breaking, but this was the only possible solution to the problems Dtimun would face. She couldn't count on Komak's assurances. The future was always in flux. "I'm not Cehn-Tahr, even if I have reserve status with your military, so your laws don't affect me," she said doggedly, despite his angry expression. "After the child was regressed, Hahnson could do a short-term memory wipe starting at the

day we came here to Memcache for the first time.
I could go back to my old life with no memories to
torture me. You could go back to the Holconcom
as its commander." She looked at him evenly, surprised to find a glimmer of some odd emotion in
dark, intense eyes. "Later, you could bond with a
Cehn-Tahr woman and have a child to inherit your
estates. Couldn't you?"

He seemed to stiffen even more. He didn't reply.
The Cehn-Tahr bonded for life, as she seemed to forget. He would not be able to bond with any female
as long as Ruszel lived. That had been a disturbing
consideration once. Now, however....

She bit her lower lip. "We could do what was necessary to save Chacon, and Princess Lyceria, and
then...forget it ever happened."

He barely heard her. He was considering things he
had never expected. He really would have the fight
of his life trying to bond permanently with an out-
worlder. Not that he'd ever run yet from a fight. Yes,
they could go back to the old life, once Chacon and
the princess were safe. The child could be regressed.
Her memory could be wiped. Sad, though, to erase
such gossamer, fragile memories as the ones she carried of their night at the Altair Embassy, the fall on
Lagana when he'd saved her, their long day on Memcache...

His whole body went taut at just the thought. Let
her give up those memories? Give up their child? No!
Not if they put him to death for it.

He turned abruptly, to look at her. The color of his
eyes was a confusion of hues that she couldn't begin
to identify. "Komak has already said that a solution

will present itself in the future. We will not dwell on such possibilities until we have to. And we will not speak of them again," he said firmly.

Now who wasn't willling to face unpleasant outcomes? she wondered. He seemed honestly disturbed by her comments. That gave her a tiny glimmer of hope. But he didn't say anything else.

Her heart was breaking inside her. She glared at him, feeling still the effects of the crash on Akaashe and the sting of his indifference toward her, despite his physical needs and that odd, infrequent, enigmatic tenderness. It was a heart-wrenching decision to have to make. She would have a few precious weeks with him, pretending a life she could never have. But her body would be altered forever. And she wouldn't even get to keep the memory. Or her child… She bit down on the pain. Still, Chacon would live and many soldiers would live, too, as well as the princess. If they didn't go… She ground her teeth together. She'd have to sleep on it. Regardless of the nobility of agreeing, it was no decision to make lightly.

He saw those thoughts in her mind and winced mentally at the pain that radiated from her. The decision to give up the child tormented her. She would do it only because she wished to spare him disgrace. She'd already sacrificed so much for him. Too much. He had told her that his interest in her was strictly physical. That was a lie, and he'd only just realized it. He'd realized something else as well. Once there was a child, it would be impossible for him to let her go, or agree to a regression. He hadn't anticipated this. He had never wanted a child so passionately. It surpassed even the pregnancy of his first bonding. He stared at her with his emotions in turmoil, his face wiped clean of expression, as shock washed over him.

She glared at him. For a few seconds, she'd thought he felt…well, something. Now he was as impassive as ever. "I'll let you know what I decide tomorrow. But I could roast you, sir," she added involuntarily, her face flushed with anger at his lack of visible emotion.

His eyes widened. They flashed green before he could control the impulse. "Roast me?"

"Roast," she said with feeling, with glittery eyes. "Over hot coals. On a spit!"

She was beautiful like that, with her face faintly flushed and her green eyes throwing off sparks. He tried and failed to contain a chuckle.

"And I swear, if it was possible for a human to eat a Cehn-Tahr, I'd have you on a toasted bun with sauce! Sir," she added flatly.

He pursed his lips, openly amused. He felt rather than saw Komak behind him.

"He would leave a terrible taste in your mouth, Madelineruszel," Komak assured her.

Dtimun turned and stared at the younger man intently. He was recalling Madeline's comment that she'd thought she saw human DNA in Komak at Ahkmau…

Komak's mind was a blank slate…a *tabula rasa* as impenetrable as his expression.

"Are you two having a staring contest?" Madeline asked. "If you are, I'd really appreciate having you take it out of here. I need some sleep. It's been a very, very long day," she added with a glare in Dtimun's direction.

Dtimun glanced back at her with a raised eyebrow.

"We can put off any further discussions until tomorrow. You do need rest."

"I won't be here," she muttered in exasperation, pulling up the covers. "I'm going to run away with Rognan and found a bird speak colony."

Komak burst out laughing. "Where is Rognan?" he asked suddenly, because he hadn't seen the bird all day.

"Gathering sticks, I imagine," Madeline piped in. "We'll have to have a nest to live in."

There was a sudden clomp of big bird feet, one hitting harder than the other as Rognan entered the room. He padded to the bed and dumped a huge, dead rodent—surprisingly clean and free of blood—on the cover at Madeline's feet. His big yellow eyes twinkled at her.

"Protein…Ruszel," Rognan croaked. "Big soldier in helmet said…Ruszel needs protein." He indicated the rodent. "Very nice. For you." He stood, waiting for praise.

Madeline looked from the rodent to the two surprised Cehn-Tahr facing her. She swallowed hard, at the sight of the dead rodent lying on the covers of her bed. "How… very thoughtful of you!" she exclaimed. "Thank you, Rognan," she added. "It looks delicious."

Rognan flapped his wings in appreciation, upending a flowerpot. He groaned as he picked it up with one big clawed foot on his undamaged leg and put it gingerly back on the table, looking so dejected that Madeline laughed.

Dtimun looked at Komak. "Perhaps we should remain long enough to watch her eat it."

Komak's eyes flashed as green as the commander's.

Rognan chuckled. "Yes. Please. Eat." He nodded again toward the rodent. "It will honor me, to give you strength."

They all stared at Madeline, whose discomfort was noticeable. She was reluctant to offend Rognan, whom she adored, but the thought of eating, uncooked, a furry rodent, was just beyond her. And the commander and Komak, standing there with those outrageous, smug expressions, looking so oddly alike, daring her....

Madeline groaned softly and pulled the covers over her head.

The two aliens laughed, recovered the rodent and shooed Rognan out of the room with soothing words before they left. The door closed behind them.

Madeline removed the covers and stared at the ceiling, her thoughts turbulent and disturbing. At least she had peace and quiet to make this most unenviable of decisions. It was, she decided somberly, going to be a very long night.

* * * * *

To be continued in
THE MORCAI BATTALION: INVICTUS,
coming in December 2015 from HQN Books!

GLOSSARY & CHARACTERS

Ahkmau: The Rojok prison complex to which enemy soldiers are transported. It is located on one of the moons of the Rojok home world, Enmehkmehk, and features some of the most diabolical tortures known to sentient beings. No one who enters its gates ever leaves. It is the pet project of the Rojok emperor, Mangus Lo, a madman who uses terror to control the populace and advance his conquest of new planetal resources for his overpopulated home world.

Altairian: A blue-skinned race noted for its stoicism, allied to the Tri-Galaxy Federation.

Ambutubes: Cylinders in which wounded and dead are placed for transport; operate on zero-point energy and can be floated to a ship through remote control.

AVBD: Audio visual bio detectors, placed in corridors and individual units aboard the *Morcai* to monitor the interior of the ship against sabotage.

The *Bellatrix*: One ship of a fleet of SSC ships, this one captained by Holt Stern, a Terravegan national. The ship's medical chief of staff is Lieutenant Commander Madeline Ruszel, who specializes in Cularian medicine. Her colleague Dr. Strick Hahnson is a specialist in human physiology and pharmacology. Both Ruszel and Hahnson, like Stern, are Terravegans, born on far-flung colonies whose settlers originated hundreds of years ago in the Sol system, on planet Earth. A planetal catastrophe reduced the human population to less than ten thousand souls; but just before it occurred, the colony ships had embarked from the international space station in orbit above Earth and were weeks away by the time the disaster occurred.

Benaski Port: The only neutral port in the vicinity of the Tri-Galaxy Fleet headquarters planet, Trimerius; listed on star charts as a favorite haunt of renegades, outcasts and deserters, with many pleasure domes, bars, gambling emporiums and a small unit of ship outfitters who can make minor repairs on spacegoing vessels. Notorious for trafficking in Dacerian women and various hallucinogenic substances. No extradition treaties with any outworlders, thus a haven for those fleeing law enforcement.

Berdache: A third sex of Terravegans who prefer their own gender as mates. They may marry at the pleasure of the state. They are also permitted to serve in the military. The term berdache is reportedly rooted in Native American language on ancient Earth.

Breeders: The Terravegan state has evolved into two classes of citizens. One class is assigned to the military, another is assigned to breeding camps. Breeders are males and females chosen for their genetics for the government baby mills. They are placed on farms, where they are given every comfort and luxury so long as they produce eggs and sperm for artificial breeding. They are not allowed to mate, but they are permitted to live together while their children are raised to the age of six—this is only for persons in the highest tier of society, such as politicians. Breeders are not permitted to produce children in the natural manner, as embryos are created free of imperfections which natural breeding can allow. Uncontrolled birth is forbidden. Marriage is permitted only in the elite classes such as political leaders. Fraternization between sexes in the military, whose members are mentally neutered for service, is punishable by death in the rare instances when the neutering is not successful. Another class of citizens allied to breeders is charged with the training and education of the children up until age six, at which time they are given over to their military units. Children are taught to revere the state, and that military service is the greatest honor available to a Terravegan. They are discouraged from any fraternization with other children, especially children who will be selected as breeders. Their education begins at birth, with implanted technology and physical conditioning a daily chore.

Centaurian: A misnomer deriving from first contact between humans and people of the Cehn-Tahr system near the Eridani solar system. They were at first believed to be natives of the Alpha Centauri system 4.3 light-years from earth. A fleet of colony ships from ancient Earth went off course due to a glitch in the programming that went undiscovered since the crew and complement were in cryosleep. The ships entered an unstable area of space, which "folded" into a system many parsecs from the Sol system. When they woke, it was to the sight of an alien vessel approaching them. The Cehn-Tahr boarded the lead colony ship and the captain assumed that they had reached their destination of the Centauri system. By the time the mistake was discovered, humans were used to calling these natives Centaurians and the name stuck. The Cehn-Tahr guided them to a planet in a nearby system that had the basic necessities of life—light, heat, water, breathable air—and introduced them to the natives who lived on the planet. They were accepted easily and blended into the existing human colony, all of whom were vegetarians, since there were no animals on the planet. They intermarried with the locals. In time, they colonized other systems, and the race as a whole became known as Terravegan. The Cehn-Tahr are humanoid, but their race traces its evolutionary roots to a species of giant cat, the galot, which was originally found in the Eridanus system. The species is also found on Memcache, the home planet of the Cehn-Tahr. The Cehn-Tahr are one race only, and their features include golden skin, jet-black hair and elongated cat's eyes that change color to mirror mood. Their ears, nose, mouth, et cetera are exactly like any human's, and they do not have either tails or fur. There is a narrow ribbon of fur that lies along the length of the spinal cord, a vestigial racial trait that is not visible, and that is never shown to outworlders. Their true physical form is only revealed to family, or, when in combat, to the enemy.

Cehn-Tahr have two system-wide military units: the regular space navy and the elite Holconcom, which is the commando force, feared by other races. They also have an elite guard, the *kehmatemer,* who are assigned to the Dectat (the Cehn-Tahr parliament) to protect the emperor and parliamentary members. Women do not serve in their military, preferring to use their talents in the political and social arenas. Each Cehn-Tahr comes from a specific Clan, which is part of the individual's social status. The commander of the Holconcom, Dtimun, has never given the name of his Clan. He is the only member of the Holconcom, except for his executive officer Komak, who is not a clone. Among the Cehn-Tahr, clones have the same status as any normally born member of the society.

Chacon: Field marshal and commander of the Rojok military, and one of the most famous of warriors in his own right. Unlike his emperor, he is an honorable and compassionate being, respected even by his enemies. He will have no part of terrorism and is openly critical of the death camp Ahkmau. He believes in the war, because the Rojoks are so overpopulated that they have no more room in their dynasty to search for natural resources. Tri-Galaxy politics made it impossible for them to petition for the right to colonize in the New Territory, so war was the only recourse. But he hates Mangus Lo's policies and refuses to send prisoners to the death camps. He is so popular with the Rojok population that the Rojok tyrant is afraid to openly oppose or criticize him.

Clones: They can be created in less than a solar day among the Rojok. The process takes longer for Terravegans and Cehn-Tahr. However, in the human colonies, clones have no official status and are used for spare parts. They are treated as subhuman. Not so among Cehn-Tahr, where they are given full official status.

Cularian medicine: A specialty of exobiology that deals with Cehn-Tahr and Rojok physiology and pharmacology. Until Ruszel began serving with the Holconcom, it was largely theoretical, because few humans had ever seen either a Cehn-Tahr or a Rojok, since the Terravegan forces were headquartered on Trimerius, in the human colonies. Not until the Rojoks invaded neutral planetary systems and then destroyed a trial colony did the Rojoks and Cehn-Tahr come into contact with humans. Cularian specialists are trained in every science, including emerillium technology and even theoretical physics and quantum mechanics, and they perform combat surgery as well as undertaking routine care of injuries.

Dacerius: A desert planet famous for its yomuth races, silver work and exotic women, many of whom are captured and sold by slavers. Famous, also, for its bureaucracy, which deals in doublespeak and exasperation. Many nomadic tribes, most of whom have no affiliation with the central government. Tribal leaders are still chosen by combat.

Dtimun: Commander in Chief of the Holconcom, the galaxy's most elite commando unit. Except for its leader, the entire unit is made up of clones. The commander has led the unit for many years and is greatly respected not only by his own men, but by allied commands as well. He and the Cehn-Tahr emperor, Tnurat Alamantimichar, are enemies; no one knows why. He has never revealed to which Clan his family claimed kinship, in a world where Clan affiliation was honor itself. He does not like humans, especially the Terravegan doctor Ruszel, who thinks of him as a barbarian because he objects to having a woman in a combat unit. Ruszel was once the captain of an elite SSC Amazon squad, the Amazons (all female) being one of the most respected and courageous of the combat elite.

Dylete: Cehn-Tahr have two hearts. There is only one heart at birth. Over a period of years approaching middle age, a new heart begins to form in concert with the original organ. At the time of halflife, approximately eighty-four to eighty-eight years of age, the first heart stops functioning and the new heart accepts the burden from the old one. The old heart is then reabsorbed into the body. Sometimes this process of changeover fails, and the patient dies. A Cehn-Tahr in his eighties is comparable to a thirty-four-year-old human male. However, some Cehn-Tahr have modifications that allow them to live to extreme age, in which case the dylete may occur more than once.

Emerillium: A crystal that, in its refined form, has electrical and magnetic properties, first used as a power source by the Cehn-Tahr, the technology was subsequently shared with the human military under treaty.

Enmehkmehk: The home planet of the Rojok dynasty. One of its moons contains the notorious prison complex Ahkmau, which translates as "place of tortures."

Galot: A huge feral cat found originally in the Eridanus system, but also on Memcache. Reports of them have been noted on a few colony planets, probably from kittens illegally transported as pets.

Great Galaxy War: Decades ago, a group of arms smugglers, tech producers and anarchists formed an alliance and secretly induced various governments to attack other governments after "incidents of terror" provoked public opinion against former allies. The Cehn-Tahr and the Terravegans joined forces, along with the Altairians and Jebobs, to combat the growing totalitarian states that were replacing republics. Eventually, alliances would be formed with governments throughout the galaxy and, when the war inevitably spread to two adjacent galaxies through the time-warp technological advances, other races joined the proponents of freedom and formed the Tri-Galaxy Federation and the Tri-Galaxy Fleet. A good portion of the original aggressors were captured and their ships confiscated. The rest fled into exile. The political wing of the Federation is the Tri-Galaxy Council, headquartered on Trimerius.

Gresham: A weapon powered by emerillium technology that uses a cartridge to shoot a cutting beam of high-intensity modulated energy at an enemy. Standard issue in the SSC.

Holconcom: The most elite, and feared, commando force in the three civilized galaxies. Created by the Cehn-Tahr emperor Tnurat Alamantimichar, and strengthened by secret nanotechnology called microcyborgs, the Holconcom is the vanguard in any battle. It is under the sole command of its leader— at present, Dtimun—and even the emperor himself may not command it. The Cehn-Tahr who serve in the unit are all clones, except for the commander, and their strength and method of combat are legendary. Few humans have ever seen them fight. They sport high-collared red uniforms. They can be attached to an ally military only with the consent of their leader, and they are difficult to command. Their leader's contempt for protocol and chain of command is well-known, as well as his refusal to follow orders. The Holconcom operate behind enemy lines, creating havoc and cutting lines of communication, as well as seeking out supply and communications networks, which are then targeted for attack. They are allowed forbidden technology that enhances speed and weaponry and is unknown to outworlders.

Hyperglas: A synthetic material that resembles glass but has the strength of steel, widely used in terraforming projects and architecture.

Jaakob Spheres: An orb containing many smaller orbs that preserve in stasis the DNA of all member Tri-Galaxy Federation races, as well as cellular specifications for exotic weaponry native to those cultures. A true prize for the Rojoks who capture them, except that the orbs are transcribed in Old High Martian, an ancient human tongue, of which the Rojoks know nothing. The orbs were in transit on a diplomatic observation tour to the Peace Planet, Terramer, just before the Rojoks attacked the planet, killed many of the colonists and one of the Cehn-Tahr observers (a young son of the Cehn-Tahr emperor) and kidnapped both the diplomatic observers and the Spheres. Among their captives is Lyceria, daughter of the Cehn-Tahr emperor.

Jebob: A member race of the Tri-Galaxy Federation. Offshoots of the Altairian race, they are also blue-skinned.

Kelekoms: A sentient race of energy beings who can attach themselves to host bodies and share information psychically. Through an ancient treaty with the Cehn-Tahr, they send emissaries to the Holconcom and host Cehn-Tahr diplomats on their home world. Only four emissaries are allowed to serve with the Holconcom. They bond with their hosts until death. Usually, due to their longevity, the hosts die long before they do—so a new host is offered in place of one who is killed in combat or dies of natural causes. The *kelekoms* are extremely susceptible to alien bacteria and have to be kept in sterile fields aboard the Holconcom ship, *Morcai*.

Komak: Dtimun's second in command of the Holconcom, an enigmatic and charming Cehn-Tahr who is overly curious and has a howling sense of humor that frequently exasperates his commanding officer. But on the front lines, he is brave and formidable. He is also very mysterious, and is fascinated with humans.

Lawson, Admiral Jeffrye: Leader of the Tri-Galaxy Fleet, composed of Terravegan, Altairian and Jebob military, but also the authority over any ally military seconded to the fleet in time of war. An old battle horse who is known for his bad temper and his soft heart. Winner of the Legion of Honor, the fleet's highest award, in the Great Galaxy War thirty years ago.

Lightsteds: Secret Cehn-Tahr technology that controls the rate of flow of emerillium power banks, much like control rods in a nuclear reactor.

Mangus Lo: Leader of the Rojok dynasty, a small misshapen Rojok who poisoned his uncle and proclaimed himself emperor, supported by a group of bloodthirsty militants who rushed in to silence any detractors. He imposes terror to control the Rojok population. It was he who constructed Ahkmau, first used to house political prisoners and then to house enemy aliens.

Memcache: Home planet of the Cehn-Tahr Empire.

Mental Neutering: The Terravegan military is mentally neutered for service, so that males, females and berdache may serve together with no sexual distraction. The process is chemical and irreversible, although there are times when the process does not work . Cadets are chosen from children in the breeder colonies for traits that enhance combat abilities. Most cadets are initiated into military school at the age of six. Type of service and specialties are chosen for them. They serve until they are of retirement age, at which time they may specify a vocation they wish to pursue. This is usually at the age of sixty, although many officers are allowed to continue to serve if their abilities are considered necessary to the state. Military may not marry. In the event that the neutering does not "take" completely, there is a statute that requires the death penalty for any fraternization between members of the military. The Cehn-Tahr government also invokes the death penalty for any fraternization between their soldiers and other races.

Microcyborgs: Implants, nanotechnology, which greatly enhance strength and endurance. Secret Cehn-Tahr technology. Usually implanted in the hair.

Milish Cone: A pocket-size water synthesizer.

Morcai: A legendary group of alien warriors who in ages past warred with a vastly superior force, and through tactics, strategy and sheer ferocity won a resounding victory. The flagship of the Holconcom is named for them: the *Morcai*.

Rigellians: A race of small humanoids descended from reptiles, with pale yellow skin and slit pupils. They are distant cousins of the Rojoks (who also have traces of reptilian DNA but deny any link to reptilian ancestors).

Rojok: An alien species in the Cularian classification of humanoids. Rojoks are one race, with reddish skin, thin mouths, slit eyes that are usually yellow or brown, and blond hair. Only officers are allowed to wear their hair long. The Rojok were a peaceful race until the Great Galaxy War, when they suffered at the hands of the renegades and were forced to study combat techniques and remake their military. They are now a military culture, having forsaken the arts in their determination never to be occupied by an alien force again. They have scientists, but are known to use spies to steal innovative technology from their enemies. They are led by an emperor, Mangus Lo, a Rojok who took power during the Great Galaxy War when he and his corps of terror troops protected the capital from being captured by the enemy. Now he rules with terror, using fear of imprisonment to keep the public in line. Every Rojok must give ten years to military service, although women are not permitted to serve; they are considered property, and the former royalty among the Rojoks are confined in camps. The system is supposed to be egalitarian, but Mangus Lo lives a life of incredible luxury and decadence, as do his ministers and bodyguards. The economy is based on military production, and property is owned by the state alone. Few dissidents are ever lucky enough to escape the military spies.

Spacing: A fatal walk in space without a space suit.

SSC: Strategic Space Command, an elite combat unit under the auspices of the Terravegan government, seconded to the Tri-Galaxy Fleet based on the planet Trimerius. Holt Stern's ship, the *Bellatrix,* was part of the SSC Fleet.

Terravega: The first and only human colony from Earth established outside the Sol solar system. Now established in many other colonies on far-flung planets. The original colony site is referred to as Terravega, and the systems that it populated are known, collectively, as the Terravegan Colonies.

Trimerius: A planet in the Alpha Trimeri system. It is the headquarters of the Tri-Galaxy Fleet and home planet of the exobiological and human life sciences complex, which also boasts one of the finest medical centers in existence. The spaceport covers several square acres of land and is bordered by barracks for the military personnel stationed on the base. Not conducive to human life in its original state, the planet has been terraformed by the addition of many city-size hyperglas domes. The weather is controlled. The vegetation is very alien.

Vegan: The Meg-Vegan colonies are near the New Territory. Vegans are very tall and have light green skin. They are notorious pacifists.

Wimbat: A small, winged mammal found on Celeb IV that hibernates for two-year periods.

Wrist Scanner: Dr. Madeline Ruszel's medical kit is embedded in her left forearm, in such a way that it is wired to her own nervous system and uses it as a power source. It contains a minibank of electronically linked instruments, along with a modem, and a minisynthesizer that can produce a limited amount of drugs in the field. With it, she can read vital signs, do surgery, contact any linked medical facility for assistance and even transfer patient information across the galaxy. The unit has a cover that mimics human flesh, so when it is not in use, it is not noticeable.

Yomuth: A giant rodent, found on Dacerius. They can go for two weeks without water in the deep deserts and they can run like the wind. If attacked, they fight standing on their hind legs, using their thick, sharp claws as weapons. They also bite. Many Dacerians race them at meets held throughout the year among nomadic tribesmen.

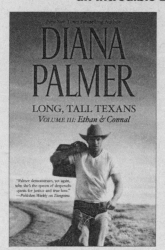

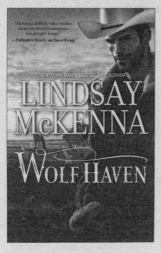

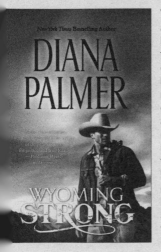

DIANA PALMER

(limited quantities available)

TOTAL AMOUNT	$_____
POSTAGE & HANDLING	$_____
($1.00 FOR 1 BOOK, 50¢ for each additional)	
APPLICABLE TAXES*	$_____
TOTAL PAYABLE	$_____

(check or money order—please do not send cash)

To order, complete this form and send it, along with a check or money order for the total above, payable to Harlequin HQN, to: **In the U.S.** 3010 Walden Avenue, P.O. Box 9077, Buffalo, NY 14269-9077 **In Canada:** P.O. Box 636, Fort Erie, Ontario, L2A 5X3.

Name: _____

Address: _____ City: _____

State/Prov.: _____ Zip/Postal Code: _____

Account Number (if applicable): _____

075 CSAS

*New York residents remit applicable sales taxes.
*Canadian residents remit applicable GST and provincial taxes.

H HARLEQUIN® HQN™
www.Harlequin.com

PHDP1